Praise for

BELLA AND THE BEAST

"Once more, Drake proves the right pair of shoes can change your life—especially if they're red and belong to the Cinderella Sisterhood. This story is both charming with its light fairy tale–based plotline, and intriguing with the dark, underlying Gothic twists. This is the perfect quick pick-me-up read."　　　　*—RT Book Reviews*

"An intriguing and passionate story full of history and tingling romance . . . another winner by author Olivia Drake."
—Romance Reviews Today

"Lush historical romance, complete with all the sprinklings of a fairy tale. Olivia Drake is an excellent writer, and this story knows how to submerge readers completely."
—Fresh Fiction

ABDUCTED BY A PRINCE

"Drake will have readers believing in the magic of not only a pair of shoes, but also love and the joy of finding your soul mate."　　　　*—RT Book Reviews* (4½ stars)

"I am a huge fan of the 'Cinderella Sisterhood.' This novel is the enchanting third book in the series, and author Olivia Drake has kept the series very much alive with lots of heartwarming romance, and enough spice to warm even the coldest nights."　　　*—Night Owl Reviews*, Top Pick

STROKE OF MIDNIGHT

"Drake's flair for mystery blended with humor and passion will delight readers . . . utterly enchanting."

—*RT Book Reviews*

"A compelling romance filled with intrigue."

—*Affaire de Coeur*

"Another wonderfully written novel by Olivia Drake."

—*My Book Addiction*

IF THE SLIPPER FITS

"Filled with romance, breathtaking passion, and a dash of mystery that will leave you wanting more."

—*Night Owl Reviews*

"A dash of danger and a dash of fairy tale in the form of a very special pair of shoes add to the romance plot, filling out *If the Slipper Fits* nicely."   —*Romance Junkies*

"Cinderella knew it was all about the shoes, and so does master storyteller Drake as she kicks off the Cinderella Sisterhood with a tale filled with gothic overtones, sensuality, sprightly dialogue, emotion, an engaging cast, and a beautiful pair of perfectly fitting slippers."

—*RT Book Reviews* (4 stars)

"I was enchanted with this story as Olivia Drake took the residents of Castle Kevern *and* this reader on an emotional, delightful journey. A magical fairy tale deserving to be read and read again!"   —*Once Upon a Romance*

ALSO BY OLIVIA DRAKE

THE CINDERELLA SISTERHOOD
Bella and the Beast
Abducted by a Prince
Stroke of Midnight
If the Slipper Fits

HEIRESS IN LONDON SERIES
Scandal of the Year
Never Trust a Rogue
Seducing the Heiress

HIS
Wicked
WISH

OLIVIA DRAKE

St. Martin's Paperbacks

This is a work of fiction. All of the characters, organizations, and events portrayed in this novel are either products of the author's imagination or are used fictitiously.

HIS WICKED WISH

Copyright © 2016 by Barbara Dawson Smith.

All rights reserved.

For information address St. Martin's Press, 175 Fifth Avenue, New York, NY 10010.

ISBN: 978-1-250-06030-3

Our books may be purchased in bulk for promotional, educational, or business use. Please contact your local bookseller or the Macmillan Corporate and Premium Sales Department at 1-800-221-7945, ext. 5442, or by e-mail at MacmillanSpecialMarkets@macmillan.com.

Printed in the United States of America

St. Martin's Paperbacks edition / June 2016

St. Martin's Paperbacks are published by St. Martin's Press, 175 Fifth Avenue, New York, NY 10010.

10 9 8 7 6 5 4 3 2 1

Chapter 1

Upon entering Lady Milford's London town house for the first time in ten years, Nathan Atwood had no notion that his aversion to marriage was about to undergo a dramatic reversal.

Rainwater dripped from his wet garments onto the marble floor of the foyer. A puddle formed around his black boots. As he tossed his cloak and hat to the butler, a gust of wind rattled the night-darkened windows on either side of the door.

Nate rubbed his cold hands together. "Good evening, Hargrove. I see you're still alive and kicking after all these years."

Expressionless as ever, Hargrove transferred Nate's sodden apparel to the arms of a footman, who bore the items away down a corridor. The white-haired butler surveyed Nate's outmoded garb and, in particular, the too long dark hair held back by a thin leather ribbon. His upper lip curled ever so slightly. "It would have been wise to send a note, instead of appearing like a drowned rat on her ladyship's doorstep."

The hint of censure on those battered features tickled Nate's fancy. He had forgotten the enjoyment of coaxing a reaction from that deadpan visage. Lady Milford's butler had never approved of him, not even when Nate had been a dashing young libertine arrayed in the latest fashion. "This early spring rain is trifling compared to the typhoons of the Far East. Now, I've just arrived back in England and I should like to see my godmother at once. Is she in?"

"Her ladyship has a prior engagement. You may pen a message if you like."

Nate ignored the man's gesture to proceed into an antechamber flanked by green marble pillars. "For pity's sake, I've traveled here all the way from China. Go and ask her if she'll spare a few moments for her godson."

The butler thinned his lips. "It would be best to return on the morrow. I'm sure she will clear a slot on her calendar—"

"That won't be necessary, Hargrove." The feminine voice floated down from the top of the staircase. "Do send him up at once."

Nate looked up to see an elegant woman standing at the first-floor balcony. A pale violet gown hugged her slim form, and her styled hair appeared as pitch-black as ever, with nary a line on the classic oval of her face. Lady Milford had to be above fifty years of age, yet she looked as eternally youthful as if she'd been wrapped in the finest tissue for the past decade.

Despite the gravity of his purpose, he couldn't stop a genuine smile. He hadn't realized until this moment how much he'd missed Lady Milford. She had always been a safe port for him in the tempest of his parents' marriage. And more of a steadfast influence in his childhood than his own frivolous mother.

Now, Nate had many questions for her that needed answering. Specifically, in regard to the letter she'd sent him over a year ago. It had taken eight months to reach him in Shanghai, then another five months for him to finish several crucial business transactions and then make the long voyage back to England.

He bounded up the staircase, taking the marble steps two at a time. Reaching the top, he caught Lady Milford in a warm embrace, inhaling the familiar scent of lilacs as he planted a kiss on her smooth cheek. "You haven't aged a whit, Godmother. You're lovelier than ever."

She laughed away the extravagant compliment. "And *you* are still the rogue, my dear Nathan. You should have warned me of your call. I'm due to leave for the theater in half an hour."

"Forgive me. I came straight from the docks." As she glanced at the untidy state of his garb, he added, "Alas, there are no proper English tailors where I've been living."

One slender eyebrow arched. "Why, India is quite civilized these days. Surely there must be many tailors in Bombay."

"Bombay was only my mail drop. Correspondence had to be forwarded to me in China."

"China!"

"I've been living there for the past two years. Trade is beginning to open up more to the Europeans. It's a treasure trove of tea and silks and gemstones."

"Have you made your fortune, then? I always thought you would."

"That and more. In truth, I'm hoping to open an import office here in London."

"That *is* good news! Perhaps it will bring you home more often." She tucked her hand in the crook of his arm. "Do come into my sitting room, Nathan. You've time enough for a drink while you tell me about your travels."

As they strolled along a carpeted corridor and into a rose and yellow room at the rear of the house, he related some of the more unusual sights he'd seen: tall temples called pagodas that were home to Buddhist priests, black-and-white bears that ate only bamboo leaves, and ex-otically robed merchants who spoke little English yet were shrewd at bartering.

Lady Milford seated herself on a rose-striped chair while he went to a side table to fill a tumbler of brandy from a cut-glass carafe. When he offered it to her, she shook her head.

Her solemn violet eyes studied him. "Enough chitchat," she said. "I presume it isn't only business that has lured you back to England. It's also the sad news conveyed in my letter."

His fingers gripped the glass. He could feel the imprint of the cut crystal against his skin. "Yes."

"Pray allow me to say that I'm so very sorry for what has happened. A letter is hardly the ideal way to convey a death in the family."

Nate took a drink from his glass and let it burn down his throat. So it was true. His father was dead. He expected to feel a rush of triumph, but his chest felt devoid of emotion. "Quite so."

"If you came straight here from the docks, then you haven't yet called at Gilmore House," she observed. "Why?"

How could he explain his reluctance to visit the place where he'd grown up as the second son of the Earl of Gilmore? After all, his father no longer held sway over the family. The tyrant was gone now. Nate had learned the news from Lady Milford's letter:

With great sorrow, I must inform you that your
father lies on his deathbed. The smallpox has
weakened his heart and the doctors have little
hope of his recovery. My dear Nathan, although I
can't pretend to know the nature of your quarrel

*with Gilmore, I do understand your desire to make
your own way in the world. Yet, as your godmother,
I dare say that you have been parted from your
brother and sister for long enough . . .*

Walking to the night-darkened window, he took another
swallow of brandy. The Earl of Gilmore—dead. It was still
hard to believe it. The man had been a harsh, godlike des-
pot who had singled out Nate as the target of his vitriol.
He had been the bane of Nate's childhood.

By nature, his elder brother, David, had been dutiful
and well behaved, the ideal son and heir, while Nate had
been the bad seed, wild and rebellious. All the gifts, the
admiration, the praise from the earl had been directed at
David. Gilmore had had nothing left for his younger son
but chilly stares and cold rebukes.

On his twenty-first birthday, Nate had had one final explosive quarrel with Gilmore. He had left England the
very next day, vowing never to return. But now, the news
of the earl's death changed everything. It was gratifying
to imagine the man moldering in his grave. No fate could
be more fitting for that vile wretch.

Lightning flashed against the night sky. For a moment
he saw the silhouetted rooftops of Mayfair, strange and yet
so familiar. Somewhere out there, his siblings were likely
at Gilmore House, where the family always stayed during
the season. Emily must be a young lady of nineteen now.
David would be thirty-three and the new Earl of Gilmore.

The prospect of seeing them again stirred a morass of
emotion in Nate's chest. David had never taken advantage
of being the favorite. There had always been a sort of ca-
maraderie between the brothers whenever their father
wasn't around. In a way, David had been as much a victim
of Gilmore's poison as Nate had.

But did David know the real reason why Nate had departed so abruptly? Had the old devil told his heir the truth? Would his brother reject him now?

As rain sluiced down the window, Nate saw Lady Milford's seated figure reflected in the glass. It struck him that she was still awaiting his response.

Brandy in hand, he walked forward and settled himself on the chaise opposite her chair. "Of course I came here first," he said, swirling his drink. "After all, it was *your* letter that brought me back to England. And I thought it best to do a bit of reconnaissance before going to Gilmore House. You can fill me in on all the household news."

"Your family has been in mourning this past year, of course. Emily is finally to make her come-out in a few weeks." Lady Milford paused, then added, "But before I say more, I must ask why you departed so abruptly—with nary a word of explanation. Your father would only say the two of you had quarreled."

Scowling, Nate tilted his head back and drained the rest of his brandy. "It was a long time ago. It's best forgotten."

"Nonsense, such a powerful disagreement cannot be swept under the rug. It will have to be resolved, or it will continue to fester."

"Fester? Why would you say that?" He sat up straight, his spine rigid. He wondered if she knew the truth. "Did the earl tell David why I left England? Did my brother say something to you?"

"No! Not a word." Her fine eyebrows drawn in a quizzical frown, she tilted her head. "Nathan, I feel we're speaking at cross-purposes. Did you and your father already clear the air? Did the two of you perhaps straighten things out by letter?"

"Absolutely not. I cut off all contact with my family when I left England. No one but you knew my address."

"I see," she said slowly. "Then you must be prepared to

make amends when you visit Gilmore House. What will you say to him?"

Nate frowned at her. He must have misheard. There could be no reason for the horrifying suspicion that lurked at the verge of his mind. "What the devil do you mean, *say to him*? My father is dead. You yourself wrote in your letter that he lay on his deathbed."

Lady Milford's face paled. She lifted her hand to her mouth. For a moment there was only the distant rumble of thunder and the hissing of the fire on the hearth. "My dear Nathan," she said faintly. "Did you not receive my second letter? I mailed it a week later, after your father had made a miraculous recovery. The doctors were truly amazed . . ."

His blood ran cold. He could feel his heart thudding in heavy strokes against his rib cage. Despite the brandy he'd just finished, his mouth felt dry as dust. "That's impossible. Only a moment ago, you said the family was in mourning this past year."

"Yes, because I thought you *knew* . . ." Lady Milford rose from the chair, seated herself beside him on the chaise, and placed her hand on his sleeve. Her violet eyes conveyed a deep compassion. "Soon after I sent that first letter, David contracted the smallpox, too, as did Emily. Your sister survived but . . . I'm afraid David did not. I'm so very sorry."

A roaring filled his ears. The air Nate drew into his lungs cut like knives. His brother was dead. David, who had slipped Nate food whenever he'd been put to bed without his supper. David, who had covered for Nate when he'd failed to complete his school assignments. David, who had been buried over twelve months ago.

A nightmarish unreality suffocated Nate. The mail service was often unreliable, especially to the Far East where few Europeans traveled. He must have departed Shanghai before the arrival of the second letter. The sympathy on Lady Milford's face confirmed that awful truth.

The Earl of Gilmore was *alive*.

Springing to his feet, Nate hurled the tumbler at the fire. The glass shattered with an earsplitting crash. Shards skittered across the marble hearth. "I should have known the wretch was too hateful to die!"

Before Lady Milford could do more than rise from the chaise, Hargrove appeared in the doorway. "Is aught amiss, my lady?"

Nate spun toward him. "What the devil! You were eavesdropping out in the corridor!"

"Quite the contrary." The butler glowered before turning to his employer. "Your visitor is waiting downstairs in the library, my lady. Shall I send a footman to clean up here?"

"Later," she said. "Kindly close the door on your way out."

The servant's pale blue eyes flicked to Nate. Hargrove made a slight bow and retreated. The door shut with a small bang that conveyed his displeasure.

Though caught up in a storm cloud of wrath, Nate felt the jab of proper manners. He toed a few splinters of glass away from his godmother. "Forgive me," he said stiffly. "I'll repay you for the damage."

Lady Milford dismissed his offer with a wave of her hand. "I never understood why Gilmore treated you so shabbily. But it's clear your feelings toward him have *not* changed."

"Nor shall they! I would never have returned to England had I known his presence still poisoned the air."

Her lips pursed, she glided to his side. She tilted her head back to look him in the eyes. "Nathan, whatever happened in the past, it is time to arrive at some sort of peace with your father. After all, you are now Gilmore's heir. You hold the title of Viscount Rowley."

Another quake ripped through him. David had always borne that courtesy title. It had been an intrinsic part of his elder brother's persona. It could never belong to the unfit second son.

At her penetrating look, he turned on his heel and prowled the confines of the feminine room. "No! I can't just step into my brother's shoes. I'm not like him."

"Of course you're not like him. You are your own man, and a fine one at that. And however distasteful it might be, you've a duty to your family."

He made a sharp, slicing sweep of his hand. "I reject that duty. And I certainly don't intend to stay in town and dance to Gilmore's tune. He can go to the devil for all I care!"

"And what of your sister? Your grandmother? Your two nieces? Will you reject them, as well?"

He pivoted sharply toward her. "Nieces?"

"I wrote to you of David's marriage after you left England. His young daughters are now fatherless. But that isn't my point." She stepped in front of him to stop his pacing. "Nathan, running away again won't solve anything. You're no longer a boy to flee at a whiff of trouble."

"Are you calling me a coward?" he snapped.

She placed her hands on her slim hips. "I'm merely saying it's time for you to put the past behind you. For the sake of your family, you *can* learn to be civil to your father. You can rejoin society as the heir to a venerable title. Perhaps in time you'll even find a young lady to wed."

Nate snorted. How like a woman to play matchmaker. They always thought a bachelor's troubles would be solved by taking a wife. But he knew the discord of marriage from observing his own parents. And he had no desire to claim a place in society, anyway.

He should return to the docks, board his ship, and depart at first tide. Let his godmother disparage him. She would never understand why he loathed the Earl of Gilmore—or why making amends with the man was impossible.

Yet, in the next breath, Nate realized he hungered for revenge. He craved payback for all the slights, the coldness, the criticisms. It wasn't enough to know that Gilmore had lost his precious eldest son. The man deserved to have his snobbish nose rubbed in the dirt.

What better way than to force him to face his new heir?

The clarity of that thought reverberated in Nate. By damn, he'd be a fool to squander this opportunity. Especially when Lady Milford had planted the seeds for the perfect plan of revenge.

Without further ado, he sprang toward the doorway. "If you'll excuse me," he flung over his shoulder.

Lady Milford hastened after him. "Where are you going?"

"I'm taking your advice. I'm staying in London for a time and entering society. And I'm getting married."

She caught hold of his sleeve as he flung open the door. "*Married?* To whom?"

"To the most loudmouthed, tawdry, unsuitable vixen I can find. A serving maid perhaps. Or a shopgirl. Maybe even a whore. It matters little so long as she's an embarrassment to Gilmore."

"That's mad! You can't truly mean to shackle yourself to such a woman for the rest of your life."

"Oh, *I* won't be the one punished." He bared his teeth in a feral smile. "You see, after foisting the trollop on Gilmore, I'll leave her in his care whilst I depart England forever. She'll remain here as a permanent reminder of how I bested him."

His godmother gave him a withering look. "It isn't like you to be so mean-spirited, Nathan. Do you care so little for the plight of that poor girl that you would throw her to the wolves of society?"

"Mean-spirited?" he said on a harsh laugh. "She'll go from living in a hovel to residing in a mansion with the prospect of someday becoming a countess. The chit will thank me!"·

Lady Milford stepped into the doorway to block his exit. Resolve firmed her fine features. "If you are intent on this wicked plan, then it seems I cannot stop you. However, I *will* insist upon one stipulation."

"What's that?"

"You must accept *my* help in choosing your bride."

Chapter 2

While the audience cheered and clapped, Madelyn Swann sank into a deep curtsy. The dramatic action caused the skirt of her costume to billow around her in a sea of rich ivory silk. The pose was carefully scripted. From a young age she'd learned that every action onstage had to be embellished, every word uttered with vivid emotion, every facial expression exaggerated.

Rising again, Maddy smiled brilliantly and threw out her arms as if to embrace all the spectators, from the unwashed masses crammed together on benches in the pit to the wealthy patrons in the upper box seats. Whistles and catcalls came from the men. A number of them tossed flowers onto the stage.

The fan-shaped theater was packed to the rafters. A thousand times in the past she had accepted the adulation of the audience. It always pleased her to know that her acting had entertained them.

But tonight was different. Tonight, she felt a lump in her throat because this had been her final performance at the Neptune Theater.

The other cast members trooped out to join her onstage. They had graciously given her a moment alone as a farewell tribute. Edmund, who had played Romeo to her Juliet, fell to one knee and made a show of kissing her hand as if they truly were star-crossed lovers.

The crowd roared its approval. They liked to imagine a real romance between the leads, though Maddy knew that Edmund, with his refined features and raffish smile, had no interest in women. It was an unspoken secret among the cast and crew that he fancied other men. Maddy cared only that he was a part of her tight-knit theater family—the family she soon would be leaving.

Taking another bow in the brightness of the gas lamps, she hid a twinge of doubt. Had she made the right choice? The stage was all she had ever known. The entire twenty-four years of her life had been spent with an acting troupe, with the smell of greasepaint and long hours of rehearsals. Her first memories were of watching her mother and father practice their lines, of sitting in the shadows while they performed, of traveling in a horse-drawn caravan from town to town. Maddy had been thirteen when her mother had died in an accident, and fifteen when her father had caught a lung ailment. He had never recovered, and Maddy had found a new home in this Covent Garden theater.

Perhaps she'd made a mistake in deciding to give it all up.

No. If truth be told, she had been yearning to spread her wings. The ritual of reciting familiar lines night after night, of capering across the boards in the guise of a character, had begun to wear on her. She had long wanted to make her own life, not play someone else's story. She wanted to be her own person, not obey the dictates of a theater manager. Most of all, she dreamed of using her skills in costuming to open a shop for ladies' apparel—if only she had the funds.

Then a recent, alarming development had forced her to

take swift action. She needed that money and she needed a protector—fast.

Her gaze flicked to a box seat on the left where a flaxen-haired gentleman sat alone. Unlike the others, he wasn't clapping and cheering. Rather, he scrutinized her through a pair of gold opera glasses.

As Maddy took another bow, a cold shiver prickled her skin. She had sensed Lord Dunham's presence from the moment she'd stepped onto the stage to deliver her first line. He was often there lately, watching her. She'd always kept a distance from the many upper-class gentlemen who desired her as their mistress. But a month earlier, she had made the mistake of singling out Lord Dunham in order to ask him a few discreet questions about his grandfather, the Duke of Houghton.

The duke was Maddy's grandfather, too, though she had never met the nobleman. Lord Dunham had no idea they were cousins, either. That fact had to remain a secret for now.

Meanwhile, Dunham had misconstrued Maddy's interest in him. He had become infatuated, stalking her at every turn, determined to seduce her. On several occasions, he had even followed her to the rooming house where she lived, only to be deterred by the formidable presence of her maid, Gertie.

The tall red velvet curtains began to close, the ropes cranked by old Rufus hidden in the wings. As the audience vanished from sight for the last time, Maddy released the breath she hadn't realized she'd been holding. She itched to be gone from here, away from being the center of attention. Away from Lord Dunham's lustful eyes.

The clapping sounded muffled now, the shouts and chants continuing unabated. His white teeth flashing in a grin, Edmund motioned to Rufus. "Let's take a bow again. Maybe I'll even sing a song!"

Maddy had no heart for another curtain call. "Without me, please. I don't think I could bear another good-bye."

Edmund gave her a sympathetic hug. "Run along, my beauty. You've earned your rest. But pray don't even think to scuttle out of our party! Gertie has gone to check on the arrangements." The cast had rented a private parlor in a nearby pub for Maddy's farewell supper.

She leaned up to peck his cheek. "I wouldn't miss it for the world."

With that, Maddy slipped through the horde of supporting players and down a few steps at the rear of the stage, exiting into a narrow corridor. A single oil lamp hung from the wood ceiling, its light low and dim. She took a quick glance around. On several occasions, Lord Dunham had been lurking here, ready to pounce. But tonight the manager had promised to bar all visitors from backstage.

Maddy started toward her dressing room. Old theater posters decorated the smudged gray walls. She had trod along this cramped passage countless times. It was as familiar to her as the pair of shabby shoes that she wore for good luck at every performance. But now the time had come to begin the next stage in her life.

A flurry of butterflies stirred in her stomach. After much deliberation, she had devised a scheme that would both enrich her and provide her protection from Lord Dunham. Several days ago, she had sent out discreet announcements to the wealthiest of her admirers. More than a dozen of them had been invited to submit bids to win her services as their mistress.

Never give yourself to a man without a ring upon your finger.

Her mother's long-ago admonishment echoed in Maddy's head, but she studiously ignored it. Yes, her plan might be unconventional and more than a little wicked. But such a liaison made perfect sense for a woman in her position. Unlike her mother, Maddy was no wellborn lady who could hold out for a proper marriage proposal. The very fact that she was an actress sullied her reputation in the eyes of the world.

Besides, Mama had hardly been a model of proper behavior, for in her youth she had eloped with a traveling actor. In a fury, the Duke of Houghton had cut off all contact with his daughter. Maddy had grown up seeing Mama's sorrow at being shunned by her noble family. She had developed a fierce loathing for Houghton and other noblemen of his ilk.

Deep in thought, Maddy turned the corner. She stopped abruptly. Her stomach took a sickening dive.

Lord Dunham lounged in the doorway to her dressing room. How well she knew his fair features: that narrow blade of a nose, the refined cheekbones, the flaxen hair. From previous encounters, she also knew that despite his languid pose, her cousin possessed a wiry strength beneath the black tailcoat and snow-white cravat of a gentleman.

"Why are you here?" she asked coolly, willing steadiness into her voice. "Only cast members are permitted backstage."

"Don't be cross, darling." Sauntering forward, Dunham presented her with a posy of red roses, the stems tied with a white ribbon. "I merely wished to congratulate you on a magnificent performance."

Maddy reluctantly accepted the bouquet. "Thank you, my lord. Now you really must go before you're discovered here."

"The cast is busy with encores. Your Romeo certainly likes to show off his singing."

He was referring to Edmund, who enjoyed entertaining the crowd with his deep baritone. She could hear him in the distance, his rich voice accompanied by cheers from the audience. There would be no help from that quarter. Even her maid Gertie had gone out to check on preparations for the farewell supper.

No one would hear Maddy if she screamed.

"They'll be finished very soon," she said with contrived certainty. "And I'm afraid my head hurts, so if you'll be so kind as to depart."

She made a sweeping gesture toward the exit door behind her. It led out into the alley where this man belonged. But Dunham merely shaped his lips into an attractive smile. No doubt some women found him charming—though she herself thought him far too snooty.

His ardent gaze raked her body as if he were imagining her naked. "Is that how you show your gratitude, Miss Swann? Surely you can grant me a kiss at the very least."

"I'm afraid not, my lord. We scarcely know one another."

"Only because you've been avoiding me of late." He edged closer and forced her to take a step backward. "You seemed so very friendly at first, inquiring about my family history, showing an interest in my pedigree. If I've done something to offend you . . ."

"I've merely been checking into the backgrounds of all the gentlemen who are pursuing me. A woman can't be too careful."

He shook his head, a hank of flaxen hair falling onto his brow so that he looked more like a choirboy than a seducer. "Nonsense, you showed me a particular attention. You invited me into your dressing room. We shared a flask of wine."

That had been a mistake, Maddy knew in retrospect. Their meeting had been the catalyst for his obsession with her. "I'm sorry if you misconstrued my purpose. Now, I really must ask you to go. You may submit your bid tomorrow evening at the auction along with the other gentlemen."

And she would toss it straight into the rubbish bin. Even if he wasn't her cousin, heir to the odious Duke of Houghton, she would still despise Lord Dunham for making her feel like a cheap whore. She had only invited him to participate in the auction so as not to alienate him. He was, after all, her one link to finding out information about their mutual grandfather.

All at once, Dunham lunged at her. Before she could do more than gasp, he pressed her back against the wall of the corridor and locked her in the prison of his sinewy body. The odor of his cologne made her gag. In a fright, she tried to wriggle free, but his arms were like iron bars.

"You're quite the feisty filly. I shall enjoy taming you to the ride." As if to relish her squirming, he nuzzled her cheek, his breath hot and moist on her skin. "Ah, Madelyn. You are so very beautiful."

"Release me at once!"

"Don't play the innocent. After all, you're selling your services to the highest bidder. I'd merely like to sample the goods and decide how much to offer. Now, that isn't unreasonable, is it?"

Maddy took a shuddery gulp of air. She still held the posy he'd given her, and her fingernails dug into the stems. Further struggling would only enflame him. Better to find a way to catch him off guard.

Drawing upon her acting ability, she pretended to go limp. She willed the tension out of her body and sagged in his arms, letting her head fall back as if to yield to his dominance. For dramatic effect, she formed her lips into an enticing bow. "As you wish, my lord," she whispered. "You're so much stronger than I am."

A blue flame flared in his eyes. "Now, there's a good girl. Or shall I say, a *bad* girl? Just the sort I like."

He crowded closer to claim his plunder. At the first repugnant touch of his wet lips to hers, she reached up and jammed the posy into the soft underside of his chin. She ground hard with all her might. The cloying odor of crushed roses burst into the air. Lord Dunham yowled as several thorns found the exposed skin of his throat.

His grip slackened and she jerked herself free, ducking under his arm and whirling around, intending to flee down the corridor and back to the safety of the stage. Instead, she found her way blocked.

A fine lady stood watching them. The woman had appeared from out of nowhere.

Maddy found herself the object of scrutiny by a pair of lovely violet eyes. Though the lady's features were mature, her skin showed only the finest of lines and it was difficult to pinpoint her age. She had coal-black hair beneath a dark berry silk bonnet that was elegant in its simplicity. In her gloved hand, she clutched a velvet reticule. Even in her befuddled state, Maddy noted the exquisite cut of that plum-hued cloak with its pearl button fastener. *This* woman had not sewn her own garments from cheap fabrics on the remnants table.

The lady gave Maddy a penetrating look before turning her attention to Lord Dunham, who was hissing curses while gingerly dabbing at his throat with a white handkerchief.

"Alfred Langley," the woman said, arching an eyebrow in regal disdain. "This is quite the unexpected surprise."

He looked up and scowled. "Lady Milford! What the devil are you doing here?"

"Better I should ask *you* that question," she responded. "Especially as it seems you are engaged in your usual sort of mischief."

Lady Milford must have been in the audience tonight, Maddy realized. But who had allowed her to come backstage? And how much had the woman seen?

Whatever the answer, she couldn't be trusted not to cause trouble. The last thing Maddy needed was a scandal on the night before the auction. "Lord Dunham was just on his way out the door," she said.

He cast an angry glare at her. "Not without redress. I've a mind to summon the constable!"

"You daren't," Maddy said, her fingers gripping the folds of her skirt. "Lest I testify as to exactly what happened here tonight."

He curled his lips into a sneer. "And who do you suppose he'll believe, a lord of the realm . . . or a guttersnipe actress?"

Lady Milford delicately cleared her throat. "Alfred, you're forgetting something. There is another witness to your actions."

"Good God, surely you can't take *her* side. She attacked me like a madwoman!" Lord Dunham gestured at the reddened streaks on his throat left by the thorns. "Look, I'm bleeding!"

Maddy bit her lip to keep from ridiculing his histrionics. He might only be suffering from injured pride, but he was a nobleman and she was in enough hot water without making him angrier.

Lady Milford appeared unimpressed by his wounds. "Be that as it may, I hardly think it in your best interests to involve the law. Especially as Houghton will then become aware that in addition to your other sins, you've taken to assaulting women!"

The mention of his grandfather had a visible effect on Lord Dunham. His flushed features turned pale and his hand froze in the act of dabbing his wounds. Maddy found that most remarkable. Was he truly so terrified of the Duke of Houghton?

Lord Dunham had revealed precious little about their mutual grandsire. But now his reaction told her more than she'd been able to weasel out of him over the course of several weeks. It confirmed her suspicions that Houghton was a harsh, fearsome nobleman who could make even his adult grandson quake in his fine leather shoes.

Dunham tucked the handkerchief back into his coat pocket. "Blast you both. I shan't stay and subject myself to this collusion of hens! As for you, Miss Swann, we will speak tomorrow."

He aimed an icy glower at Maddy, a look that chilled her to the marrow. Then he stalked to the exit door, wrenched it open, and vanished into the alley behind the theater. The door closed with a loud bang that reverberated down the narrow corridor.

The incident left Maddy shaken. Glancing at Lady Milford, she rubbed her arms in an effort to restore warmth to her skin. "I'm sorry you had to be privy to that scene, my lady," she said stiffly. "But I do appreciate your aid."

"It was my pleasure. And pray don't give Lord Dunham another thought. Men seldom react well when their vanity is injured."

Maddy didn't know quite how to respond to the woman's kindness. An awkward silence ensued, in which she was keenly aware of the vast social gulf between them. She had never before engaged in conversation with a noblewoman other than her late mother.

Lady Milford made no move to depart. She stood with her gloved hands folded at her waist and her expression serene, studying Maddy as if she were an exotic creature in a zoo.

Perhaps she *was* outlandish to a lady who'd never seen

from close-up an actress prepped for the stage. Because the gas lamps washed out a performer's complexion, Maddy had applied a heavy dose of cosmetics to enhance her features. She had rouged her cheeks and reddened her lips and darkened her brows with soot.

To play the tragic Juliet, she had twisted up her blond hair with gold ribbons in medieval fashion. The décolleté of her ivory gown revealed a generous display of bosom that must be shocking to a lady of refinement.

Despite her discomfort at the woman's scrutiny, Maddy held her head high. "Were you looking for someone, my lady?" she asked coolly. "You must have come backstage for a reason."

"I'm here to see *you*, Miss Swann. On a matter of great importance."

Chapter 3

Maddy led the way into her dressing room. What could this elegant lady want with her? Whatever it was, it couldn't be to Maddy's benefit. Aristocrats often exploited the lower classes for their own selfish purposes. Yet Lady Milford had come to her rescue and it would be churlish to refuse to hear her out.

Maddy usually felt a sense of tranquility when entering this cozy chamber. It was her refuge from the hustle and bustle of the theater. Tonight, however, she was aware of the dingy cabbage roses on the wallpaper, torn in places and stained by soot from years of burning oil lamps in close quarters. Articles of clothing were scattered around from her quick wardrobe changes between scenes. Gertie must have been too busy helping the other performers with their costumes to tidy up.

Maddy cleared a ruffled petticoat off the single wooden chair in the corner. "I'm afraid you'll have to pardon the disorder. I wasn't expecting any visitors."

Lady Milford gracefully seated herself. "It is I who should beg pardon, Miss Swann. It was discourteous of me not to have arranged this meeting in advance."

Maddy pulled out the stool by the dressing table, and

the legs scraped noisily on the wood floor. Sitting down, she noted the clutter of cosmetics and reached out to re- place the cap on an open jar of rouge. It irked her that she felt embarrassed by the mess. What did it matter what this woman thought of her?

Nevertheless, she straightened the hairbrush and hand mirror, then put a cork in a bottle of perfume. "Perhaps you had better tell me why you're here."

The woman folded her gloved hands around the velvet reticule in her lap, her posture straight and her gaze direct. "Allow me to be frank. I understand you are soon to hold an auction for select gentlemen of the ton. An auction in which you yourself are to be the prize."

A pot of greasepaint dropped from Maddy's nerveless fingers. She caught it just as it rolled off the edge of the dressing table. Was her ladyship an angry wife come on a mission of rebuke?

No, Lady Milford appeared to be in her middle years. The noblemen were all bachelors in their prime.

Was she an irate mother, then, wanting to protect her son from a conniving actress?

But Lady Milford didn't look livid. Serious, perhaps, but not on the verge of explosive fury. None of the men were named Milford, anyway.

"Indeed," Maddy murmured cautiously. "The gentle- men are to bring their sealed bids to me tomorrow night, and in due course, I shall select the winner. But . . . how did *you* find out about the auction?"

"My source is of no consequence," Lady Milford said with a flutter of her fingers. "However, I should like to ask, is it true that only those men who have received an invita- tion will be permitted to submit a bid?"

"I—yes. I could hardly open it to the general public." She'd chosen only a dozen or so nobles who were proper and well heeled, men powerful enough to protect her from

Lord Dunham, yet not cruel in nature. If she was to embark on an illicit affair, it would be with a gentleman who would treat her with a measure of decency.

"I see," said Lady Milford. "That is why I'm here, Miss Swann. I wondered if you would consider extending an invitation to my godson, Viscount Rowley. With the death of his brother over a year ago, he is now heir to the Earl of Gilmore."

Maddy's jaw dropped. Not because she knew who Viscount Rowley was—she had never heard of him—but rather, because Lady Milford actually seemed to be expressing *approval* of the auction. So much so that she would come here to solicit an invitation on behalf of her godson!

The situation was so mind-boggling that Maddy couldn't make sense of it. Ladies often turned a blind eye to the peccadilles of their male relatives. Yet they would never dream of helping those men actually *acquire* a mistress.

"I—I hardly know what to say, my lady. I know nothing about Viscount Rowley."

"My godson has been abroad for the past ten years on a trip to the Far East. He has only recently returned. But I can assure you, he is a very wealthy man. Whatever compensation you hope to receive, he has the means to exceed it."

"A monetary settlement is only a part of my requirement." Maddy balked at the notion of trying to explain her selection process to this stranger. It was just too private, too personal. Especially when it came to her most secret desires. In the dark of night, she had burned to discover what it was like to lie naked with a handsome man. To experience the glories of lust in his heated embrace . . .

However, she had never felt inclined to be free with her favors as other actresses often were. Promiscuity had always been distasteful to her, perhaps because of the influence of her lady mother. Over the years, Maddy had developed a reputation for rebuffing offers from even the finest gentlemen. Consequently, many of them had clamored to participate in this auction of her virginity.

"What *are* your other requirements?" Lady Milford asked.

Under the woman's direct stare, Maddy battled a blush. "The gentleman must be someone I can admire, someone who is fine-looking but also adept at intelligent conversation." A thought occurred to her. Perhaps Lord Rowley was some sort of imbecile who could not speak for himself. "May I ask, why are you acting as the viscount's emissary? Is he incapable of pleading his own case?"

Lady Milford laughed. "Hardly. If you must know, he's busy unloading his ships and is quite unaware that I am here tonight. With the auction scheduled for tomorrow evening, I deemed it wise to act swiftly."

"Do you mean to say he's never even seen me?"

"No, but when he mentioned his desire to attain a . . . woman, I immediately thought of you, Miss Swann. I've attended your plays in the past and I've been most impressed by both your talent and your beauty."

"Oh—thank you."

"You no doubt find my intrusion into his affairs to be rather odd," Lady Milford went on. "To that, let me say that my godson's happiness is of the utmost importance to me. And I am of the belief that you are the perfect match for him."

Maddy blinked. The perfect match? The woman spoke as if she were negotiating for a bride, not a mistress. "I'm pleased you would think so highly of me, my lady. But I've only your word to go on. With me never having made Lord Rowley's acquaintance . . ."

"Ah, but you *can* meet him when he delivers his sealed

bid. I'm certain you'll find him to be a charming, handsome gentleman with a quick mind and a noble heart. And far superior to any of those on your list."

"Of course you would believe so. He *is* your godson."

Lady Milford smiled with genuine warmth. "Excellent point, Miss Swann, though you should know that I've something of a reputation as a matchmaker. As such, I am very well acquainted with all of the eligible bachelors that you have chosen. Shall I read their names aloud and enumerate each man's weaknesses?"

She reached into her reticule and withdrew a folded piece of paper.

"No! No, that won't be necessary!" Irked, Maddy crossed her arms. Really, this had gone too far. It was disconcerting enough to discuss the auction with such a fine lady, let alone to feel maneuvered by her. Clearly, Lady Milford would not surrender when it came to fighting for her godson. Yet in spite of it all, Maddy found her curiosity stirred about this paragon of manhood.

What real harm could there be in allowing one more bid?

She blew out a breath. "All right, if Lord Rowley wishes to participate, then so be it. Have him bring his written offer here himself tomorrow evening at eight, at the same time as the other gentlemen. But I will make you no promises."

"Excellent." Looking pleased, Lady Milford tucked the paper back into her reticule. Then, oddly enough, she drew out something else. Something that sparkled a rich reddish hue in the light of the oil lamp.

A pair of shoes?

Forgetting her wariness, Maddy found herself leaning forward on the stool. Yes, they *were* shoes. Exquisite dancing slippers, each with a glittery buckle, and much finer than anything she'd ever admired in a shop window. She couldn't take her eyes from them. They seemed almost . . . alive. Countless tiny crystal beads frosted the garnet satin, giving the shoes a shimmering glow.

Lady Milford placed the pair on the floor in front of Maddy. "As a token of my gratitude, perhaps you'd like to borrow these for a time."

"Borrow them—"

The token reeked of a bribe, and Maddy didn't think it fair to the other gentlemen. Yet before she'd even completed that thought, she was kicking off her scuffed old shoes and sliding her stockinged toes into the elegant garnet slippers.

At once, a feeling of happiness flowed through her veins. She sprang up from the stool and twirled around, marveling at how gloriously comfortable the shoes felt. The weariness of standing for hours during the play vanished completely. It was as if her feet were enveloped in the softest cotton batting.

"They fit perfectly, my lady! How did you know my size?"

A hint of mystery tinged Lady Milford's half smile. "It was good luck, I suppose. They shall be yours until you no longer need them."

Until she no longer needed them?

The conversation had taken another peculiar turn as Maddy sensed an underlying message that she didn't quite understand. It was rather like reading a play with a page missing from the script.

Lady Milford arose from the chair and glided to the doorway. There, she turned to give Maddy a keen look. "I do hope you'll grant me one more wish, Miss Swann."

"What is that?"

"You'll wear the slippers tomorrow while you accept your bids."

With a flick of her rich plum cloak, the woman vanished

into the corridor, leaving Maddy with her lips parted in unspoken refusal. Lady Milford asked the impossible. It would be folly to wear such beautiful shoes on the following evening. Not that Maddy dared to explain why.

No one must know about her secret plan for the auction.

Chapter 4

In her dressing room the following evening, Maddy stood in her petticoats and corset. She held her arms extended straight out while Gertie tied thick padding around Maddy's slender waist. The wool-stuffed burlap sack was a vital part of her disguise. But the task of fastening it in place seemed to be taking forever.

Craning her neck, she peered over her shoulder at the maid who was stooped down, fussing with the strings. She could see only the woman's salt-and-pepper hair. "Is something amiss?" Maddy asked, controlling the urge to fidget. "We really do have to hurry. The gentlemen will be arriving in half an hour."

"If ye don't wish t' lose yer fatty bits on stage, ye'd best be patient." Gertie gave one final pat and straightened up. "There, 'tis done."

"Thank goodness. Now the dress, and quickly please."

With Gertie's help, Maddy drew the black bombazine gown over her head and stuck her arms into the long sleeves. The maid tugged the skirt down over the heavy padding. While Gertie fastened the buttons at the back, Maddy adjusted the severe bodice. Next, she stepped to the dressing table and donned a wig made of coarse gray horsehair, tucking every last strand of her own blond locks firmly out of sight.

Only then did she peer into the age-spotted mirror to assess her transformation.

A portly old biddy with sausage curls and a thick waist stared back at her. The drab gown was perfectly suited to an ancient servant. She had applied a good deal of makeup earlier, and her face felt heavy from the layers of putty she'd used to create numerous wrinkles.

Pleased with the disguise, Maddy spun around toward the maid. "What do you think, Gertie? Shall I add a wart to my chin, perhaps?"

The woman glanced down at the sparkly garnet slippers that peeped out from beneath Maddy's black skirt. "Them shoes. They ain't fittin' fer a servant. Where'd they come from, anyhow? I don't recall ever seein' 'em in the costumes room."

Maddy was loath to explain the particulars of Lady Milford's visit, or her own strange compulsion to wear the gorgeous slippers no matter how risky it might be to give away her real identity. She simply couldn't bring herself to exchange them for the sturdy pair of half-boots she'd intended to wear. "Never mind, they're just for luck," she said evasively, arranging her hem to hide the shoes. "No one will notice them."

Gertie harrumphed. "Don't see why ye need any o' this," she grumbled as she turned to gather the discarded clothing from the floor. " 'Tis a right load of foolishness, that it is."

"You *know* why." Maddy sat down at the dressing table, dipped her forefinger in the jar of putty, and began to sculpt a wart on her chin. "I explained it all to you before. I want to scrutinize the gentlemen without their knowledge."

The masquerade was a way to separate the wheat from the chaff. If she went out there as herself, they would all be toadying to her and vying for her attention. So she had decided to pose as a servant assigned to gathering the bids. That way, it would be easier to judge each man's character by observing how he reacted to an old crone. It was all part of her strategy to acquire a benevolent man as her lover, one who treated the underclass with dignity and respect.

"That ain't what I meant," Gertie said, hanging a petticoat from a wall hook. " 'Tis this whole scheme o' yers that's folly. Sellin' yerself t' the highest bidder! As if ye was a milk cow! Why, yer dear sweet mam must be turnin' over in her grave."

As Maddy leaned forward to examine the new wart in the mirror, she could see Gertie reflected behind her, a husky, broad-faced woman who had grown up on a farm and had once labored as a maid at the Duke of Houghton's estate in Hampshire. When Maddy's mother had run away to marry a traveling actor, Gertie had loyally accompanied her. The faithful woman had been a fixture in Maddy's life forever, and her criticism felt as horrid as disappointing her own mother.

But they had been through all this before, and Maddy didn't want another quarrel, not when her stomach was already tied in a knot.

"Mama came from a different world," she said. "I must make my own way in the world in which *I* was born."

"Ye should stay on as an actress, then. 'Tis a worthy calling. And they want ye here, girl. Poor Edmund was about to weep his eyes out last night."

The troupe had held the farewell supper at a local pub, with cast and crew members alike making toasts to her. Maddy had shed a few tears, too. But it was time for a change of scene. Time to set her life onto a new and exciting course.

"And how long would it take for me to save enough money to open my shop? Another ten years? Twenty?"

Maddy added a touch of gray soot to her eyebrows. "Besides, I need a protector, as well you know."

Hands planted on her sturdy hips, Gertie shook her head. "Tell Lord Dunham ye're his cousin, then. Mayhap he'll quit pesterin' ye."

"No. It wouldn't matter to him. You didn't see the look in his eyes last night." Maddy shuddered at the memory of him forcing his kiss on her. Next time, she might not be so successful in fending off his attack.

She had another reason for keeping their kinship a secret. If he knew, Lord Dunham would tell his grandfather—*their* grandfather—and that would ruin her opportunity to catch the Duke of Houghton by surprise. Once this auction was settled, she would have the leisure to formulate a scheme in which to confront the duke before all society . . .

But Gertie needn't know all that.

Maddy arose from the stool and went to the woman, patting her big chapped hand. "Everything will go well tonight, you'll see. I'll have a fine town house in which to live. It would be a tremendous help if you'd accompany me as my personal servant." Maddy paused, searching those familiar weathered features. "Unless, of course, you'd rather stay on here with the troupe."

"Bosh, I wouldn't leave ye, not ever! I promised yer mam on her deathbed."

Gratified, Maddy hugged the robust woman. "Thank you, dearest. You can't imagine how much that means to me."

Gertie harrumphed again, her brown eyes tender with concern. "Ye've made yer bed an' ye'll lie in it, then. Let's hope ye don't come to regret it!"

A short while later, leaning heavily on a walking stick, Maddy shuffled out of the wings and onto the stage. Only a few gas lamps had been lit along the edge of the stage. With the cast and crew taking a night off, she had been allowed to use the premises this one last time.

Already a score of gentlemen occupied seats on the benches in the pit of the shadowed theater. They looked up as Maddy appeared, then lost interest at once. To them, she was merely a creaky old maidservant to be ignored.

So far, so good.

Pausing as if to catch her breath, she used the opportunity to scan the crop of contenders. Several men chatted among themselves, but most were busy eyeing each other like rival cocks in a fighting pen.

As well they should be. Only one of them would become her lover.

Her insides clenched with anxiety. Would she make the right choice? Who among them would submit the most lucrative offer? Who would be most suited to her? Who would be eliminated?

The first name already had been crossed off her list. Lord Dunham sat in the first row, his marine-blue coat a perfect foil for his flaxen hair and narrow aristocratic features. A diamond stickpin winked in his lapel and his foot tapped impatiently. Her cousin could offer her the crown jewels, and she still wouldn't have him.

Nearby, ginger-haired Lord Netherfield turned a folded paper over and over in his hand, brushing it almost lovingly. Behind him sat Mr. Stanford, the boyish heir to a baronet, cradling an enormous bouquet in his lap. A short distance away, the scholarly Marquess of Herrington had his nose in a book, though he slid wary glances at his fellow competitors from time to time.

Only one arrival remained standing in the gloom at the back of the theater. He was leaning against a pillar in a casual pose of attention. With the gaslights shining in her eyes, Maddy couldn't identify him. But she had the impression of a tall, well-built man.

Was *he* Viscount Rowley?

Lady Milford's godson was the only candidate who was a stranger to Maddy, for she knew all the others present. But she couldn't be certain it was him because there were two gentlemen on her list who were not among the throng.

It was just past eight o'clock and she wouldn't wait for latecomers.

Using the cane, she tottered to the front of the stage and cleared her throat with a rusty, rattling noise. She was forced to do so a second time, even louder, before the men deigned to look up at her. "Ye've all come to see Miss Swann, then," she said.

Murmurs of assent rippled from the group.

"Where is she?" Mr. Gerald Jenkins called out in a hearty tone that matched his stout form. "We've laid wagers as to which of us will win the prize, so run along and fetch her. We want to see Beauty, not the Beast."

A few men chuckled at the crude quip, while others were polite enough to refrain. Mr. Jenkins slipped down a few slots on Maddy's list.

"I fear me mistress is indisposed," she uttered in a quivery voice. "She cannot be with ye this night."

A buzz of protests erupted from the gentlemen. Several of them shook fists in the air. The Marquess of Herrington clapped his book shut, while Lord Netherfield cried out, "This is most inconvenient. I turned down a dinner invitation to be here!"

Maddy projected her voice over the hubbub. "Never fear, milords, never fear! Miss Swann has instructed me to gather the offers from the lot of ye. Now, if ye'll be so kind as to wait, I'll make me way down there. Mind, the stairs ain't easy fer an old biddy like meself."

With that, Maddy limped toward one side of the stage. She stooped over the cane and grimaced as the padding beneath her black gown pinched her ribs. Concentrating on her performance, she kept her back hunched and took a series of short, shuffling steps. Little did these aristocrats realize, the act was a test to see if any of them had the heart to lend assistance to an ancient servant.

When the gentlemen began rising from their seats, she had high hopes of witnessing a skirmish over which one of them was to be her knight in shining armor. Then she realized they were merely jockeying for position in a queue to present their bids.

Blast the lot of them. Were they so ignorant of common courtesy toward their elders? So blind to the humanity of servants?

It would seem they all deserved a black mark by their names.

To hide her displeasure, she glared down at the floorboards, pretending to watch for obstacles. Now and then, the garnet slippers kicked up the hem of her gown. So much for expecting the shoes might bring her good luck.

Lady Milford's bribe had gone to waste. Her much-vaunted godson had failed to make an appearance. Unless . . .

Maddy slid a glance toward the rear of the fan-shaped theater. The mysterious figure was gone now from the shadows. If that had been Viscount Rowley, he'd scuttled out like a bashful coward without even delivering his bid.

Charming, handsome gentleman with a quick mind and a noble heart—hah! It seemed far more likely that Lord Rowley was nothing at all as Lady Milford had described. Rather, he must be a drooling, cross-eyed, sniveling, chinless buffoon.

Her cane tap-tapping, Maddy reached the short flight

of stairs and pretended to teeter on her descent to the first step. She was half tempted to fake a tumble to see if any of the gentlemen would even notice her lying in a heap at the bottom of the stairs. While aiming a glower in their direction, she detected a faint sound from behind her.

Half a second later, a hand gripped her elbow.

Startled, she jerked up her head and found herself staring into the most arresting pair of male eyes she'd ever seen. They were forest green with flecks of gold beneath strong dark eyebrows, and set in boldly chiseled features. The stranger had shoulder-length black hair tied back neatly in a queue like the men in portraits of half a century ago. Although his garb was well tailored, it was plain and utilitarian: a charcoal-gray coat, black trousers, and white cravat.

He must have come up the matching stairs on the other side of the stage, Maddy realized. How had she not heard his approach until the last instant? More to the point, who was he?

Viscount Rowley.

No, it couldn't be him. Lady Milford's godson was a half-witted dolt . . . wasn't he?

Wasn't he?

This man's face looked attractively bronzed from the sun . . . as if he'd just undergone a long sea voyage from the Far East. He was the only participant whom she'd never met. That led her to one inescapable conclusion.

Dear God. It *was* him.

Viscount Rowley bent his head nearer. "Trust me, madam. I shan't allow you to fall."

His deep charismatic voice sent a shiver over her skin. And those eyes . . . they were too keen, too intelligent, too observant. They caused a quivery twist in the pit of her stomach, a sensation Maddy attributed to the fear of discovery. She hadn't intended for any of the gentlemen to have quite so close a look at her face. If he were to detect that her wrinkles were sculpted from putty . . .

Quickly, she tucked her chin into her bosom and said in a rusty voice, "Thank ye, sir. 'Tis most kind of ye to aid a poor old soul."

"It's my pleasure."

As he assisted her down the stairs, his closeness made her so skittish that she wanted to abandon the pretense and scramble nimbly to the bottom. The steps were narrow and their hips bumped at the slightest movement. Maddy was acutely aware of his superior height, the heat of his body, and the firmness of his fingers around her upper arm. To make matters worse, she caught a whiff of sandalwood along with something mysterious, something that could only be called the deep dark allure of masculinity.

So intent was her focus on him that Maddy failed to notice they'd reached the base of the stairs. She took another step, expecting her foot to descend. Instead, her sole struck the floor hard and she stumbled in actuality this time, nearly dropping her cane.

Lord Rowley grabbed her close to him. "Steady there," he said. "It could be tragic for a woman of your advanced years to suffer a fall."

Was he teasing her? Had he guessed—

She didn't dare risk a peek up at his face to read his expression. And his arm! It lay firmly around her waist now. Heaven help her if he detected the padding of her disguise.

Maddy contrived a cackle of laughter. "There be no need to fuss, milord. I ain't in me grave yet."

Using the cane, she waddled away as swiftly as the masquerade would allow. Only then did she breathe a sigh of relief. *Handsome and charming . . . a good heart.* Well, he *had* been the only one to help her. She would give him good marks for that. But the time had come to focus her attention on the other participants.

They had formed a line down the center aisle of the theater. It was just as well, for she could take up a stance with her back to the stage lights so the men would be less likely to notice her heavy makeup. Had Lord Rowley seen through her masquerade?

The question nagged at her like a sore tooth. But surely that fear was only a trick of her overactive imagination . . .

Out of the corner of her eye, she observed his tall figure as he headed down the outer aisle toward the back of the theater. He must be taking the long way around in order to go to the end of the line.

Or not.

Gertie had seated herself in the shadows of the last row to observe the proceedings. Much to Maddy's dismay, Lord Rowley sat down beside the maid and proceeded to engage her in conversation. What could he possibly have to say to her?

Despite the fine acoustics, Maddy couldn't detect a word of their discourse. But at least Gertie's stiffly upright posture proved she wasn't charmed in the least.

"You there," Mr. Gerald Jenkins snapped in an aggrieved tone. "Will you require us to stand here all night?"

Maddy snapped to attention, realizing the loudmouth had pushed his way into the first position. "Beg pardon, milord. Have ye a bid, then? If ye'd be so kind as to put it on the bench o'er there."

With an arrogant flick of his wrist, the stout man tossed down a folded paper sealed with red wax. "You make certain Miss Swann gets mine first."

For that, she'd fling it into the rubbish bin and strike Mr. Jenkins off the list, Maddy decided. She'd never be able to tolerate the company of such an arrogant fool. " 'Tain't me place to give me mistress any such order," she said. "Next, please!"

The Marquess of Herrington stepped forward. Brown-haired with unremarkable features, he seemed a mild-mannered man and unlikely to cause any drama. Her research had revealed him to be a scholar on a wide range of topics, which boded well for stimulating conversations.

He opened his book to show her the inscribed flyleaf. "I should like to present this treatise on astronomy to Miss Swann, for she shines brighter than any star in the heavens."

Maddy swallowed a bubble of mirth. She had only ever encountered such melodramatic nonsense in poorly written scripts. But she couldn't laugh, not when he looked so serious.

"I say!" chimed a fellow halfway down the line. "*I* was never told we were allowed to give trinkets. It isn't very sporting to the rest of us."

Rumbles of agreement came from the others. A number of men began to crowd forward, their faces angry and aggressive.

Faced with mutiny in the ranks, Maddie acknowledged their point. " 'Tis right kind of ye, milord," she told Lord Herrington. "But Miss Swann said there's to be only the written bids. No gifts allowed."

As Herrington sighed and stepped away to add his folded paper to the pile, Mr. Stanford stood next in line, his shoulders drooping in boyish dejection as he stared unhappily at his huge bouquet of flowers. "The devil you say! I tucked my proposal inside all these blasted ribbons. It was to be a game for Miss Swann to unravel them."

While he fussed with untying the pink streamers, Maddy felt sorry for the young man who had put such time and effort into pleasing her. That ought to elevate Mr. Stanford as a solid prospect—except for the fact that she couldn't honestly say he awakened her lusts. Rather, she felt the urge to mother him, to give him a sympathetic pat on the head and send him back to the nursery.

As the others came forward to tender their bids, a titter of laughter drifted from the rear of the theater. Maddy craned her neck to peer around the line of gentlemen. She blinked, unable to believe her eyes.

Gertie was *giggling*. The maid had half turned in her seat to face Lord Rowley, and they appeared to be enjoying quite the lively chat.

Maddy compressed her lips. Like a debutante at her first dance, the middle-aged woman was flirting with Lord Rowley. How on earth had the viscount managed to charm her in the space of a few minutes? And more curious, what could be the topic of their conversation? The two surely could have nothing in common . . .

"When can we expect Miss Swann to announce her decision?"

The snooty, aristocratic voice yanked Maddy's attention back to the auction. Lord Dunham stood in front of her, one pale eyebrow arched in disdain as if he were annoyed by the need to address a servant.

Maddy leaned heavily on the cane, playing the crone and peering up at him through slitted eyes. "Dunno, milord," she rasped. "Could take a day or a week for her to weigh the offers. 'Twill be a lucky man, indeed, who wins her favor."

"Tell your mistress that Lord Dunham trusts that she will make a prudent decision." He dropped a sealed paper onto the pile, then turned on his heel and strolled up the aisle.

Maddy controlled a shiver. His tone had held an unmistakable threat. How angry her cousin would be if he knew he'd already been cut from her list of prospects. In truth, he'd never really been on it. She had only invited him to the auction so as not to stir his suspicions.

Much to her surprise, he stopped at the last row of seats to address Lord Rowley. The viscount rose and the two men exchanged a few words while the last stragglers deposited their bids and filed out of the theater. Then Lord Dunham departed as well, with Gertie also heading into the lobby, presumably to see the men out.

The only one left was Lord Rowley. He alone had not submitted his offer.

Maddy found herself intensely curious. Were he and Lord Dunham cronies? That would be a black mark against Lord Rowley. Then again, the viscount had been halfway around the world for the past ten years, so they could hardly be very close.

She tensed as Lord Rowley started toward her. He advanced down the center aisle with a self-assured stride, giving her a moment to assess him. Lady Milford certainly hadn't overstated his attractiveness. He had strong masculine features, a firm jaw, and faint indentations on either side of his mouth that made her wonder if he had dimples when he smiled. The overlong black hair and green eyes were an unusual and alluring combination.

Her knees softening to jelly, Maddy tightened her gloved fingers around the knob of the cane. She hunched her back and worked her heavily wrinkled face into a sour glare. It was a difficult pose to maintain once he stopped in front of her. His superior height forced her to twist her neck in order to peer up at him.

"Laggard," she croaked. "There always be one in every crowd."

"Pray forgive me." He made a slight bow. "Nathan Atwood, at your service."

Maddy's heart sank like a stone. So he *wasn't* the viscount, after all? She felt unaccountably disappointed to realize her mistake. She would have liked to have reviewed this man's offer and compared it to the others.

After all, he possessed physical attributes in abundance. And he deserved a gold star for his courtesy toward servants, too.

Who was he, then? Her vivid imagination leaped with possibilities. Could he be a journalist from one of the tittle-tattle news sheets writing an undercover story on the auction? Heavens, maybe that was why he'd been chatting with Gertie, to pump her for information.

"Weren't no Atwood on Miss Swann's list," Maddy said. "Ye best be gone, sir. Ye ain't allowed here."

She shook her cane at him, then hobbled over to the bench and started to gather up the dozen or so bids.

"I am indeed on the list. Miss Swann will know me as . . . Viscount Rowley."

Maddy fumbled the papers. Several dropped to the wood planks of the floor. He sprang to her side at once, collecting the folded sheets and handing them back to her. It was a good thing because she could scarcely bend over with the dense padding constricting her midsection.

It was a bad thing, too, because Viscount Rowley was crouched right in front of her. Once again, he gazed into her face. He was close, so close she could see the golden flecks in his gorgeous green eyes.

Clutching the papers to her severe bodice, Maddy backed away and assumed the humble pose of a servant. "Thank ye, milord. Ye be most kind. Have ye a bid, then?"

"I do, indeed." He paused, his eyes narrowed slightly. "However, I've a request to make. That's why I waited to be the last one here."

Maddy found her curiosity piqued. "Aye, an' what might that be?"

"I've been abroad for the past ten years. The other gentlemen have all had the pleasure of making Miss Swann's acquaintance—which puts me at a distinct disadvantage.

It seems only fair that I should be allowed to meet her in person before tendering my offer."

"Nay!" she snapped. "I already said she's indisposed—she's ill."

"I'm very sorry to hear it." His expression reflected sympathy, though his sincerity immediately became suspect as he continued, "I won't keep her very long. It need be only a brief introduction. Enough for me to determine for myself if we are well suited."

" 'Tis impossible! She ain't here, anyhow, and that's that."

"Then pray take me to her." His mouth curved into a smile, proving that he did indeed have a matching set of attractive dimples. "Surely it can't hurt for you to ask her on my behalf. Please, madam, I'd greatly appreciate your help in the matter."

The charm of that smile caused a quake inside of her. For one feverish moment, she was tempted to agree to his demand, to dash back to her dressing room and transform herself into a fashionable actress. But it would take far too long to untangle herself from this contraption around her waist and to scrub off her sticky makeup. She would need a bath to get the smell of the horsehair wig out of her tresses.

Why should she humor Lord Rowley, anyway? She already had granted him a special favor by allowing him to participate. He had no right to wheedle her for another.

He was probably hoping for a chance to use that dazzling smile on Madelyn Swann and gain an advantage over the other men. Well, she would call his bluff.

Maddy shook her head. "Beg pardon, milord. But I have me orders. Ye'll give me yer bid now or be cut out of the auction entirely."

Lord Rowley's smile vanished. He studied her for a moment. Then, to her great satisfaction, he reached into an inner pocket of his coat and brought forth a folded paper. He tapped the edge against his open palm, his face serious as if he were deep in thought.

Excitement tingled inside her. He *had* been bluffing. He *would* give it to her. She'd have the chance to see just how much he was willing to offer for her.

He extended the bid to Maddy. She reached out to snatch it. Just as her fingers brushed the paper, however, he abruptly withdrew it, tucking the envelope back inside his coat.

"No," he said decisively. "I'm afraid I must stand by my condition. No meeting, no offer."

"But—"

"I'll bid you adieu, madam. Pray convey my sincere regrets to Miss Swann."

With that, the viscount turned on his heel and strode away down the aisle. He didn't look back, not even once. A moment later, his tall figure disappeared into the shadows of the lobby.

Chapter 5

Maddy straightened up, abandoning the stooped posture of her disguise. She frowned at the darkened doorway and willed the viscount to reappear. He couldn't just walk away like that. He'd had the proposal right in his hand. Her fingers had touched it!

She wanted to march after him, to tell him that he could have his audience with Madelyn Swann on the morrow. Yes. Why hadn't she suggested that as an option? She need only hurry and catch him before he exited the theater . . .

Maddy darted three steps, then stopped in the aisle. Blast it, she couldn't go running after him as if she'd undergone a miraculous healing of her half-crippled state. She'd give away the masquerade. And why should she humiliate herself by chasing him down, anyway?

She had plenty of offers from the finest gentlemen in society. One less wouldn't matter.

Her lips pursed, Maddy laid the cane on the nearest bench. She took a moment to straighten the mess of folded papers that she'd been clutching against her bosom. There were fourteen of them in all. Discounting her cousin's and Lord Gerald's, that left twelve choices.

A full dozen who were every bit as eligible as Lord Rowley.

She aimed another scowl at the doorway where he had vanished. It was just as well he'd gone. Giving up so easily on the auction proved him to be a fickle man. It didn't speak well for his determination to acquire Madelyn Swann as his mistress.

She listed his faults. He was far too good-looking, which meant he was likely vain. In addition, he was entirely too charming. He must be accustomed to getting his own way, using his spellbinding smile as a tactic to entice women, even ancient hunchback crones.

It wouldn't work on her.

A woman of her station had to be practical in matters of the heart. In fact, Lord Rowley had done her a favor. He had made her realize that it would be best to choose a dull, unremarkable man as her lover. Such a fellow would appreciate her and not use his dimples to cajole her into doing his bidding.

She intended to be the one in charge. Not a strutting cock with a flashy smile and fascinating green eyes.

With that resolve firmly in mind, Maddy took the stack of bids and headed back toward the short flight of steps to the stage. She'd go to her dressing room, remove this irksome disguise, and then return to her boardinghouse for the night. She could scarcely wait to sit down and peruse all the offers in private.

Several promising prospects came to mind. The Marquess of Herrington, in particular. He was a placid scholar and likely would spend most of his time with his nose in a book. So long as he provided her with the funds she needed, he would be one of her prime choices.

Ascending to the stage, Maddy tried to conjure Lord Herrington's image in her mind. But his nondescript features remained hazy. Did he have black hair or choco-late brown? A square jaw or rounded? Thin brows or bushy ones?

No matter. It would be dark in their bedchamber. When they cuddled together beneath the covers, she wouldn't be able to tell if he had plain brown eyes or brilliant green with gold flecks.

She wouldn't care, either, and that was that. She'd had enough drama to last a lifetime. Instead of learning her lines and participating in endless rehearsals, she would en-joy being pampered by a malleable man like Lord Her-rington. He might not have dimples—she was certain of *that*—but he would provide her with the means to secure her future. Then, once she'd served as his mistress for a year's time, they'd part ways and she would be free to become an independent entrepreneur.

Satisfied with the plan, Maddy walked across the stage and headed toward the door that led backstage. The heels of the garnet slippers tap-tapped on the floorboards. How quiet and gloomy it was here, in stark contrast to most nights when the place teemed with activity.

She paused a moment to breathe deeply of the smells of wooden sets and musty paint, and to say a silent good-bye. She would miss this theater, the only real home she'd known since traveling all over England with Mama and Papa in a small troupe of actors. Yet it was time to go. Already the place felt like a part of her past, some-thing to be remembered with fond nostalgia.

All of a sudden, a faint noise in the wings startled her. The small scrape sounded like a footstep.

Maddy called out, "Gertie? Is that you?"

No one answered. Nor should anyone. By now, the maid would be far away down the corridor, packing Maddy's belongings in the dressing room. The sound was likely a mouse, scrabbling for a crumb dropped by one of the crew members.

Then, as Maddy walked past the red curtains, something moved in the corner of her eye. She turned sharply. A few feet away, a black shadow shifted in the deep darkness of the wings.

The tall, hulking figure of a man.

He lunged at Maddy.

Her heart catapulted into her throat. Dropping the bids, she threw up her hands in self-defense and sucked in a breath. Even as she uttered a strangled yelp, she felt the wig being plucked from her head. Her blond hair sprang free and spilled down her back.

Frantic, she beat at her attacker's chest with her fists. It was like hammering a brick wall. He clamped his hands onto her shoulders and pushed her away, holding her at arm's length. A deep chuckle emanated from the darkness. "Calm down, Miss Swann. I mean you no harm."

That voice. It sounded familiar . . .

"Let me go," she snapped.

Her attacker complied at once. He stepped out of the gloom of the curtains. The dim gaslight fell upon his face, illuminating the dimples on either side of his mouth.

Viscount Rowley smirked at her. "It's just as I thought. You *are* Miss Swann."

Stunned, Maddy could only gawk. He had gone out into the lobby. She'd seen him walk away. How had he stolen into the wings without her knowledge? He must have come through the service door hidden behind a column by the ticket booth.

How had he known it was there?

He bent down and picked up the horsehair wig from the floorboards, twirling it in his hand. "A clever disguise," he said. "But your blue eyes gave you away. They're far too bright and youthful. Once I noticed that, it was easy to spot the rest—the smooth hands, the lack of a double chin, the areas that ought to sag but don't."

With rakish boldness, he glanced down at her bosom. Her breasts tingled in response, and a hot flush spread beneath the putty wrinkles on her face. How was it that he could make her feel breathless with just one look?

Maddy despised his effect on her. She despised *him* for his arrogance in unmasking her. She felt naked without the wig. Exposed to his ridicule. She'd been right to suspect he had seen through the disguise. Right to think him conceited and superior. That wasn't an amiable smile on his face.

It was a grin of triumph.

Lord Rowley was pleased with himself. He was enjoying her embarrassment. He believed he'd bested her.

A tide of fury boiled up in Maddy. She snatched the wig from his hand. With all her might, she swung the hairpiece like a club to smack the grin off his face. "Scoundrel! Devilish trickster! How dare you sneak in here and frighten me half to death!"

He backed up a step and clapped his hand over his reddened cheek. "Pray forgive me, Miss Swann. However, I must object to being labeled a trickster when it was *you* who tricked *me*—and all those other fellows. We were the victims of *your* ruse."

"Victim? You're a filthy, pig-headed jackanapes, that's what. A nasty, arrogant clodpate!"

"I've never before been cursed by a Shakespearean actress. I must compliment you on your phraseology."

Humor still played at the corners of his mouth. He found her tirade amusing. *Amusing!*

Infuriated, she beat him about the shoulders and neck with the curled gray wig. "Don't you mock me, you horrid coxcomb!" *Whack!* "You thought you were so clever, pretending to be gentlemanly, assisting the old crone down the stairs." *Whack, whack!* "As if I'd ever choose a vile, despicable scapegrace like you." *Whack, whack, whack!*

At that point, the wig broke apart into pieces, which she flung at his chest. He brushed a few horsehair curls off his coat, and then with an earnest look, he flattened his hand over his heart. "I swear on my mother's grave, I didn't know about the disguise when I first came to your aid. It was only as I was helping you descend that I observed certain . . . anomalies."

"Stop trying to bamboozle me! I'd sooner believe a forger handing me a fistful of banknotes." She fixed him with a scathing glare. "Speaking of bamboozling, why were you talking to my maid at the back of the theater? What were you saying to her?"

Lord Rowley arched an eyebrow. "I'm not at liberty to reveal a private conversation."

His caginess only fed Maddy's anger. He was grinning at her again, the deep indentations that bracketed his mouth making him revoltingly handsome. "Devious rascal! You're naught but a strutting cock, showing your dimples and flashing your pretty smile to charm every woman you meet!"

"Have you been gazing at my lips, Miss Swann? They can be yours to enjoy if you so desire."

"I'd rather kiss a slimy toad."

As Maddy glanced about the shadowy stage for something to throw at him, her eyes widened. The bids! They were scattered over the floor. She had forgotten all about them.

"Blast it!" she muttered.

She crouched down and grabbed about half of the folded papers, but the others lay beyond her reach. Hampered by the stout padding around her waist and her voluminous black skirt, she struggled to crawl on hands and knees to collect the rest.

The last one had an *H* embossed in the red seal. That must be Lord Herrington's bid. The one that interested her the most. He was a dull sort who would cause her no trouble.

As she stretched out her fingers, Lord Rowley brought his shoe down onto the paper to anchor it in place. "You won't be needing that," he said.

"I beg your pardon," she said heatedly, tugging in vain at the folded paper. "Move aside, you rotten varlet!"

"Only if you promise to consider *my* offer, too."

She angled a glare up at him, resenting the way he towered over her. "I've no intention of indulging a shameless cheater. You had your chance to give me a bid and you squandered it. The auction is now officially closed."

"It isn't over until you make your selection. And I'll wager you won't want any of those others once you have a look at mine."

"Well, I won't read your offer, so we'll never know, will we? Now, move your blasted foot."

When his polished black shoe remained firmly in place, Maddy yanked so hard on Lord Herrington's proposal that it ripped. To make matters worse, she lost her balance and tumbled backward, landing on her bottom with her legs akimbo and a ragged half of paper clutched in her fingers. The surprise of it knocked the breath out of her.

At once, Lord Rowley bent over her. "Are you all right, Miss Swann?"

His concerned question was marred by the suggestion of a grin at the corners of his mouth. He was so close she could see the individual black lashes around those intense green eyes. A flush spread from her core and up into her face. A flush that could only be anger—she wouldn't allow it to be anything else. "I'm perfectly fine, no thanks to you." Maddy waved the torn piece at him. "And look what you've done, you worthless dolt!"

The viscount made no apology for the damage he'd caused. As she struggled to right herself, the precious bids clutched to her bosom, he took hold of her arm and easily hauled her to her feet. "I daresay that roll of stuffing around your middle protected you from harm."

His reference to the disguise set her teeth on edge. It was as if he were deliberately trying to needle her, which made no sense if he hoped to procure her as his mistress.

Before she could formulate a suitable retort, he leaned closer and scrutinized her face. "Perchance, are you feeling overheated?"

"Certainly not!" The last thing she wanted was for him to presume she was burning with lust. "Why would you ask?"

"The mole on your chin appears to be melting—along with the rest of your face."

With a small gasp, Maddy lifted her hand and touched the makeshift wart. The pads of her fingers came away gummy with flesh-colored putty. She tentatively explored her cheeks to find the same gooey mess. Dear heavens, she must look a fright.

Her gaze flashed to Lord Rowley. Naturally, the sewer rat appeared to be enjoying her plight, judging by the gleam in his eyes.

"At least now I'm getting a glimpse of the real Madelyn Swann," he said. "It would be helpful if you were to remove the rest of the disguise, as well."

"With great pleasure."

Maddy scraped a sticky wad off her chin and flung it at him. He glanced down at the damage. The blob left a whitish trail down the front of his tailored, charcoal-gray coat.

Her action had a startling effect on him. For the first

time, that rakish smile vanished and a thunderous expression darkened his face. His lips compressed into a thin line and his jaw hardened.

He looked fit to kill.

Alarm buried her anger. She'd gone too far this time. He was a powerfully built man and she was alone with him. Alone in this deserted theater where he could do with her as he willed.

Nevertheless, she lifted her chin and ordered, "Leave here at once, my lord. The auction is over, and I've nothing more to say to you."

Clutching the bids in one hand, Maddy headed for the door at the back of the stage, struggling against the impulse to run for her life. She turned the knob with sticky fingers and went into the narrow corridor that led to the dressing rooms. A single lantern cast a dim, cheerless light over the old theater posters tacked to the dingy walls.

Where was Gertie? Surely the maid hadn't gone home. Surely she must be waiting in the dressing room. Unless by some charming ploy he had convinced the woman to vacate the premises : . .

The heavy tread of footsteps sounded behind Maddy. Her heart jerked against her tight corset. A glance back revealed Lord Rowley's dark, broad-shouldered form coming through the doorway in pursuit of her.

"Don't you dare follow me," she snapped over her shoulder. "You aren't permitted backstage. Now get out!"

He made no response, only continued to pace after her. She swallowed a glut of fear. He was a far more formidable opponent than Lord Dunham. She had caught her cousin off guard the previous evening by striking him with the bouquet of roses. But she'd already used the element of surprise on Lord Rowley, and she had an uneasy suspicion he would not be fooled again.

Maddy quickened her steps. So did he. It occurred to

her that he could have easily caught her by now, but he kept a circumspect distance. Perhaps he was toying with her. Like a lion with his prey in sight.

He must believe he had her cornered. She prayed he did not.

A welcome wedge of light spilled from her dressing room. She rushed into the small chamber and slammed the door shut. To her immense relief, Gertie was kneeling before the trunk, folding items to be packed.

"I'm so glad you're here!" Maddy uttered fervently. She tossed the bids onto her dressing table and then grabbed the single wooden chair.

"Be there somethin' wrong, dearie?" The maidservant frowned as she pushed to her feet. "Why, ye look a fright. What happened t' yer wig?"

"Never mind. It's Lord Rowley—he's coming, and he's very angry. I must bar him from entering!"

Maddy wedged the back of the chair under the door handle. Just in time.

A hard rapping sounded. "Miss Swann, let me in. I've something to give to you."

"Go away!" she called, glowering at the wooden panel. "I won't read your proposal. As I told you, it's too late. The auction is closed."

Gertie came to stand beside her. She gave Maddy a keen stare. "Ye ain't heard his lordship's offer yet?"

"No." Feeling safer now in company, Maddy resorted to her earlier anger, speaking loudly enough so that he would hear out in the corridor. "He's a conceited, self-satisfied churl and I want nothing to do with him!"

Much to Maddy's shock, Gertie walked forward and moved the chair out of the way. She opened the door and bobbed a curtsy to Lord Rowley. "Beggin' yer pardon, milord. Miss Swann will indeed talk t' ye. 'Tis only polite since ye took the time t' write up a bid."

The maid gave Maddy a chiding look, the same one she'd used when Maddy was a child and had sneaked an extra sweet.

Dumbfounded, Maddy felt as if the world had shifted on its axis. Why would Gertie take his side? Lord Rowley might be handsome—insufferably so—but how had he charmed the no-nonsense maidservant in one brief conversation at the back of the theater?

His wide shoulders and overwhelming presence filled the doorway. He had to duck his head slightly while stepping into the dressing room. The smear of putty on his lapel looked like a badge of dishonor.

As he glanced at Gertie, a silent message passed between them.

"I'll wait right outside," the maid declared, taking the chair with her. "Holler if ye need me, miss."

"Don't go—" Maddy objected.

But the door was already closing behind the woman. Once again, she was alone with Lord Rowley.

Chapter 6

The viscount strolled around the little dressing room. With great interest, he eyed the costumes that hung from hooks on the wall, the piles of folded accessories in the trunk, the chipped china pitcher on the washstand, the collection of cosmetics on the dressing table.

Maddy clenched her teeth and watched him scrutinize her private space. His presence seemed to suck the very air out of the room—that had to be why she found it difficult to draw breath into her lungs. She ought to make a dash for the door while his back was turned.

Yet curiosity rooted her in place. How had he managed to hoodwink Gertie into cooperating in his scheme? What exactly had he said to the maid?

Grabbing a rag, Maddy used it to wipe her sticky fingers. "You had no right to follow me," she snapped. "You aren't wanted here."

He fixed his keen gaze on her. "I followed you because I have something that belongs to you."

"If you're referring to your bid," she said, rubbing furiously at a spot on her thumb, "I've already said I won't take it."

"Then perhaps you'll take this."

A provocative smile playing on his lips, he held out the ripped half of Lord Herrington's offer. The one that had been stuck under his shoe. The one she had totally forgotten about.

She snatched it from him. "If you think to soften me, you're sadly mistaken. That phony charm won't work on me as it did on Gertie. So you may as well save your breath."

Maddy marched to the dressing table and added the ripped piece to the other bids. Too bad she lacked the bodily strength to evict Lord Rowley. Well, she would simply ignore him. She'd pretend he wasn't even there. Eventually he would be forced to depart in frustration.

Seating herself on the stool, she pinned up her messy blond locks, securing them in a loose bun on top of her head. Then she dipped a corner of the rag into a pot of linseed oil, using it to scrub the makeup from her face. The task of removing the wrinkles kept her busy for several long minutes. All the while, she sensed Lord Rowley's nearness like an impending calamity.

From this angle, she couldn't see him in the oval mirror. Yet the fine hairs prickled at the nape of her neck. What was he doing? What if he was a madman? What if he drew a knife and murdered her?

Maybe then Gertie would be sorry for deserting her!

On the pretext of cleaning a stubborn place beside her nose, Maddy leaned forward to peer more closely into the mirror. She spied him standing to one side behind her, his shoulder propped against the wall in a relaxed pose. The filthy beast was watching her. His gaze roved over her as if he were trying to peer through the dense padding beneath her black gown.

She pivoted on the stool. "Blast you! Just go! I've already made my choice, anyway."

"Without reading the bids? You're bluffing."

"Actually, I'm not."

"Who's the lucky fellow, then?"

"It's none of your concern."

In utter disregard for her wishes, Lord Rowley sauntered closer, coming to stand by the dressing table. There, he leaned against the wall with his arms crossed. An enticing hint of his masculine scent drifted to her, and his nearness caused an irksome pulse in her loins.

"I did a bit of research on the men you invited to the auction," he said. "Bachelors, all of them. You must have an aversion to engaging in an affair with a married man."

Paying him no heed, Maddy resumed cleansing her face. It wouldn't do to admit he was right, that she could never steal another woman's husband. The very thought repelled her.

"So who *is* the chosen one?" the viscount asked. "I can't imagine you'd pick Lord Netherfield. He's too much the whiner."

She ignored Lord Rowley. Any answer would only encourage him.

"I also very much doubt you'd favor a loudmouthed boor like Gerald Jenkins," he mused. "Or a nefarious rake like Dunham, no matter that he's heir to a dukedom."

Lord Rowley and her cousin had spoken to each other as Dunham had been leaving the theater. She badly wanted to ask what they had said, but restrained herself.

"No," he went on in a speculative tone, "you'd go for a man *you* can control. A fledgling like Mr. Stanford, perhaps."

She rubbed the last of the putty from her chin. Let Lord Rowley blather all he liked. She had the training and discipline to pretend he wasn't even there.

"The trouble is, young Stanford lacks the funds to keep you in high style. I rather doubt his offer will suffice."

Maddy concentrated on her image in the mirror. Her skin was rosy from all the scrubbing and shiny from the linseed oil. So much the better. Maybe if Lord Rowley deemed her unattractive, he'd go away.

"That narrows the field," he continued. "I'm guessing you'd select a dull dog who's rich enough to keep you in jewels, yet will allow you free rein to do as you please. Perhaps a scholar who spends most of his time in the library. Like the Marquess of Herrington."

Her fingers paused ever so slightly while wiping a trace of putty from her hairline. Quickly she schooled her expression into blankness.

He leaned down suddenly, planting his hands on the edge of the dressing table. "I've guessed him, haven't I? It *is* Herrington you favor."

Maddy thinned her lips. This time, she couldn't help but turn her head to glare at him, only to find his green eyes on level with hers. They seemed to peer into her very soul. How was it that he could read her thoughts so well?

Flustered, she jumped up from the stool. "And what if it is him? He's a marquess and a gentleman and I'll be exceedingly happy as his mistress!"

Maddy stomped over to the washstand, grabbed the pitcher, and filled the basin with water. She seized the sliver of soap and lathered her hands vigorously, then bent over the basin and scrubbed the last traces of makeup from her face. How foolish of her to answer Lord Rowley. She should *not* have let him goad her like that. And if he imagined his mockery of her suitors would induce her to change her mind in his favor, he'd be sorely disappointed.

The soap suds burned her eyes. Blinded, she splashed water over her face, then groped for the towel where it always hung on its hook. Her fingers found only bare wood. "Blast it . . . Gertie! Where's the—"

A linen cloth made its way into her hand, and she felt the unexpected touch of Lord Rowley's warm, rough skin against hers. Startled, she backed away while blotting the water from her face and rubbing her eyes.

Through damp lashes, she glowered at him. "Are you still here, my lord? I vow, you're like a swollen pustule that won't go away."

Rather than take offense, he chuckled. "I wonder if Herrington knows that you can hurl insults like a fishwife. He won't be happy to have his peace and quiet disturbed."

"There will be no outbursts with the marquess, for *he* merits being treated as a gentleman." Maddy flung the wet towel at him. "Unlike a tedious wretch like you who deserves to be cursed from here to perdition."

He easily caught the towel with one hand. "Call me whatever you please, Miss Swann. I happen to like your colorful curses."

His grin held a genuine appreciation that Maddy found perplexing. Any other gentleman would be insulted, infuriated, affronted. Perhaps he truly *was* a madman.

"I've had quite enough of this nonsense," she said crisply. She tried to cross her arms, but it was awkward with the padding around her midsection. "I should like you to go now."

"So you can piece together Herrington's bid and see how much he's offered you to warm his bed? Don't waste your time."

With that, Lord Rowley strode to the dressing table, gathered up the proposals, and tossed the lot into the rubbish bin.

Maddy lunged forward to rescue them, but his long legs blocked her access to the container beneath the dressing table. "What do you think you're doing?" she asked. "Move out of the way, you tyrant."

"None of them can possibly match my offer." The viscount reached inside his coat and produced a folded paper. "Here, do yourself a favor and have a look."

He thrust the folded bid into her hand. She felt a strong compulsion to rip it into shreds and throw it at his too handsome face. But then he would continue to plague her with his presence. It was clear Lord Rowley wouldn't leave until he'd had his way.

As much as she disliked being forced to capitulate, reading the proposal might be her best course of action. Then she could reject it soundly and send him packing.

"Oh, for pity's sake!" Hissing out a breath, Maddy broke the silver wax seal and unfolded the sheet of paper. She angled it close to the oil lamp on the dressing table. Written in bold black penmanship, the offer was brief, concise . . . and utterly astounding. Her legs wilted and she sank down onto the stool to scan the words a second time.

She cast a disbelieving look up at him. "You want me to be your *wife*—not your mistress? This must be a jest."

"Oh, it's quite true, Miss Swann. All the other bidders will keep you hidden away like a dirty little secret. I, on the other hand, want you at my side as I enter society. I'm offering you the honor of my name along with a generous stipend. You will be Lady Rowley—and a wealthy woman in your own right."

The masculine angles of his face revealed a firm resolve. As an actress, she'd made a study of facial expressions so that she could reproduce them on stage. Lord Rowley was indeed telling the truth.

All of a sudden she understood why Gertie approved of him. He must have told her of his plan to offer marriage. Nothing would make the maidservant happier than to see Maddy with a ring on her finger and a title to her name.

But that didn't explain *his* motive for the startling proposition.

Why would a nobleman wish to wed a lowborn actress whom he had only just met? In fact, he hadn't even met her when he'd written up the bid. One possibility jumped to the forefront of her mind. Perhaps he was like Edmund. Perhaps Lord Rowley needed a convenient wife to cover up his secret predilections. "Are you one of those men who prefers . . . other men?"

He stared at her, then chuckled softly. His hand reached out to caress her cheek. "Hardly. I can assure you, Miss Swann, this marriage *will* be consummated. I've every intention of making love to you. Thoroughly and completely."

His light touch unfurled a ribbon of heat that descended deep into her body. The sensation was so potent, so pleasurable, that she immediately pictured herself lying naked in his arms while he explored her most forbidden places. It was a disturbing fantasy, for she couldn't deny that a part of her burned with lust for him. Another part, however, rejected the prospect of submitting to such a conceited rogue.

She sprang up from the stool again. "I haven't agreed to this marriage. How can you expect me to commit the rest of my life to you on the basis of one meeting? We don't even like each other—or at least I don't much like you!"

Lord Rowley shrugged. "You need only tolerate me for one season—perhaps three months in all. Then I will leave England for good. And I shan't ever return."

"Leave? Why?"

"I've numerous business interests abroad. As part of our agreement, you will be required to remain here in London. You'll have the income and the title—along with the expectation of becoming Countess of Gilmore upon the death of my father."

When Lord Rowley mentioned his sire, his jaw tightened slightly and his lips firmed. That hint of tension in his expression sparked a realization in her. Slowly, she guessed, "You intend to use me to embarrass your noble family."

"Indeed." He prowled the confines of the dressing room

before turning to face her. "You strike me as a clever woman, Miss Swann, so I shan't mince words. The Earl of Gilmore will be livid to learn that his heir has taken a notorious actress as a bride. He'll be even angrier when he discovers we'll be living at Gilmore House with him."

"Why do you despise your father so much?"

"My reasons are my own," he said sharply. "You are not to question me on the matter. In return for my generosity, I'll expect you to perform as you've done tonight—by hurling insults and playing the guttersnipe. The more outrageously you behave, the better. Feel free to swing from the chandeliers if it suits you."

A deep anger underscored his words. Lord Rowley truly hated his father. Enough to foist a low-class female into the earl's household as a member of the family.

She wondered what terrible circumstances could have inspired such a powerful animosity in him. Was that why he'd been abroad for the past ten years? Had he come back to England for the express purpose of setting into motion this odious plot to punish his father?

Her every instinct warned Maddy not to entangle herself in the scheme. Lord Rowley expected her to behave as a coarse, foulmouthed termagant. No wonder he had found her actions tonight so entertaining. She had played right into his hands. She fit the profile of the slattern he wanted to wed.

He intended to parade her before his aristocratic family and all of society, too. They would scorn her as an ill-mannered commoner. She would be snubbed at every ball, every dinner party, every drive in the park. They would never accept her as one of their own. No matter how lofty her title, she would always be the scandalous actress who'd been purchased at auction by the Earl of Gilmore's heir.

So why did she feel tempted to accept?

It wasn't the money. One of the other noblemen could provide her the funds to open her shop. In a year's time, the affair would be over and she would gain her freedom.

But Lord Rowley would set her free, too, and much sooner. He would leave England forever in a few months and then she could open the ladies' apparel shop she'd always wanted to own. Her elevated status would bring the wives of merchants flocking to her store. *They* wouldn't care that society had shunned her. It would be enough for them to rub elbows with a lady of high rank . . .

"Well?" he prompted as he came to stand in front of her. "I need your answer, Miss Swann. In exchange for a title and wealth, will you be the trollop who causes an uproar in my father's household?"

"It's more likely you and I will be at each other's throats."

"So much the better." Taking her hand in his, he brought it to his lips for a smooth kiss. "This is your chance to play the greatest role of your career. Only think of all the ingenious ways you can irritate my father. It shall be great fun, I promise you."

He gave her that heart-stopping smile, complete with dimples and a flash of white teeth. It was absurd for one man to be so gorgeous—and to cause her blood to heat at his slightest touch. She must be a fool even to consider participating in his despicable plot of vengeance.

Yet who was she to stand in judgment of him? She had long dreamed of taking her own revenge—though he must never know it.

Unlike the other bidders, Lord Rowley was offering her the chance to enter society. The chance to mingle with the nobility. The chance to seek out her grandfather, the Duke of Houghton, and to punish him for disowning her mother.

"All right," Maddy said. "I accept."

Chapter 7

While the ancient cleric droned his way through the marriage service, Nate cast a sideways glance at his bride. Madelyn Swann stood beside him at the altar, her sapphire-blue eyes fixed on the minister. Late afternoon sunlight filtered through one of the chapel windows and illuminated her fine profile, the pert nose, the rosy lips, the long lashes. A cherry-red bonnet covered her hair, though a few blond strands had escaped to frame her face.

Good God, she was beautiful. A most delectable bit of muslin. Her disguise at the auction two nights ago had kept him from fully comprehending that fact until today.

His gaze flicked downward. *Oh, yes.* He'd selected that tawdry crimson dress from her trunk of costumes. The gown hugged the curves of her waist and hips while her breasts pushed in creamy abundance against the low-cut bodice. No wonder men had flocked to the auction for the chance to bid on her as their mistress.

She looked ravishing. And he could scarcely wait to ravish her.

The minister's voice echoed in the chapel. " 'If any man can shew any just cause why they may not lawfully be joined together, let him now speak, or else hereafter for-ever hold his peace.'"

The balding clergyman looked up from his black book. A long pause ensued while he squinted through his round spectacles at the chapel door, as if expecting someone to come dashing down the aisle with a long list of Nate's sins.

Nate didn't need to glance back over his shoulder to know that the near-empty pews held only the two requi-site witnesses: Gertie, the dour maidservant, and Elias Josephson, a grizzled ship's mate whom Nate had com-mandeered to act as his valet. No other guests had been invited, for no gossip must reach the ears of the ton. Not yet, anyway. Not until he had presented his scandalous wife to his family and savored the horrified shock on the Earl of Gilmore's face.

Impatience gnawed at him, and Nate controlled the urge to snap at the minister. He wanted this church service to be over with and done. He wanted to take Madelyn Swann to Gilmore House and witness the unfolding of his re-venge.

The minister resumed in a thundering tone, "'I charge ye both, as ye will answer at the dreadful day of judg-ment when the secrets of all hearts shall be disclosed, that if either of ye know any impediment why ye may not be lawfully joined together in matrimony, ye do now confess it.'"

This time, instead of looking at the church door, he stared back and forth between Nate and his bride. No doubt the cleric was suspicious at the speed and secrecy of the nuptials. Under normal circumstances, the church required the posting of banns for three successive Sundays. But Nate had acquired a special license the previous day, thanks to a note from Lady Milford to the archbishop.

His godmother had been surprisingly helpful. Although

she disapproved of his purpose, she had arranged for his participation in the auction. No doubt she'd feared that he might pluck a scruffy beggar out of the gutter to be his wife.

Nate had to concede that Lady Milford had been right to insist upon advising him. He was quite satisfied with her selection. Madelyn Swann could enunciate well due to her training as a Shakespearean actress. Yet she also could spew curses like a seasoned harpy. And nothing would be more offensive to the Earl of Gilmore than to learn that his new daughter-in-law was a commoner who'd auctioned her body to the highest bidder.

The minister cleared his throat. " 'Wilt thou have this woman to thy wedded wife—' "

Nathan cut off the rest. "I will."

The cleric pursed his lips, then turned to Madelyn Swann. " 'Wilt thou have this man to thy wedded husband, to live together after God's ordinance in the holy estate of matrimony? Wilt thou obey him and serve him, love, honor and keep him in sickness and in health, and forsaking all others, keep thee only unto him so long as ye both shall live?' "

Madelyn Swann cast a guarded glance at Nate. Once again, he felt bowled over by her lush beauty. Those deep blue eyes. Those delicate features. Those soft lips that had blistered him with reproaches when he'd lunged out of the darkness and yanked off her wig.

She'd scarcely spoken a word to him today when he'd fetched her from her cheap rooming house. Unlike the furious vixen of the night of the auction, she had been solemn and reticent. What if she was harboring second thoughts about the marriage?

How absurd.

Madelyn Swann was a fortune hunter. The chit had agreed to his demands because she craved the status of a lady and all its attendant luxuries. What lowborn female would not? No doubt her mind must be preoccupied with daydreams of fancy balls and an extravagant wardrobe, of lording her newly elevated place over those of lesser rank.

She would not, *she could not,* say no.

Could she?

Her lips parted. Her voice rang out clearly. "I will."

Nate released the breath he hadn't realized he'd been holding. His heart was thudding against his ribs. He hadn't truly been afraid of her refusal. It was just that her cantankerous nature made her unpredictable.

On the instructions of the minister, they turned face-to-face and repeated their vows, first Nate and then her. *For richer, for poorer, in sickness and in health, to love and to cherish, till death us do part . . .*

What rot. Neither of them had any intention of honoring such a pledge. They might be wed in the eyes of the law, and he certainly meant to exercise his conjugal rights, but otherwise their union might as well be a business contract.

He would use her for revenge. She would use him for his wealth and position. All the rest of this ritual was pure claptrap.

When the minister prompted him to produce a ring, Nate realized that he'd never thought to purchase one. "There is none," he hissed. "Get on with it."

For a moment it looked as though the fusty old fellow would put a halt to the entire ceremony. But Nate stared him down.

The cleric cleared his throat. " 'Those whom God hath joined together let no man put asunder . . . I now pronounce ye man and wife.' "

Madelyn's blue eyes lifted to Nate in cool disdain. She clearly intended to maintain a wall between them. To keep him at arm's length as she'd done the evening of the auction.

Her aloofness irked him. Madelyn was his wife now. He wouldn't allow her to dictate the terms of their marriage. She needed to learn who was in charge.

Pulling her against his body, Nate bent his head and subjected her to a deep kiss. Her lips parted as if to protest, and he seized the opportunity to slide his tongue inside her mouth. She was warm, soft, delectable. As he moved his hands down her slender back, his blood heated. At the auction, she had disguised her feminine curves beneath a mountain of padding. He wouldn't allow such a crime ever again.

Madelyn stood rigidly for a moment; then with a little purr of pleasure she arched on tiptoes to return his kiss. Her fingers threaded into his hair and she melted against him. *Yes.* She lusted for him as much as he did for her.

Tonight, he would take her to his bed. Such a beautiful actress must have had a harem of lovers. She would be well versed in the art of lovemaking. She likely knew a host of ways to please a man. He couldn't wait to discover them— and to teach her some of his own.

Though revenge was the primary purpose of this marriage, bedding her would be a satisfying bonus. They would have a few months in which to enjoy each other's bodies. By then, he no doubt would tire of her carping and be ready to depart England for good, leaving his inappropriate wife as a thorn in his father's side. And with luck, Nate would have planted a son in her. Gilmore would be especially irate at the earldom's bloodline being diluted . . .

The minister loudly cleared his throat.

Nate reluctantly drew back. To his satisfaction, Madelyn looked dazed, her lips reddened. A blush tinted her cheeks; she must have realized the spectacle they'd made in front of the rector and the witnesses. He felt not a particle of regret. She belonged to him now.

His wife. Lady Rowley.

The name caused a twist in his gut. Viscount Rowley had been David's courtesy title. Throughout their childhood, his elder brother had been addressed as such by the servants. David had deserved the honor, for he had been the good son: proper, kind, well behaved.

Nate couldn't shake the guilty sense that he'd somehow stolen the title. He loathed having the noble distinction thrust upon him. He'd far rather have his brother alive and well.

As he gave Madelyn his arm and they proceeded into the vestry to sign the register, he took a deep, revitalizing breath. It was better to concentrate on his revenge than to dwell on regrets. His plan had been set into motion. Within the hour, he would face the Earl of Gilmore for the first time in ten years.

Today, Nate would not be the scorned second son. Today, he was the heir. And today, he had the perfect weapon of retaliation in his highly unsuitable bride.

Maddy tried not to gawk as they stepped out of the carriage in front of Gilmore House. It had been daunting enough to ride in the luxurious vehicle with its plush cushions and gilt fittings when she was accustomed to ancient hackney cabs. She cast a glance upward at the columned marble façade and wondered for the umpteenth time why she'd been foolish enough to embroil herself in such a mad scheme.

Lord Rowley barked an order to the driver to take the coach around to the mews. He looked strikingly handsome in the white cravat and forest-green coat, a tall black hat on his head, his long dark hair tied back in a queue. She wondered why he favored the old-fashioned style. Yet it suited him. It made him look dangerous and distinctive, quite unlike any other gentleman she'd ever met.

He was her husband now.

A quake of unreality turned her knees to jelly. Maddy felt as if she were acting out a play, that at any moment the curtains would swing shut and she would walk back to her cluttered dressing room at the theater. It was difficult to believe that only two days ago, she had been preparing for the auction and planning to choose a temporary lover.

Now, she was married. To a powerful peer who craved revenge on his father.

Dear God. What had she done?

Lord Rowley turned to her and offered his arm. His face was taut, his jaw set. For a moment she couldn't move. He was wholly unlike the charming man of two evenings ago, chuckling at her curses and uttering jests of his own. During the half-hour ride from the chapel near the Strand, he had been largely silent. He'd sat staring out the window, his fingers tapping impatiently on the velvet cushion. Now that he had entrapped her, he clearly no longer felt the need to sweet-talk her or to flash his dimpled smiles.

Maddy rather regretted that. As much as he'd irked her at their first meeting, she had enjoyed sparring with him. He had made her feel warm and alive. Not filled with cold misgivings.

"Take my arm," he ordered in an undertone. "Lest you trip on your skirts walking up the stairs."

"Wouldn't that suit your purpose?" she taunted, while curling her fingers around the hard crook of his sleeve. "For me to make an embarrassing spectacle of myself?"

"Not if you land on your face and bloody your nose. I shan't give Gilmore any reason to accuse me of mistreating you."

The Earl of Gilmore. How sad that Lord Rowley referred to his sire in such a chilly manner. Maddy's father had always been "Papa" to her, a man who'd deserved her love and respect.

As they proceeded up the wide stone steps, Lord Rowley continued in a low growl, "Once we're inside, you're to play the crass, prattling fishwife. It's imperative that you stay in character at all times."

"That oughtn't be a problem. After all, it *is* my true character. Isn't that why you chose me, my lord?"

He scowled at her as if suspicious of her sarcasm. "The more tactless blunders you commit, the better. And you're to babble, too."

"Babble?"

"Yes. Gilmore has a particular loathing for chatterboxes."

Well, that was fine by her, Maddy thought. She'd had experience in playing a variety of roles, and today she didn't even have to memorize a script. She could just pretend to be the loudmouthed vixen and behave accordingly. Provoking his father's disgust ought to be simple enough.

Yet a coil of nerves squeezed her stomach. Events were proceeding far too quickly. If only she could have a day or two in which to settle into her new life and adjust to the novelty of being a married lady. If only she didn't have to face this dreadful scene on the very afternoon of her wedding . . .

As they reached the portico, she stopped just short of the massive white door. "Lord Rowley, wait. What if your father isn't at home? Have you sent word ahead?"

He glowered down at her, and the sunlight illuminated the gold specks in his green eyes. "He's here. Lady Milford assured me of that. And you had better call me Nate. Gilmore must be deceived into believing we're madly in love."

Nate. It didn't quite suit him. It was too small, too

ordinary for an aggressive, self-important nobleman like him. "I'll call you Nathan. And if you continue to glare at me like that, *you'll* be the one to ruin this ruse. You'll spoil the image of the blissful bridegroom."

A grin suddenly tilted his mouth, lightening his stark expression and causing his dimples to deepen attractively. Bending his head closer, he murmured, "I'll play the blissful bridegroom, to be sure. Especially in our bedchamber tonight."

Her breath lodged in her throat. For one heart-pounding moment, Maddy thought he meant to kiss her again. Right here on the porch, in front of all the fancy carriages and posh passersby on the street. His passionate embrace in church had caught her by surprise. She had not expected the shockingly wonderful assault of his mouth, the intense rush of heat, or her irresistible impulse to kiss him back.

I can assure you, Miss Swann, this marriage will be consummated. I've every intention of making love to you. Thoroughly and completely.

A pleasurable shiver tingled over her skin as she remembered his promise to her on the night of the auction. Having never lain with a man, she had only a rudimentary knowledge of what would transpire between them tonight. Pondering it made her both edgy and eager. In the darkened privacy of their bedchamber, they would cuddle under the covers while he kissed her again. His hands would rove over her nightdress and then delve beneath it . . .

The abrupt click of an opening door interrupted the immodest fantasy. Her cheeks burning, she jerked her gaze away from Lord Rowley. No, *Nathan*. She had to train herself to address him by his first name.

A barrel-chested older man in black tails stood in the doorway, one sparse eyebrow raised in inquiry. His aura of cool hauteur vanished as a smile creased his jowly features and lit up his brown eyes. "Master Nathan! Can it truly be you, returned home at last?" The man paused a fraction, then corrected himself with a servile bow. "Forgive me, my lord. I spoke out of turn."

Grinning, Nathan clapped the man on the shoulder. "It's been a devil of a long time, Shawshank. But I should have known you'd still be here on duty."

"No rocking chair for me or Mrs. Shawshank just yet—though his lordship *has* hired a new cook from Paris." The servant's gaze flicked to Maddy as if to puzzle out her identity. "Pray, come inside at once, my lord."

Shawshank must be the butler, Maddy surmised, as Lord Rowley—Nathan—placed his hand at the small of her back and urged her to precede him into the house. The warm pressure of his touch felt unbearably intimate. As if he were branding her as his own.

Of course, he was making his claim on her perfectly clear to the servant. The charade had commenced. The thought caused a quivery sensation in the pit of her belly.

Then she forgot all else as they entered a magnificent foyer. The spacious room soared upward for three stories to a domed ceiling that was painted with cherubs and angels frolicking among clouds. An enormous crystal chandelier glinted in the late afternoon sunlight. The pale green walls displayed a selection of portraits and landscapes in gilded frames, along with several busts on pedestals. In the center of the hall, a marble staircase curved up to the next floor, the stone banister continuing along an upper balcony on either side.

Maddy had passed many grand houses in her time in London. But never before had she actually set foot inside one. Lord—*Nathan* had said they would be living here at Gilmore House.

Once again, that peculiar dreamlike state enveloped

her. She couldn't imagine calling this splendid dwelling her home. It seemed more like a palace occupied by kings and queens and nobles.

She was now a member of the upper crust, Maddy reminded herself. Yet she felt like an intruder. A part of her wanted to flee out the door and return to the familiarity of the theater.

Nathan removed his hat and handed it to a footman, along with his gloves. "Do give him your cloak, darling," he said to Maddy. To the butler, he added, "I'm afraid you'll have to be patient with Lady Rowley. She isn't familiar with the ways of a noble house."

The butler's eyes widened on Maddy. Clearly, he'd just realized she was Nathan's wife. "Er . . . felicitations, my lord."

Lady Rowley. She mulled over the new name while unfastening the frog loop at her throat. It seemed to belong to another person, someone far loftier than herself, or perhaps a character in a play. But, of course, that was the point. She was here to perform a role.

And there was no time like the present to begin.

She tossed her cloak to the footman. Then she turned to the butler and seized his gloved hand, pumping it up and down. "May I say, 'tis a pleasure to meet you, Mr. Shawshank. I hope we can become fast friends."

His jowly face turned crimson. Especially when his gaze dipped to the scandalous cut of her bodice. The servant recovered swiftly, his expression reverting to stoic politeness. "Thank you, my lady. Might I take your bonnet as well?"

She untied the ribbons beneath her chin and pitched the hat to him. "Certainly, sir. But have a care not to crush the cherries. They cost me a pretty penny!"

He shifted his hands so as not to touch the jaunty cluster as he transferred the bonnet to the footman. "You've naught to fear, my lady. The staff shall take excellent care with your belongings."

The young footman in his smart blue livery and formal white wig openly gawked at her before scurrying away down a long corridor. Maddy could only imagine the gossip that would ensue shortly in the servants' hall. Everyone would crowd around belowstairs to hear the lurid details of Lord Rowley's outrageous bride.

Would Gertie have the sense to hold her sharp tongue?

With any luck, the maid wouldn't have arrived just yet. After the wedding ceremony, she had gone to collect Maddy's belongings from the boardinghouse. Maddy would have to caution the woman later . . .

"Is my father at home?" Nathan asked the butler.

"The family is presently in the drawing room, taking tea. If you'll wait in the antechamber, I'll see if his lordship is still with them."

"Pray don't tell him I've brought company," Nathan ordered. He slid his arm around Maddy's waist and gave her the warm smile of a besotted lover. "I want my new wife to be a surprise."

"As you wish, my lord."

After making a deferential bow, Shawshank turned away and headed at a measured pace up the marble stairway. His posture was so ramrod straight he resembled a soldier on parade.

The moment he was out of earshot, Maddy pulled away from Nathan's staged embrace and scowled at him. "The *family*?" she whispered. "Do you mean to say there'll be others present besides your father?"

Nathan shrugged. "My grandmother, the dowager countess, lives here at Gilmore House. So does my brother's widow, Sophia, though I've never met the woman. And there's my sister, Emily. She'll be nineteen now and no longer in the nursery."

The prospect of facing a trio of snooty aristocratic ladies unnerved Maddy. She felt unprepared for such an ordeal. "You never mentioned I'd be seeing anyone but the earl today."

He cocked an eyebrow. "So? You ought to feel right at home in front of an audience."

"Perhaps, but . . ." Aside from her mother and Lady Milford, the few ladies she'd encountered had been haughty and condescending, scorning to speak to her. "You ought to have warned me I'd be performing to a group. Had I known, I'd never have agreed to wear this ghastly gown. It's designed for a stage production, not fashionable society!"

His appreciative gaze dipped to her near-naked bosom. "On the contrary, it's perfect for a scandalous actress. A woman should always show off her best assets."

"My best asset is my mind."

He chuckled. "Well, try not to act too intelligent today. As part of the ruse, of course." Catching hold of her elbow, he tugged her toward the staircase. "Come along now."

Maddy struggled to keep up with his long strides. "What are you doing? We're supposed to wait down here."

"And let Gilmore refuse to see me? No. Absolutely not."

Clutching her skirts while ascending the broad stairs, she slanted a glance up at Nathan, who was looking grim-faced again. "Surely he wouldn't be so rude. He hasn't seen you in ten years."

"You don't know the Earl of Gilmore. Now, stop arguing. You're supposed to vex my father, not me!"

Reaching the top of the staircase, he propelled her down a wide corridor. Shell-shaped sconces for candles decorated the walls, while gilt chairs sat at intervals. Their feet made no sound on the thick carpet with its pattern of roses and ivy. To either side of her lay palatial rooms, one of them a dining chamber with a table longer than the stage at the Neptune Theater.

Maddy was hard-pressed not to gape in awe. The size and splendor of this house was as alien to her as the moon. Mama had grown up in such a palace. How had she ever adjusted to life with a troupe of actors, staying in a tiny caravan while they traveled from town to town? No wonder she had spoken wistfully of her past life—especially the father who'd coldly told her she was dead to him.

Maddy clenched her teeth. As Lady Rowley, she would enter high society. She would go to parties and balls and dinners, and at some point, she would encounter the almighty Duke of Houghton.

Her grandfather. The villain who had shunned Mama.

That was the one quality she and Nathan shared, Maddy reflected. They both craved revenge on a family member. But her husband must never learn of her connection to the nobility. Her true background must remain shrouded in secrecy until just the right moment.

Nathan brought her to a halt in the corridor just outside an arched doorway. Though she couldn't quite see inside, Maddy heard muffled voices emanate from within the room: the angry rumble of a man, then the higher-pitched, shocked tone of a woman.

The butler must have just announced Lord Rowley's arrival.

She glanced up. Nathan's face was a hard mask, and it seemed for a moment that he'd forgotten her presence. The whalebone corset beneath the tawdry gown squeezed her rib cage. If only she could read his thoughts . . .

His fingers tightened around her arm. As he guided her toward the doorway, his eyes glinted with the hardness of emeralds. "Smile, darling," he hissed. "The show is about to begin."

Chapter 8

They stepped into an immense, long chamber with gold brocade draperies on the many tall windows. Enormous tapestries hung on the walls. Formal groupings of chaises and chairs provided places for family and visitors to sit. The numerous side tables displayed an array of curios that Maddy would have liked to examine more closely had Nathan not steered her toward the far end of the chamber.

Several people clustered near a marble fireplace where flames danced on the hearth to ward off the chill of the early spring afternoon. A silver tea service rested upon a trolley, and a slender brunette lady stood with the pot in hand, filling a cup. Nearby, a middle-aged gentleman and an elderly woman sat in a pair of thronelike chairs.

Their attention was trained on the butler.

Shawshank bowed, then started to walk away. He stopped upon seeing Maddy and Nathan coming toward the group. "Lord Rowley!" The hapless butler glanced back at the seated gentleman. "Pardon me, your lordship. I did ask him to wait downstairs."

As one, the three aristocrats turned to stare at the newcomers. The younger woman frowned—no, they *all* frowned.

No one uttered a word of greeting. Nor did anyone smile or exclaim joyfully or open their arms to welcome Nathan home.

The older man set aside his teacup and rose from his chair. His build somewhat burly, his thinning auburn hair sprinkled with gray, he wore a tailored black suit with a crisp white cravat. His lips were compressed, his eyes dark brown, his cheeks pitted with a few pockmarks. He exuded the hostile contempt that one might direct at a bill collector—not a long-lost son and heir.

He must be Nathan's father, the Earl of Gilmore.

Maddy's stomach clenched. As Shawshank exited the drawing room, she wanted to go with the butler. But she'd committed herself to this ruse in exchange for a lavish stipend and a place in society. There was no turning back now.

Arm in arm, Nathan strolled with Maddy to join the gathering. He bowed to the two ladies in turn, then gave a sardonic nod to the earl.

"Hullo, Father. I trust you've told Shawshank to kill the fatted calf in honor of the prodigal son's return."

Gilmore's nostrils flared. He stood rigidly still, his fingers clenched into fists at his sides. "You would dare to make jests after vanishing for an entire decade. Where the deuce have you been these past ten years?"

"Traveling through the Far East. And you may congratulate me. I've become quite the wealthy businessman."

"An Atwood, in trade?" the senior woman said with disapproval. The gnarled claws of one hand wrapped around the gold knob of a cane; she had hazel eyes that squinted from a mass of wrinkles on her face. "I cannot believe even *you* would stoop so low, Nathan."

He favored her with a cool smile. "Ah, but it's true, Grandmamma. I deal in tea, silk, spices, whatever goods can be used to turn a profit. I've been selling briskly to

European markets, and I'm looking to expand into England."

"Well! We will speak of this matter later." Looking none too pleased by his success, his grandmother turned her sour attention to Maddy. She lifted the quizzing glass pinned to her bodice and held the gold-rimmed lens to one eye. "But first, who is this tawdry creature?"

"That's no way to describe the newest member of our family." Nathan slipped his arm around Maddy's waist, drawing her close to his side in the manner of a love-struck bridegroom. "Allow me to introduce my wife, Madelyn. As of today, she is Lady Rowley."

An audible gasp swept the gathering. The earl's face turned ghastly pale, making his pockmarks more prominent. The dowager clutched a lace handkerchief to her mouth, while the pretty brunette lady wilted onto the nearest chair in a rustle of dove-gray silk.

Maddy recognized her cue.

She rushed straight to the Earl of Gilmore and threw her arms around him, planting a loud smack on his pitted cheek. He smelled of starch and expensive cologne. " 'Tis a pleasure to meet such a grand personage as yourself, milord." She affected a girlish giggle. "But I needn't address you as 'milord,' eh? After all, you're *my* father now, too, and 'twould be only right and proper for me to call you 'Papa.' "

A thunderous flush replaced the whiteness of shock on his proud features. But before he could condemn her brazen behavior, Maddy turned her back on him and swooped toward the seated dowager.

The landscape of wrinkles on the woman's face was truly remarkable. Maddy would have liked to have used them as a model when she'd disguised herself as a crone. "And you must be dear old Granny," she said, projecting her voice as if on stage. "Why, I've never had a real grandmother before. I can't wait for us to become better acquainted. Just think of all the cozy chats we can have."

As Maddy leaned down to hug the woman, Lady Gilmore recoiled, thrusting up her cane as a shield. "Keep your distance, girl! You're far too impertinent!"

Maddy strove for a bewildered look. "Have I done something wrong, milady? Pardon me, but it's just that I'm so excited to become one of the Quality. Who would've thought a poor girl from Covent Garden would be married to an earl's heir? And to become the granddaughter of a countess!" Cocking her head, she tapped her chin with her forefinger. "Or perhaps I am your *step*-granddaughter. I fear I don't know what the nobs would call our connection. Do you?"

"Deplorable, that's what," Lady Gilmore hissed. Her poisonous gaze shifted from Maddy to Nathan and then to her son, the earl. Gilmore looked furious enough to spit nails.

Maddy wasn't finished. She whirled toward the younger lady in the next chair. But the chirpy greeting died on her lips as she realized the gray silk of the woman's gown indicated half-mourning. According to Nathan, his elder brother had died a little more than a year ago, and Maddy felt reluctant to play the strident harpy with his widow.

Nevertheless, she pasted on a bright smile. "And you, milady, who might you be? Perhaps you're my husband's sister, Emily? Or his sister-in-law, the one he said he's never met?"

"She's David's widow, I presume," Nathan said. He came forward to soberly kiss the woman's hand. "It's a pleasure to make your acquaintance, Lady Sophia. May I present Lady Rowley to you? Pray accept our deepest condolences on your bereavement."

Lady Sophia yanked back her hand. She jutted out her

small chin, and her china-blue eyes stared resentfully from a peaches-and-cream complexion. "*I'm* still Lady Rowley. And how dare you introduce me to this . . . this trollop!"

The room fell silent except for the crackle of the fire. *Trollop.* The ugly slur hung in the air.

"Now, now," Nathan chided, "that's no way to speak of my dear wife." Saying nothing more in Maddy's defense, he stepped back to stand by the fireplace, resting his elbow on the marble chimneypiece, a faint smirk on his handsome features.

The rat was enjoying this.

Maddy fought to maintain a frivolous smile. She resented the injustice of being called a trollop, though the malice of these aristocrats came as no surprise. She *was* behaving badly; that was the whole point of the charade, to make them despise her. Any vitriol they spewed only meant that her acting had been a success.

"But *I* am Lady Rowley," she said in feigned bewilderment. "Yet you say *you* are Lady Rowley, as well. How very peculiar! Will there be two of us with the same name, then?"

"Yes, Sophia retains her title," Lady Gilmore confirmed in a clipped tone. "*She* is well deserving of it."

Implying, of course, that Nathan's bride was *not* worthy.

Maddy let the nasty insinuation sail right over her head. She might as well play the chatterbox that Nathan said the earl abhorred.

She clapped her hands. "Oh, splendid! We'll be just like twins, then! I've always wanted a sister." She beamed at an appalled Lady Sophia, then rattled on. "Perhaps we can visit the shops together, milady. I love to try on hats and gloves and other pretty things, don't you? Do you like my gown, by the by? It's very elegant, isn't it?"

She twirled around the tea trolley so that the crimson skirt billowed out in an indecorous manner.

Lady Sophia's gaze raked over the tight-fitting gown with its indecently low neckline. "I doubt you know the meaning of the word 'elegant'."

"Well, Nathan thinks it's beautiful. He picked it out especially for me. Didn't you, darling?" Since the ruse was his invention, Maddy deemed it time to direct the attention back to him. Her hips swaying, she sauntered over to him by the fireplace. "He has excellent taste. Only look at how handsome he is in his wedding clothes."

Nathan's mouth tilted in a slight smile that showed a hint of dimples. "The sentiment is mutual, for no other woman has such beautiful assets as you, my sweet."

Assets. She didn't need for him to glance at her bosom for her to remember their earlier conversation. A hot blush penetrated the deepest part of her body. Other men had looked lustfully at her, but none of them had ever made her so flustered. Her involuntary reaction was only made worse by the fact that his family was present, watching them. When she would have turned away, Nathan caught her waist in a firm grip. He glanced over her head at his father. "I'm sure you can tell that Madelyn was very popular with the gentlemen," he said. "More than a dozen vied to have her all to themselves."

A trickle of ice replaced the flush of heat. Did he really intend to tell his family about the auction? Of course he did, for he knew they would scorn her all the more.

"Please, darling, you'll embarrass me," she murmured.

He looked down at her. To the others it must seem a tender glance, yet she saw the glitter of anticipation in his eyes. "There's no need to be shy about our whirlwind romance, my love," Nathan said before returning his gaze to the earl. "You see, I'm extremely fortunate to have won Madelyn's hand. She had quite a harem of enthusiastic suitors."

"Not so very many," Maddy demurred. "And perhaps

now isn't the time to relate all the details. We should let your family finish their tea." She pried his hands off her waist. "Do be a dear and escort me on a tour of the house. I can't wait to have a peek into all the fancy rooms. Why, there must be dozens of them!"

But Nathan wasn't listening. Nor was Gilmore.

The earl flicked her a look so icy she felt chilled to the bone. "Where did you find her?" he asked. "In a brothel?"

Nathan chuckled. "Hardly. You might know her as Madelyn Swann, celebrated star of the Neptune Theater in Covent Garden. Perhaps you've seen her plays?"

Lady Sophia huffed out an indignant breath. The dowager fanned her wrinkled face with a handkerchief, muttering, "Good heavens!"

As the two women stared at her, Maddy held her head high. She very much doubted either of them had ever had to labor for a living. What were *their* accomplishments, to think themselves her better?

"An *actress*." Gilmore spat the word as if naming a particularly distasteful type of vermin. "Well, I wouldn't know of her. I haven't attended the theater in quite a long while. We've been in mourning this past year, in case you don't recall."

She saw Nathan's jaw tighten at the reference to his brother's death. "Then you can't have heard about the auction," he said.

"Auction?"

"Nathan, darling, I really *do* wish to tour the house—"

As Maddy tried again to intervene, he pressed his forefinger to her lips while keeping his determined gaze fixed on his father. "Recently, Madelyn solicited bids from a select group of gentlemen. Her purpose was to sell her services to the highest bidder. Luckily, I was the only one who offered her marriage instead of carte blanche."

Lady Sophia uttered a squeak of horror. Lady Gilmore

stared, slack-jawed. Lord Gilmore's face turned red with fury.

"You *purchased* this . . . this female?" he sputtered. "Then you dared to grant her the honor of my name?"

"Not yours, Father. *Mine*. I'm an Atwood, too, pray recall. Your son and heir."

His father took a step toward him. "What, is this some sort of twisted plot of revenge? To wed the most unsuitable tart you could find and make our family a laughingstock?" He stabbed his forefinger in his son's direction. "I won't have it!"

"You must have it. The deed is done. We've spoken our vows in church." Clearly relishing his father's rage, Nathan slid his arm around Maddy's waist again. "And I'd call my wife eminently suitable. After all, she's a very attractive woman and this family could use some fresh blood in its pedigree. She'll make a fine countess someday."

The earl turned to scowl at Maddy, and she felt his wrath like a physical force. His face flushed, he glared daggers at her, as did the dowager in the chair behind him.

Maddy held her chin high and forced herself to preen at Nathan's praise like the silly twit she was supposed to be playing. The truth was out now and there was no refuting it. She *had* sold herself to the highest bidder—and if these aristocrats despised her for that, then so be it.

All of a sudden, Lady Sophia loosed a choked sob. "*He* doesn't care that David's dead. Nor does she! Look at them, they're both *glad*!" She lurched up from her chair. "Oh, I cannot bear this a moment longer!" Tears spilling down her cheeks, she clutched her skirts and fled the drawing room.

Maddy's bravado abruptly deflated. In spite of the woman's earlier venom, she felt a twist of sympathy for Lady Sophia, who had lost her husband and all her prospects with him. At one time, Lady Sophia had anticipated becoming the Countess of Gilmore. How horrifying it must be for her to watch another woman usurp her place—and a lowly, loudmouthed actress at that.

It was only a role, Maddy reminded herself. She had to think of herself as a character in a dramatic production. Yet on stage, even when she'd played a villainess like Lady Macbeth, she wasn't hurting real people. If she made someone weep, those were merely crocodile tears, not evidence of true, heartfelt pain.

The moment Lady Sophia vanished out the door, the earl turned toward the dowager. "You should go after her, Mama. You've both suffered a terrible shock."

Lady Gilmore remained on her gilded throne, sitting stiffly upright with her hands clutching the gold knob of her cane. "Nonsense, Hector. I shall remain right here. I won't be driven away by a reckless troublemaker like him."

"That's no way to speak of the successor to the earldom, Grandmamma," Nathan mocked. "Madelyn will think us little better than street brawlers."

Lady Gilmore harrumphed. "You're hardly one to lecture me on manners, young man! Especially when you bring such a wicked woman into this house."

"It cannot be good manners to insult the newest member of our family," he retorted.

Like an angry bull about to charge, Lord Gilmore swung toward Nathan. "Stop this right now. Your grandmother has every right to be distraught. Look at what you've done, appearing here without warning after ten years' absence, stirring up chaos in my household, foisting this . . . this *female* on us. You're a disgrace as always. You haven't changed a whit."

"Nor have you, Father." Nathan strolled to the tea tray and grabbed a slice of cake, wolfing it down with his fingers. "We're both doomed to relive our past, I fear. Only this time, I'm not a boy to be bullied into obedience."

Gilmore watched him in obvious disgust. "Sophia's right, you don't care a whit about David. You're pleased he's dead so that you can claim his rank."

His jaw tight, Nathan paced to the earl. He stood half a head taller than his father, forcing Gilmore to tilt up his chin. "Leave my brother out of this. You always did try to turn us against each other."

"Bosh. I expected you to behave like a gentleman, as he did. But you were determined to be the bad seed."

"The bad seed is now your heir," Nathan taunted. "And it gives me great satisfaction to know there's not a damned thing you can do to change that fact!"

The earl's face turned a deeper crimson. His chest heaved beneath the tailored black coat. "Say what you will to me—but don't curse in front of your grandmother. She deserves your respect!"

"Sit down at once, Hector, lest you suffer an apoplexy," urged the dowager. To Nathan, she chided, "His health is not what it was before his illness. *You* may wish to send him to an early grave, but I most certainly do not!"

His illness? Maddy wondered what the woman meant.

Nathan didn't inquire, so he must have understood the reference. He stood in moody silence as Lord Gilmore sank heavily into the chair beside his mother and groped for his teacup.

Standing at the edge of the gathering, Maddy felt momentarily forgotten. That was fine with her. She would sooner observe the scene from the wings than be drawn back onto the stage of their bitter squabble. The powerful, destructive emotions between father and son both repelled and fascinated her. She'd always liked to observe people in order to glean insights for playing characters onstage.

But seldom had she had the opportunity to witness such a clash of wills.

Clearly, the Earl of Gilmore was a haughty, demanding man. But why did he hate Nathan with such ferocity? What lay at the root of their quarrel? Was it just a case of two strong-minded men butting heads? Or was there something more, something deeper? There seemed to be a dark undercurrent between them that defied her observational skills.

And she couldn't place the entirety of the blame on Gilmore. Nathan appeared to take considerable pleasure in provoking his father.

The earl drained his teacup, his hand shaking slightly. The man truly *did* look ill, with a grayish tinge to his skin beneath the flush of fury.

Nudged by concern, she went to the trolley and fetched the pot, bringing it to Lord Gilmore and refilling his cup. "There you go, milord." She judged it best not to call him "Papa" at this particular moment. "Do you wish sugar or cream? Shall I bring you a slice of cake?"

"No," he snapped, eyeing her irritably. "And you're not to take on the role of hostess in this house. That is Lady Sophia's place."

Maddy affected a bright smile. "But her ladyship ain't here, milord, and I would very much like to be helpful. Since I'm now a member of your fine family, you see."

Turning away from his glare, she replenished the dowager's cup as well. Lady Gilmore peered suspiciously into her tea as if suspecting poison before she raised it to her withered lips and took a tiny sip.

Maddy would have liked refreshment herself, but there were no additional cups on the tray and she certainly wouldn't ask for one. Let these snoots shun her, she thought, marching back to replace the pot on the trolley. Their nasty opinion of her only proved that she was earning her generous stipend from Nathan.

Her husband strolled forward to join her, linking his arm with hers in another display of sham affection. Though she knew it was all for show, the contact of his hard muscles and warm flesh made her quiver inside as if her skin were sensitized, her every pore alert to his nearness. The reaction irked her, for she didn't much like him at the moment.

Not that he noticed. His attention was aimed at his father. "I trust you'll allow my wife and me to stay at Gilmore House. As I've just recently arrived in London, it will take some time to procure a place of our own."

Gilmore set down his teacup with a clatter. "Go to a hotel. You'll be more comfortable there."

Nathan's mouth formed a sly smile. "Then you won't care if people speculate as to why you've shunned your own heir?"

"He has a point, Hector," the dowager said in an undertone. "We can allow nothing to mar Emily's debut."

"That's precisely why I *don't* want them here. Look at the woman, she's a disgrace!"

"Indeed," his mother concurred. "Yet they're bound to go out into society. And under my strict tutelage, her vulgarity *might* be modified. At least to some degree."

They were discussing her as if she weren't even present, Maddy thought with a stab of resentment. These highbrow aristocrats viewed themselves as the arbiters of proper behavior, yet they couldn't grasp the irony of their own rudeness.

Then a movement in the doorway snared her attention. A slender young woman in a pale peach gown hovered there. Russet-brown curls framed the oval of her face, though she was too far away for Maddy to discern her features.

The girl darted into the room, wending a path through the clusters of chairs and chaises. "You mustn't send him away, Papa. Please!"

At the sound of her voice, Nathan turned. He sprang in swift steps to meet her halfway, grabbing hold of her dainty waist and twirling her around in a circle. "Who is this interloper? Surely it cannot be . . . Emily? But she was only a little sprout when I departed England."

Smiling, his sister wriggled free. "Nathan, *why* have you stayed away so long? You didn't even give me an address to write to you!"

"I've been very busy building an import firm. And you . . . you've been ill, I've heard." He gently cupped her cheek in his hand. "Pray forgive me for not being here."

During their brief conversation, Maddy had been walking closer to them, and with a shock she noticed the pockmarks on the girl's face that resembled those on the earl's cheeks. Emily's blemishes were even more noticeable, likely because of the fairness of her skin.

The girl's eyes widened on Maddy and she shyly ducked her chin as if to hide her disfigurement.

Nathan looked over his shoulder to give Maddy a warning glance. "Allow me to introduce you to my wife, Madelyn. But you needn't concern yourself with her. I'm sure your paths won't cross very often."

Maddy's heart went out to the girl even as annoyance pricked her. Did he truly think she'd act the crude termagant with his disfigured sister? "It's a pleasure to meet you, Lady Emily," she said. "What pretty russet hair you have. It enhances the hazel of your eyes."

Nathan's sister gave her a startled look. She touched her glossy curls self-consciously. "Oh, I—"

"Come here, Emily," the dowager ordered. "You mustn't speak to that woman."

Emily left her brother and ran lightly to the earl,

kneeling before him. "Papa, I haven't seen Nathan in so very long. Please do let him stay."

A brief softening on his haughty face, Gilmore squeezed her hands. "If it makes you happy, then so be it." His dark gaze narrowed on Nathan. "But only for a short while until he finds his own residence."

Chapter 9

Standing at the newel post, Nate watched as Madelyn, led by a maidservant, ascended the staircase on the way to her bedchamber. The saucy sway of her hips beneath the cherry-red gown stirred his blood. He was tempted to go after her. To lock the bedroom door and avail himself of that curvaceous female body at once.

But his lust could wait until nighttime. His wife had served her purpose for now. All in all, her performance in the drawing room had been brilliant. Addressing the earl as "Papa" had been a particular stroke of genius.

Gilmore had been enraged by Nate's marriage. The revulsion on his face had been priceless. His father had been especially disgusted to learn about the auction, for nothing could have been better designed to create a permanent blot on the family honor.

Nate had arranged for the other gentlemen who had bid on Madelyn to be informed of the marriage. The scandal would spread like wildfire. Everyone of consequence soon would know that Gilmore's heir had purchased a notorious actress for his bride. In the coming days, there would be an invasion of visitors as nosy members of the ton came here to gawk at Madelyn.

Nate allowed a smile of satisfaction as he slipped into a shadowed antechamber. He leaned his shoulder against the wall and settled there to wait. From this vantage point, he could peer out into the main corridor and watch the doorway of the drawing room. A part of him despised skulking in dark corners as if he didn't belong at Gilmore House. He had every right to be here. Yet this subterfuge was necessary.

A few minutes later, his patience was rewarded. Gilmore walked out of the drawing room, the dowager clinging to his arm as she hobbled along with the aid of her cane. Emily trailed behind them like a forgotten ghost.

The trio headed toward the staircase where Madelyn had vanished. Perfect. It appeared the earl meant to escort Grandmamma upstairs to rest before dinner.

Nate retreated out of sight as the sound of voices approached. His grandmother was saying, ". . . so cheap and gaudy! I must write a note to my seamstress at once."

"Stylish garb cannot change a sow's ear into a silk purse," the earl grumbled. "I fear that woman is a hopeless tart . . ."

Their conversation faded after they'd passed by the antechamber. Nate poked his head out and saw his sister still following behind their father and grandmother.

"Psst," he hissed softly.

Emily glanced over her shoulder. He beckoned to her, crooking his forefinger. She looked back at the older couple who were engrossed in their nasty tête-à-tête; then she scampered toward Nate.

He pulled her into the antechamber. Peering out once more, he was gratified to see Gilmore and the dowager heading up the stairs, unaware of Emily's disappearance. By the time they noticed, they wouldn't know where she'd gone.

Or who she was with.

"What's the matter?" Emily whispered. "Why are you being so secretive?"

His gut wrenched at the sight of her standing in the shadows. Ten years ago, she'd been an inquisitive little scamp who'd pestered him with a thousand questions about everything under the sun. Now, she'd grown into a beautiful woman, if only one could overlook the pockmarks that marred her creamy skin. "I wanted a moment alone with you, that's all. To tell you that I'm sorry you had to witness that scene in the drawing room. I'm afraid Father and Grandmamma don't approve of my new wife."

"Well, *I* like Madelyn. She was very kind to me. They shouldn't be so mean to her just because she's an actress."

"They're trying to protect you. Madelyn has a rather unsavory reputation with the gentlemen, you see."

"Only because she's so very beautiful." Emily clasped her hands to her bosom. "*I* think it's wonderful that the two of you fell in love. And I'm glad you married her no matter what other people might think."

Her starry-eyed mien troubled Nate. Not because Emily had mistakenly assumed that love had prompted his hasty marriage. Rather, he was loath to see his naïve sister admire a worldly woman like Madelyn. When he'd concocted his scheme of revenge, he hadn't even considered how it would affect Emily.

"Like it or not, it *does* matter what people think," he said. "In fact, it would be best if you kept a prudent distance from my wife. You especially oughtn't be seen in public with her."

"What? You sound just like Papa!"

Nate clenched his jaw at the unwelcome comparison. He was nothing like the Earl of Gilmore. Nothing at all.

He caught hold of her slender shoulders. "Listen to me, Em. He's right in this particular matter. My marriage is bound to stir up a scandal. I won't have you caught in the fireworks, not when you're about to make your debut. It will harm your marital prospects."

"Bah, I haven't any real prospects," she said with a toss of her chin. "My only admirers will be fortune hunters sniffing after my marriage portion. I heard Grandmamma and Sophia say so when they thought I wasn't listening."

Fury stabbed into Nate. Blast those two biddies! "Never mind them. You'll find a good husband, I'm sure." At least he hoped so.

"Well, if I don't," she said archly, "I shall run away and join a convent. I'll give my dowry to the nuns and spend the remainder of my days in cloistered prayer."

Nate restrained a laugh. "So you'll renounce all your worldly goods? You'll have no use for jewelry?" He reached into an inner pocket of his coat and brought out a miniature black-enameled box. "It seems I shall have to give this to someone else, then."

Emily's eyes brightened. "What is that? A gift for me?"

She grabbed for the box, but he held it high out of her reach. "First, you'll have to promise not to become a nun—at least not for a good long while."

"I promise! Oh, *please* give it to me."

Chuckling, he placed the small box into the palm of her hand.

Emily eagerly undid the tiny catch and opened the lid. On a nest of white silk lay a jade figurine on a delicate gold chain. She stepped out into the corridor where there was more light to examine the necklace. "Oh, my gracious, it's a little dragon. How precious! Is it truly mine?"

"Absolutely." Nate stepped behind her to secure the hook at the back of her neck. "It came all the way from China. Over there, the dragon is a symbol of power and courage. It will give you great luck when you make your debut."

"Perhaps it will keep me from tripping on my hem." Her

face fell suddenly. "But Grandmamma won't allow me to have this. She says that debutantes should wear only pearls."

"Keep it in your reticule, then. It'll be our little secret."

Emily smiled. "Yes, indeed. But first I want to go look at it in the mirror." Standing on tiptoes, she landed a butterfly kiss on his cheek. "Thank you, Nathan. You're the best of brothers."

Rooted in place, he watched as his sister flew up the staircase and vanished, leaving him alone in the ornate corridor. Emily was wrong. He wasn't the best of brothers. The best brother had stayed here at Gilmore House while Nate had gone off to seek his fortune. The best brother had died from the same illness that had befallen Emily and the earl.

Maybe if he had stayed, *he* would have been the one with the pockmarks instead of his sister. Maybe he would have died instead of David.

Nate pulled a deep breath into his lungs. The air felt as thick and oppressive as the inside of a mausoleum. Dammit, he was supposed to be gloating today, not wallowing in gloom.

He stalked down the corridor toward the library. He needed a strong drink. He needed to forget his mawkish thoughts. Most of all, he needed to celebrate the success of his revenge on the Earl of Gilmore.

Maddy arrived late to dinner.

She dashed into the dining room to find everyone already seated at the far end of the long table. For a moment she paused in the doorway, overwhelmed by the affluence on display. Cobalt-blue curtains framed the darkened windows, while family portraits hung on the walls. On the linen-draped table, crystal glasses and china plates gleamed in the soft glow from an extravagance of candles.

It was a far cry from the rough plank table and overturned crates used for quick meals by the cast and crew of the Neptune Theater.

The Earl of Gilmore occupied the head of the table with nineteen-year-old Lady Emily to his left and his mother to his right. Prim-faced Lady Sophia sat beside the wrinkled dowager with Nathan opposite her.

Sipping from a wine goblet, Nathan smirked at his wife's tardy entry. He had planned this, Maddy realized. She had waited alone for hours upstairs in the large, lavish bedchamber, but he'd never so much as poked his head in the doorway to check on her. After the dramatic reunion with his family in the drawing room, the devil had vanished to the bowels of the netherworld with nary a word to his new bride.

Maddy had been told by a footman to listen for the sound of the gong before going down to dinner. But she had taken a wrong turn and had become lost in the maze of corridors and staircases until her wanderings had brought her here.

Nathan's abandonment annoyed her, though not because she desired his company. After all, they were hardly typical newlyweds who yearned to spend every moment together. But he ought to have warned her of his plan to neglect her. She felt as if he'd thrust her onto the stage of his life without offering adequate instruction.

Well, then. Since he hadn't told her otherwise, she would simply continue in her role of the shallow, talkative, ill-mannered commoner.

Shaping her lips into an alluring smile, she minced toward the diners. She noticed two things in quick succession. No one had any food on their plates yet, which meant she'd kept everyone waiting. And secondly, the women had changed into exquisitely beautiful gowns, Lady Emily in pale yellow organza, Lady Sophia in lavender silk, and the dowager in celery-green satin.

Maddy felt horribly conspicuous in the crimson dress with its plunging neckline. But even if she'd known to change, she couldn't have worn anything else because Gertie was still absent. The maid had been charged with collecting Maddy's belongings from both the rooming house and the theater. She didn't know what was keeping Gertie. Everything had been packed beforehand, and she'd had only to arrange for transportation of the trunks.

The earl rose from his chair in grudging courtesy. "I see you've finally deigned to join us, Madelyn. You've kept us waiting for a quarter hour."

"I'm so sorry, Papa," she said brightly. "I fell asleep for a while and lost all track of the time."

His lips thinned at her too familiar address, but he didn't correct her. He merely resumed his seat and gave an imperious nod to the two blue-liveried footmen on duty. Both sprang into action, one of them picking up a large silver urn, the other a ladle with which to transfer soup into everyone's bowls.

Nathan jumped up to draw out a chair for Maddy. "So there you are, darling. I was just about to come looking for you."

"Thank you, my dearest." She puckered her lips and blew a kiss in his direction. "You've been so very attentive. I couldn't ask for a more considerate husband than you."

His green eyes glinted at her. He wasn't put off in the least by her syrupy drivel; the scoundrel was enjoying the spectacle. She had an awareness of a close, conspiratorial connection between them. They were in this ruse together to hoodwink his family. And Maddy didn't know if she liked the collusion or not.

Yet it was necessary to earn her rich stipend. In a few months, he would leave England forever and she would be free to live as she chose. Until then, however, she had to play his game.

As a footman ladled a clear mushroom broth into her bowl, she picked up her silver spoon and held it close to the candlelight, examining the ornate leaf pattern on the handle. "This must be solid sterling," she said to Nathan in a loud whisper designed to project to the others. "And these plates, they're the finest porcelain. Oh, I do hope I don't break anything."

The dowager harrumphed. "If you would prefer to eat from cheap crockery down in the kitchen, then feel free to run along and do so."

Maddy blew on her steamy bowl of mushroom soup. "Me, dine with the servants?" she asked in wide-eyed surprise. "Why, that won't do at all. My place is here with my new family. Right beside my dear husband."

Fluttering her lashes at Nathan, she spied the earl glowering at the end of the table. Beside him, the dowager arched a haughty gray eyebrow. Sophia pruned her lips as if the spoonful of soup she'd just swallowed tasted of vinegar.

Lady Emily peered past her brother, the candlelight shining on her pockmarked face. "I'm very glad you're here, Madelyn," she asserted. "If Nathan loves you, then so should we all."

Maddy's heart squeezed. The girl's kindness was refreshing in this cesspool of hostility. And regrettably misplaced, for she was wrong in her naïve assumption that it was a love match. "How lovely of you to say so—"

"It is best to refrain from commenting on matters beyond your ken," Lady Gilmore chided the girl. "Tend to your dinner now."

Emily blushed and returned her attention to her soup.

Maddy itched to fling the hot contents of her bowl at

the bitter old woman. No wonder the Earl of Gilmore was so pompous. He had learned his cold, selfish conduct at his mother's knee. How could these people think themselves the masters of refined taste? She'd known street urchins with better manners.

Nathan signaled to the footman to refill his wine goblet, then said testily, "Leave Emily be, Grandmamma. She only means well."

"She must learn to keep her opinions to herself," the dowager decreed. "Especially in situations where she contradicts her elders."

The scolding only made Emily hunch her shoulders as if she wanted to slide under the table. She looked so distraught that something had to be done to draw attention away from her.

Maddy purposely made slurping noises with her spoon. "Mmm, this mushroom broth is so delicious! It's nothing like the cabbage soup we ate at the theater. That slop often gave me a case of the belches, it did."

Everyone stared wide-eyed at her, even Emily. Nathan's mouth twitched as if he were biting back a chuckle.

The Earl of Gilmore sharply put down his spoon. "There are some things one does not discuss in company," he snapped. "Have you no manners at all?"

"What? Oh! I'm so sorry, Papa. I'll try to be more polite." Maddy held out her empty bowl to the footman. "Could I have more, please, sir? I'm still rather hungry."

Nathan leaned closer so that she caught an enticing whiff of his sandalwood scent. "Be patient, darling," he said. "We've five more courses yet."

"Five—"

"A veritable feast awaits you," he promised. "The earl has always believed in no less than six courses for dinner."

On cue, a white-gloved footman came around to collect the soup bowls, while the other servant brought a platter of whole baked fish to the dowager, who used the silver serving fork to transfer a dainty portion to her plate. When it came time to dish out her own helping, Maddy thrust her nose close to sniff it.

"Stuffed pike! I must say, it smells considerably better than the fried cod from Billingsgate Market. At the theater, we always bought day-old fish in order to save money, you see. But I suppose you needn't practice such economies in such a fine house as this one." She grabbed one of the forks at random from beside her plate. "Mr. Shawshank said you even have a fancy cook, come here all the way from France."

The tension around the candlelit table was palpable. Clearly annoyed by her chatter, the Earl of Gilmore compressed his lips. He and the others no doubt also were offended at her calling the footman "sir" and the butler "mister." Little could they guess, she had made those blunders on purpose. Over the years, Gertie had entertained her with stories about the workings of a noble household, including the petty rules for addressing the staff members.

"We have David to thank for hiring the chef," Lady Sophia said, gazing down her dainty nose at Maddy. "My late husband had superior taste in all matters."

Lord Gilmore gave Sophia a brief smile that warmed his cold features. "Indeed, David was accomplished in a wide variety of areas, from cultivating friendships among the politically connected to managing the tenants on my estate. He is sorely missed." The earl glanced up at a portrait over the fireplace, and a brooding cloud descended over his face.

Maddy followed his somber gaze to the painting of a handsome young gentleman in a red coat and black breeches standing beside a glossy brown horse, the reins held loosely in his gloved hands. With his noble bearing, dark auburn hair, and medium build, the man bore a strong resemblance to Gilmore.

With a jolt, she realized his identity. He must be the eldest son. Nathan's brother, David. The image of him shook her to the core, for the smiling man in the painting looked so vital, so alive.

How had he died? Nathan had never told her. Nor had he informed her of exactly why he despised his father, though she was beginning to have an inkling that it might have something to do with his elder brother. There was so much she didn't know . . .

Though reluctant to stir up painful memories, she felt too curious to bide her tongue. She said in a stage whisper to Nathan, "Your father was gazing at the portrait over the fireplace just now. Is that your brother, David?"

Nathan's gaze flicked to the painting before he glanced away, appearing troubled as he took a swallow of wine. "Yes."

"He was a fine-looking gent, to be sure." She added in sincere sympathy, "I'm so very sorry for your loss. I never had any brothers or sisters, so I can't imagine how you must feel—all of you."

No one responded. A frigid hush dampened the conversation at the table, the silence disturbed only by the clink of silver utensils. Everyone attended to their plates, while Maddy nibbled on a tender slice of fish without really tasting it.

A quagmire of gloom seemed to have swallowed everyone present except for her. Clearly no one wished to speak of the late departed heir. Ought she make more commentary? Poking her nose into their private grief certainly would prove her to be a crass, unladylike boor.

Yet the constraints of conscience kept her quiet. It was

one thing to behave like a silly ninny, but she drew the line at causing pain to others. Even if they *were* snobs.

"Who told you about David's passing?" Lord Gilmore asked suddenly, his sharp gaze pinning Nathan. "No one in this household wrote to you."

That disturbed Maddy. Had his family made no attempt to inform Nathan of his brother's death? Why not?

"I have my sources," Nathan said cagily.

"Lady Milford, no doubt," the dowager said with a moue of distaste. "She's his godmother, she doted on him, and she'd know how to contact him. She's always been one to meddle in other people's affairs."

"Apprising me of a death in the family hardly constitutes *meddling*," Nathan said. "Did it never occur to any of you to ask Lady Milford if she knew my whereabouts?"

"You will not pin any blame on us," the earl blustered. "You were the one who walked out. You were the one who cut off all contact."

"Quite so." Nathan gazed speculatively from his grandmother to his father. "Yet I can't help but wonder if you two were hoping I wouldn't ever find out about David. Was that the plan? If I hadn't returned to England, you could have had me declared dead and my toadying cousin named the heir."

Silence spread like a poisonous fog. Maddy's stomach twisted when the Earl of Gilmore failed to deny the shocking accusation. Had that truly been his scheme, then?

"Papa wouldn't be so cruel," Lady Emily burst out, clearly upset. "Tell him, Papa. Tell Nathan he's wrong."

"Of course, darling." The earl reached out to pat his daughter's hand. "Your brother is most certainly mistaken. I can't imagine what would have put such an appalling notion into his mind."

As the footman came around with a course of roasted chicken and spring peas, Maddy wasn't quite sure who to believe. Especially when she noticed the Earl of Gilmore exchanging a veiled glance with his old dragon of a mother. Had he lied in order to appease Emily?

His expression cynical, Nathan tended to his food without saying another word. Maddy didn't want to become involved in his personal problems. She had wed him as a means to her own ends, to gain the funds to open a dress shop and also to have the chance to confront her estranged grandfather in society.

Yet despite her resolve to remain detached, she felt a stirring of sympathy for Nathan. What had his childhood been like in this cold, gloomy atmosphere? Was that why he'd gone away for the past ten years? Because his father and grandmother had favored the elder brother—to the point of denying Nathan any love at all?

And the real question was, what exactly had he done to earn their hatred?

Chapter 10

As the ladies arose after a dessert of apricot cake, Nate stood up, too. He was relieved to have this lengthy dinner over at last. It had been a trial to make stilted conversation, to abide by civilized manners when several times he'd wanted to plant his fist in the Earl of Gilmore's face.

He would not call the man "Father" or "Papa." Not ever again. Not after the punishing words Gilmore had flung at him ten years ago. And not after the man had all but admitted he'd have preferred Nate to be declared dead in order to bar him from inheriting.

But at least Madelyn's performance had made the evening worthwhile. She had a remarkable knack for irritating the earl. Nathan didn't know how much of it was pretense, and how much was her true character, though he suspected she was far more intelligent than his family had been led to believe. He was impatient to discover the real Madelyn—in particular, the nubile body beneath that indecent gown.

He went to Madelyn's side and set her soft hand on his arm. She glanced up at him, her eyes a deep, mysterious blue. He caught an alluring whiff of her scent, and thoughts of the night ahead stirred a keen impatience in him. She belonged to him now; he could enjoy her as he willed. No doubt a woman of her experience knew many ways to please a man. At the first opportunity, he would concoct an excuse for them to retire early . . .

"The ladies will take tea in the drawing room," Gilmore announced. "Emily, if you'll be so good as to escort your grandmother." As the girl hastened to the dowager's side, he added sharply, "Nathan, have you forgotten the custom in this household? The gentlemen remain in the dining chamber."

"I prefer to accompany my bride."

"Sit down. It won't harm you to drink a brandy in my company."

As the earl resumed his seat, Madelyn gave Nate a sassy smile and tugged her arm free. She whirled around, and with an impudent twitch of her cherry-red skirts, she headed after the other women. Her hips swayed as she vanished out the door.

He wasn't sure if it she was just playing a role, or if the minx was deliberately teasing him. Whatever the case, he relished her playfulness. But if she intended to try to wrap him around her little finger, it wouldn't work. He'd had plenty of practice in taming strong-minded women. Madelyn would be no different.

One of the footmen placed a decanter and two crystal glasses in front of Gilmore. The other retainer brought forth a humidor and offered it to the earl, who opened the box and selected a cigar. Then Gilmore waved both servants out of the dining chamber.

Still standing, Nate found himself alone with the one man he loathed more than any other in the world. The urge to leave the room burned in him. He didn't owe this man any courtesy.

But if he walked out, Gilmore would brand him a coward.

Nate yanked out his chair and sat down. An expanse of white linen separated them. Gilmore uncorked the decanter and poured a generous splash into each tumbler.

He nudged one glass in Nate's direction. "Go on, take it. It seems we shall have to learn to tolerate one another's company."

His words were an echo of what Lady Milford had said only a few days ago. Yet everything in Nate rejected the notion of a ceasefire. He didn't want to reestablish a relationship with this man; he preferred to be a perpetual thorn in Gilmore's side.

Nevertheless, he seized the glass and took a quick swallow, letting the brandy burn down his throat. "What could we possibly have to discuss? Everything I had to say to you was uttered ten years ago. I presume you recall that scene since you instigated it."

One corner of Gilmore's mouth curled in a familiar haughty look that harkened back to Nate's youth. The earl picked up a small knife and trimmed one end of his cigar, frowning as if reflecting upon that ugly episode from the past. Their heated clash had resulted in Nate storming out of Gilmore House and boarding a ship to India. He had wandered for a time throughout Asia before using his talent for bartering to develop a thriving business.

But Gilmore didn't know that part of the story. Nor would he care.

The earl set the knife aside, pulled a candle closer, and lit the cigar at the flame, puffing out a cloud of smoke. "That long mane of yours needs barbering," he said abruptly. "I'll send my valet to you tomorrow morning."

Nate sat up straight. He shouldn't be surprised that Gilmore had ignored the past and launched a personal attack. "Be thankful I don't braid it anymore like the merchants in Shanghai. By emulating their style, I earned their trust and made a fortune in trade with them."

"You're in England now and you'll conform to the standards of a gentleman. You cannot be seen in public looking like a heathen."

"I'll do whatever I damned well please."

The earl irritably tapped ash from his cigar into a saucer. "Will you harm your sister's reputation, then? Emily will be making her debut in a fortnight. She will have difficulty enough attracting a husband without *you* complicating the matter."

With that, he'd struck a direct blow. Not for the world did Nate wish to ruin Emily's chance to make a good marriage. Yet he wouldn't be bullied. "If the length of my hair frightens off one of Emily's suitors, then the fellow is too gutless to be worthy of her."

"And what of your unsuitable bride? The scandal of your marriage is certain to taint Emily. What the devil were you thinking to wed such a vulgar female?" His eyebrows clashing in a frown, Gilmore puffed on the cigar. "Never mind, your purpose is clear. You wish to strike a blow at me. You seek to bring shame down upon this household and damn the consequences."

Now here was a topic that Nate relished. He settled back in his chair and savored his brandy, eyeing the earl over the rim of the glass. "Madelyn is a trifle unconventional, I'll grant you. But give her a chance. She'll charm everyone as she's charmed me."

"Charm? I'm sure that strumpet has *charmed* quite a few men in her time. Especially the reprobates who tried to buy her services at auction!"

"Mind your tongue," Nate snapped, wondering at his flare of anger when he ought to be rejoicing in Gilmore's disgust. "You're speaking of my wife—the next Lady Gilmore, I might add."

Gilmore's nostrils flared as he sucked in several breaths. He appeared to be striving to contain his explosive fury.

Excellent. The man deserved to suffer for the way he'd treated Nate all those years ago. The earl had brought this disaster upon himself.

Gilmore put down his cigar in the saucer. "Enough with this quarreling," he said sharply. "It serves no purpose. It is time for us to set aside our animosity and speak civilly."

"You first."

"Your sister has had a difficult time this past year. She lost a beloved brother. She also lost her beauty—along with the prospect of making a good marriage and having a happy life."

"Emily will find someone. Not all men care about appearances." Nate hoped that was true, anyway. He himself had been guilty of choosing women based upon their physical allure. He hoped to God his sister would find a better man than him.

"Every gentleman cares about the reputation of his chosen lady," Gilmore stated. "Emily's standing in society will suffer greatly from your folly today!"

"Increase her dowry, then. That ought to attract men like flies to honey. She'll have her pick of suitors."

The earl made a quick, sharp shake of his head. "No, there's a far better solution. I hope to God you'll give it serious consideration."

"Go on."

Gilmore leaned forward, his hands gripping the edge of the table as he pinned Nate with a piercing stare. "You were wed only today. That means there's still time to act. I shall summon my lawyers in the morning. If you love your sister, you'll annul this disastrous marriage."

Maddy stared at her reflection in the dressing room mirror. It had been a relief to shed the gaudy red gown and the whalebone corset. But her present garb could hardly be deemed any less of an embarrassment.

The new nightdress clung to her every curve. Sewn of shimmery white gauze, it hinted at her underlying nakedness. The peaks of her breasts thrust against the sheer material, while lower, the shadowy triangle of her privates could be seen.

"Gertie! Come here at once!"

A mobcap on her salt-and-pepper hair, the middle-aged maidservant bustled through the doorway to the bedchamber. A smile wreathed her plain features as she caught sight of Maddy. "Why, 'tis a perfect fit. His lordship will be most pleased."

"It's far too revealing!"

"Bah, 'tis what Lord Rowley bade me purchase. 'Somethin' fine that'll please a bridegroom,' he said. And then he winked at me." She giggled. " 'Tis what he wanted ye t' wear on yer weddin' night."

Nathan must have won over the dour maidservant with one of his dimpled smiles, Maddy thought in exasperation. "Well, I would prefer my usual nightdress. Where is it?"

" 'Tis buried somewhere, I suppose," Gertie said, with a vague wave at the three trunks that had been delivered while Maddy was at dinner. The maid trotted over to one and returned with a flimsy robe made of white silk trimmed with costly lace. "But this'll help cover ye. 'Tis another bride gift from his lordship."

Maddy suspected it would be useless to ask the maid to search for the more modest nightgown. Gertie would only claim it was lost. And the robe *did* look exquisitely soft and beautiful.

Slipping her arms into the flowing sleeves, she tied the sash tightly at her waist and drew the lapels together to camouflage her bosom. In the pier glass, she looked somewhat more respectable, though the garment still skimmed her figure in a most provocative manner. She blushed to

imagine standing before Nathan in such scanty attire and
being ogled by those intense green eyes.

A contrary mix of desire and doubt churned inside her.
She *wanted* to experience the intimate act of lovemaking,
Maddy reminded herself. After all, she had arranged the
auction for the purpose of choosing a lover. What difference should it make that she'd ended up with a husband
instead?

Because she had not foreseen all the drama, that was
why.

From the start, she'd known of his desire to punish his
aristocratic family. But the full extent of his hatred for his
father hadn't become clear until she'd entered Gilmore
House today and witnessed the clash between the two men.
Nathan was using her to inflict turmoil upon the orderly
routine of this household. And it disturbed Maddy that
sweet, naïve Lady Emily could be hurt in the process . . .

"Poor thing, ye look a bundle of nerves," Gertie said in
a kindly tone. "Sit now an' I'll brush yer hair. Like I used
t' do when ye was a little girl."

Maddy plopped down on the stool in front of the dressing table. The surface was far too pristine, and she felt a
sudden keen ache for the familiarity of her cluttered room
at the theater with its abundance of pots and jars. The oval
mirror reflected her pale features as she helped Gertie
pluck out the pins, letting her blond locks tumble down her
back.

"I can see now why you weren't here before dinner-
time," Maddy said to distract herself. "You went shopping
at Lord Rowley's request."

The maid ran the bristled brush through Maddy's long
hair. " 'Twasn't just that. He also bade me deliver the rejections, too."

"Rejections?"

"Aye, t' the other lords who bid on ye."

Maddy frowned at the maid's reflection in the mirror. "*What?* I never wrote any such notes."

"Lord Rowley did so on yer behalf." Clearly approving of his highhandedness, Gertie resumed her brushing. "He told those gents ye're his wife now an' they're not t' bother ye no more."

Maddy was too stunned to be calmed by the rhythmic strokes of the brush. In all the preparations for the hasty wedding, she hadn't spared a thought to notifying the disqualified gentlemen. She ought to be incensed that Nathan would make such a move without consulting her. The auction was, after all, *her* doing.

Yet if truth be told, she felt relieved at being spared that chore.

In particular, Lord Dunham would no longer pursue her now that she had a husband. Her cousin wouldn't be lurking around every corner, waiting to force his attentions on her. But how would he react when—if—they met in society?

Maddy refused to think about that now. Nothing else mattered except this night when she would give herself to a man she scarcely knew. A man who could smile and charm when it suited him, yet who regarded his own father with brutal loathing.

Restless, she jumped up from the stool. "His lordship should be here soon. You had better finish unpacking."

"Aye, milady."

Her bare feet silent on the soft carpet, Maddy paced through the doorway and into the vast bedchamber with its rose and green décor. Never in her life had she imagined living in such luxury. Numerous candles cast a warm glow over the French-style furnishings, the chaise by the tall windows, the upholstered chairs by the fire. On the large canopied bed, the apple-green coverlet had been turned down invitingly, while a sea of plump feather pillows lined the gilt headboard.

Very soon, she would lie there with Nathan.

Her insides squeezed again. When would he come to her? What would he say? Was he still fuming?

He and his father had joined the ladies in the drawing room not long after dinner. Both men had looked furious after their brief time alone together. It was clear they'd quarreled, and she burned to know the source of their enmity.

At the earl's request, Emily had entertained the group by playing the pianoforte for the better part of an hour. Afterward, Nathan had declared it time for him and his bride to retire for the night. He'd aimed a hard stare at his father before pressing a warm kiss to Maddy's cheek. *Go on up, darling. I'll join you very soon.*

It had all been for show, she knew. All the lovey-dovey nonsense was merely a trick to needle his father. She'd returned here over half an hour ago, and with every tick of the ormolu clock on the marble mantel, she wondered where Nathan was, what could be delaying him.

Had he and the earl quarreled about *her*?

She felt uncomfortable in the role that had been assigned to her. Playing the uncouth, jabbering strumpet would only taint Lady Emily with scandal when the girl made her debut. But the stage had been set, the first act set in motion, and how could the script be altered now?

Troubled, Maddy paced back into the dressing room to find Gertie arranging unmentionables in a drawer. It occurred to Maddy that she'd seen nothing of Nathan's belongings. "Where are his lordship's things?"

"In the connecting room. 'Tis the way of the gentry fer a husband and wife t' sleep in separate chambers."

"Oh?" That was welcome news. It meant she'd have a

private retreat from him—and this gloomy household. "Well, I'm glad to hear it."

Gertie chuckled. "Ye might change yer mind once his lordship has his way with ye."

"I very much doubt that."

"Time will tell, milady." The maid's smile took on a certain wistfulness. "Ah, 'tis a fine thing t' address ye as 'milady.' Yer mam would be so proud t' see ye take yer rightful place in society."

Maddy grasped the woman's chapped hands. "Gertie, I meant to warn you. You must never mention my connection to the Duke of Houghton, not to anyone. Nobody here must know about my past."

"But Lord Gilmore would be happy t' learn of yer blue blood."

"Nevertheless, you'll promise me. *Please.*"

Gertie gave a reluctant nod. "Aye, milady, I won't betray ye." She shooed Maddy out of the dressing chamber. "Now, run along t' bed. 'Tis best ye wait for his lordship there."

Returning to the bedchamber, Maddy spied a door half hidden in the shadows of the far corner. That must be the one connected to Nathan's quarters. The coil of tension inside her tightened. A part of her yearned for him to join her—yet another part hoped he would stay away.

Perhaps getting into bed had its merits. If she was ensconced beneath the covers, he couldn't gawk at her in this revealing nightdress. Darkness would be preferable, as well.

Intending to blow out all the candles, Maddy headed toward a table near the fireplace. She was halfway there when the rattle of a doorknob froze her in place. In the next instant, the connecting door swung open.

Chapter 11

Her husband stepped into the bedchamber. Their eyes locked as he paused in the doorway. Tall and intimidating, he wore a robe of forest-green silk tied with a gold cord at his lean waist. He wasn't smiling. The harsh angles of his face hid all trace of those attractive dimples.

No one would mistake Nathan Atwood, Viscount Rowley, for a proper gentleman. Not with his shoulder-length black hair drawn back by a leather thong at the back of his neck. Not with his brawny muscled build and the sunburnished tone of his skin. And certainly not with the avid manner in which he eyed her.

His bold gaze swept over her as if he could see right through both her negligee and the gossamer nightgown beneath it. Perhaps he could.

Maddy crossed her arms in an instinctive attempt to shield herself. Other men had looked at her with lust, but none had seen her in such scanty attire with her hair unbound. It was jarring to reflect that she'd met Nathan only two nights ago.

Although they'd exchanged solemn vows in church, he was still very much a stranger to her. She knew little of his private thoughts. When she'd agreed to participate in his scheme, Maddy had only had a glimpse of his dark side. Rather, he'd seemed to possess the arrogantly charming nature of many noblemen. But the witty gentleman who'd coaxed her into this hasty marriage had vanished.

Perhaps he had never truly existed.

In his place was a ruthless lord who'd wed her for the purpose of vengeance. The hatred he'd directed toward his father today had been unsettling, to say the least. If Nathan was capable of holding such a powerful grudge for so many years, it stood to reason he might be dangerous, volatile, aggressive.

How much could she really trust him?

Shutting the door, he walked toward her, watching her closely as if to identify her weaknesses. Fear leaped inside her, the fear of being at the mercy of such a dominant male. Would he take her straight to bed? Would he strip her naked and ravish her? A sizzle of excitement scorched her veins. Her knees wobbled and she reached out to grip the back of a chair. The clash of emotions within her made no sense. How could she dread him and crave him all at the same time?

As he drew near, Nathan veered suddenly toward the fireplace. Only then did she notice that he carried a champagne bottle and two glasses, which he placed on a side table. There was something civilized about his action that helped to assuage her nerves.

Coming closer, he put his hands on her shoulders. The warmth of the contact quickened her heartbeat. But if he intended to seduce her, he made no move to do so. "Madelyn, I must say—"

He broke off at the sound of footsteps behind her. Gertie trotted into sight and bobbed a curtsy, her manner respectful. "Good evening, Lord Rowley. Should ye or milady be wantin' anything else?"

His attention flicked to the maid. "No. And pray see to it that we are not disturbed for the remainder of the night."

His deep voice held the promise of intimate secrets soon to be unveiled. He still gripped Maddy's shoulders, and she wondered what it would feel like for his hands to slide all over her body. She wanted him kiss her again as he'd done at the close of their wedding ceremony. To overwhelm her so that she didn't have to think.

The maid left, the door shutting quietly. Nathan stepped away, leaving Maddy frustrated. As he went to pour champagne, she said rather breathlessly, "What did you mean to tell me just now?"

He brought a glass and pressed it into her hand. Their fingers brushed and a spark scurried up her arm, raising the fine hairs on her skin. Nathan lifted his own flute in a toast, clinking glasses with her. "I wanted to offer you my compliments on a fine performance today. You could not have been more perfect in your role."

She took a sip of champagne, the bubbles bursting on her tongue. "I'm not sure your family would agree with you."

"That's the plan." He reached out to catch a lock of her unbound hair, letting the golden strands sift through his fingers. "May I say, your beauty is an unexpected bonus. It will make this marriage so much more enjoyable."

The cool calculation in his tone crept down her spine. It was a reminder that first and foremost, she was his tool of retaliation. Any desire he felt for her was merely sweet icing on the bitter cake of his hatred for his father.

She took a step back, out of his reach. "Nathan, I must ask you. Why does your father despise you so much? He can't be entirely coldhearted. He appears to love your sister. And at dinner, he had no end of praise for your late brother."

Nathan's face hardened. "Never mind why. Our agreement is for you to play your prescribed role without question."

"But shouldn't I at least have an inkling as to what caused the strife between you and your father? You both looked fit to kill when you came into the drawing room after dinner. You must have quarreled about *something*."

He paced to the table to refill his glass. "You really wish to know? Then I'll tell you. Gilmore wants me to meet with his lawyers in the morning. He's pressuring me to annul my marriage to you."

"Annul!" Maddy gripped her wineglass. If the marriage was invalidated, would Nathan still pay her the stipend? Would she lose the funds to open her shop? Would Lord Dunham once again prey upon her? "Well, what did you say to him? Surely you refused."

"Good God, of course I refused. I won't play into that devil's hands."

A measure of tension seeped out of Maddy, and she sank down into one of the plush chairs by the fire. Sipping her champagne, she watched Nathan prowl the bedchamber like a caged lion. Perhaps this was her chance. She might never have a better opportunity to improve her distasteful role in the household.

"I imagine the earl was only considering your sister's situation," she said. "Lady Emily is making her debut, and even *I* know that our marriage is bound to harm her reputation."

Nathan sent her a fierce glare. "Emily will be fine. I'll make certain of it."

"How? By turning that scowl on some hapless young stripling until he agrees to court her? Honestly, Nathan, that's hardly a sensible plan."

"So what do you suggest? That I should reconsider the annulment?" He stepped aggressively to her. "No, you wouldn't want that. You're a fortune hunter, Madelyn. You need this marriage as much as I do."

Unnerved by his attack, she stared up at him towering over her. His temper was a powder keg set off by the smallest spark. She wanted to defend herself, but that would mean exposing her private plans, plans he must not know. "All I meant was that perhaps there's a way to improve the present state of affairs—at least somewhat. So that I'm not such a ruinous liability."

He paced away a few steps and turned to glower at her. "How? You're a common actress, a woman of ill repute. I purchased you at an auction where other men were bidding to win you as their mistress. By tomorrow morning, all of society will be buzzing with the scandal."

"Yes, I'm well aware of that." Maddy cringed to think of being branded the villainess who'd enticed the Earl of Gilmore's heir. She would be the target of every vicious gossip in London. Draining the last of her champagne, she held out her empty glass. While Nathan refilled it, she went on, "However, I've been thinking. Perhaps it isn't necessary for me to behave in quite such a vulgar manner. Perhaps I could tone down my act. I'm sure your father would still detest me even if I were to pretend to be a refined, dignified lady."

Nathan frowned. "You speak like one already. Where the devil did you learn the diction of the upper class?"

At the quizzical look on his face, she strove for a wide-eyed, innocent expression. He mustn't guess that her mother had been born and bred a lady. Or that Maddy hoped to confront her grandfather, the Duke of Houghton, sometime in the near future.

If Nathan kept secrets, then she could do likewise.

"I'm an actress, aren't I? My talent is mimicking speech and mannerisms. With your permission, I'll convince the dowager to give me lessons in deportment. Over the course of a week or two, I'll transform myself into the epitome of propriety."

She braced herself for his attack. After all, her idiotic behavior today had been Nathan's idea, a key component of his plot against his father, though for what reason Maddy still didn't know.

But Nathan only gave her a keen stare. "And you truly think this will improve matters for Emily?"

"If I don't slurp my soup or blather like a silly chatterbox, then I won't be a constant embarrassment to the family. And it will perplex the gossips if the notorious Lady Rowley proves to be quiet and circumspect, the model of ladylike behavior."

Unexpectedly, Nathan chuckled. "You, quiet and circumspect? I'll wager you could never manage that."

She gazed up at him from her chair. His lips were tilted slightly, not quite a smile but enough to reveal a beguiling hint of dimples. The champagne must be having an effect, for she suddenly felt giddy and vibrant. "Then I accept your wager. And you will pay me a token if I succeed."

"A token."

"Yes. Something with diamonds, perhaps." Had she really said that? Maddy wanted to call it back. Demanding jewels would fortify his view of her as a fortune hunter.

But it was too late. He set down his glass and extended his hand to her. "Agreed. We'll shake on it to seal the bargain."

She stared at his outstretched hand. His fingers were long and masculine, the nails neatly trimmed, his skin bronzed by the sun. The prospect of touching him reawakened that earlier tug-of-war in her, the battle between the need to flee and the desire to stay. "That isn't necessary," she demurred.

"I'll be the judge of that," he said in a commanding tone. "Come, give me your hand now."

By the shrewd gleam in his eyes, it was clear that he'd noticed her hesitancy about their night together. He was challenging her to reach out and touch him. And why shouldn't she do so? She'd made her choice upon agreeing to this marriage. In church, she had vowed to be his wife in every sense of the word. And if truth be told, she wanted to lie with Nathan, to learn everything he could teach her.

No matter how much the darkness in him might alarm her.

Leaning forward in the chair, she lifted her hand and his fingers firmly closed around hers. The contact sent a flash of warmth up her arm and over her skin, tightening her breasts and hitching her breath. He must have felt it, too, for the fire in his eyes scorched her.

Rather than shake her hand, he firmed his grip and tugged her up out of the chair, using momentum to propel her into his arms. He plucked the champagne glass from her fingers and set it down on the table before drawing her fully into his embrace.

Her heart hammered at his sudden closeness. With every inhalation, she drew in his scent of soap and sandalwood. As she clutched at his muscled shoulders to steady herself, the pattern on his dressing gown suddenly caught her attention.

Seizing the distraction, Maddy traced the embroidered design with her fingertips. No wonder she hadn't noticed it until now. It was very subtle since the mythical winged creatures were sewn of the same rich green threads as the garment itself. "Dragons?"

His eyes gleamed an identical green. "Indeed. The Chinese are quite fond of them."

A hundred questions about his travels in China crowded her mind. But now was not the time to ask them.

"The workmanship is exquisite." She slid her fingers across the broad expanse of his chest, appreciating both the fabric and the warmth imbued by his skin. "The silk is amazingly soft. It's finer than anything I've ever seen in a shop."

"My warehouse is full of silk. I'll give you as many bolts as you like so long as you keep fondling me like that."

He looked quite rakish with a smile playing on his lips, reminding her of the dashing gentleman he'd been at the auction. Maddy's insides tightened into an aching knot. The deep V of his collar revealed a swath of his chest. She had been trying not to dwell too much on the bare flesh beneath his dressing gown.

But now she could think of nothing else.

He seemed to be waiting for her to say something, so she murmured, "I do very much want to be here with you tonight."

By way of response, his hands skimmed downward to cup her bottom and lock her against the solid column of his body. They stood with his chest to her breasts, his loins to hers. Her breathing grew shallow as the heat of him penetrated her flimsy nightdress.

He stared down at her, his gaze intensifying, desire evident on his face. A thrill unfurled inside her. He'd kept his hot-blooded passion hidden behind a mask of caustic wit and cool authority. But now he looked ready to take what he desired.

His eyes glittered in the candlelight. "We're in perfect accord, then," he stated. "There will be no annulment. I intend to make certain of that. Tonight. *Now.*"

The wild hunger she sensed in him called to her deepest feminine urges. Warmth flowed through her in a knee-weakening rush. "Yes," she whispered.

His head swooped down and he took her mouth with aggressive fire. One of his hands moved upward to hold the back of her head while his tongue delved between her lips to explore her thoroughly. Her blood quickened and surged. It felt as if he were branding her as his personal property. And in the doing, he awakened every forbidden part of her. Clinging to his shoulders, she felt the burn of his kiss spread throughout her body until her breasts ached and her privates throbbed.

In the midst of it all, Maddy knew his primary purpose tonight was to thwart his father. To make the marriage real so that no man, no matter how devious, could tear their vows asunder. But she no longer cared what drove Nathan. She only knew what drove herself, and that was a keen desire to experience physical union with this man.

Her husband.

A moan rose from deep inside her throat. Her fingers traced over his chest and up to his face to stroke the roughness of his shaven cheek. She found the slight indentions that she so loved on either side of his mouth. How divine it was to touch him at last, to feel his arms clasping her so close. She wanted to absorb his heat and strength into her very core.

He broke off the kiss and moved his lips down over her jaw, her throat, her collarbone, and she tilted her head back to accommodate him. He was right; they were in perfect accord. It seemed he couldn't get enough of her taste, and she couldn't get enough of his kisses. The damp hunger of his mouth made her quiver with yearning.

Dimly, she felt his hands at her waist. With one expert tug, he untied her robe. He pushed the garment from her shoulders, letting it slither to the floor. Then he drew back slightly to stare down at the jut of her breasts against the sheer fabric of her nightdress.

His fingers traced over the gauzy material, trekking over one lavish mound, traversing the valley in between, and arriving at the second peak. There, the play of his fingers unleashed a storm of sensations that made her gasp. Before she could even catch a shuddering breath, he deftly freed both breasts from the confinement of her bodice.

Just like that, the wisp of a nightdress slipped down to pool at her hips. Only the filmy skirt protected her from full nudity.

The rush of cool air on her bare skin penetrated the stupor of her passion. Maddy trembled, aware that candlelight bathed her naked bosom. All the flames that she'd meant to blow out before his arrival were still lit. Whenever she'd imagined her first time with a man, it had always been under the covers, in the darkness, with long ardent kisses preceding furtive caresses.

But they still stood by the fireplace, and Nathan had disrobed her with the practiced skill of a seducer. She had never expected him to proceed so swiftly. Or to stare so boldly at the decadent display of her breasts. His teeth were slightly bared, his face ravenous, a dragon intent on devouring her.

He lowered his head as if to consume her.

Her heart drumming, she reached out to stop him. One of her palms flattened over the exposed skin between the folds of his dressing gown. His chest felt like the furnace for a fire-breathing monster. "Nathan, wait!"

He glanced up at her, frowning, the dragon denied his feast. "What is it?"

Her gaze flicked to the four-poster with its turned-down coverlet and plump pillows. "Oughtn't we retire to the bed?"

He cocked his head in a faintly quizzical look. His eyes bored into her as if he were trying to comprehend her meaning. Had she said something wrong?

Then he moved his rough-textured fingers over her breast, leaving a trail of sparks over her sensitive skin. Under the insistent caress of his thumb, her nipple shrank into a taut, tender bead. "Am I not pleasing you here, darling? I could swear that I am."

Maddy could scarcely think when he stroked her like that. If not for his arm wrapped around her waist, holding her upright, she might have melted into a puddle at his feet. The raspy pads of his fingers aroused a keen craving in her that only he could soothe. He seemed to know exactly how to touch her in order to wrest a response.

But he also seemed to expect *her* to know things.

She blinked in startled realization. Of course. Nathan believed her to be experienced in the bedchamber. He had not lived in London these past ten years, so he was unaware that she was famous for rebuffing many gentlemen. He would assume her to be a strumpet as other actresses often were. And because Lady Milford had interceded on his behalf, he had not received a written invitation to the auction.

His fingers feathered over her nipple, stirring a deep shiver that rippled through her body. As he watched her, his teeth gleamed in a provocative smile. "You *do* like this," he said. "Don't deny it."

She caught hold of his wrist to still the delightful action. It was impossible to think coherently while he caressed her. "Yes. Yes, I do. It's just that . . . I'm not accustomed to this. I've never done it before."

His dark brows lifted. He looked truly puzzled. "This? It?"

A blush warmed her cheeks. "I've never lain with a man. The auction was for . . . my virginity."

He straightened up to stare down at her from his superior height. His gaze probed into her, his chiseled features fraught with stunned skepticism. Maddy felt uncomfortable under his scrutiny, and embarrassed by the need to make such an intimate admission. If only the wedding hadn't been so rushed, if only she hadn't been so distracted by the turmoil in his family, perhaps she'd have come to this realization earlier.

All at once, his thunderous disbelief cleared and his mouth twisted in wry irony. Much to her astonishment, he threw back his head and laughed. "Of course. I see what you've been about tonight, why you're acting so shy and missish."

His mirth mortified her. Did he find her innocence amusing?

She yanked a handful of flimsy bodice back up over her bosom. "Jackanapes! I should hope you understand since I just *told* you why."

He chuckled again. "You're practicing your new role, that's what. The model of ladylike behavior . . . refined and circumspect . . . the epitome of propriety. But you needn't playact with me, Madelyn. Not when we're alone together."

Her eyes widened. How could he have misunderstood her so completely? "That isn't what—Oh!"

In a swift move, he snatched her up into his arms. His smirk gleamed down at her. "However, if you wish to retire to the bed, my lady, then so be it."

Maddy clung to his neck as he carried her across the room. Her head nestled in the lee of his shoulder, her cheek to his hot neck. For a moment, she couldn't form a clear thought. Her senses swam with his masculine aroma of sandalwood, the beat of his pulse in her ear, the feel of his strong arms cradling her to his chest.

With great fanfare, he laid her down on the mattress. The coverlet felt cool beneath her bare back, while the front of her burned from the torch of his skin. Nathan loomed over her, his arms braced on either side of her waist, as he brushed an intoxicating kiss over her lips. The taste of him was a dizzying effervescence that bubbled through her veins.

"I may just change my mind," he murmured against her mouth.

"Change . . . ?"

"Indeed, I see how it can be stimulating for you to play the fair maiden, untouched by any man. So I will do my part and be the lusty conqueror, intent upon ravishing you."

Maddy snapped to attention. He didn't believe her. He still thought her virtue was a pretense, that she was concealing her expertise at lovemaking for the purpose of some erotic fantasy. It irked her that Nathan would brush off her honest confession—especially one that had so flustered her to admit.

The rat!

She parted her lips to blister him with a reproach.

But he chose that moment to step back from the bed. He unfastened the sash at his waist. The green dragon robe slithered down his body and dropped to the carpet.

Her eyes widened at her first view of a naked man. Without conscious thought, she pushed up on her elbows, the better to see him. Candlelight glowed on the sculpted muscles of his arms and torso. Across his wide chest, a light furring narrowed to a thin line on his flat abdomen. It led her gaze on an irresistible downward path to his loins. There, in a nest of black hair, his manhood jutted in all its glory.

She stared, transfixed by that virile thickness, the ropy veins, the smooth head. Never had she imagined a mature man could be so imposing. A heated dampness softened her nether region, and she trembled inwardly. How was it even possible that he would fit inside her?

He stepped closer, affording her an even more spectacular view. "There's naught to fear, my lady. You may touch me if you like."

Maddy averted her face. A blush swept through every crevice of her body. Her fingers curled into fists to keep from doing as he suggested. "Coxcomb!" she chided breathlessly. "Have you no shame?"

"None at all," he said, amusement in his deep voice. "But I imagine the sight must be quite shocking for an untried innocent like yourself."

He spoke teasingly, a nod to the game he assumed she was playing. The game that was utterly, frustratingly false. But how was she to convince such a pig-headed man?

She tried again. "Nathan, truly, you must believe me—"

"Methinks the lady doth protest too much."

As he joined her on the bed, the thread of her thoughts unraveled. He pressed her back against the coverlet, crooking his knee over her legs to pin them in place. She was keenly aware of his member resting hot and heavy against her upper thigh. He bent his head and his hungry mouth sought her bosom, tasting one peak as if it were a rare delicacy.

Unable to resist him, she stroked the black silk of his hair. The pleasure he ignited in her was so seductive she felt on the verge of swooning. Honeyed lava coursed through her veins, flowing downward to her loins. He blew lightly on her dampened nipple and a feverish shiver swept over her skin.

As he applied the same ardent attention to her other breast, she gave up trying to persuade him of her purity. Let Nathan believe what he willed. It didn't matter anymore. She wanted only to satisfy the gnawing ache inside herself, to experience more of the irresistible sensations he'd awakened in her.

With his knee, he nudged her legs open. Somewhere, she'd lost her nightdress and she couldn't remember how, perhaps when he'd carried her here to the bed. The fleeting thought vanished as his hand glided downward, over her smooth belly and lower still, to play with the silken thatch at the apex of her thighs.

She tensed, her fingers gripping his shoulders, her entire being focused on that one spot. His fingers probed her with light strokes, feathering over the place that no other man had ever touched. A sigh arose from the depths of her being. "Ahhh, *Nathan*."

He seemed to take pleasure from her response, rubbing his raspy cheek against her bosom. He kissed her throat, licking the hollow there, nuzzling her neck, nipping at the tender lobe of her ear. But it was the masterful caresses below that drove her half mad with desire. She closed her eyes, the better to appreciate them. Her hips strained toward his hand, seeking more of the delight.

He moved his mouth downward, his kisses leaving a trail of sparks over her bare abdomen. As he neared her privates, she opened slumberous eyes to gaze down at his dark head. A dim awareness of his intention seeped into her passion-beleaguered brain.

He couldn't . . . he wouldn't . . . yes, he *would*.

He parted her soft folds and blew lightly on her dampness. That one simple action unleashed a torrent of intense pleasure. It was so unexpected, so darkly alluring, that she gasped and tried to squirm away. Her hands pushed at his hard shoulders. "You mustn't . . . !"

He looked up over her naked form, a fierce passion on his chiseled face. "Enough pretense, Madelyn. You want this. You know you do."

He bent his head between her open legs again, and at the first lap of his tongue, she was lost. Her insides clenched with a heat so powerful that she melted onto the bed. Nothing in her tame fantasies had prepared her for the wicked joy of his mouth on her. With panting whimpers, she strove for something beyond her reach. She teetered on the verge of a precipice, and her fingers grasped at the satin coverlet to anchor herself. Then a sudden series of rapturous spasms flooded her. She felt herself being swept away on a wave

of pleasure so deep, so intense that it blotted out awareness of all else.

As the ripples ebbed, Maddy came back to herself.
Dazed and blissful, she lay sprawled in the bed, her heartbeat slowing. She blinked up at the canopy overhead, trying
to grasp what had just happened. So *that* was the pleasure she'd heard whispered . . .

Nathan slid his heavy body over hers. A few strands of
his black hair had come loose from the fastening at the
nape of his neck. The angles of his face looked taut and
strained, his green eyes glittering with unquenched passion. Through her languor, it struck her that he had not
experienced that ecstasy. Wanting to soothe him, she
reached up and cupped his cheek in the palm of her hand.

At the same moment, she felt a burning pressure between her legs as he pushed himself partway inside her.
He stopped and frowned, his jaw rigid as he stared down
at her with an uncomprehending look. His harsh breaths
filled the silence.

Growling deep in his chest, he gave a quick, hard thrust.
A flash of pain wrenched a cry from her. She clutched at
him, gasping, aware that his heated length had penetrated
fully into the depths of her body.

His eyes went unfocused, the black lashes lowering
slightly as he began to move inside her. He bent his head
close to her, burying his face in her neck. Heat came off
him in waves. In a guttural tone, he whispered her name,
"Madelyn."

The discomfort of his entry had subsided to a slight
sting. She instinctively tilted her hips, the better to feel him
inside her. His plunges increased in intensity, and a sheen
of sweat made his skin slick. The rub of his chest hairs
against her breasts fanned the embers inside her. She
wanted to experience that bliss again, yes, she craved it
with unladylike fervor.

But it was not to be. With one last fierce thrust, he gave a hoarse cry. His powerful body convulsed in the throes of release. Then his weight settled heavily over her.

She had been a virgin, after all.

Nate pushed away the intrusive thought. He didn't want to reflect on his blunder. Not while he was still sheathed inside Madelyn, his body relaxed and replete in the aftermath of their coupling. Not while he lay with his face tucked in the fragrant disarray of her hair. Beneath him, her skin felt as smooth and warm as melted candlewax. Everything about her was feminine perfection, from the soft globes of her breasts to the shapeliness of her legs entangled with his.

She had been untouched. More insistent this time, the thought pulled him back to cold reality. He had only realized the truth upon meeting the resistance of her maidenhead. Even then, he had been too caught up in passion to absorb that fact.

But he did now. Fully, completely, gallingly.

No wonder she'd had that charming hesitation about her, the shy reluctance to touch him, the qualms when he'd caressed her intimately. Looking back, he could see that she'd behaved exactly as one would expect of a virgin. But he'd convinced himself she was acting.

Blast it. He felt like a cad. To make matters worse, he'd lost control at the end in a fit of madness. He should have taken the time to pleasure her again. That, at least, might have compensated for his mistake.

He rolled onto his side, separating their bodies. Glancing down, he spied the rusty smear of blood on her thighs, proof of her plundered innocence. She gazed at him, her eyes big and blue in the perfect oval of her face. Her blond hair was rumpled, her lips moist and rosy from his kisses.

He wanted to kiss her again. To make it all up to her.

The notion irked him. What the hell was he thinking? He had nothing for which to atone. Madelyn was his wife, bought and paid for. He could use her as he willed.

He pushed up onto his elbow. Without preamble, he said, "If you'd told me you were a virgin when we first made our bargain, I'd have been gentler with you."

She turned toward him, and he tried not to ogle her beautiful breasts. "I thought you *did* know," she said. "I'd made it clear in the invitation to the auction that I sent to the other gentlemen. But then, just a little while ago, I realized I never wrote one to you."

It annoyed Nate all the more to think of her sending out invitations as if to a party. "How the devil did you word such a note? *Please submit your bid for the chance to plough my virgin soil?*"

A pink blush swept over her cheeks. She drew the covers up to her chin. "Of course not. I put it more delicately than that. The gentlemen knew, anyway, because I'd spurned every one of them in the past. I had a reputation, you see."

"A reputation."

"Yes, for being chaste. Apparently everyone knew it but you. And I *did* try to tell you, Nathan." Her expression softened in a dreamy look. "Nevertheless, I can't say that I have any regrets. Being with you tonight was truly . . . sublime."

Her lashes were half lowered, her lips tilted in a heartfelt smile. His cock stirred. The rest of him recoiled. He didn't want Madelyn to look at him that way—as if she adored him. As if she hoped their mating meant much more than just satisfying a raw sexual need.

Rising from the bed, he yanked on his dressing gown and secured the sash firmly at his waist. "As I said, you should have made certain from the start that I knew that you were a virgin. I might have offered you a larger sum for your services."

As he'd intended, the warmth in her eyes cooled at the reminder that she'd sold herself to him. She stared at him a moment, then lifted her chin. "I'll be the Countess of Gilmore someday. And you'll be long gone from England. So tell me again, who has the better end of our bargain?"

A chuckle stirred in his chest, but he stifled it. Dammit, he didn't want to trade wits with her. She was supposed to be offended, to blister him with one of her colorful curses.

He bade her a terse good night and strode out of her bedchamber, firmly closing the door on temptation. Madelyn had turned out to be quite different from his initial assessment of her. She wasn't the vulgar strumpet, free with her favors, opening her legs to the highest bidder.

No. She *had* opened her legs to the highest bidder. She had married him in order to further her social-climbing ambitions.

And that was all he needed to remember.

Chapter 12

"Ouch!"

The exclamation escaped Maddy as a pin pricked her bare foot. She stood on a stool in her bedchamber while a middle-aged seamstress crouched before her, adjusting the hem of a ready-made gown in a putrid shade of brown.

The woman looked up, her gray eyes alarmed in a care-worn face. "Pray forgive me, milady. I didn't mean to hurt you."

Maddy was dismayed by the woman's cringing demeanor. It was as if she expected to be flogged with a whip. Though perhaps it wasn't Maddy she feared but the crotchety Countess of Gilmore, who sat enthroned in a chair by the hearth. For the past few hours, the dowager had been selecting a new wardrobe for Maddy while uttering critical commentary. At present, she was bent over the fashion book in her lap, studying the pages through her quizzing glass.

"It was merely a little pinprick, Mrs. Dobbs," Maddy said, playing the silly chatterbox. "There's no harm done. I'm sure it's hard for you to concentrate in such unfamiliar surroundings. If only Grandmamma had warned me of this appointment, I'd have come to your shop instead and saved you the trouble of dragging all your supplies here."

The bed was covered in fabric swaths, boxes of buttons, rolls of ribbons, and numerous fashion periodicals. Without conscious intent, Maddy's mind flashed to an image of her lying there in Nathan's arms while he did all those wickedly wonderful things to her. Her body tingled at the memory even though she was vexed with him. She had not seen him since the previous night, when he had insulted her.

You should have made certain from the start that I knew that you were a virgin. I might have offered you a larger sum for your services.

The tactless clodpate! She *had* told him—albeit a little late—yet he had not listened. It was his fault, not hers. Then, without apology, he had walked out, leaving her to stew alone.

Mrs. Dobbs sent a small, grateful smile up at Maddy. A smile that instantly vanished when Lady Gilmore thumped the tip of her cane on the carpet.

"Bide your tongue, Madelyn. Tradesfolk are obliged to come here if we request it of them. And it is highly improper of you to comment on their welfare."

"I merely thought—"

"Enough of your trivial thoughts. As for venturing out to the shops, that is strictly forbidden. You will not be seen in public until you are in possession of a decent wardrobe."

"That will take weeks, Grandmamma. What am I to do until then?" Maddy felt the impish urge to vex the woman. "I suppose I can wear this gown for daytime and my crimson dress in the evenings. The gentlemen seem to like it—the crimson one, I mean."

Lady Gilmore curled her lips in disgust, the network of wrinkles shifting on her face. "That tawdry rag should be burned. Indeed, it *shall* be burned."

Maddy swiveled her position on the stool to give Mrs. Dobbs better access to the back of the gown. "Burned? But what if I'm invited to a party before any of my new gowns arrive?" Hoping to glean a tidbit about the Duke of Houghton, she clasped her hands to her bosom. "Oh, Grandmamma, do you suppose I'll be introduced to a duke when I go into society? It's always been a dream of mine, to meet such an exalted figure. Do you know any dukes? Will they host balls that I'll attend? Oh, please do tell me their names."

Lady Gilmore dropped the quizzing glass and glared. "Cease this babbling at once, girl. It is unbecoming for the wife of a viscount. And as for dukes, I shall say a prayer you don't ever encounter one. You would be a disgrace to this family!"

It was the perfect opportunity for Maddy to propose her metamorphosis into a proper lady, as she'd discussed with Nathan the previous evening. But even as she parted her lips to speak, a knock sounded on the door.

Gertie bustled out of the dressing room. Apparently having overheard the dowager's rantings, she rolled her eyes at Maddy. Then the maid opened the door.

Shawshank stepped into the bedchamber and bowed first to Lady Gilmore, then to Maddy. "Pardon the interruption, Lady Rowley," the portly butler said to Maddy. "Where shall we put the silk?"

"The silk?"

"Indeed, Lord Rowley had it delivered from his warehouse just now. He said to give it directly to you, my lady."

Nonplussed, she waved at the bed. "You may place it right here, I suppose, with the other sewing supplies."

Her eyes widened as a line of footmen came marching through the doorway, each servant hefting several rolls of colorful fabric. She quickly jumped down from the stool to give the footmen better access, and Mrs. Dobbs scrambled to her feet, too, stepping back out of their way. Before Maddy's astonished gaze, the many spools of cloth piled up as high as the top of the gilt headboard.

"My word!" the dowager exclaimed as the team of servants departed. Using her cane, she levered herself to her feet and shuffled to the bed to regard the hoard. "What is all of this?"

Maddy stifled a smile. Not even in the role of talkative vixen would she tell the fusty old woman what Nathan had said to her the previous night when she'd stroked her fingers over the dragons embroidered on his dressing gown. *My warehouse is full of silk. I'll give you as many bolts as you like so long as you keep fondling me like that.*

Her insides contracted at the memory. Why had he sent her such an extravagant gift? Was he merely fulfilling a promise? Or did he mean for it to be an apology for doubting her virtue?

Oh, she hoped it was the latter. The offering would go a long way toward mollifying her annoyance at him.

She went to the bed and fingered a length of cobalt-blue silk, then another of rich bronze. "I suppose my husband wishes me to make my gowns out of the cloth he brought from China."

The dowager harrumphed. "Did he think *my* selections would not be good enough?"

Maddy held her tongue. That was another reason she was thrilled to receive his gift. The fabrics that Lady Gilmore had chosen from the dressmaker's samples were the drabbest, dowdiest shades in the color palette, like the mustard-brown frock that Maddy was wearing at present. Apparently, the dowager's plan was to make the infamous Lady Rowley appear matronly and nondescript in the hopes that she would fade into the background.

"What is going on here?" Lady Emily asked, her hazel eyes bright with curiosity as she peeped around the door.

"I saw the footmen carrying many bolts of cloth up the staircase."

"You should be practicing the pianoforte at this hour," Lady Gilmore chided. "I gave you strict orders not to come in here."

"I've finished my lesson already," Emily said. "I just wanted to see . . . oh, heavens! Look at that treasure trove!"

She darted to the bed to examine the rolls of fabrics. In particular, she seemed drawn to a bolt of fine cream silk, rubbing it reverently between her fingers. Tiny pink roses had been stitched all over it.

"Do you like that one?" Maddy asked.

Her pockmarked face glowed with an inner beauty. "Oh, yes. It would be perfect for my presentation gown when I meet the queen."

"We have already selected a white satin for you," Lady Gilmore said sharply. "The embroidery on this would be highly inappropriate."

"Then perhaps it will do for something else," Maddy told the dowager. "I'm sure Nathan would love for her to have it. So would I. Would you like that, Lady Emily? Perhaps it can be used to fashion a ball gown."

"Truly? Thank you!" The girl ran to Maddy and folded her in a warm embrace redolent of soap and lilacs. "I'm so very glad that we're sisters now."

Maddy's heart ached as she returned the hug. She had never had a sibling; the theater troupe had been her family after the deaths of her parents. Now, it was an unexpected pleasure to find that she could actually *like* one of these aristocrats. But oh, if only she could fix the unsightly pit marks on that fresh, pretty face.

"That is quite enough," the dowager said sternly. "If you are finished with the pianoforte, Emily, then you may begin addressing the invitations to your debut ball."

"Of course, Grandmamma." Emily dipped a graceful

curtsy to the old woman. She started toward the door, then spun around, her pink skirts whirling. "Oh, I nearly forgot. We've been swamped with callers today. They've left their cards downstairs. I suspect they all wish an introduction to Nathan's new wife."

So he was right. The news had spread like wildfire through society. Maddy felt a lurch in her stomach as she wondered if the Duke of Houghton might have been among the visitors. Had she missed a golden opportunity to come face-to-face with her grandfather?

"How exciting that all the nobles want to meet me," she said with contrived frivolity. "Perhaps I should go straight downstairs in case anyone else comes to call. I wouldn't want all those fancy grandees to think I'm dodging them."

"Get back onto the stool and finish your fitting," the dowager ordered. "Until further notice, you are to remain right here in your bedchamber when anyone other than family is in the house. Now, run along, Emily. And pray don't burst in here again like a hooligan—else I shall blame it on Madelyn's bad influence!"

Obediently, the girl vanished out the door, closing it behind her.

While Mrs. Dobbs knelt down to resume her pinning of the hem, Maddy stepped onto the stool. She hated seeing the dowager crush her granddaughter's high spirits. With her skin disfigurement, poor Emily had enough troubles already.

Maddy reminded herself she was only here to play a role—and not to interfere in the lives of Nathan's relatives. Nevertheless, she found herself saying, "Lady Emily is such a sweet girl, isn't she? It's dreadful to see those pit marks on her face. Has she tried powder or paint to cover them?"

Lady Gilmore looked up from her surly inspection of

the silks on the bed. "Cosmetics are inappropriate for a young girl."

Maddy disagreed wholeheartedly, but decided now was not the time to quarrel. Better she should use the opening to delve for more information. "May I ask what happened to her? I noticed the earl has similar blemishes on his face as well. Did they both suffer from the same illness?"

"Smallpox." Uttering that one word seemed to deflate the dowager's spitefulness. The old woman hobbled back to the fireplace and eased herself back into the chair. With a heavy sigh, she added, "It happened in late winter, just over a year ago."

Nathan's brother David had died a year ago. It all began to make horrible sense to Maddy. "What about my husband's older brother? Did he catch the smallpox, too? Is that what happened to him?"

Lady Gilmore's wrinkled face drooped and she glanced down at her gnarled fingers wrapped around the cane. "Unfortunately so. David was an honorable, upstanding nobleman with great possibilities. His premature death was a terrible blow to this family."

Having lost her parents, Maddy understood the grief of saying good-bye to a loved one. But did the earl and his mother have to show such favoritism toward the elder son? Did they have nothing left for the younger one? "Then perhaps we can be thankful that Nathan was away from England at the time. At least he was spared."

"That one," Lady Gilmore spat out with bitter force. "He was always the wild, reckless profligate. While David was learning to run my son's estates, Nathan was gambling and carousing, often staying out all night. His only interest in his father's lands was how much he could milk from them to pay his debts."

Maddy lifted her arms to allow Mrs. Dobbs to pin the loose waist. Yes, it was easy to picture Nathan as a rogue, flashing those dimples and seducing loose women. Perhaps she was wrong to sense a deep, dark reason behind his father's scorn of him. Perhaps it was nothing more than a reaction to Nathan's past wicked behavior.

But she wouldn't criticize him in front of this sour old lady. Not when they were supposed to be madly in love.

"Then it's a good thing he went away and grew up," she prattled. "I'm sure you'll soon see that he's changed for the better. After all, he's become an exceedingly wealthy tradesman. And now that he is Viscount Rowley, and a married man, I feel certain he will settle down and conduct himself like a fine and proper gent."

When Lady Gilmore pursed her lips as if preparing to spew more vitriol, Maddy deemed it time to propose her plan to transform herself.

She hopped down from the stool and went to kneel before the dowager, heedless of a pinprick in her side as she took those cold, gnarled fingers in hers. "Oh, milady, I do hope you'll help me. I feel unworthy of such a lofty man as my dear husband. I fear that I might embarrass him when we go out in society to hobnob with all the gentry. A new wardrobe won't be enough to change my common ways. That's why I was thinking you might be so kind as to give me lady lessons."

Grimacing, the dowager extracted her fingers. "Lady lessons?"

"Yes. I doubt there will be time for me to learn how to play the pianoforte like Emily. But I can study other things. I will need to know which fork to use at dinner, the proper way to serve tea, and how to converse with noble folk—"

"You need only practice the old maxim 'hear much and talk little.'"

Lady Gilmore sounded crotchety, but at least she hadn't outright refused. Encouraged, Maddy plunged onward.

"There's also how to dance, how to curtsy, and how to address a duke—"

"No. That part shall be unnecessary."

"What part?"

With rheumy hazel eyes, the dowager stared down her snooty nose. "Allow me to be blunt, Madelyn. I should have made this perfectly clear during your earlier outburst. As a figure of notoriety, you will *not* be invited to the best houses. You will *not* be invited to many parties. And you most certainly will *not* be meeting any dukes at all!"

Nate's steps slowed as he neared the open door in the upstairs passageway. He dreaded this encounter. He didn't much like children. They tended to be sticky and loud and tiresome. But like all unpleasant chores, it was best to get this over with and done.

He stepped into the doorway. The nursery looked much as it did in his youth. The schoolroom with its low shelves of books formed the main area with the bedchambers located down a corridor to the right. The same alphabet animals were framed on the walls, and a globe of the world sat on a pedestal. But the room seemed to have shrunk compared to the vast space he remembered from his childhood.

Of course, he had been much smaller then, a mischievous rascal who had spent a good deal of time banished to a stool in the corner and facing the wall. Sitting still for hours had been the absolute worst punishment for an active lad. The whippings administered by the Earl of Gilmore had hurt much more, but at least they'd been over swiftly.

The tableau on the far side of the room drew his attention. There, a young girl sat at a child-sized oak table by the windows, swinging her feet and kicking up the hem of her yellow gown, while she wrote with chalk on a slate.

Nearby, a plump nursemaid dozed in a rocking chair with a tiny redheaded girl cuddled on her ample lap. The little one was sucking her thumb while watching the other girl.

Nate felt rooted in the doorway. These must be his nieces. The two daughters that his brother had sired.

His throat tightened unexpectedly. A hot moisture prickled his eyes. Aghast, he looked away and swallowed several times. How absurd to feel moved by the sight. They were merely children.

And they were not his responsibility. That burden fell to the head of the family, their grandfather, the Earl of Gilmore. Yet Nate felt a duty toward them nonetheless. Long ago, David had watched over him, protecting him whenever possible from the earl's wrath. And this was Nate's chance to return the favor.

A deep breath expanded his chest. With determined steps, he started toward the children. As he approached, the girl at the table twisted around in her miniature chair to watch him. The nursemaid awoke and spied him, her eyes like two black currants in a doughy face.

With the toddler in arms, she struggled to wrest her fleshy form out of the rocking chair. "Oh, milord! Pardon me!"

"Pray remain seated," Nate said. "There's no need to get up."

Clearly discomfited, the servant settled back down to her rocking.

He squatted down on his haunches by the girl at the table. She was a fairy-child with reddish-brown hair tied back with a yellow ribbon and hazel eyes exactly like David's. A smudge of chalk dust adorned her minuscule nose. She didn't appear frightened, only curious.

"Hello," he said. "I'm your uncle Nate. What is your name?"

She stared at him. Her expression had a quiet solemnity

that reminded him again of his brother. A weight sat on his chest, making it difficult to breathe.

Blast, why had he come here? He didn't know how to hold a conversation with a child. "Perhaps you'll tell me your sister's name, then," he tried.

She regarded him for another long moment, until he was almost ready to give up and leave. Then she said in a clear, bell-like voice, "I'm Caroline. And she's Laura. She cries at night sometimes. But *I* never do."

"That's very good of you. I suppose that means you're not a baby anymore." He fumbled for a topic, then spotted the slate where she had been practicing her ABCs. "I see you're learning to write."

"I'm on *Q*. It's a circle with a tongue." Caroline bent her head over the slate again and laboriously drew the letter, a bit crooked but recognizable.

"Excellent," he said. "Do you know any words that begin with *Q*?"

She thought a moment, then announced, "Queen! Like Queen Victory."

He grinned, using his thumb to wipe the smear of chalk dust from her pert little nose. "Queen Victoria, indeed. Well done."

Even as a sweet smile bloomed on Caroline's face, the tap of footsteps sounded behind him. Lady Sophia's sharp voice rang out. "What is going on here?"

Nate jumped to his feet and turned around. He hadn't known anyone else was here. Gowned in somber gray, his widowed sister-in-law stood in the doorway to the children's bedchambers. He could appreciate why his brother had married her. Sophia had delicate features, lustrous brown hair, and a fine figure—though the effect was spoiled by the vinegary look on her face. Directly behind her trailed a thin, fortyish woman clad in black, her dark hair in a severe bun.

"I was just observing Caroline at her work," he said. "She's doing a marvelous job with her writing."

Sophia glided over to Caroline to pat her hair and fuss over her, before going to the rocking chair. The red-haired toddler stretched out chubby arms, and Sophia picked her up, hugging her close and crooning in her ear before handing the child back to the nursemaid.

Nate had the distinct impression that his sister-in-law was checking to make certain he hadn't harmed the girls in any way.

He tried not to be annoyed. She seemed an attentive mother, if a trifle overprotective. And he was a stranger to her, after all. Over the years, she'd known only the poison disgorged by the Earl of Gilmore.

Though by now she'd probably also figured out that Nate had married a common actress for the purpose of revenge.

"Miss Jameson will take over now." Sophia gave a nod to the governess, who scurried toward the child. "We were just consulting on Caroline's progress in her schoolwork."

He bowed. "Then I'll leave you to your occupation."

As he turned to go, she said, "One moment, if you please. May I have a word with you?"

"As you wish."

Sophia marched toward the other end of the schoolroom, stopping near the door to the outer passageway. As he joined her there, she lifted her chin and said in a hushed tone, "I confess to being very surprised to find you here. You don't seem the sort to be interested in children."

"I wanted to meet my brother's brood. They're lovely girls. How old are they?"

"Caroline is five and Laura is two." Like a mother hen guarding her chicks, Sophia regarded him combatively. "It would have been proper for you to ask my permission to come here. That would have allowed me to prepare my daughters."

"Prepare?"

"Caroline is often shy with strangers. They frighten her."

"Really? She wasn't frightened of me." Nate was rather proud of that now. "We conversed quite well."

Sophia didn't appear mollified in the least. She said stiffly, "Nevertheless, I must ask that your . . . wife refrain from visiting the nursery. I trust you can see that a woman of her kind might have an unwelcome influence on my daughters."

Nate stiffened. The audacity of this woman, to suggest that Madelyn would corrupt his young nieces. He'd never heard anything so ridiculous. His mind conjured the image of his wife, the look of wonder in her big blue eyes as he'd entered her for the first time. The shock of her innocence was seared into his memory.

But Sophia wouldn't care about that. He'd known many ladies like her in the past. Only bloodlines mattered to them.

It took every bit of effort to hold his temper in check. Aware that he and Madelyn would have to live under the same roof with this woman for the coming months, he told himself to choose his words carefully. "I don't believe you've stopped to consider—"

The retort died on his tongue. Madelyn stepped into the doorway. A vision in blue silk, her blond hair in a simple knot atop her head, she looked from Sophia to him and smiled brilliantly. "Oh, dear me! Have I interrupted something?"

Chapter 13

A moment earlier, Maddy had stopped in the passageway outside the nursery. Detecting the murmur of voices, she'd hesitated to intrude upon a private conversation between Nathan and his sister-in-law. At least until Lady Sophia had said, *A woman of her kind might have an unwelcome influence on my daughters.*

The comment cut deeply into Maddy's heart. It confirmed everything she had ever known about the snobbery of the upper class. A woman of her kind, indeed!

When Nathan did not respond, she knew she ought to retreat, to pretend she hadn't been eavesdropping, if only by accident. But she would not tolerate such shabby treatment. If her own husband wouldn't stand up for her, then she must do so herself.

Maddy stepped through the doorway of the nursery just as Nathan said, "I don't believe you've stopped to consider—"

He fell silent as his gaze flashed to her, his green eyes intent. Her heart skipped a beat. He looked exceptionally attractive today in a blue-gray coat and white cravat that enhanced the sun-burnished angles of his face. Though he wore the elegant garb of a gentleman, there was always

something uncivilized about him. Perhaps it was the boldness of his stare or the way he tied back his black hair
with a leather thong.

Both he and Lady Sophia appeared startled by her
abrupt appearance. They must be wondering what she'd
overheard. Good, Maddy thought. They oughtn't be talking about her behind her back.

She shaped her lips into a dazzling smile. "Oh, dear me,
have I interrupted something?"

"Certainly not," Nathan said. "I was just on my way
out."

"Well, I'm so glad to have found you, darling," Maddy
gushed, gliding to his side. "I've been looking all over the
house. And Lady Sophia, how lovely to see you again."

Turning her attention to the woman, Maddy felt an unwelcome twist of envy. David's widow oozed refinement
from her glossy brown curls to the fashionable cut of her
gray gown. It made Maddy keenly aware of the old blue
dress she'd donned after her fitting. The style was several
years out of date, though recently she had added a bit of
lace at the bodice and adjusted the sleeves to give it a more
modish flair.

Nathan dropped a kiss on her cheek. "Speaking of
lovely, you're looking quite beautiful today."

The gravelly sound of his voice flowed through her as
a primal thrill. She accepted his compliment with a grain
of salt; he was playing the role of devoted husband. Yet the
masculine scent of him, redolent of sandalwood and
leather, sparked vivid memories of the pleasure they'd
shared the previous night, when she had buried her face in
the crook of his neck while he'd moved inside her. Now, she
blushed as a throb of desire heated the place where they'd
been joined. Her flustered feeling intensified when he
slipped his arm around her waist, his fingers idly rubbing
the small of her back.

But he was gazing at his sister-in-law. "As I was saying, Sophia, I don't believe you've stopped to consider. At this time next year, my child—Madelyn's child—may be sharing this nursery with your daughters. They'll be cousins. Won't that be splendid?"

The idea of bearing his baby caused a quake inside Maddy. Before the auction, when she had been intending to enter into a temporary arrangement as a gentleman's mistress, she had learned from one of the other actresses how to avoid pregnancy with a vinegar-soaked sponge. But Maddy had taken no such precautions the previous night.

Should she have?

No. She was a married woman now, and a child would be a boon to her bargain with Nathan. How wonderful to contemplate motherhood. Her heart melted at the notion of cradling his baby in her arms, a tiny boy with a thatch of black hair and miniature dimples . . .

"Splendid, indeed," Lady Sophia said in a brittle tone.

Maddy came out of her reverie to see that the woman's face had gone pale. And no wonder, for Nathan was the heir now. His child would take precedence over Lady Sophia's daughters.

It had to be a bitter pill to swallow.

Maddy looked across the schoolroom at the two little girls. A nanny in a black gown sat with the older child, helping her as she drew on a slate. The younger one napped in the nursemaid's ample arms.

The sight brought a smile to her lips. "Are those your daughters, my lady? How precious they are. Quite the prettiest children I've ever seen. You must be so proud of them."

"Yes, thank you." Lady Sophia hesitated, then pursed her lips and said with rigid politeness, "Would you care to meet them?"

Maddy would have liked that if not for the woman's

obvious reluctance. As infuriating as Lady Sophia might be, Maddy decided not to push herself where she wasn't wanted. "Perhaps another time," she demurred. "I wouldn't dream of disturbing the sweet little darlings. And anyway, I must steal my husband away from you. He and I have an important matter to discuss."

In the guise of devoted wife, she slipped her hand into the crook of Nathan's arm, then tilted up her head and batted her lashes at him for good measure. One corner of his mouth twitched in a faint grin and his eyes warmed with appreciation. A wave of intense attraction washed through Maddy. To regain her equilibrium, she had to lower her gaze to the starched white folds of his cravat.

"Wait," Lady Sophia said sharply as they turned to go. "Lord Rowley, did you not promise the earl that you'd find your own place of residence very soon?"

"I did," he said. "However, all the best homes are likely to have been let for the season. So who knows, perhaps we'll stay right here for some time to come. Good day."

With that, he whisked Madelyn out of the nursery and down the narrow passageway. Their footsteps echoed on the uncarpeted floorboards. Despite the weighty matter pressing on her mind, Maddy needed to keep all of his subterfuge straight. There were things he hadn't made clear to her yet.

"You aren't intending to look for a town house at all, are you?" she asked. "Your plan has always been to remain here."

"How astute of you. To remove my disreputable bride from Gilmore House would defeat my purpose."

"And you haven't told anyone that you're planning to leave England for good at the end of the season?"

"Not a living soul beyond you, Madelyn. It's our little secret."

His cavalier smile shouldn't bother her. Their eventual parting suited her plans, as well as his. With the generous stipend he'd promised her, she could move into her own house after he was gone. If she'd conceived his child by that time, she would have sufficient funds to hire a staff of servants and still fulfill her dream of opening a dress shop.

Yet one key part of her purpose in marrying him was already in jeopardy. All because of his grandmother's shocking decree.

As a figure of notoriety, you will not be invited to the best houses. You will not be invited to many parties. And you most certainly will not be meeting any dukes at all!

Anxiety twisted in Maddy. If she couldn't mingle with the aristocracy, then how was she to meet the Duke of Houghton? How was she to confront the haughty man who had shunned her mother for eloping with an actor?

Although Lady Gilmore had consented to teach her, the dowager believed that no matter how much Maddy studied and practiced, a common actress could never become a true lady and the ton would never accept her. No amount of cajoling from Maddy had swayed the old woman from that conviction.

Yet Maddy wasn't ready to give up.

As she and Nathan started down a flight of stairs, she glanced up at him. "We need to speak in private," she said. "Someplace where no one else can overhear."

"How intriguing. I'd never turn down a tryst with a beautiful woman."

In the midst of her worries, she warmed to him. That was the second time today he'd complimented her. It was gallant of him, for she wore a shabby gown and felt frazzled from the long hours being poked and fitted by the dressmaker. She wondered how many women he'd charmed with such flattery, how many more he would seduce in the future, for once Nathan went abroad again she doubted he would honor their wedding vows.

The notion vaguely disturbed her. Surely vows made before God were not meant to be broken.

But at least her husband seemed in a better humor today. Most likely because he had won the battle with his father over the issue of annulling the marriage. Last night's consummation had ensured that.

Upon reaching the bottom of the stairs, they started down the long, empty corridor where the bedchambers were located. Her room might be a quiet place to talk. Unless Gertie and Mrs. Dobbs hadn't yet cleared away all the sewing supplies . . .

She swung toward Nathan. "Oh, I nearly forgot! Thank you for the bolts of silk. I can't tell you how very much I appreciate them."

"If you can't tell me, then you may show me."

His hand at the small of her back, he abruptly steered her to the first doorway, turned the latch, and escorted her inside, closing the door behind them. The spacious room appeared to be an unused bedchamber. The tall draperies were drawn, shutting out the mid-afternoon sun and rendering the space dim and shadowed. She had a glimpse of a four-poster bed and chairs shrouded in protective cloth.

Then Nathan pulled her into his arms and passionately kissed her. After an initial shyness, she succumbed to the clamoring sensations within her and returned the kiss. The hot pressure of his mouth felt heavenly and the excitement of his unexpected sensual assault awakened her desires. But when he slid his fingers inside her bodice to caress her bosom, she was brought to an awareness of his intentions.

She drew back, breathless, to push at his shoulders. "Do stop. I told you, I need to speak to you. It's very important!"

"Ah, but lovemaking is so much more fun than talking."

He tried to nuzzle her throat, and she ducked, slipping out from the circle of his arms and backing away until her spine met one of the bedposts. She collected the unraveled threads of her thoughts. "You *will* hear me out, Nathan. Your grandmother told me today that I'm to be stuck in this house for the entire season. It doesn't matter if I transform myself into a fine lady. I still won't receive invitations to the best parties."

He sauntered toward her. "Balls are hot and over-crowded affairs, full of preening snobs. You won't be missing much."

Her heartbeat quickened at his rakish smile and she re-treated farther into the bedchamber. "But that was part of our bargain," she said, glancing back to avoid stumbling into the furniture. "We were to attend fancy parties, to mingle with the nobility. You promised that as your wife, I would enter society."

He arched a dark eyebrow as he prowled after her. "Did I? I don't recall saying that."

"It was implied, then. It was a big part of my reason for marrying you."

"And here I was hoping it was your lust for my manly form."

Nathan made a quick grab for her arm. His fingers brushed her sleeve, and with a gasp, she scrambled for ref-uge behind a chair. The faint smile on his face aroused her passion. He could easily overpower her, she knew he could, but he relished toying with her as a tiger stalks its prey.

How she yearned for him to catch her. She longed for his mouth on hers again, his touch on her body. But not yet. Not until she'd convinced him to help her.

As he came closer, she held up her hand. "*Please* stop chasing me, Nathan, and think for a moment. How am I to be an embarrassment to your father if I'm kept out of the public eye? It's to your advantage to make certain that I'm included in *all* the invitations. So that I'm seen everywhere, even at the most exclusive parties."

Halting, he stared at her through the shadows of the bedchamber. From his hard, calculating expression, Maddy knew she'd finally reached him. "I'll take care of the matter," he said after a moment. "You needn't fret about it."

"But what will you do? How will you manage it? Your grandmother says that you have a terrible reputation. If you're not invited to parties, then I won't be, either—*Oh!*"

He lunged, and this time, he caught her by the waist and brought her flush against his hard form. His smile gleamed through the gloom, his dimples in attractive display. "I said I'll take care of it. You'll dance at as many parties as you like. Trust me."

With that, he sank into an overstuffed chair and brought her down onto his lap. Maddy found herself sprawled over him, her bosom crushed to his chest. She looped her arms around his neck to steady herself. But Nathan wasn't done. He reached beneath her skirts and nudged her legs apart so that she straddled him. "Ah, that's better."

His hard length pressed against her aching center, with only the cloth of his trousers and her lace-edged underdrawers as a barrier. "Nathan!" Scandalized, she glanced over her shoulder at the closed door across the dim-lit bedchamber. "What if someone walks in here?"

"Never mind that. Let's live dangerously."

Their lips joined in a deep kiss, and a sense of wicked adventure enhanced her enjoyment. His hands were still beneath her skirts, stroking her bare thighs above her garters before delving between her legs. His fingers found the slit in her undergarments and caressed her with great delicacy, his thumb gliding through her wetness, stimulating exquisitely sensitive flesh. Craving release, she moaned into his mouth.

She almost wept when he took his hand away to open the buttons of his trousers. But the knowledge of his intention filled her with fire. Feverishly, she braced her hands on his shoulders and raised herself as he fitted himself into her. She sank down, sighing with pleasure as he filled her, shuddering with the perfection of their union.

Succumbing to an instinctive urge, she swiveled her hips and relished the ripples of heat that eddied through every part of her body. Nathan sucked in a breath through his teeth. Beneath her skirts, his hands gripped her thighs and she moved again, awash in the glory of pleasuring him as well as herself. It was her turn today to direct the action, and she embraced the role with great relish, sliding up and down his shaft until she could scarcely bear any more of the divine friction.

She pressed her forehead to his. "Nathan, *please . . .*"

Reaching between them, he stroked the place of their joining. At once, a bolt of hot bliss shot through her and she cried out from the onrush of ecstasy. Hazily she was aware of him giving a quick upward thrust of his hips as he, too, shuddered in the frenzy of release.

Utterly spent, she melted against him, her head resting on his shoulder until her heart slowed and she could catch a breath again. Never in her life had she felt so happy as this moment, cradled in his arms. How had she ever lived without this pleasure?

"That was heaven," she said on a sigh, kissing his jaw. "No wonder you have such a bad reputation. It comes from carousing with women."

His eyelashes half lowered, he regarded her. "Jealous?"

She was, just a little, but that defied logic. Whatever he'd done in the past shouldn't concern her. "Certainly not! It's only that I heard from your grandmother that you'd misbehaved quite a lot in your youth. I confess to speculating as to why."

He idly caressed her bottom. "Misbehaving is fun. You should know that by now."

"Mmm." For a moment, she couldn't string two thoughts together. The languor of release had cast her mind adrift. "I wonder if that's all. I wonder if perhaps you were deliberately trying to rile your father, even back then."

His hand ceased its delicious play. He leaned back to give her a sharp stare. "You will not mention him when we're together like this. Not ever. We will speak of nothing consequential at all. Is that clear?"

The hard flare in his eyes jolted her back to reality, as did his harsh tone. She had not meant to anger him. The comment had tumbled out in an unguarded moment. How foolish of her to reference the Earl of Gilmore at such a time.

Though his outburst stung, Maddy subdued her curiosity. She had no right to probe into Nathan's private past. They weren't devoted partners, building a long life together. They each had their own purposes, their own secrets.

It would be best to keep their relationship light and playful. After all, he'd be departing from her life in a few months' time. Until then, she might as well revel in sensual passion.

She curved her lips into a provocative smile, letting her fingers trace the hard angles of his jaw. "As you wish, my lord. There shall be nothing between us but pleasure."

Chapter 14

The coach inched forward in the queue of fine vehicles. Maddy put her face close to the window. Looking ahead, she could see a throng of people gathered in the torchlight outside a town house. They appeared to be common folk, hoping to catch a glimpse of the luminaries descending from their carriages.

A frisson of anticipation capered over her skin. Her plan was about to be set in motion. Tonight, for the first time, *she* would be one of the favored few allowed to enter the rarefied realm of the nobility. She finally would have a chance to search for her grandfather . . .

"Madelyn!" the dowager groused. "Don't press your nose to the glass. That is most improper."

She looked across the coach to see Lady Gilmore glaring in the pale light of the lanterns, her gloved hands grasping the gold knob of the cane, the ostrich feathers on her olive-hued hat wagging above her wrinkled features. A stern-faced Lord Gilmore sat beside her, then Lady Sophia in dark mulberry silk, the beauty of her dainty form spoiled by the haughty set of her chin.

The luxurious coach comfortably seated all six of them, with Maddy on Nathan's right and Emily on his left.

Nathan said nothing in Maddy's defense; he merely looked aloof, although she knew him well enough by now to detect the faint twitch of amusement at the corners of his mouth. After two weeks of marriage, the rascal still enjoyed seeing how much she irritated his family.

Maddy sat back demurely and folded her kid-gloved hands in her lap. Let them all sneer. She was determined not to be a liability for Emily's sake. "Forgive me, Grandmamma. I quite forgot myself for a moment."

"You must be on your best behavior tonight," Lady Gilmore scolded. "I would not like to think that I've squandered the past fortnight instructing you in proper manners."

"*I* think she'll do famously," Emily piped up. "She's a very quick learner and the dancing master said she's his best pupil."

"Pish-posh. A monkey can be taught to dance. It is how she behaves among her betters that concerns me. And at this party in particular! Lady Milford invites only the crème of the crème."

"Indeed, she's the premier hostess of the ton," Sophia said, turning her cool blue eyes on Maddy. "I cannot imagine that Lady Milford has ever before felt obliged to include a common actress on her guest list."

Maddy hid her annoyance behind a regal manner. "Then I shall endeavor to be worthy of the honor."

Nathan chuckled. "Since I am recently married, it would be peculiar for my bride *not* to attend." He placed his hand over Maddy's in her lap. "And we can be thankful for the opportunity. An invitation from my godmother is guaranteed to make Madelyn acceptable to the ton."

He was gazing at his father, no doubt savoring Gilmore's disapproving expression. Maddy had not quite grown accustomed to the tension between the two men. It loomed like a dark cloud over every meal, every family gathering

in the drawing room, every chance encounter in the corridor.

Nevertheless, the firmness of Nathan's hand on hers
stirred a melting warmth in her. He had come through on
his promise to help her, after all. Somehow, he had persuaded Lady Milford to host a party to pave Maddy's entry into society. It was the perfect remedy to the dowager's
poisonous decree that would have kept Maddy hidden
away at Gilmore House.

"This is the first grand event of the season," Emily said,
her face aglow with excitement. "I can scarcely wait to see
who's here. Oh, I do hope I'm asked to dance."

A fond smile eased the earl's taut features. "You are
looking exceptionally lovely tonight, my dear. I'm sure the
gentlemen will be clamoring for introductions."

Maddy allowed herself a secret smile of satisfaction. No
one seemed to have noticed exactly *why* Emily appeared
so radiant, or looked closely enough to see that it was due
to a clever application of cosmetics. Earlier, Maddy had
brought the girl into her dressing room and used a minuscule amount of putty to fill her pockmarks. The pits were
still there, but they were far less evident, especially with a
dusting of powder and a touch of rouge on Emily's cheekbones to enhance her youthful luminosity.

Lady Gilmore had expressly forbidden the use of face
paint. But luckily, the dowager's poor eyesight had prevented her from detecting the subterfuge. Maddy had no
intention of enlightening her.

The coach crept forward and came to a halt in front of
the brick town house. A footman opened the door and
stood stiffly at attention. He extended his gloved hand to
help the ladies exit, first Lady Gilmore, and then Maddy.

As she stepped out, the petticoats beneath her evening
gown rustled. The peacock-blue dress had been sewn from
one of the lengths of silk that Nathan had given her, and

she'd had to cajole the dowager for the right to wear such a vibrant hue. But the effort had been well worth the trouble. She knew from the mirror in her dressing chamber that the off-the-shoulder gown complemented her upswept blond curls. Lady Gilmore had even grudgingly allowed Maddy to borrow a delicate sapphire teardrop necklace from the collection of family jewels.

In the glow of the torches, a red carpet runner had been laid to protect the ladies' hems. She had a swift view of the many admiring onlookers; then Nathan took hold of her arm and they followed the Earl of Gilmore and his mother past a line of liveried servants and into the house.

Throngs of richly garbed aristocrats crowded the spacious foyer with its high ceiling, and the air buzzed with conversation. The crystals of a huge chandelier glittered with the light of a hundred candles. A nervous excitement flowed through her veins. This had been her mother's world—and Maddy had long been curious to view it.

She handed her wrap to a waiting footman. Clutching a small reticule, she took a position with Nathan behind the earl and dowager in the receiving line. Lady Milford stood at the base of the marble staircase and welcomed each of her guests. Resplendent in lilac satin, a diamond tiara on her coal-black hair, she was clearly the doyenne of high society.

Maddy drew a shaky breath. She hadn't seen Lady Milford since the woman had come to the dressing room at the theater and requested that Nathan be included in the auction. Would her ladyship acknowledge their prior meeting? How would Maddy explain that acquaintance to the others—especially Nathan's grandmother?

Nathan lowered his lips close to her ear and whispered, "Don't look so frightened, darling. My godmother won't bite."

"Perhaps not her, but someone else, then."

He laughed softly. "Stay close and I'll guard against the wolves."

He turned to speak to Emily and Sophia, who stood behind them in line. All the while he kept his hand at the small of Maddy's back in a possessive gesture. Even in the midst of so many people, a pulse of attraction heated her. The carnal delight she had found with him these past few weeks had far surpassed her tame, virginal fantasies.

Since their marriage was one of mutual convenience, she had diligently ignored the darkness in him, the part of himself that he kept closed off to the world. It wouldn't do to wonder at the source of his hatred for his father. Nor to yearn for any more than physical pleasure with Nathan. After all, he would only be in her life for a few months.

The line moved forward. After greeting their hostess, the dowager hobbled several steps away and then stopped to wait with Lord Gilmore. Her wrinkled face alert, she held the quizzing glass to her eye and closely watched Maddy to see that no mistakes were committed.

Nathan made the introductions. "Lady Milford, may I present my wife, Madelyn, Lady Rowley. Madelyn, this is my godmother."

Maddy sank into the curtsy that she'd spent hours practicing. As she arose, Lady Milford gave her a warm smile and clasped Maddy's gloved hand. "It's a pleasure to make your acquaintance, Lady Rowley. I'm intrigued to finally meet the woman who caught my dashing godson."

The shrewd light in those violet eyes told Maddy that the secret of their earlier meeting was safe. With great relief, she returned the smile. "The pleasure is all mine, my lady."

"You appear to have made Nathan very happy," Lady Milford added. "Perhaps you and I might have a chance to chat more later."

"Thank you, I would enjoy that very much."

Then the little exchange was over and Maddy could breathe again. As Nathan drew her away, the dowager gave her a terse nod of approval. The Earl of Gilmore merely compressed his lips and averted his gaze to the milling throng. He was likely checking to see who might have noted her identity, Maddy thought in vexation.

She realized there were indeed many people looking her way, ladies whispering in small groups and gentlemen boldly eyeing her. They were all strangers to her. She saw no one familiar among them.

Was the Duke of Houghton present? He might be in the company of his grandson, her cousin. But Lord Dunham was nowhere in sight.

She held Nathan's arm as they started up the grand staircase with the rest of their party. "You're in," he murmured for her ears alone. "You've officially breached the walls of society. Everyone will have to accept you now that you have my godmother's stamp of approval."

Maddy allowed herself a moment of triumph, although another concern weighed on her mind. She glanced around to make certain no one could overhear. "Nathan, I have to ask. Do you know if any of the gentlemen from the auction were invited here?"

His mouth tilted in a grin. "Worried?"

"Of course I am. It could prove awkward. Should I pretend not to know them?"

"Do as you wish. So long as it displeases Gilmore."

His careless manner irked her. As happy as he'd made her in the bedchamber, he could be exasperating in his quest to use her to shame his father. "Don't tease. If anyone openly denounces me over that auction, it could cause a horrid scandal and reflect badly on your sister."

As they reached a reception area at the top of the staircase, he brought her gloved hand to his and kissed the back. "Set your mind at ease, darling," he murmured. "I

very much doubt any of those men would wish their pec-
cadilloes revealed in public. They'll pretend not to know
you for fear of landing in hot water with the ladies in their
life."

The reassurance eased her qualms. The last thing she
needed was for one of the gentlemen to reproach her in
front of everyone for spurning him. Or worse, to catch her
alone and attempt to grope her as Lord Dunham had done
at the theater.

"Why are you two whispering?" Lady Gilmore grumbled, huffing and puffing from the climb up the steps.
"What are you saying?"

"I was merely asking Nathan to tell me who is here,"
Maddy improvised. "But I fear he's been away from
society for so long, many are unknown to him."

"You will sit by me with the matrons," the dowager declared. "I will provide any necessary names. Come along
now. You will hold my arm while Gilmore and Sophia introduce Emily to the right people."

Maddy had envisioned herself strolling through the
crowd with Nathan, admiring the gowns of the other ladies,
viewing the opulent surroundings, and most of all, searching for the Duke of Houghton. Was she really doomed to be
stuck in a corner with the grumpy dowager?

She frowned up at her husband in attempt to convey her
displeasure, but he merely gave her that maddeningly
handsome smile and handed her over to his grandmother.
"Take good care of her, Grandmamma, while I go in
search of a card game." He leaned close and gave Maddy
a kiss on the cheek, whispering, "You'll be bored, but I'll
make up for it later when we're alone."

The warmth of his breath tickled her ear and sent a
feathery tingle over her skin. Leaving her frustrated
in more ways than one, he sauntered off into the multitude. He looked tall and attractive in his dark coat, his

shoulder-length black hair drawn back at his nape with a leather ribbon, setting him apart from all the other gentlemen. He drew quite a few glances, she noticed, especially from the women, and just as he stopped to turn his dimpled smile on a brunette beauty, Maddy heard the dreaded thud of the cane on the floor.

"Don't stand there gawking," Lady Gilmore hissed. "Help me into the drawing room."

Maddy dutifully grasped the old woman's arm. The dowager had stringy muscles beneath her olive-green sleeve, and she seemed sturdier than her appearance, tottering along with the aid of her cane. They went through an arched doorway and entered a long chamber, apparently two large drawing rooms that had been opened up for the purpose of this party. The rich décor of gold and blue formed a fitting backdrop for the many elegant guests.

At one end of the room, occupying several rows of chairs, a gaggle of middle-aged and elderly matrons sat with their fans waving and their tongues wagging.

"This is the true test," Lady Gilmore muttered. "You are to sit quietly and speak only when addressed. And no babbling whatsoever!"

It had to be the hundredth time Maddy had heard that particular directive. She swallowed her exasperation and said meekly, "Yes, Grandmamma."

As they neared the women, the whispers intensified. Many pairs of sharp eyes dissected her dress, her posture, her manners. It was obvious that every one of these pretentious snobs knew Lord Rowley had had the audacity to wed an upstart actress and then thrust her into their exalted midst.

Lady Gilmore stopped in front of them and presented Maddy. As each lady was introduced to her, she smiled politely and sketched a graceful curtsy. When the ordeal was over, she and Lady Gilmore found seats at the edge of the gathering, and the dowager bade Maddy sit near a large fern on a pedestal by the wall.

Maddy had to tilt her head to see past the leafy vegetation. She had been placed far enough away from the other ladies so that no one spoke to her, though they continued to stare disapprovingly in her direction while murmuring behind their fans. The veil of greenery also effectively separated her from the other guests in the drawing room.

Clearly, the dowager's plan was to hide Maddy in plain sight.

Perhaps it wouldn't be so bad, she told herself. At least she had a partial view of the party. A footman brought around a tray of drinks, and she sipped on champagne, the bubbles bursting on her tongue. For a time, she entertained herself by studying the array of gorgeous gowns on the other ladies, noting the cut of the sleeves and bodices, the accessories like gloves and reticules. When she opened her shop, she would have to be well versed in the latest fashions.

She also kept a watch for elderly gentlemen. But if the Duke of Houghton was present, she had no idea which one he might be. The barrel-chested man with the gray muttonchop whiskers? The stoop-shouldered octogenarian with a cane? The craggy old lecher who gawked openly at the ladies?

When a small ensemble began to play, Maddy surreptitiously tapped her feet in time to the music. She was wearing the fancy slippers given to her by Lady Milford, and every so often, the sparkly toe kicked up the hem of her peacock-blue skirt. From her vantage point behind the fern, there appeared to be dancing at the far end of the chamber. With all her heart, she longed to be in the thick of the other guests, whirling around the floor in Nathan's arms.

Impatience sizzled in her veins. Where *was* her husband? He'd mentioned something about cards, but that had been well over an hour ago. Had he joined a foursome? Or was he squiring that pretty brunette in a dance? It grated on Maddy to think of him aiming his heart-melting smile at another woman. He surely would be renewing acquaintances with members of the ton tonight. Ten years ago, he'd had a wild reputation, and if he were to meet an old flame . . .

At that moment, the crowd shifted and she spied a familiar gentleman in the doorway. All other thought fled her mind. That narrow aristocratic face beneath the neatly combed flaxen hair belonged to her cousin Alfred Langley, Lord Dunham.

She sat up straight, her gloved fingers digging into the reticule in her lap. Lord Dunham stood in conversation with someone. Who? Straining to see past the foliage, she spotted another gentleman with similar bone structure and sandy-brown hair, though he wore gold-rimmed spectacles and his face looked younger, his features lacking the sharpness of Lord Dunham's.

Were the two men related? More importantly, did Lord Dunham's presence mean that the Duke of Houghton was also in attendance?

Her heart thumped. This could be her big chance. While deciding on a scheme to escape Lady Gilmore's watchful protection, she noticed Emily standing a short distance away with Lady Sophia, exchanging pleasantries with a middle-aged couple.

The younger gentleman with Lord Dunham cast several furtive glances at Emily. A hint of yearning played on his face. The girl did indeed look like a vision, her slim figure garbed in cream silk, pearls at her throat, the candlelight shining on her russet-brown hair.

Lady Gilmore was gossiping with a matron, and Maddy

waited until there was a break in conversation. She leaned closer and asked, "Grandmamma, pardon me. Might I ask if you know those two gentlemen standing over there by the doorway? They look enough alike to be twins." Not really, but Maddy needed an excuse to single them out.

Lady Gilmore picked up the quizzing glass and squinted through it. "Twins? Hardly, they are eight years apart in age. The fair-haired one is Lord Dunham, heir to the Duke of Houghton. The other is his younger brother, Lord Theodore Langley."

Maddy sat in stunned surprise. So she had *two* cousins, not just one. She debated whether or not to inquire about the duke's presence, too, then decided against it, not wishing to arouse Lady Gilmore's suspicions. "I was curious because Lord Theodore appears to be gazing rather admiringly at Emily."

"Humph. I should rather Lord Dunham take a fancy to the girl. He may be a rapscallion, but he *is* the heir to one of the grandest titles in England."

"I wonder if Emily has met them," Maddy said. "I shall go find Nathan or the earl and ask one of them to do the honors."

The dowager grasped the knob of her cane. "Nonsense, I can introduce them myself."

"Oh, pray don't disturb yourself, my lady. I'm sure the earl is somewhere nearby."

Without further ado, Maddy arose from her chair and glided into the swarm of guests before Lady Gilmore could voice another objection. A heady sense of freedom swept through her. She would likely catch a scolding later for leaving without permission. But that risk was well worth the chance to cut herself loose from that clutch of old biddies.

She made a wide berth around her two cousins. Lord Dunham mustn't spot her—at least not yet. Of all the gentlemen from the auction, he was the one most likely to harass her and stir up unwelcome gossip.

The lilt of music lured her toward the far end of the room. She didn't see Nathan or his father anywhere. People stared and whispered, but she pretended not to notice. Her chin held high, Maddy imagined herself in the role of a highborn lady as she strolled through the multitude. She felt rather like an actress stepping off the stage and walking among the audience.

If anyone caught her eye, she smiled coolly and gave a regal nod. No one spoke to her since convention dictated a lady be formally introduced before engaging in conversation. Maddy didn't mind in the least. It was a blessing they were all strangers because she hadn't entered society to make friends.

She wanted a glimpse of her grandfather. *If* he was here.

This was the glittering world in which her mother had grown up. Had any of these people known Mama when she'd made her debut nearly thirty years ago? They would be shocked to the depths of their snooty souls to learn that the scandalous commoner in their midst was the daughter of Lady Sarah Langley, disgraced for eloping with an actor.

But no one must know just yet.

Approaching the dance floor, she spied another man familiar to her. The Marquess of Herrington was squiring a horse-faced girl in amber satin with a tail of ribbons at the back of her gown.

Maddy took her time selecting another glass of champagne from a tray while she surreptitiously observed him. Brown hair, brown eyes, ordinary features. Of all the gentlemen who had submitted bids in the auction, Lord Herrington had been the most dull and unremarkable. For that reason she had believed he would suit her well, a quiet scholar who would not make many demands on her. She had all but settled upon him as her lover when Nathan had presented his offer of marriage.

How different her life would be now had she kept to her original choice. She would not be a wife, but a mistress.

The music stopped. Lord Herrington bowed to his partner. Leaving the dance floor, the couple strolled into the milling assembly and headed straight toward Maddy.

She tensed. There was no time to turn and flee. That might attract undue attention, anyway.

She knew the moment the marquess saw her. His eyes widened ever so slightly. His nondescript features turned rigid. Yet his gaze flicked over her as if she were invisible.

She found his action unexpectedly amusing. He must be squirming inside, wondering if she would embarrass him by offering a greeting or making reference to the auction.

Maddy was half tempted to raise her champagne glass in a salute. Instead, she merely took a sip as the couple walked past her. What a relief that she had spurned his offer. Nothing about the lackluster man stirred her in the least. She shuddered inwardly to think of allowing him the intimate pleasures she'd shared with Nathan.

"Any regrets?"

A familiar male voice rumbled in her ear, and she choked on a bubbly swallow of champagne. She whirled around to see the smirking features of her husband, the gold flecks in his green eyes gleaming in the candlelight. Her heart took a wild leap. "Nathan! I thought you were playing cards."

"I was. Then I spotted you here, making moon eyes at Herrington."

"Pardon me? After your grandmother's lessons, I'm far too refined to make moon eyes."

He took hold of her hand and rubbed his thumb over her gloved palm. "Your dreamy expression must have been for me, then. You were reflecting on your good fortune in selecting me instead of him."

Nathan had deduced her very thoughts. Maddy was indeed thrilled with her choice. She couldn't imagine being with any other man. But she didn't want him to guess just how much the world sparkled whenever he was near. "Conceited jackanapes. You have an overblown sense of your own worth."

Chuckling, he plucked the champagne glass from her hand and set it on a table. "Well, my overblown senses tell me you're keen to practice your dancing skills. Come, the next one is a waltz."

Chapter 15

As the music commenced, Nate had his wife exactly where he wanted, clasped in his arms, one of his hands at the small of her back and the other laced with her fingers. After prowling through the party and reacquainting himself with a few old friends, he had found himself gravitating back to Madelyn. And why shouldn't he? If his scheme was to embarrass Gilmore, better he should stay close to his infamous bride.

Better he should pretend they were madly in love.

It was hardly a difficult task, for she was the perfect partner, light on her feet and easy on his eyes. Her soft blond hair had been drawn up in a coil at the back of her head with wispy ringlets framing her delicate features. The peacock-blue gown enhanced the milky skin of her bosom. He liked knowing that she belonged to him alone, that no other man had made her cry out in ecstasy. She smiled as they whirled around the dance floor, the picture of a sensual woman who enjoyed life to the fullest.

Yet he couldn't shake the image of her watching Herrington.

"You never answered me," he murmured while deftly guiding her past another couple. "Have you any regrets?"

"About giving up the marquess in favor of you? Of course not. I wouldn't have been invited to this party if I was merely a mistress." She spoke in a soft, breathy tone that required him to bend close to hear. Her eyes glimmered up at him, her lashes slightly lowered in a coy look. "However, you'll be leaving England in a few months. I'll be lonely. Perhaps I shall seek out Herrington as a lover."

Taken aback, Nate forced out a laugh. "That dull dog? He'd bore you inside of two minutes."

"Would he? I happen to find his intelligence to be highly stimulating. In fact, there are any number of gentlemen here who might be good company for an abandoned wife." Madelyn glanced around the dance floor as if seeking prospects for future trysts.

The minx was provoking him on purpose, Nate told himself. He wouldn't let her get away with it. Putting his mouth close to her ear, he breathed in the sweet scent of her skin. "You may not realize it yet, darling, but I've spoiled you for any other man."

"No, what you've done is to awaken my desires." Those big blue eyes challenged him. "And after showing me such pleasure, you can't expect me to live as a nun in the years to come. That hardly seems fair since *you* very likely will take lovers in your travels."

Nate found the topic more disturbing than it ought to be. He didn't want to acknowledge any truth in her words. And he certainly didn't want to imagine Madelyn in the arms of a lover, moaning another man's name in the throes of passion. It was time he called her bluff. "This conversation is absurd. You've studied to be a lady for the past fortnight in order to help Emily. You wouldn't do anything to hurt my sister."

"Emily will marry eventually, perhaps even by the end of this year. Once her future is settled, I'll be free to pursue my own interests. Anyway, you ought to encourage me to have affairs once you're gone. Then I shall be a perpetual disgrace to your father."

When she flashed that brilliant smile at him, Nate wanted to shake her. Madelyn was teasing him, she had to be, yet his insides felt tied in knots. She was an incredibly lovely, vivacious woman who took great pleasure in sexual intimacy. Without him around to fend off the sniffing dogs, she might very well fall prey to seduction.

As the waltz came to a close, he took a deep breath to dispel the tightness in his chest. Perhaps the root cause of his disquiet came from his childhood. His mother had had affairs; he remembered her as a beautiful, frivolous flirt whose indiscretions had caused much strife between his parents.

But Nathan's marriage was not based on fidelity to wedding vows. He shouldn't give a damn what Madelyn did after he left or with whom she did it. Let her open a bordello in Piccadilly Circus if she liked. It mattered nothing to him.

Her fingers pressed into his sleeve. "There's Lord Dunham and his brother by the fireplace," she murmured, peering into the crowd. "I lost sight of them while we were dancing."

His resolve went up in smoke. Dunham had been one of Nate's cronies in his dissipated youth. The reprobate had been a participant in the auction, the second one tonight who had caught Madelyn's interest.

Leaning down, he hissed in her ear, "For pity's sake, can't you wait with the trysts until I'm gone?"

She blinked at him and then laughed. "I'm sorry, you've misconstrued my meaning. Earlier, I noticed Lord Dunham's brother, Lord Theodore, admiring Emily. He looks to be an agreeable gentleman, and I hope you'll introduce them."

Nate looked at her suspiciously. "My sister?"

"Yes, I think she may have gone this way a few minutes ago."

Her gloved fingers curling around the crook of his arm, Madelyn urged him through the jam-packed room. They found Emily out in the corridor chatting with a fortyish gentleman whose balding head proved him to be far too old for her. Nate had no qualms about drawing his sister away to a quiet corner. As a debutante, she was supposed to be in the company of a family member at all times.

"Why were you left alone?" he demanded. "Where the devil is Gilmore? And Sophia?"

"Papa went to the library to smoke with the gentlemen," Emily said. "Sophia is upstairs in the ladies' retiring room. I'm sure she'll be back soon."

"In the meantime, there's someone you should meet—" Madelyn began.

"Dunham's brother," Nate broke in, still mistrustful of his wife's eagerness to make the introduction. "Do you know him?"

Emily's hazel eyes lit up. "Lord Theo? I've been *pining* for an introduction." Her fingers fluttered self-consciously over her pitted cheek. "But he's so handsome and clever. He attends Oxford, did you know? Do you truly think he would care to meet me?"

"Absolutely," Madelyn said, taking a handkerchief from her reticule and using it to discreetly dab a spot on the girl's cheek. "You look beautiful and, anyway, I saw him admiring you earlier."

As Emily smiled, her face took on a radiance that made Nathan study her more closely in the candlelight. The pit marks looked less obvious tonight, and he wondered if it was Madelyn's doing. If she had the skill with cosmetics to transform herself into a wrinkled old servant, as she'd done the night of the auction, then minimizing a few scars would have been a snap for her.

Once again, she had surprised him. She wasn't the shallow, heartless trollop that he'd initially thought. Of course, that was why he couldn't entirely trust her, either. She was too much the freethinker for her own good.

"Shall we go?" Madelyn said, looping her arm through Emily's.

"Wait." Nate stepped in front of them. He didn't want his wife anywhere near Dunham. Especially not when she looked so delectable. "Leave this to me, Madelyn. You should return to Grandmamma. Remember, it's best you're not seen in Emily's company."

"Oh, la! Everyone knows that Emily and I live under the same roof. It will seem odd if we're *not* friendly toward each other."

"I quite agree," his sister asserted. "And if anyone dares to snub Madelyn, then *I* shall snub *them*!"

Nathan had been certain that mentioning Emily's reputation would succeed in discouraging Madelyn. But she seemed hell-bent on seeing Dunham. At least Nathan could make sure the meeting was under his supervision. "No one is snubbing anyone," he said tersely. "We'll go together, then."

He offered an arm to each lady and they strolled back into the crowded drawing room. His mind continued to analyze Madelyn's motive. Was it just that she wanted to help his sister? Or was she angling for an official introduction to Dunham?

That had to be it. Although she and Dunham had been acquainted during her time as an actress, no one in society could be privy to that prior association. Therefore, they would have to meet again formally in order for her to converse with Dunham without raising eyebrows.

Why the hell did she want to chat with Dunham, anyway? Was the scoundrel on her list of potential lovers?

Blast it, she shouldn't be planning tête-à-têtes in front of her husband.

Much to Nate's satisfaction, however, Lord Theodore Langley stood alone by the fireplace, gazing into the flames. Dunham was nowhere in sight—and good riddance.

Nate hadn't spoken to Theo since he was a timid, gawky lad of twelve, home from Eton during the holidays, with his nose buried in a book. Apparently the years hadn't changed him much, for he still looked a trifle awkward in company.

"Well, well, if it isn't Theo Langley," Nate said, offering his hand. "Nathan Atwood here, in case you've forgotten me."

Theo looked around in surprise, his dark blue eyes rounded behind his spectacles, a lock of sandy-brown hair tumbled onto his brow. "Oh . . . hullo." His gaze flicked to Madelyn and then to Emily, lingering a moment on her before he belatedly shook Nate's hand. "Um . . . you're Lord Rowley now, aren't you?"

"Indeed, and I've lately returned from a long journey through the Far East. Lord Theo, if I might introduce my wife, Madelyn, and my sister, Lady Emily. Madelyn and Emily, Lord Theo Langley."

Theo turned hesitantly to Emily. He took her gloved hand almost reverently. "Hullo. It's—it's a pleasure to make your acquaintance."

Madelyn offered her hand as well. Her full attention on him, she studied him closely as if inordinately thrilled to meet Dunham's brother. "It's an honor, Lord Theo. Your grandfather is the Duke of Houghton, is he not? May I ask, is he here tonight?"

The second question struck Nate as odd—except in the context of her being a social climber. Did that explain her interest in Dunham? Had she selected that rogue as a future conquest on the basis of his bloodline? Nate clenched his jaw. As Houghton's grandson and heir, Dunham would be a feather in her cap.

And a rich one, too, for Houghton had deep pockets.

"I'm afraid Grandpapa doesn't get around very well these days," Theo said. "But I'm sure you'll meet him at our ball."

"Ball?" Madelyn inquired.

"It's in May. You must come, everyone does. It's always the biggest crush of the season." He blinked owlishly behind his glasses. "Not that *I* like great crowds of people. But the ladies seem to enjoy it."

Theo and Emily were stealing glances at each other and Nate decided the lad needed a nudge. "Ladies like dancing, that's why," he said pointedly. "Perhaps you and Emily should go practice your skills right now."

"Practice? Oh, yes, right, a capital notion." He bowed to the girl. "Lady Emily, would you care to dance?"

"Yes, I would, thank you!"

Arm in arm, they headed off toward the music, Theo looking tall and lanky beside petite, slender Emily. The young blade had better treat her well, or he'd have to answer to Nate.

He turned to see Madelyn smiling warmly after them. "They're such an attractive couple. They do seem enamored of each other, don't you think?"

"It would appear so."

Nate reflected that *he* was the one enamored—of Madelyn. That soft smile made him hunger to whisk her upstairs and find a bedchamber in which to make love to her. Even a dark corner or a linen closet would do, anywhere that they could be alone. The blood burned hotly in his veins. He could lift her skirts, press her up against the wall, and thrust into her tight velvet heat . . .

"Rowley," spoke a male voice from behind Nate. "You always did have a beautiful woman on your arm. This time, I see she is the scandalous Madelyn Swann."

Dunham joined them, a drink in his hand, his narrow features exuding a sly snobbery as he glanced from Nate to Madelyn and back again. He looked dapper in a black coat with a ruby stickpin in his cravat, his blond hair neatly combed. The slight sneer on his lips revealed his resentment at being the loser in the auction.

Nate slid his arm around Madelyn in a deliberate display of ownership. "Dunham. You will kindly address my wife as Lady Rowley. Darling, this is the disreputable Lord Dunham."

"How do you do, my lord?" she said.

Madelyn was still smiling but with tense civility. She didn't extend her hand as politeness demanded, nor did she curtsy. She watched Dunham almost warily, and Nate wondered if he'd been wrong to think her interested in the man. Rather, there seemed to be an undercurrent of dislike between them.

Why would she have invited him to participate in the auction if she had an aversion to him? Was it just his rank that had attracted her? Whatever the reason, Nate felt disturbed by it.

Dunham waved his glass toward the dance floor. "Was that Theo I saw going off with your sister just now? I'm afraid it won't do."

"Won't do?" Nate repeated coldly.

"I hate to be the bearer of bad tidings, but my brother shan't be permitted to court her. Houghton would never allow his grandson to have any connection to a family that has been tainted by common blood."

The direct slap at Madelyn made Nate's fingers clench into fists. "If you insist upon insulting my wife, then let's settle the matter in the boxing ring. Just name the time and place."

Those pale blue eyes widened slightly. "Fisticuffs," Dunham scoffed. "That was always *your* manner of solving disputes, not mine. I ask only that you warn your sister not to expect Theo to come calling."

With that, he walked away into the horde of guests. The stinking coward. Nate would have enjoyed planting a hook into that weaselly face. It was hard to believe they'd once been cronies, drinking and gambling and carousing together. He must have been out of his mind to associate with such a ne'er-do-well.

He looked down at Madelyn. As she stared after Dunham, her face was pale, her lips compressed. Nate had never seen her so wounded that she could not speak.

The sight stirred a protective instinct in him. "I'm sorry you had to be subjected to that," he murmured, gently squeezing her hand. "I'll make certain Dunham never again comes near you."

She lifted her chin and looked at him. Her blue eyes blazed with anger. "You needn't coddle me. I'm perfectly capable of watching out for myself. If you'll excuse me now, I shall return to Lady Gilmore."

Stunned, Nate stared as she glided away, the incomparable lady as she sailed through the crowd and sat down with his grandmother and the other matrons. He'd been wrong to think Madelyn distressed. She was furious. At him? What the devil had he done but defend her?

No, surely her anger was directed at Dunham. She must be incensed at him for barring Theo from seeing Emily. And she'd be affronted at being dismissed as *common*.

Whatever the reason for her ire, Nate resolved to keep a closer eye on his wife. Not just tonight but in the coming days as well. There was something between

Dunham and Madelyn, something that didn't quite make sense.

And he intended to find out exactly what it was.

The following morning at nine, Maddy entered the dining room to see the Earl of Gilmore sitting alone at the head of the table.

She stopped, tempted to make a quiet retreat. The newspaper he was holding blocked him from seeing her in the doorway. What was he doing here at this hour? The earl usually breakfasted promptly at eight. By nine, he was ensconced in the library with his papers and books. She had learned his daily routine in order to avoid his company. But their late return from the party the previous evening must have caused him to alter his strict schedule.

She balked at the notion of making stilted conversation with her father-in-law over the breakfast table. Frankly, the man intimidated her. According to Nathan, the earl had tried to have their marriage annulled. Keenly aware of his resentment of her, she often felt tongue-tied around him. She could do nothing to improve their strained relationship, either, for she had been charged with the task of irritating him.

She was being paid handsomely for her efforts, Maddy reminded herself. It was necessary for her to earn her keep. Besides, the footman standing on duty by the sideboard kept flicking glances at her. And the food laid out there smelled delicious, making her stomach rumble.

She pasted on a chipper smile and advanced into the room. "Good morning, Papa. I trust you are feeling well today."

Gilmore lowered the newspaper to regard her. Maddy knew she looked respectable in the stylish morning gown of bronze silk. Yet not even the tiniest hint of welcome cracked that dour façade. He merely gave her a nod, then lifted his cup to the footman, who scurried over to refill it from a silver coffeepot.

Maddy proceeded to the sideboard. The chafing dishes held a vast array of kippers and sausages, eggs and deviled kidneys, porridge and toast. Even after a few weeks living here, she never failed to be awed by the lavish meals. At the theater, she'd felt lucky to break her fast with stale bread and a sliver of cheese. Now she filled a plate with coddled eggs and bacon. Then she marched boldly forward to seat herself at the earl's right hand.

The footman came to pour steaming tea into her cup, and Maddy added a trickle of cream, stirring it with a silver spoon. Gilmore continued to read his newspaper as if she weren't even present.

She buttered a slice of toast. If there was to be a conversation, she would have to start it. "Lady Milford's party was a brilliant success, was it not? It seemed we all enjoyed it very much."

The earl glared over the top of his newspaper. "You behaved adequately last night. Is that what you wish to hear from me? Then consider it said."

Maddy tried not to quail under that unfriendly stare. *Adequately.* Was that all? But she hadn't been fishing for a compliment, anyway. "I was thinking of Lady Emily in particular. She danced with quite a few young gentlemen. She seemed especially taken with Lord Theodore Langley."

Instantly, she was sorry to have spoken that name, although Gilmore merely grunted and returned to his newspaper. Lord Theo was her cousin and she mustn't single him out lest someone guess the connection or glimpse a family resemblance. Besides, Lord Dunham had forbidden the courtship.

Houghton would never allow his grandson to have any connection to a family that has been tainted by common blood.

She took a bite of egg without really tasting it. His crass statement had lit the fuse of her fury. She had barely been able to contain herself from blurting out that she and Dunham shared the same blue blood.

But that revelation must wait for the moment when she came face-to-face with their mutual grandfather, the Duke of Houghton. Perhaps at the ball he was giving sometime in May.

Gilmore folded his newspaper and laid it down beside his empty plate. His dark brown eyes penetrated her. Abruptly, he asked, "Who are your people?"

Maddy's heart pounded. She took her time slathering gooseberry jam on her toast. "My people?"

"Your relatives, your family," he said in irritation. "Who taught you to speak like a lady? You could not have learned such refinement in your short time here in this house."

"Oh." She felt on familiar ground now. "I'm an actress, as were my parents before me. I grew up in the theater. From an early age, I learned to imitate speech patterns, to play many different roles. It was a necessary part of my work."

His flinty stare made her uncomfortable. It was hard not to look away, to pretend a brashness that she didn't really feel.

He dabbed his mouth with a linen serviette. "I presume you also became adept with the use of cosmetics at the theater."

"Why, yes."

"Emily was wearing face paint last night. My mother would never have allowed it. None of the servants would have dared to disobey her. And Sophia denied any complicity. That leaves only you, Madelyn."

She clutched her fork, the whorled pattern pressing into her fingers. His stern expression daunted her. His face bore a network of the same unfortunate pits as Emily's, a legacy of the illness that had claimed the life of his eldest son. How could he be angry over the improvement in his daughter's looks?

Maddy refused to apologize for helping the girl. "Yes, I did use a bit of powder and paint to minimize Emily's scars. You mustn't hold her to blame, either. It was entirely my doing. I can be quite insistent and persuasive, you see!"

"I am not blaming anyone," he said testily. "My daughter looked exceptionally fine last night. It seems I am obliged to thank *you* for that."

Rising, the earl pushed back his chair. Maddy gawked at him in astonishment. Before she could articulate a reply, he walked away and vanished out the door.

Chapter 16

Two hours later, Maddy was still mulling over the possibility that the Earl of Gilmore might have a trace of humanity in him, after all, when his son stepped into the morning room.

Nathan's broad shoulders and tall form made the spacious chamber seem suddenly smaller. The walnut-brown coat brought out the gold flecks in his green eyes, while tan breeches and black knee boots outlined his long legs. A warm attraction pulled at her, a testament to his magnetism. It was hard to believe that less than a month ago, she had not even known he existed.

When he opened his mouth to speak, however, she held her finger to her lips and glanced meaningfully at Lady Gilmore, who sat dozing in the chair opposite Maddy.

The dowager's chin sagged to the bosom of her pigeon-gray gown. Her eyes were closed in her wrinkled face, and a light, rhythmic snoring emanated from her. She had fallen asleep some ten minutes earlier and Maddy was loath to awaken her.

She quietly closed the book in her lap and set it aside. Then she arose from the chaise and tiptoed to the door to join Nathan. Catching hold of his arm, she steered him down the corridor toward the front of the house.

"What a relief," Maddy said with feeling. "Your grandmother has been especially petulant this morning."

"Exhaustion from the late party, perhaps?" Smiling, Nathan ran the backs of his fingers down her cheek. "It doesn't seem to have affected you. And you certainly had less sleep than her."

A delicious shiver coursed through Maddy. He had been especially attentive to her in bed last night, taking care to arouse her so completely that she fancied the aftereffects of pleasure still softened her body. Or perhaps it was just that smile of his now that made her so weak-kneed.

She strove for control. "Actually, I was growing quite drowsy myself while reading to her. A book of dry sermons isn't designed to keep a person awake for very long."

He frowned slightly as they strolled down the sumptuous passageway. "I thought the book was for your own enjoyment. But you were reading aloud to Grandmamma?"

"I always do so each morning. She claims it's good for me to practice my diction. But the truth is, she won't admit her eyesight is poor. She insists she doesn't need spectacles, only that silly quizzing glass."

Nathan stopped just outside the door to the drawing room and took hold of her upper arms. "You needn't feel compelled to do her bidding, Madelyn. If Grandmamma needs a companion, I'll speak to the earl about hiring one."

"I don't mind helping out. I'm used to staying busy." At the theater she'd had rehearsals and costume fittings and a hundred other duties to occupy her days.

"Nonsense, you're a lady now. I won't have my wife treated as a servant. You're free to occupy your days as you wish."

"What else am I to do? I can't shop or go to the park. The dowager expressly forbade me to leave this house."

"That was before you passed your test with flying colors last night."

To Maddy's surprise, Nathan pulled her into the quiet drawing room, guiding her to the one of the windows that looked out over the square. It was late morning, and people were out strolling or walking their dogs in the sunshine. The squeeze of his hand around hers drew her attention back to him. "That's why I sought you out just now," he went on. "To commend you on winning our wager."

"Wager?"

"On our wedding night, you vowed to transform yourself into the perfect lady. We agreed that if you succeeded, then I would reward you with diamonds."

Maddy blinked. She had made that thoughtless demand in a fit of nervousness about the night ahead. But she didn't want him to continue to think her a fortune hunter.

She placed her hand on his cheek, loving the faintly raspy feel of it even though he had shaved that morning. "Nathan, that really isn't necessary. You've given me enough already with the new wardrobe and the stipend. I don't require anything else."

"Quite the contrary. There is indeed something you need." A half smile playing on his lips, he reached into an inner pocket of his coat. "It occurred to me that you were shortchanged at our nuptials. I should like to rectify the matter."

He held out his hand. Between his forefinger and thumb, he held a gold circlet with a large, square-cut diamond and two smaller diamonds on either side. The gemstones winked in the sunlight.

Her eyes widened on the ring. A rush of tender emotion filled her throat. Of all the jewels he could have given her, she had never expected something that called to her heart. Something that hinted he might have deeper feelings for her than mere lust.

She tore her gaze from the ring and looked up, trying to read his enigmatic expression. "It's . . . beautiful."

"I'm glad you approve. Shall we complete the ceremony, then?" Taking her left hand, he slid the circlet onto her finger. "With this ring I thee wed."

Her heart thudded as she gazed down at the diamonds sparkling on her hand. She blinked against a hot prickling in her eyes. It was foolish to feel a tightness in her bosom, to wonder if Nathan might be falling in love with her. It was imprudent to wish their marriage could be more than one of convenience, for she must not want something that could never be. Yet she felt more newly married in this moment than she'd felt that cold day in church.

She lifted her soft gaze to his face. "Thank you, Nathan."

Standing on tiptoes, she brushed her lips across his. He pulled her close and deepened the kiss, his mouth playing with hers for one heartfelt moment of tenderness. Then he drew away all too soon.

He took a step back and regarded her with a look of aloof satisfaction. "Last night, you were wearing gloves, so no one noticed your lack of a ring. But that won't always be the case. It would raise eyebrows in society if you're seen without my wedding band."

So that was his true purpose. To brand her as his. The gift had no romantic significance to it whatsoever.

The bubble of wistful yearning burst, leaving her deflated. She thought back to their waltz at the party, when she had teased him about taking a lover once he left England. He had appeared displeased by the notion, and the heady thought that he might be jealous had prompted her to needle him all the more. Now, it struck her that he intended for the ring to be a constant reminder that she belonged only to him.

Not out of love, but because he'd bought and paid for her.

Little did Nathan realize, though, she desired no man but him. The prospect of an affair repulsed her. She didn't know if the muddle of emotions he stirred inside her ought to be labeled love or fondness or friendship. All she knew for certain was that she craved to be with him, to talk to him, to probe behind the cool façade he showed to the world.

"I must be going now," he said briskly, taking out a gold watch and consulting it before replacing it in his pocket. "I've some pressing business at my warehouse. I shall be back in time for tea."

He turned to leave the drawing room, but on impulse Maddy caught hold of his sleeve. "May I go, too?"

Nathan frowned. "There will likely be callers this afternoon, wanting to have a closer look at you after last night's party. Grandmamma will require you to be here."

"So that I might be examined like an exotic creature in a zoo? All the more reason for me to escape this house for a while."

"I have paperwork and you'll be bored silly."

"Not nearly as bored as I'd be listening to the gossip of catty aristocrats." Smiling, she stroked his cheek, conscious of the ring weighing on her finger. "Please, Nathan, I haven't been out in the daylight for over two weeks. Won't you take me with you?"

He stared at her a moment before nodding. "As you wish, then."

The London docks were no place for a lady. Nate was sorry he hadn't considered that before letting himself be wheedled by his wife. But he didn't seem to have the fortitude to deny Madelyn anything. Especially when she aimed that dazzling smile at him.

She was smiling now as she alighted from the carriage with the assistance of his hand. The elegance of her bronze-hued gown looked incongruous against the filthy cobblestones. Her ocean-blue eyes glowed inside the brim of a chocolate-brown bonnet tied beneath her chin with an amber ribbon. She lifted her face to the midday sun and breathed deeply as if savoring the rotten stench off the Thames.

He found it impossible to believe she could enjoy these rough surroundings. But she was glancing around with interest at the many ships and the activities of the dockworkers.

He himself liked the hustle and bustle of the docks. He liked hearing the shouts of the sailors, seeing the forest of masts, smelling the tang of salt in the damp, fishy air. He especially liked the sense of being a useful part of this well-oiled machine that brought in goods to fill the demands of a great city.

A male whistle of appreciation came from somewhere behind them. Nate turned around with a scowl, but couldn't tell if it was one of the stevedores unloading a nearby ship or a dockworker rolling a barrel along the busy waterfront.

Leaving the carriage in the care of a coachman and footman, he guided Madelyn around a series of dirty puddles and toward a warehouse, the bricks blackened from soot. "I oughtn't have brought you here," he muttered. "The men who frequent the docks are coarse fellows, and I don't like the way they're looking at you."

"Oh, la," she said. "It's not so very different from the way the nobility was staring at me last night. Just pretend they're not there."

As Madelyn made a small, dismissing gesture, the sun

winked off the diamond on her hand. His mind flashed back to the pleasure on her face as he'd slid the ring onto her finger. She'd been delighted by the gift, so delighted that the dreamy warmth in her eyes had alarmed him.

God help him if she were to believe the ring had any profound meaning. Of course it didn't. Rather, he intended for it to act as a warning to any lecherous gentleman with seduction on his mind.

Madelyn belonged to him and to him alone.

At least until he left England. He refused to consider what might happen after that—because thinking about it made him grit his teeth and feel the urge to punch something.

He rapped hard on a door with peeling green paint. An eye peered through a peephole, and a moment later the door swung open.

A hugely muscled giant stepped back to allow them entry into the dimness of the warehouse. He had a patch over one eye, a torn ear that had healed jaggedly, and a mug that looked as if it had been rearranged by a potato masher. " 'Ello, guvnor," he said in a deeply gravelly voice. " 'Oo's the pretty bird?"

"The *bird* is my wife, Lady Rowley. Madelyn, this is Yancy, my watchman."

"It's a pleasure to make your acquaintance, Yancy."

She extended her hand and the man gingerly shook it, her dainty fingers like a tiny wren caught in his meaty fist. No other lady of Nate's acquaintance would have been so gracious to such a fearsome lout. In fact, they'd have run screaming at the sight of his battered face.

But Madelyn seemed to view Yancy in a more favorable light than some of the finest gentlemen in society. She looked interested and friendly, as she did with everyone she met.

Except Dunham. What had happened between her and that reprobate? Nate pushed away the nagging question for another time.

As they walked through the warehouse, she asked in a hushed tone, "What happened to cause his terrible injuries?"

"Yancy used to be a prizefighter until he lost the eye."

"Where did you find him?"

"He was a sailor aboard my ship, earning his passage back here to England. I came to trust him when . . . I saw what a hard worker he was." Nate felt loath to share the real story. Yancy had risked his own life during a terrible storm at sea to save several seamen from being washed overboard, including Nate himself.

Madelyn glanced around the small warehouse with its high, grimy windows. Dust motes danced in the meager sunshine, the rays of light illuminating the crates and barrels stacked against the brick walls. "Do you really need a guard on duty even during the day?" she asked.

"Thievery is a way of life in this part of London. It pays to be careful." Nate took her over to a large cask and pried open the lid with his pocket knife. "There's a small fortune in these containers. Dip your hand inside and you'll see."

She gazed askance at him, as if expecting some trick. Then she reached into the cask and brought forth a palm full of dark, loose leaves. With a smile, she lifted the substance to her nose and breathed deeply. "Tea!"

"The variety is called *keemun,* from the Anhui region of China. All the crates over there contain silk." Stacked up three high, the oblong containers ran the entire length of the back wall.

Her face alight, she asked, "That's quite a lot of cloth! May I look?"

"I'm afraid it would take far too long to pry off the lids. I warned you, I have papers that require my attention in the office."

"Then perhaps Yancy wouldn't mind helping me."

Nate shouldn't be surprised at her willingness to tolerate the company of the hulking man. But at least it would keep her busy while he worked. "If it pleases you."

Summoning the watchman, Nate instructed him to assist Madelyn.

Then he went into the small office in the corner of the warehouse and pulled a sheaf of papers from a drawer in the old oak desk. Picking up a quill, he set to work reading the clauses of the topmost contract. The murmur of voices drifted to him, one deep and rumbly, the other lively and feminine.

He had left the door open and he could see Yancy's colossal figure popping open a lid with a crowbar, while Madelyn chatted with him. What the devil did she find to talk about with such a man? Despite her common blood, she had lived in the insulated realm of the theater, not the rough-and-tumble world of ex-pugilists.

Nate focused again on the paper in front of him. It was a contract for the sale of tea to a merchant who wished to blend it with Indian varieties. Dipping the quill into the ink pot, he made some notations to the payment schedule. A short while later, a tinkle of laughter disturbed his concentration.

Disgruntled, he peered through the doorway at Madelyn as she continued to chatter with Yancy while fingering one length of silk after another. Did she intend to coax more cloth from Nate? Hadn't he given her enough already?

Or was she assessing his fortune? Trying to calculate the net worth of her rich husband?

Nate didn't want to think badly of her. He had a habit

of doing so. Every time he tried to fit her into a category, she proved him wrong. He had believed her to be a strumpet until their wedding night. He'd thought her a social climber, yet she deigned to befriend a man who hailed from the foulest part of London. He'd thought her self-absorbed, yet she'd used her skill with cosmetics on his sister and read sermons to his half-blind grandmother.

She was as keen for illicit affairs as Mama had been . . .

Nate shut down that thought at once. It was wrong to draw a parallel to his mother. Madelyn was incomparable. She was like no other woman he'd ever met. Perhaps that was why she fascinated him. He never quite knew what she would say or do next.

But he never should have allowed her to come to this warehouse. Better he should enjoy his wife in bed and keep her separated from every other aspect of his life. She was too much of a distraction.

He forced his mind back to the papers and managed to work his way through them by sheer determination. He was signing the last one, his pen scratching across the document, when the light tap of footsteps penetrated his awareness.

"You're left-handed," Madelyn observed.

He tensed to see her standing in the doorway. All during his youth, he'd heard criticism from instructors who'd forced him to learn penmanship with his right hand. "Actually, I can use either hand, although I prefer the left. Will you denounce me as the devil's spawn?"

She raised an eyebrow. "Of course not. Who called you that? Was it your father?"

"Actually, a governess. Gilmore took little interest in the schoolroom. Other than to thrash me if I failed to complete my work in a timely manner." Nate could still remember his dread as a boy at being sent down to the library to face the earl, who had kept a willow switch in his desk for the purpose of whippings.

Madelyn tilted her head to the side, looking curious as if she wanted to probe further into his past. Nate quickly changed the subject. "You and Yancy seemed to rub along quite well. What have you two been talking about all this time?"

"For one thing, he told me that he saved your life during a storm at sea. An enormous wave crashed over the ship, and you were about to slide over the rail when he grabbed you by the seat of your trousers—"

"That's quite enough." He could see by the twinkle in her eyes that she knew the part about how Yancy's quick action had stripped the breeches right off Nate. "You needn't go on about it."

She ventured a step closer. "Why? Am I disturbing you?"

At the half smile on her face, all the blood in his brain rushed to his groin. "Indeed you are. But if you close the door, I can take care of that quickly enough." He moved aside the papers and patted the scarred surface of the desk. "Right here."

Her eyes widened as she caught his meaning. The desire he saw there fed his own lust. "Hush," she whispered, with a glance over her shoulder. "Yancy is just outside. He'll hear you."

Nate enjoyed her scandalized reaction. For all her unfettered behavior in the bedchamber, Madelyn could be charmingly prudish. "I shall send him out on an errand."

"No! This warehouse is filthy."

"So are my thoughts right now."

"Do stop teasing, Nathan. This is a place of business." She sat down in the chair opposite him. Inside the frame of her bonnet, her blue eyes sparkled with a warmth that touched a place deep inside of him. Then the curve of her mouth turned pensive as she glanced at his papers. "Speaking of business, I wonder if your father has any idea how hard you've worked here, how much effort you've put into this enterprise. If he were to visit this warehouse and see how industrious you've become, perhaps he would learn to respect you."

Her words struck him cold. Every vestige of humor died away. "Gilmore would despise this place. He would use it as ammunition against me. Gentlemen do not engage in commerce."

"But he has to be made to realize that you're not a wild youth anymore. So that the rift between you two can be mended."

"Enough." Nate stood up, gathering the papers into a stack. "I will not speak of him with you. Not now or ever. Shall we go?"

Her lips firmed, Madelyn rose from the chair. She radiated curiosity, but he didn't give a damn. She had no idea what had happened in the past, nor did he intend to enlighten her.

The rift was an abyss that could never be bridged. It had little to do with his misspent youth. That was precisely why he didn't want to foster closeness with Madelyn outside of carnal lust. He didn't want her poking and prying.

Because then she might uncover the secret that stained his soul.

Chapter 17

Maddy stared down at the invitation in her hands. It had been addressed to all in the household: Lord Gilmore, Lady Gilmore, Lady Sophia, Lady Emily, Lord and Lady Rowley. Sitting at the dainty desk in the morning room, she read the inscription on the heavy cream card several times to savor its brief message.

The pleasure of your company is requested by the Duke of Houghton at a ball to be given on . . .

Her heart thumped against her breastbone. In a little more than three weeks' time, she would be entering her grandfather's house. At last she would come face-to-face with the Duke of Houghton. She finally would have the chance to confront the haughty nobleman who had disowned her mother for marrying a lowborn actor.

She vividly remembered the day when she had come upon her father weeping at the gravesite of her mother. Maddy had been thirteen years old and her beloved mama had just been laid to rest after a terrible accident in which the axle of their wagon had broken, throwing her beneath the wheels. They had been traveling with a troupe of actors at the time, touring the north of England, and Maddy had gone looking for her father because the other players wished to start on the road to their next performance in a distant village.

Catching sight of Papa kneeling over the fresh grave, Maddy hurried through the tiny cemetery. Her shoes crunched on the autumn leaves that carpeted the quiet graveyard beside the old stone church. The sound of his sobbing wrenched Maddy's chest. Struggling to contain her own grief, she crouched down and put her arms around his broad back.

"Oh, Papa, I miss her, too. So very much."

"I don't know how I can leave her here. She was my life."

"I know, Papa. But we have to go. The others are waiting for us."

He turned to her, his ruggedly handsome face damp with tears in the light of the overcast day. Despair shone in his blue eyes. "I should never have taken your mother from her home. She deserved better than to live as a nomad all these years. So do you. You should be living as a lady with your grandfather, the Duke of Houghton."

Maddy had grown up hearing tales of the fearsome aristocrat who had rejected his daughter upon her elopement with an actor. "No, I won't leave you! The troupe needs me now. I can play Mama's parts. I've memorized all of them."

Smoothing back her hair, he kissed her brow. "You are a blessing, Maddy. You look like Sarah and you have her gift for the stage, as well." Then his expression hardened, a muscle working in his strong jaw. "And you needn't fret, I would never take you to Houghton. He'd spit in my face. Then he'd toss you into the gutter as he did to your mother . . ."

"What is the matter with you?" a crotchety voice demanded. "Why have you not written the acceptance note?"

Jolted back to the present, Maddy glanced over from her

chair at the desk to see the dowager glaring through her quizzing glass from the chaise. "Oh. I'm sorry. I was contemplating the wording of the reply, that's all."

Lady Sophia looked up from her embroidery tambour frame. Arrayed in dove gray, she embodied the stylish widow in half-mourning. "There is nothing to contemplate. The example I wrote out is right in front of you." To Lady Gilmore, she added, "Perhaps she isn't proficient enough, Grandmamma. I should be happy to complete the task myself."

"Nonsense, Madelyn has demonstrated her penmanship and it is perfectly adequate. She must learn the responsibilities of a countess so that she will not disgrace the venerable title of Gilmore someday."

Two small stacks of invitations sat before Maddy on the desk. One pile required acceptances and the other, rejections. She had been assigned the tedious job of writing out replies to all of them.

For the past few days, after having been scolded for accompanying Nathan to the docks the previous week, she had been required to resume her lady lessons. According to the dowager, a titled lady had to approve the daily menus, settle disputes with the servants, supervise the tallying of the linen closets, and perform a host of other activities like responding to the invitations that arrived daily.

Maddy deemed it wise not to mention that her training was an exercise in futility. She wouldn't be staying at Gilmore House once Nathan left England at the end of the season. She would take his stipend, lease her own home, and fulfill her dream of opening a shop.

She doubted the Earl of Gilmore would want her here, anyway, once she caused a scandal by berating the Duke of Houghton in full view of the ton.

She picked up her quill and dipped the tip into the silver inkwell. While writing out the acceptance note, she said over her shoulder, "This invitation is to the Duke of Houghton's ball. I met both of his grandsons at Lady Milford's party. Lord Theodore mentioned that His Grace isn't feeling well."

"He's hale enough to host his annual ball," Lady Gilmore said. "And if you are contemplating what to say to His Grace in the receiving line, there is no need. You will not speak to the duke at all. You are to smile and curtsy and move on."

That was *not* Maddy's plan. She had every intention of addressing the man in no uncertain terms. Her primary purpose in marrying Nathan was to enter society and confront her grandfather.

Or at least it *had* been the reason. With each passing day, she found herself becoming more and more absorbed by her husband's life. She yearned to know everything about him, to learn his thoughts and emotions, to understand what had made him the exciting, exasperating man that he was. The visit to his warehouse had opened her eyes to the fact that Nathan wasn't just another indolent, privileged nobleman. He worked diligently at his business, and it irked her that his father didn't appreciate his son's accomplishments. It also frustrated her that Nathan was so closemouthed about his past.

I will not speak of him with you. Not now or ever.

She wouldn't find out anything from Nathan. He simply wouldn't talk about his father. If ever she was to fathom the family undercurrents, she needed a different source— like the two ladies here in this morning room.

Maddy finished the acceptance, sanded it, and then started on the next one. Glancing over her shoulder, she said in a conversational tone, "I imagine that as countess, Nathan's mother had to answer invitations, too, perhaps at this very desk. He's never said much about her. What was she like, Grandmamma?"

"She was the daughter of a marquess," the dowager said with a sniff, "though one would never have known it by her actions."

"What do you mean?" Maddy asked in surprise.

"Camellia was far too lively and giddy to be a proper lady. And she was quite the accomplished flirt, as well. That frivolous woman did not give my son the fidelity he deserved. Not, of course, that I am wont to speak ill of the dead."

Maddy turned in the chair to stare at her. "Are you saying that she engaged in indiscretions during her marriage?"

"Do not flap your tongue like a gossip," the dowager snapped. "Let this teach you only that a lady must behave in a sober and moral manner at all times. There is no other point in resurrecting the past. It is best forgotten."

Maddy glanced down at the diamond ring on her left hand. Nathan had given it to her to brand her as his. She'd assumed he'd been jealous because of her teasing about taking a lover. But had his disapproval been rooted in the memory of his own mother's affairs?

She tried another avenue of questioning. "How old was Nathan when she died?"

"It was shortly after Emily's birth." Lady Gilmore blinked at Sophia, who sat beside her on the chaise, intent on her embroidery. "What age would that have been, my dear?"

"David was fourteen at the time," Sophia said. "That means Nathan would have been twelve."

Twelve. Almost the age Maddy had been when her own mother had died. At least she'd had a loving father. Her heart ached to imagine his grief as a boy growing up in this cold household. "Was that when . . . the strife between him and his father began?"

Lady Gilmore raised an eyebrow, causing a movement

of the multiple wrinkles on her brow. "Certainly not. Nathan took after his mother. He was a difficult child from the very beginning, always disobeying the rules, playing pranks, speaking out of turn. More than once he tried to drag David into trouble, too, although the earl and I saw through those schemes."

As Maddy finished writing out another reply, she felt compelled to defend her husband. "I was under the impression that Nathan and David were friends as well as brothers. What do *you* know of the matter, Sophia? Did David ever speak favorably of Nathan?"

Sophia jabbed her needle into the stretched cloth. "My husband had more pressing things on his mind than a brother who had forsaken his duties to the family. Had David not fallen so wretchedly ill, he would have become a great earl someday."

Her lips compressed, Maddy dipped the tip of the quill into the inkwell. The woman seemed determined to say nothing complimentary about Nathan. Yet Maddy hesitated to criticize Sophia, for the lady had suffered greatly in losing her beloved husband, the father of her two young daughters. Conscious of the woman's disdain, Maddy had stayed away from the nursery, though she knew Nathan went up there sometimes to visit his nieces.

Indeed, it must be very difficult for Sophia to watch another woman usurp her coveted role as the wife of the heir. All because David had died so young from a tragic illness. That made Maddy wonder about something that had been nagging at the edge of her mind.

She set down her quill and turned to face the other two women. "It must have been a terrible time for you, Sophia. But I have to ask, why wasn't this family inoculated against the smallpox? After all, the procedure is hardly experimental anymore. These days, many people are inoculated—and especially the nobility, I should think."

Sophia stared wide-eyed at her, then glanced over at the dowager.

Lady Gilmore uttered a small sound of distress as she glared at Maddy. "*Must* you ask so many intrusive questions? *Must* you plague me so! I cannot bear your company another moment!"

The dowager levered herself to her feet with the aid of the cane. Her back hunched, she hobbled out of the morning room.

Maddy sat in stunned confusion. She turned her gaze to Sophia who remained rigidly on the chaise. "What did I say? I—I didn't mean to upset her. I'm so sorry."

"Don't apologize to me, but to her ladyship," Sophia said coldly. "Shortly after they were married, her husband died of the smallpox from receiving a faulty inoculation. So Grandmamma never allowed them to be administered to her son or her grandchildren. And now, she blames herself for David's death."

The revelation troubled Maddy for the remainder of the day. She was still thinking about it as she readied herself for bed with the assistance of her maid. While Gertie put away clothing, Maddy sat at the dressing table, braiding her long blond hair.

She had regarded the dowager as a haughty, snappish old lady who embodied the snootiness of the upper class. But with this new disclosure, Maddy could see a chink in Lady Gilmore's armor. The woman was not entirely hard-hearted, after all. How dreadful it must be to suffer the guilt of knowing one had been instrumental in the loss of a beloved grandson.

"I heard a scrap o' news in the servants' hall tonight," Gertie said.

Jolted from her musings, Maddy glanced over at the maidservant, who was folding a petticoat. "News?"

"Ye're t' attend the Duke of Houghton's ball next month."

"Oh . . . yes. I had to write out the acceptance note today."

"What will ye say t' His Grace? Have ye decided yet?"

Maddy hesitated, then shook her head. "Not precisely. But I've ample time to consider it."

For a moment, the only sound was the closing of a drawer. Then Gertie said in a motherly tone, "Perhaps ye should tell Lord Rowley about this. He's yer husband and he deserves t' know."

Maddy firmed her lips. Increasingly, she didn't like keeping the secret from Nathan. Yet what could she say to him on this matter? He believed her to be a commoner. That was why he had married her. He would be shocked and likely even angry to learn that she had blue blood, that her mother had been born a lady. Worse, he might even try to stop her from confronting the duke . . .

"I deserve to know what?" Nathan asked.

Her heart jumped. She looked over, startled to see her husband standing in the doorway of the dressing room. His hands on his lean hips, he wore the jade-green silk robe with its subtle pattern of dragons. The deep V of the collar revealed a swath of broad, bare chest.

How much had he overheard?

Gertie bobbed a curtsy and smiled at him. "Evenin', milord. I'll be out o' yer way right quick." Grabbing a pile of laundry, she slipped past him and went out into the bed-chamber. A moment later, the outer door clicked shut as the maid departed.

Nathan was still regarding Maddy with a questioning look. Heaven help her. She would have to brazen it out and pray he hadn't heard the duke's name mentioned.

She arose from the stool, the braid draped over the shoulder of her nightdress. His gaze flicked to her bosom, where the thin lawn of her gown clung to her breasts. Hoping to distract him, Maddy gave him a mollifying smile. "Gertie's right, there *is* something you deserve to know. It concerns a blunder I made today with your grandmother."

"Blunder?"

"Come, and I'll tell you."

Her hips swaying, she sauntered forward and laced her fingers with his, drawing him into the bedchamber. On the canopied bed, the covers had been turned down, the pillows plumped. A branch of candles on a nearby table cast a soft, golden light over the intimate setting. How she longed to be lying there with Nathan, to lose herself in passion.

But if they went to bed, they'd never talk. And she *did* have something to broach to him. He always departed after they'd made love, so this might be her only opportunity.

Leading him to the fireplace, Maddy bade him sit in a chair. Then she drew a footstool close and sat down, their knees almost touching. "This morning, I asked her ladyship why no one in the family had been protected from the smallpox. That's when I found out it was *her* doing."

A shadow crossed Nathan's face. He looked away a moment into the gloom beyond the firelight, as if he were thinking of his brother's needless death. "Ah. Well, you couldn't have known."

She breathed a sigh of relief that he hadn't mentioned the duke. He must not have heard the entirety of her conversation with Gertie. "I never meant to cause your grandmother pain. I merely thought the nobility would have been inoculated. After all, even *I* was, as the child of traveling actors."

Leaning forward, he slipped his fingers inside the loose neckline of her nightgown, stroking lightly over a small, smooth scar on her upper arm. "So that's what this is. I'd wondered."

Her skin tingled and her body softened, but Maddy would not allow him to divert her. She caught hold of his wrist to stay the tempting caress of his hand on her bare shoulder. "Nathan, it made me realize *you* were never inoculated, either. I do hope you'll rectify that soon."

"You needn't fret, darling. If I were to die, you'd be a rich widow."

His cavalier comment exasperated her. "Don't be stupid. I would never wish for you to suffer the same fate as your brother."

"My family would say that fate erred when the good brother died, leaving the bad one to inherit."

Maddy shook her head at his cynicism. "David may have been a good man, but so are you, Nathan. I suspect David knew that, too. You were friends as well as brothers, were you not? I've seen it in your eyes when you've spoken of him."

Nathan sat back in the chair, his expression stony. "I was grateful to him. He covered for me when I hadn't finished school assignments. He smuggled food to me when I'd been put to bed without supper. But I never did a blasted thing for him in return. So how could it be called friendship?"

That was more than he'd ever admitted to her before. Encouraged, she asked, "Was he ever caught helping you?"

"Sometimes. To his credit, he always accepted the blame, though the earl punished me instead."

"Then you took David's thrashings for him. That's something."

"It's nothing. And my brother was never one to quarrel with Gilmore's edicts. Unlike me." Nathan reached out and caressed her cheek. "But I have had my revenge. I have foisted *you* upon my family."

His cold smile troubled her, for it was part of the hard shell that hid his inner torment. He had never overcome his past. Returning to England had brought out the wounded little boy in him. "You're still hurt by your father's favoritism toward your elder brother, aren't you?"

A dark frown flitted over his face. Then he moved his hand to the nape of her neck, his fingers stroking, sending pleasurable chills over her skin. "Enough of your foolish talk. That isn't why I came here."

Maddy resisted the seductive sensations. He always did this; he shut down the discussion every time she probed his thoughts and feelings. Somehow, she had to break through the wall of his distrust. To encourage him to open his mind and heart to her.

Perhaps she could foster closeness between them by making a confession of her own. She could reveal her own hopes and dreams. She could tell him about her plan to open a shop.

Sitting on the stool, Maddy caught hold of his hand and brought it to rest on his knee, entwining their fingers. "If you won't speak of yourself, then there's something else I wanted to tell you. I've thought long and hard about this ever since we visited your warehouse. And . . ."

"And?"

He looked at her inquiringly, his expression guarded. What if he scoffed at her? Or forbade her from proceeding with her plan? Yet if ever she hoped to win his trust, she had to take that risk.

"I want you to know the real reason why I sold myself at auction," she said, "and why I needed the funds. I've allowed you to believe my purpose to be merely greed. But the truth is . . . I've long wanted to go into trade. You see, even while I was on stage, it was always my dream to open a shop that caters to women."

As she spoke, his cool smile faded away and he regarded her with an enigmatic stare. "That's quite a lot of money for a little dress shop."

"I intend to sell more than just gowns." Maddy plunged on, determined to reveal the whole of her vision, even if he believed her mad. "I'll rent a large space, perhaps on Bond Street, and stock all the things that women purchase, gloves and hats and gowns and shoes and perfumes, even cosmetics. That way, instead of having to visit a dozen different shops, a lady will find everything she needs under one roof."

Nathan raised a dark eyebrow. For a moment he didn't say anything and she sat on pins and needles, wondering what he was thinking. He was looking at her as if seeing her in a new light.

"That's quite the novel concept," he said. "However, I must point out that rich Londoners are accustomed to specialty shops. They may very well believe the quality of the products will suffer by having the whole lot in one place. A Chinese philosopher named Confucius once said 'to know everything is to know nothing.' In your case, to *have* everything is to be good at nothing."

"That is why I intend to stock only the finest items," she asserted. "The shop will be divided into sections, each area devoted to a different specialty. So you see, your concern shouldn't be a problem."

"You'll still have to overcome preconceptions. People don't like change. They prefer to go along as they've always done."

Just as he and his father were locked in a quarrel that dated back to his childhood. But now was not the time to bring that up. "You're a businessman. How would *you* suggest I proceed?"

Nathan steepled his hands beneath his chin. "First and foremost, I'd hire an experienced staff. To accomplish that, I'd offer a higher salary than other shops. It's the best way to attract skilled employees."

"Of course! I hadn't considered that."

"Then you'll need advertisements, handbills perhaps. To let the public know what's unique about your place."

Excited, Maddy leaned forward on the stool and hugged her knees. "What do you think of offering women a complete transformation? You know, put yourself in the hands of my experts and we'll change an ugly duckling into a swan."

"As you did for my sister?"

She blinked in surprise. "You know about that?"

"I know your talents. If a beautiful woman can turn herself into a wrinkled old woman with the use of cosmetics, then concealing a few pit marks ought to be simple."

The Earl of Gilmore had guessed, too, but before Maddy could mention it, Nathan added in a musing tone, "Swann's. There's the perfect name for your shop, Madelyn Swann."

She smiled back at him. "Yes! I thought so, too. Though perhaps your father won't be pleased for me to use my maiden name."

Nathan's face hardened. "The earl will loathe having his daughter-in-law in trade. He will forbid you to open the establishment. For that reason alone, you must do it. And don't be surprised if he discourages the ton from patronizing your shop."

Maddy had never meant to stir up more conflict in the family. But she was glad for Nathan's support—even if it arose from his animosity toward his father. She simply could not abide the notion of playing the refined lady for the rest of her life. "Actually, I'm hoping to appeal to the wives of wealthy merchants," she said. "Since they're not members of the ton, they'll be eager to rub elbows with a future countess, no matter how scandalous she might be."

"An excellent strategy." A smirk deepening his dimples, he began to undo her long braid. "And I suppose you will be wanting me to supply you with the finest Chinese silks, hmm? No wonder you were so eager to poke through the crates in my warehouse."

Maddy gave him a sultry look from beneath her eyelashes. "Will you? I'll pay, of course. I don't expect anything for free."

"We can work out a fair bargain, I'm sure. I'll be happy to be a provider, though I'll leave the actual dressing of women to you. *I* much prefer *un*dressing them."

Reaching around, Nathan began to unfasten the tiny buttons down the back of her nightgown. He was smiling slightly, his green eyes gleaming with wickedness. Her breath caught. She, too, had had enough of talking for one night. As he drew the wispy fabric down her shoulders, she eagerly slid her arms out of the sleeves.

She arose from the stool and the gown slithered to the fine rug. His expression darkened as he gazed up at her nakedness, his hands caressing the curve of her hips. How she loved seeing that passionate admiration on his face as if he were viewing her for the first time.

Maddy held out her hand. "Shall we seal our bargain in bed?"

He stood up at once and subjected her to a deep, drowning kiss that left them both gasping. She could feel the heavy pounding of his heart against her bare bosom. Especially when she untied his robe and rendered him naked, as well. He was all hard muscles and hot skin, the spear of his manhood arousing a keen anticipation in her. They kissed their way across the bedchamber, then he laid her down on the sheets and began to caress her in all the ways that she adored.

Their lovemaking held an enhanced richness for her tonight. Perhaps because she basked in the glow of his approval of her dream. He'd even offered to help her, too. Though he might only be wanting to get back at his father, she fancied it to be more than that. Like her,

Nathan was an entrepreneur, and she felt now that they were on equal footing, true partners in this marriage.

A warm ache resided in her heart. Parting her legs to receive him, she reminded herself that this was all he desired from her, this lovely, perfect passion. He would be leaving her forever at the end of the season.

And until then, she must be very careful not to fall in love with her husband.

Chapter 18

Maddy added the final touches to Lady Emily's face. Then she stepped back to view her handiwork while Nathan's sister turned her head to and fro, admiring herself in the dressing table mirror. Each unsightly pit had been filled with a tiny dab of putty, her face dusted with powder. A hint of rouge enhanced the girl's high cheekbones.

Emily was in Maddy's dressing room because the dowager seldom ventured here. Due to her poor eyesight, Lady Gilmore still hadn't noticed the subtle transformation, and Maddy intended to keep it that way.

"It's even better than what you did for the other parties," Emily said, beaming. "Thank you so much!"

The girl's russet-brown hair had been pinned up with a cluster of blush-pink rosebuds tucked into the curls. Her white silk gown had an off-the-shoulder neckline with demisleeves trimmed in lace. Pale pink ribbons decorated the bodice and the flounces in the skirt.

Pleased, Maddy went to the washstand to rinse her hands. "Every girl should be beautiful at her debut ball. And tonight, you look perfect."

Gertie removed the protective linen cloth that had been draped across the girl's shoulders. "Nobody else has milady's magic touch. I was always ham-fisted with the greasepaint."

"I had many years of practice in preparing for performances," Maddy said as she dried her hands, careful not to drip on her own gown of wisteria-blue silk.

Emily fingered the strand of pearls at her throat. "It's only a shame that the necklace Nathan gave me doesn't match my gown. Though I suppose Grandmamma would condemn it anyway for being made by heathens."

Maddy handed the damp towel to the maid. "Heathens?"

"Let me show you. I carry it everywhere for luck, so it's right here in my reticule." Seated on the stool, the girl picked up the tiny beaded bag and drew out a dainty necklace, letting it rest in her palm. "My brother brought this for me all the way from China."

Maddy bent down to examine the tiny jade figurine on a simple gold chain. "Why, it's a little dragon! How charming!"

"Nathan swore it will bring me good fortune." The brilliance dimmed in Emily's expressive hazel eyes. "But I'm afraid it hasn't helped with Lord Theo. I truly thought he admired me when we danced at Lady Milford's. Yet he's never even come to call."

Emily didn't know that Lord Dunham had forbidden the relationship. *My brother shan't be permitted to court her. Houghton would never allow his grandson to have any connection to a family that has been tainted by common blood.*

The memory made Maddy seethe. It was yet another reason for her to despise Dunham—and her arrogant grandfather. But she didn't want Emily to be downcast on the night of her debut ball. "Lord Theo attends Oxford, does he not? If he hasn't been around, perhaps it's because his studies required him to go back and finish the term."

Emily brightened slightly as she replaced the dragon necklace in her bag. "Yes, but he should have written to me at least. And I didn't see his name or his brother's name on the list of acceptances for tonight. Do you suppose Lord Theo might show up, anyway?"

"I wouldn't count on it, darling, I'm sorry." Maddy leaned down to give her a hug. "You must dance with all the other young gentlemen instead. It'll be a wonderful evening, you'll see. Now do practice your smile. It's nearly time to go downstairs and welcome your guests."

As Maddy began to cap the many bottles and jars on the dressing table, Gertie came scurrying forward to help. At that moment, a muffled thumping approached from the bedchamber.

Startled, Maddy whirled around to see the dowager hobble into the doorway. Emily sat at the dressing table, fussing with her curls while trying out silly smiles in the mirror.

Lady Gilmore's gnarled fingers thrust a small crimson bag at Maddy. "I will lend you this, Madelyn, so that you do not disgrace the family. You will return it to me at the end of the evening."

Maddy opened the drawstrings and drew out a fine necklace. The classic design had many diamonds that winked in the lamplight. "Oh! It's lovely!"

Even as she lifted the necklace to fasten it at the nape of her neck, Lady Gilmore raised her quizzing glass and peered owlishly at the dressing table. Gertie was trying valiantly to stuff the many pots and containers into a bottom drawer. "What is that you're hiding, maid? What are all those jars? Stand back!"

Gertie retreated as the dowager shuffled forward and seized a small pot made of green glass, uncorking the lid. She brought it to her nose and sniffed. "Face paint!" A frown shifting her wrinkles, she aimed the quizzing glass at Emily, who still sat on the stool. In a scandalized tone, Lady Gilmore uttered, "Have *you* been using this paint?"

Emily's eyes rounded. "Ah . . ."

Maddy stepped forward to shield Emily from the woman's wrath. "It's entirely my doing, Grandmamma. For some time now, I've been applying cosmetics to conceal her scars. Have you not noticed the improvement? Ever since Lady Milford's party, everyone has been remarking on how beautiful Emily looks."

The dowager thumped her cane. "Young ladies must never wear face paint! Remove it at once."

"Perhaps that is true for most debutantes. However, in Emily's case, surely you can see that an exception must be made." Bluntly, Maddy added, "Besides, I have the earl's permission."

"My son defers to my judgment in such matters. He would never agree to this without consulting me."

"Nevertheless it's true, my lady. He told me so himself." At breakfast the morning after Lady Milford's party, he had *implied* approval, anyway, when he had thanked Maddy. "Perhaps we should go downstairs and ask him?"

Lady Gilmore pursed her lips in suspicion. The gold quizzing glass she held up to her face magnified one of her hazel eyes.

Emily jumped up from the stool. "Please, Grandmamma. None of the other girls had the smallpox. None of them have any scars. My skin looks so much prettier this way."

The dowager's harsh expression softened. For a moment, her eyes actually grew teary and Maddy knew the woman must be blaming herself for failing to protect Emily from the disease.

"Well! Girls never behaved so fast in *my* day. But I suppose it is too late to make changes. Come along, then."

Letting the quizzing glass drop, Lady Gilmore turned around and tottered out of the dressing room with the aid of her cane. Maddy grabbed her kidskin gloves and drew them on. As she and Emily followed the dowager out the door, they shared a sweet smile of victory.

The receiving line seemed endless. The Earl of Gilmore stood with his mother and Emily at the base of the grand staircase. Beside them were Nathan and Maddy, then Lady Sophia at the end. For once, Maddy was grateful to Sophia, who greeted each guest by name and spared Maddy the embarrassment of failing to recognize an important personage.

Her head spun from all the titles and names and faces. She shook countless hands and uttered various polite greetings the dowager had instructed her to memorize, though from time to time Maddy couldn't resist embellishing the stock phrases. Especially when someone came along who clearly resented the lowborn actress who had ensnared the Earl of Gilmore's heir.

One such guest had been a participant in the auction. He was the loudmouthed gentleman who'd poked fun at Maddy in her guise of the wrinkled old maidservant. He had a receding hairline and a stout chest that strained at the waistcoat beneath his formal dark coat. His companion was his mother, an even stouter gray-haired woman in an orangey-brown dress with a patronizing tilt to her double chin.

Maddy graciously offered him her gloved hand. "Mr. Gerald Jenkins, what a pleasure it is to see you again."

The woman cast a sidelong glare at him. "Again? We have been in the country this past fortnight. This is our first ball. I cannot imagine where my son would have met you, Lady Rowley."

Mr. Jenkins turned crimson. "Nor can I," he blustered.

"Oh, la!" Maddy said. "You are a sly one, Mr. Jenkins, pretending not to remember. I do hope you enjoy the ball."

As the pair moved on, and there was a lull while Maddy awaited the next arrival, Nathan bent down to whisper in her ear, "Stop it at once or you'll make me laugh out loud."

She smiled artfully up at him. "Oh la, sir, do I know you? I'm sure we must have met somewhere."

"I'll be pleased to remind you later tonight."

His wicked promise triggered a warm pulse deep within her womb. His eyes gleamed at her, his dimples adding a breathtaking charm to his starkly masculine features. With his coal-black hair tied at the nape of his neck, he looked like a brigand masquerading as a gentleman in formal at-tire. How she yearned to abandon the party and escape up-stairs with him.

Not later. Right this very moment.

She saw that same desire reflected in his gaze, too. He wanted to be alone with her, to strip off their fancy garb and join their heated flesh. Then another group of guests entered the foyer, and she was forced to return her atten-tion to duty.

Summoning a courteous smile, Maddy suppressed the allure of passion. It was amazing how her husband could arouse her even in a crowd of people. And even when they both had obligations here.

Despite the revenge that ruled his life, Nathan needed to be on his best behavior for this ball. So did she. Noth-ing scandalous must mar this special night for Emily.

Near midnight, Maddy almost created a scandal after all.

The evening had been a smash success for Emily. The chandeliers in the ballroom cast a golden light over her reddish-brown hair and lovely features as she danced every set with a different gentleman. Maddy checked on her from time to time, prepared to do a quick repair of makeup if necessary, though the girl's face still looked fresh and natural.

Too often, though, Maddy noticed Emily glancing hopefully toward the doorway. As if she expected someone to walk in at any moment. *Do you suppose Lord Theo might show up?*

The girl's naïveté made Maddy's heart squeeze. She hesitated to tell Emily the truth, that Lord Dunham had forbidden the connection. She could only pray that Emily would find a special admirer among all the gentlemen squiring her on the dance floor.

Maddy herself had joined the dancers only once, when Nathan had escorted her for the first set while Lord Gilmore had partnered Emily. Afterward, Nathan had disappeared into the card room, leaving Maddy to her own devices. She tried not to let his neglect irk her. She was determined to enjoy the splendor of this ball.

After all, how many women of her common background ever had such a stellar opportunity? She might be the only one.

As Maddy glided through the masses with a champagne glass in hand, it pleased her to imagine she was the queen, and they her subjects. She greeted people with a nod and a smile, sometimes exchanging a few words about the crush of guests or the beauty of the ballroom, which had been decorated with Grecian columns and large vases of white roses. Beyond that, though, no one seemed willing to associate with her. It was clear that although the ton would allow her into their midst as a courtesy to the Earl of Gilmore, they had no interest in forging friendships.

That was fine with Maddy. She had not married Nathan to find companionship among the aristocracy. Still, it would have been nice to share her thoughts with someone, or to dance with one of the many gentlemen. But other than a few brief conversations with family members, and one with Lady Milford, Maddy had been alone.

She amused herself by assessing all the ladies' gowns and deciding which ones she liked and which needed alteration. Their accessories and hairstyles interested her as well, for she would need to know the latest fashions when she opened her shop. Lady Gilmore beckoned to her once from across the room, but Maddy pretended not to notice. She refused to sit with the matrons in the corner. They were a gaggle of hens, squawking gossip about people who didn't interest her.

They would be screeching to the high heavens in a few weeks when she confronted the Duke of Houghton at his ball. But she mustn't think about that now.

Then, as she turned to make another circuit of the ballroom, Maddy spied a familiar face in the arched doorway. The stark black of his coat made his flaxen hair shine almost white above his sharp, narrow features.

Houghton's heir. Her cousin, Alfred, Lord Dunham.

Her fingers tightened around her glass. Dunham had sent his regrets. He was not supposed to be in attendance tonight. And he must be a late arrival, for he had not come through the receiving line.

Now, he leaned casually against the door frame, his upper lip curled in his usual smug manner. He scanned the swarm of guests like a predator searching for prey.

She really ought to avoid him. His conceit always grated on her nerves. She didn't trust him, either, not after the time when he had cornered her at the theater and forced his kiss on her.

Yet she walked toward him anyway. He was the one responsible for Emily's unhappiness. He was the one who had cast a sour note onto her debut ball by forbidding his brother to attend.

And Maddy had something to say to him on the matter.

As she approached, his eyes narrowed on her, then flicked to her bosom in an insolent manner that made her skin crawl.

She stopped in front of him and inclined her head in a gracious nod. "Lord Dunham. I don't recall seeing you on the list of acceptances."

"I changed my mind. Will you toss me out on my ear?"

She ignored the question. No doubt he would relish seeing her do something so crass. She peered past him, hoping to spy his brother among the milling guests. "Is Lord Theo with you?"

"No." Dunham bent his head close and hissed into her ear, "As I told you before, I will not allow my brother within a mile of Lady Emily. My grandfather would frown upon him associating with a family that would allow an actress to marry into the nobility."

"Yet you yourself are associating with me right now."

"I am not a green boy like Theo. And unlike Rowley, I'd never allow myself to be trapped into marriage by a scheming female."

If only he knew, Nathan had enticed her, rather than vice versa. Aware of the many curious glances around them, Maddy smiled pleasantly while clenching her teeth. "Will you walk with me for a moment? There are too many listening ears around us."

His mouth curled in a sly smile. He caught her hand and tucked it in the crook of his arm. "Tired of Rowley already? Now that he's broken you to the saddle, I would be happy to ride you in his stead."

His disgusting comment made her fume. But she could hardly slap his face in full view of the ton. "What a vile thing to say. Nathan would call you out if he knew."

"But he won't know. And you're too fascinated by me to tell him."

He was right about her not telling Nathan, though not

for the reason he believed. Dunham was conceited enough to think she wanted an affair with him. He didn't know they were cousins. Or that there was too much at stake for her to risk telling Nathan about the insult.

Lord Dunham led her out of the ballroom and through the throngs of people in the reception area at the head of the staircase. He kept his hand locked firmly over hers so that she could not escape without causing a scene. To anyone else, it would look as if they were enjoying a pleasant stroll.

Maddy felt a jab of alarm. He was guiding her toward the corridor that led to the back of the house. "Look, there are two chairs against the wall where we can sit and talk."

She tried to steer him to the private corner, protected from eavesdroppers by two large ferns on pedestals, but he hauled her onward down the passageway. "It's far too visible," he said. "We need somewhere more secluded. After all, you wouldn't wish to create a scandal at Lady Emily's debut ball."

"This is absurd, Lord Dunham," she said forcefully, keeping her voice low. "I will not leave this party in your company."

"Call me Alfred. And we need a quiet place for this meeting. Ah, here we go."

Her cousin hauled her through a doorway and into the morning room. A fire burned low on the hearth, though no one occupied the chamber. By day, the green and gold décor was soothing and pleasant with a view of the back garden. By night, the room took on a sinister aspect with deeply shadowed corners despite the glow from a candle lamp on a table.

Or perhaps it was merely her dislike of her companion that made Maddy feel uneasy. And the fact that Dunham closed the door.

She wrenched her arm free and took several steps back. She mustn't be afraid of him. Though it would cause gossip if they'd been spotted coming in here, she must avail herself of the opportunity to speak her piece quickly.

She drew a calming breath. "I wanted to talk to you for one reason, and one reason only. You said that *you* will not allow Lord Theo to court Emily, that your grandfather would not approve. Did you ever actually *ask* the Duke of Houghton about the matter? Or are you merely presuming to know his will?"

Dunham's brow furrowed in a frown. "As his heir, I speak for my grandfather on all issues. Especially now that his health is failing."

The news jolted Maddy. Her plan would be ruined if she was too late to confront the duke. "Failing? What's wrong with him? Is he dying?"

"I shouldn't think that would matter to you."

"It matters if his ball is canceled. It's an opportunity for Lord Theo to dance with Emily. And I do think you're making a mistake by keeping them apart. There's nothing more guaranteed to make them yearn for each other than forced separation."

"Never mind those two. I'd rather speak of us." He started toward her. "I was angry at first that you'd chosen Rowley over me. But now I can see the potential for quite the tidy arrangement."

Her heart thudding, Maddy backed away from his advance. He blocked her access to the door. There was no way to dart past him without risking capture. "Tidy arrangement?"

"If we're careful, you and I can enjoy an illicit affair right under his nose. I'll make it well worth your while."

She laughed. She couldn't help herself. What monumental vanity he had. "Why would you think I'd choose you over Nathan?" Seeing his pale eyebrows clash in a frown, she said firmly, "I assure you, Lord Dunham, I've no interest in an affair with you or any other man."

"You sought me out. You said that you wanted to speak in private."

"Only so that I might plead for Emily and your brother." Reaching behind, she closed her fingers around the metal rod of the fire iron. As he stepped closer, she brought the makeshift weapon around in front of her skirt, ready to raise it if necessary. "Keep your distance, sir!"

Her cousin stopped, anger on his face. "What the devil—"

The door banged open. Nathan stepped into the room.

Though startled, Maddy felt a rush of relief. She had never been more glad to see him. In the same instant, she realized how damning the scene must look, with her clutching the fire iron and Dunham about to grab her.

Nathan's face darkened with rage. He lunged at her cousin. "You bastard! What are you doing with my wife?"

"Nothing!" Dunham blustered, taking refuge behind a sturdy armchair. "We were merely talking."

"The hell you were!"

As her husband drew back his fist, Maddy sprang in between the two men. She grabbed hold of his sleeve and dug her fingers into his arm. "Nathan, no! You can't be fighting. Not at your sister's ball!"

"He was attacking you!"

In a flash, she realized that he mustn't be allowed to think that. If he started a feud with Dunham, Nathan might rescind their acceptance to the Duke of Houghton's ball. She would never have the chance to confront her grandfather.

She shook her head vehemently. "That isn't what happened. You misread the situation. Lord Dunham and I were having a brief chat, that's all."

"With a fire iron in your hand?"

"Yes, I was about to stir up the fire." She marched to the hearth and jabbed the coals. The flames flared and a shower of sparks flew up the chimney. "See? I'm sure that Lord Dunham would like to go now. Our conversation is over."

"Indeed, I've never been more insulted," her cousin said. He straightened his lapels, his wary gaze on Nathan as he sidled toward the door. "Good evening, Lady Rowley. I can't say it's been a pleasure."

As soon as he vanished out the doorway, Nathan swung toward her. Suspicion burned in his green eyes. "You were protecting him. Why?"

Maddy took her time putting the fire iron back in its proper place. "Protecting?" She affected a laugh. "No. I only spoke to him in private because I was hoping to convince him to allow his brother to court Emily. How did you find us, anyway?"

"The two of you walked past the card room. You looked quite cozy."

His fingers were still clenched into fists. His jaw was taut, his gaze hard and angry. Reaching up, she stroked his cheek to soothe him. "It was a misunderstanding, that's all. He and I had a short conversation. A few minutes, nothing more."

He looked only slightly placated. "It was foolish of you to come in here with him. He's a reprobate of the worst ilk. Even if you *did* only mean to talk, you could have been seen by one of the guests."

"Perhaps, but a bit of outrageous behavior will only be an embarrassment to your father. So why would you object?"

"Because you're my wife, that's why. You're to stay away from miscreants like him. Is that clear?"

Maddy knew he was possessive of her, perhaps because

of his mother's affairs. Yet she couldn't resist playing with fire. She stepped closer to him, gliding her fingertips over his lips. "Very clear. I'm sorry if I made you jealous."

He caught hold of her wrist and gripped it. His stony gaze lowered to her mouth. His chest heaved with barely restrained emotion, and her insides contracted with eager anticipation. He would kiss her. He would wrap his arms around her and subject her to his passion.

But he didn't. Instead, he released her arm, turned away, and stalked out of the room.

Chapter 19

Nate cupped the pair of dice in one palm and blew on them before flinging the ivory cubes onto the green baize cloth of the hazard table. He struggled to focus his bleary eyes. To his displeasure, the numbers came up a one and a two.

Groans erupted from the other five gentlemen around the table. "Crabs!" one of them shouted. "You've lost, Rowley."

"That's it, I'm out," Nate muttered.

Grabbing his glass, he stood up, swaying on his feet from far too much brandy. Aside from a few hoots, no one really objected to his departure. Another fellow immediately slid into his chair and scooped up the dice. Although he'd once been cronies with these men, they already had forgotten him in anticipation of the next roll.

Nate ambled drunkenly away. He had lost nearly five hundred after several hours' play. He could afford to lose more, but the notion sickened him. He had known men who had played through the night and lost a hundred thousand or more. Back in his youth, he had gone deeply into debt playing hazard. It hadn't mattered to him because Gilmore had been forced to pay off those obligations.

But now, the funds came out of his own pocket. And

Nate worked too damned hard to squander his wealth on a roll of the dice.

He set down his empty glass and took another from a passing waiter. Smoke from cigars formed a haze in the low-ceilinged chamber. The gaming club was located in the back room of a brothel. While a number of the patrons played dice or cards, women in scanty attire nuzzled with gentlemen in dark corners.

This was his old hunting ground. The place where he had whiled away his dissipated youth. The hellhole where he'd drilled countless whores in the upstairs bedchambers and had mistakenly thought that made him a man.

What a damned fool he had been. He didn't belong here anymore. Especially when he was unsteady on his feet. He ought to be home in bed. With Madelyn.

I'm sorry if I made you jealous.

Her infuriating apology of the previous night still irked him. He tilted his glass and drained it, the brandy sliding down his throat. Like hell he was jealous. Jealousy implied devotion to his wife. It meant he adored her so much he couldn't bear to see her with another man.

Utter nonsense.

Jealousy had nothing whatsoever to do with his violent reaction to finding her with Dunham. Rather, Nate had paid a steep price for her in the form of a generous stipend and the honor of his name. He expected Madelyn to please *him,* not engage in trysts with other men.

Especially Dunham.

Nate burned to know what was going on between those two. She claimed to have no interest in Houghton's heir. Yet something there wasn't right and Nate couldn't quite put his finger on what. Especially not now when he was in his cups. He bitterly regretted not planting his fist in the man's face while he'd had the chance.

Nate felt a caressing touch on his arm. He turned to see

a curvy brunette smiling at him. She had pretty features, a Cupid's-bow mouth, and a large bosom that strained at the low-cut bodice of her green gown. Like a cat wanting to be petted, she rubbed herself against him, her flowery perfume like a cloud around her. "You appear in need of companionship, my lord. Perhaps you'll join me upstairs."

Her invitation left him unmoved. At one time, he would have jumped at the chance to bed such a comely female. Now, however, he could only think she wasn't Madelyn.

I'm sorry if I made you jealous.

The sly jab of his wife's words continued to gnaw at him. It implied that Madelyn thought she had him on a short leash. That she could lead him wherever she pleased. Dammit, *he* owned *her,* not vice versa. He couldn't allow her to rule him.

He put down his glass and grabbed the woman's arm. "Let's go."

As they proceeded toward the door, he tried not to weave. He'd bed this doxy, by God, and prove that Madelyn had no control over him. One female was as good as any other in the dark.

At that moment, they passed a twosome snuggled together on a chaise in a darkened corner. The fair-haired man looked familiar. With a nasty jolt, Nate recognized those sharp, narrow features.

He stopped dead. He blinked, certain his muddled brain must be playing tricks. But no. It really *was* Dunham.

The scoundrel had his hands beneath the skirts of a blond woman. She was sitting astride his lap, whispering and giggling as she undulated against him. She was slim and shapely and in that crimson gown with her back turned, she looked like . . .

Madelyn.

Nate didn't stop to question the logic of his wife visiting a brothel. He didn't stop to think at all. In a rage, he charged toward the pair. "Blast you, Dunham! Ge' away from m' wife!"

He caught hold of the woman's shoulders and yanked her away. She squealed in alarm. The face that looked up at him was sloe-eyed with a tiny doll nose and a rather vacant expression.

She wasn't Madelyn.

Dunham scowled. "What the devil—Rowley?" Then he barked out a laugh. "You can't truly have thought this whore was your wife."

Nate felt like a fool, and that fact only deepened his fury. "Filthy dog. I wouldn't put it past you."

Dunham curled his upper lip in a wily expression. "Well, I do prefer whorish blondes, after all. Especially when they kiss well."

He reached for the prostitute to settle her back onto his lap.

Even in his befuddled state, Nate recognized the insult. Dunham was calling Madelyn a whore. He was implying he'd kissed her, too.

Was *that* what had happened the other night, when Nate had caught them together? It had to be.

In a red mist of fury, he seized hold of Dunham's lapels and yanked him to his feet. He hauled back his arm and drove his fist at the man's jaw. A solid crack resounded, the satisfying force of it traveling up his arm. Dunham staggered sideways into a small table and overturned it, glassware crashing to the floor.

Men shouted, women shrieked.

Nate paid no heed. He went after his nemesis, pummeling him with both fists. From out of nowhere, Dunham struck a glancing blow to Nate's nose. Tasting blood, Nate shook his woozy head and tried to land a jab, but Dunham ducked and Nate's fist swooshed through the air.

The momentum of the missed strike sent him barreling

into the wall. He banged his shoulder and the side of his face so hard that his teeth rattled. His head spun as he turned around. Even as he started to lunge again, several men rushed forward to clamp onto his arms. Nate howled in rage and struggled to free himself.

Especially when lily-livered Dunham escaped out the door.

Maddy had arrived home after midnight in the company of Nathan's family. They had attended a musical evening featuring an opera singer and a harpist at a neighboring town house. She would have enjoyed the entertainment much more had she not been annoyed that Nathan had begged off at the last minute.

Prior engagement, indeed, Maddy thought as she scanned the titles of the few books on a shelf in her bed-chamber. He'd claimed to be joining some old friends, though he hadn't specified who.

Could he have gone on the prowl for another woman?

The possibility disturbed her much more than she cared to admit. His behavior had been rather cool toward her since the previous evening at Emily's debut ball when Maddy had implied he was jealous. Perhaps she oughtn't have provoked him. But she had not been able to stop herself. The words had just come out.

She had tried to atone for her blunder by being seductive in bed. Their lovemaking had been sensational last night—yet he'd departed directly afterward as he always did.

Sexual pleasure was all he would ever give her of himself, Maddy reminded herself. Theirs was not a marriage based on love and affection. It was a business arrangement, and he would be departing from her life forever in a matter of weeks. The sooner she reconciled herself to that fact, the happier she would be.

Too wide awake to sleep, she paced the room. None of the books on the shelf appealed to her. Especially since she had come to crave Nathan's company in bed. But he likely would be out late tonight, and she needed a distraction to allay a sense of loneliness.

Perhaps she would go down to the library and find a play to reread. She had always enjoyed Shakespeare in particular, and it would be pleasant to forget her troubles in one of the Bard's lighter comedies. As she donned a wrap over her nightdress, nostalgia for the theater tugged at her. It was at times like this, when she was alone in her lavish bedchamber, that she missed the excitement of performing, the friendships with the other actors, the close confines of her untidy little dressing room. If only she could attend a play at the Neptune Theater.

But perhaps it was best to make a clean break. That was her old life. And her stay here at Gilmore House soon would be over. Her real adventure would begin at the end of the season, when she opened her shop. Then she would be so busy and fulfilled that she need never dwell on the past—or pine for the companionship of her husband.

Taking the candle lamp from her bedside table, she opened the door and went out into the corridor. An occasional flickering taper in a wall sconce lit the long passageway, leaving swaths of deep shadow here and there. The other bedroom doors were all closed. She wasn't likely to run into anyone, for the family would be fast asleep by now.

Yet upon walking toward the staircase, she was proven wrong. From somewhere ahead of her came a heavy thump. It was followed by a muffled, disembodied curse that echoed off the walls.

She froze. It sounded as if something had fallen.

No, not some*thing*. Some*one*.

With visions of half-crippled Lady Gilmore lying in

a heap at the bottom of the stairs, Maddy hastened forward with the candle. She couldn't imagine why the dowager would be wandering the house at such an hour. Was she ill?

Arriving at the stairs, she peered down into the gloom. Her eyes widened. A dark, monstrous shape crawled up the steps.

Her heart raced. Her first impulse was to turn and flee. Worry kept her rooted in place. "Lady Gilmore?" she called. "Is that you? Are you hurt?"

A growl issued from the monster. The creature lifted its shaggy head. The feeble light of the candle fell upon bloodied features. Familiar features with green eyes and a strong jaw.

"Nathan!" She set down the candle lamp on a side table and hastened down the few steps to reach him. The smears of rusty red on his lower face alarmed her. So did the raw scrapes on his knuckles. "What happened? Did you fall?"

He muttered something unintelligible.

As she slid her arm around his back to help him to his feet, Maddy caught a strong whiff of spirits. "Oh, for pity's sake! You're drunk!"

"So wha' if I am?" he said loudly. "I won' be your dog on a leash."

She struggled to assist him in mounting the stairs. He was swaying, a heavy weight that threatened to topple her. "Stop babbling," she hissed. "You'll wake everyone."

"Wake 'em, then." He made no attempt to moderate his tone. "Tell 'em that you're mine. All mine."

"You're speaking nonsense," she whispered. "Close your mouth and concentrate on walking."

They reached the top of the stairs. Somehow, she would have to guide him down the long corridor and get him into bed. Then he took a wrong step, stumbled, and crashed into the wall. As another curse echoed, she caught hold of his arm. It would be a miracle if no one heard him. "Quiet! Lean on me."

A nearby door swung open. So much for miracles.

The Earl of Gilmore stepped out, clad in a blue silk dressing gown, a look of irritation on his stark, pitted features. "What is all this racket out here?" He held up the candlestick in his hand and let the light fall on Nathan. His expression hardened into a look of disgust.

Maddy didn't want him to realize how drunk Nathan was. He'd only despise his son all the more. "He fell on the stairs and hurt himself," she said quickly. "I was taking him to my room."

"That isn't why he's injured. He's been out brawling."

At that icy tone, she put it all together. The bloodied nose. The skinned knuckles on Nathan's hands. The smell of drink.

"Yes, well, I still need to see if a doctor should be summoned."

"No. I won't have the entire household disrupted because of his folly." Gilmore put down his candle and came forward. "I'll help you get him into bed."

As he put his arm around his son, Nathan tried to shy away. "Don' want yer help. Never did."

"Silence!" the earl snapped. "Lest I toss you out of this house at once."

Amazingly, Nathan clamped his mouth shut. He lowered his head and scowled like a sullen little boy.

Maddy grabbed her own candle and followed them. Her husband was half a head taller than his father, though Gilmore was huskier and managed to keep Nathan upright and walking. As they neared her chamber, she ran ahead to open the door.

A fire still burned on the hearth. She set down the candle lamp by the bedside and made haste to throw back the covers. Gilmore guided his son there and settled him onto the sheets, lying on his back.

Nathan groaned. He threw his arm over his face as if the scanty light from the candle hurt his eyes. Maddy went to his side, her anxious gaze sweeping over him. But other than his bloodied nose and battered hands, he appeared to be hale enough.

"I'll ring for a servant to bring towels and hot water," the earl said. "That and sleep should fix him."

"A pot of strong tea, too, if you don't mind," Maddy added. As he walked to the door, she scurried after him. His assistance had been kind, and she needed for him to know that. "Thank you, my lord. I'm truly sorry to have involved you."

Gilmore's mouth twisted. His gaze flicked to the man lying on the bed. Then his dark brown eyes pierced Maddy, and he looked as if he wanted to say something. Instead, he merely nodded and went out the door, closing it behind him.

What had he been about to say? That he was disappointed in his heir? That Nathan fell far short of his paragon of a brother, David? Oh, she hoped not. It broke her heart to see the strife between father and son. Neither of them seemed ready to budge an inch, and tonight certainly hadn't helped matters.

She couldn't blame the earl for being disgusted. This *had* been a monumental folly. Where had Nathan been all evening? Who had he been with? Most of all, why had he been fighting?

Torn between anger and concern, she padded to the bed. He lay unmoving, his arm still over his eyes, only the rhythmic rise and fall of his chest giving testament to life. He must have fallen into a drunken stupor. His clothes were untidy, his cravat bloodstained and crooked. Blood also smeared the lower half of his face. One cheekbone showed the darkness of a rising bruise.

He looked like a ne'er-do-well after a long, hard night of debauchery. Was this the way he'd behaved as a young man? Was that why his father resented him? The dowager had said he'd been a difficult child, quick-tempered and re-bellious.

That was not who Nathan was anymore, Maddy thought in frustration. Now, he was a diligent, dedicated entrepre-neur who had traveled to China and made his own fortune. Yet tonight he had shown his worst side to his father and had given Gilmore even more reason to dislike him.

Perhaps this was all part of Nathan's plan. Perhaps he'd *wanted* to irk his father. She still didn't understand why he refused to make amends with the earl. Was his antago-nism just an entrenched habit?

She didn't know and he wouldn't tell her. She herself had loved her own father. She'd give anything now to have her dear papa back again, and it bothered her to see Nathan spurn his chance to have that close paternal love.

Bending over him, she tugged off his shoes, one at a time, and dropped them onto the floor. He groaned, but didn't move. She shifted her attention to his neck cloth. It took her a few minutes to untie the intricate folds, and as she leaned closer to him, Maddy caught a whiff of flow-ery perfume.

The scent jabbed her like a red-hot wire. It proved that her earlier suspicion was correct. He *had* been with a woman tonight, damn him.

In a fit of pique, she tugged hard on the untied strip of crumpled linen. It caught on something at the back of his neck, perhaps the leather thong that secured his long hair. He uttered a growl of protest.

His arm lashed out and he caught her wrist in a pun-ishing hold. "Stop," he muttered. "I'll kill you."

"Let me go, you rotten varlet."

His groggy eyes blinked up at her. "Mad'lyn?"

"Indeed. You passed out on my bed. Now kindly cease manhandling me."

His arm fell away. Then he lifted his head slightly to survey the bedchamber before dropping back onto the pillow with a groan. "Gilmore . . . wasn't he here?"

"I'm surprised you remember." She dropped the bloodied cravat in a wrinkled heap on top of his shoes. "He helped you into bed and then departed."

His lips twisted with contempt. "No scolding?"

"You're married now. He left that task to me. And I will happily fulfill it." She jerked open the buttons of his coat and then his waistcoat. "It was selfish and stupid of you to drink and brawl. And then to make noise and wake up your father, to let him see you this way."

"Don' care wha' he thinks. Blast him."

"No, blast *you*. Sit up now so that I can remove your coat before you ruin it."

He gingerly levered himself up, swaying a little and scowling. "You're angry."

"A brilliant observation." Maddy worked the form-fitting coat off his shoulders and down his arms, then flung the garment onto a nearby chair. She did the same to his waistcoat, leaving him clad in only shirt and trousers. "I've every right to be furious, and so does your father. You behaved foolishly tonight. You drank too much and you engaged in a fistfight."

"I won' be led around on a leash."

He'd said that earlier, and now it only irritated her all the more. Especially when he gazed at her so sullenly— as if *she* were the one at fault. "You're free to do as you please," she snapped. "So long as you show respect to me and to your family. Which you did *not* do tonight. Where did you go, anyway?"

Frowning, Nathan rubbed his eyes as if trying to call forth the memory. "Played hazard. Had a few drinks. Tha's all."

"That isn't all. You reek of perfume. I wonder if you went to a brothel."

His eyes widened. He glanced away as if unable to meet her gaze. His guilty reaction only confirmed what she already knew. He had sought his pleasure in the arms of another woman. Maddy's throat felt taut, her heart aching. His actions shouldn't hurt—yet they did.

A low knock sounded on the door. Grateful for the chance to pull herself together, she went to answer the summons. A footman entered with a silver tray. On it sat a jug of water and a small stack of linens, along with a pot of tea and two cups.

She drew a small table nearer to the bed for the tray. Seeing the young servant flick a curious glance at Nathan's bloodied face, she dismissed the fellow at once and he vanished out the door. No doubt the conversation in the servants' hall tomorrow morning would be animated, but Maddy didn't care. Nathan had only himself to thank for that.

She unfolded one of the cloths and dipped it into the hot water. Going to the bed, she found him sitting up and leaning back against the pillows, his eyes shut again. She bent close and began scrubbing the rusty smears from around his nose and mouth.

His eyelids snapped open. "Ouch! Have a care!"

"Oh, did I hurt you?"

Even in his befuddled state, he must have detected the sarcasm in her tone, for he snatched the cloth from her and dabbed more gently at his lower face, wiping away the blood. Maddy went to pour a cup of tea, straining out the leaves and adding a lump of sugar. As she stirred vigorously, Nathan spoke in a lowered tone. "Nothing happened . . . just so y' know."

"Nothing? Is that what you call coming home injured and staggering?" Marching to him, she thrust the cup into his hand, trading it for the soiled cloth. "Here, drink this. It will help sober you."

He sipped obediently at his tea, wincing slightly as if his face hurt. "I meant . . . the woman. Nothin' happened with her."

Even if that was true, Maddy wasn't ready to forgive him. "So why did nothing happen? Because you and another man fought over her, and he won?"

"No! That wasn't why I punched Dunham."

The damp cloth dropped from her nerveless fingers and fell onto his cravat on the floor. Dismayed, she stared at Nathan. "You were scuffling with the Duke of Houghton's heir?"

"He insulted you. And worse." Grimacing, Nathan shoved the empty teacup onto the bedside table. "He said he'd kissed you."

Startled, she sank down onto the edge of the bed. Her fingers clutched at the folds of her nightdress. Nathan looked furious and a part of her heart sang that he could be so upset at the notion of her with another man. It proved he *did* care for her . . . didn't it?

Or maybe he just thought he owned her.

"Yes, Lord Dunham kissed me," she confessed. "But it was *not* at Emily's ball, if that's what you're thinking. It was the evening before the auction. I hadn't even met you yet."

He glowered, looking only slightly mollified. "Did you enjoy it?"

Maddy considered lying just to punish him. But that would only feed his anger at her cousin. "No, I did not."

She paused, then added, "And if you don't believe me, ask Lady Milford. She came backstage just as I hit Lord Dunham with the rose bouquet he'd given me."

Nathan studied her as if assessing the veracity of her statement. His white shirt was open at the collar and exposed part of his chest. She changed her mind about him looking like a ne'er-do-well. With his black hair mussed and his face bruised, he brought to mind a warrior after a hard battle. A battle to defend *her* honor.

Unexpectedly, he groped for her hand and held it. His knuckles were raw and reddened, his eyes clearer now. With his face scrubbed free of blood, he looked more like his old self. He smiled grimly, his dimples causing an untimely stirring of desire in her. "So I was right," he said. "The rat *did* try to force himself on you. You're never to go near him again. Is that clear?"

A lurch of alarm assailed Maddy. If Nathan forbade her to see Dunham, she'd lose the chance to confront her grandfather.

"I'm likely to encounter him in society," she pointed out. "In fact, the entire family is attending the Duke of Houghton's ball in a few weeks. The acceptance has already been sent out."

"Then cancel it."

His inflexible decree must not stand, Maddy knew. Determined to use any means to woo him to her will, she scooted closer on the bed and flattened her palms over his shirt, looking into his eyes. "Darling, listen to me. Emily is very much looking forward to this ball. It will be an excellent opportunity for her to see Lord Theo again. And I must accompany her . . . in case she needs assistance with her makeup."

He glared. "I won't have m' sister dangling after Dunham's brother."

"But Emily is set on him. I believe Lord Theo is terribly

fond of her, too. And he seems so much nicer than his brother." Maddy draped her arms around Nathan's neck, her fingers playing with his hair. "I want her to find a good husband who will cherish her, don't you? Someone who will make her as happy as you've made me."

She brushed her lips across the bruise on his cheek. With a deep groan, he wrapped his arms around her and kissed her, his tongue sweeping her mouth with hungry intensity. He tasted of brandy and she felt the rise of passion, the quickening of heat that only he could stir in her. Then Nathan drew back to growl, "Fine, we'll go t' the damn ball. But Dunham had best not come within ten feet of you, or by God, I'll rip his face off."

It was hardly a romantic declaration. Yet his fierce tone made Maddy glow with pleasure. "I'll be sure to warn him if he tries."

Nathan pulled her down fully onto the bed so that she lay half draped over his hard form. His hands gripped her possessively, moving up and down her back. "You're mine."

"You're mine, as well," she declared just as fiercely. "There will be no more brothels."

He stared at her a moment. Then his mouth curled into a rather sheepish smile. "No brothels. Don' want anyone else. Only you."

A rush of tender emotion brought a lump to her throat. Unable to speak, she tucked her head into the crook of his shoulder, relishing the strong beating of his heart against her breasts. Maybe it was just the liquor talking, but it was the closest he'd ever come to admitting he cared for her.

Maddy squeezed her eyes shut. If only he loved her as she loved him. The truth of that revelation shook her. She *did* love Nathan, for better or for worse. Somehow, despite all the friction between him and his father, despite the coldhearted arrangement of their marriage, she had grown fonder of her husband than she could ever have imagined possible. Yet he would be leaving her in a matter of weeks.

His hands lay heavy and still on her back. She lifted up slightly to see that his eyes were closed again. He had fallen asleep and wouldn't be making love to her tonight. Nevertheless, she was content just to hold him, happy to savor the joy of his presence. If only she could find a way to win his heart. Yet all of her wishes in that regard might come crashing down once he found out her secret.

Maddy knew she was playing a dangerous game. For Nathan would be furious when he learned her real purpose in wanting to attend the Duke of Houghton's ball.

Chapter 20

While the Earl of Gilmore assisted his mother out of the coach, Maddy tilted her head back to gaze up at the grand edifice. Tall pillars flanked the double front doors and supported a classically designed portico. Torchlight played over the footmen in crimson livery and the procession of finely garbed guests going up the marble steps.

She drew an unsteady breath. Though the mid-May evening was mild, a shiver prickled her skin. This magnificent residence belonged to her grandfather, the Duke of Houghton. Long ago, her mother had lived here as a child, whenever the ducal family had been in London.

This was the moment Maddy had long anticipated. At last, she would be entering the belly of the beast. Instead of a sense of triumph, however, she'd felt tense and queasy for the past few days, her stomach twisted into knots. She wanted this confrontation, she craved it with all her heart and soul. Yet now that the time had come, she dreaded it as well.

Emily joined her, leaning close to whisper, "Are you quite certain Lord Theo will be here?"

Nathan's sister looked especially beautiful tonight with her russet-brown curls pinned up and her face glowing from the skillful application of cosmetics. Tiny embroidered roses decorated her cream silk gown, the fabric from one of the bolts that Nathan had brought from China.

Maddy summoned a smile. "He's bound to be at his grandfather's ball. Don't worry, darling. Everything will be just fine."

If only she herself could stop worrying. When she confronted her grandfather, how would it affect Nathan's family? Would it cause a huge scandal? What if she ruined all hope of Lord Theo ever courting Emily?

Whenever Maddy had contemplated this night, she'd envisioned a dramatic scene in which she rebuked the Duke of Houghton for his cruelty in disowning his daughter for the sin of falling in love with a commoner. Then she would announce to the astonished guests that Lady Sarah Langley was her mother. Everyone would be dumbfounded to learn that the actress they had scorned had a close blood connection to one of the most exalted families in England.

But now Maddy had second thoughts. Perhaps it would be best to make her curtsy to the duke without revealing her true identity. Then she could find a quiet moment in which to address him alone. She could still speak her mind to him, but she would do so in private.

Yes. That would be far more sensible.

The new plan eased a portion of her tension. She mustn't let her desire for revenge harm those around her. Somehow, she had begun to think of Nathan's family as her own. She could see now that the dowager showed love in her own gruff way, that Lady Sophia's discontent was rooted in grief for her husband. Surprisingly, Maddy also felt a certain fondness for Lord Gilmore ever since he'd helped Nathan to bed on the night of his drunken debauchery.

She couldn't hurt them. She *wouldn't* hurt them.

Especially not sweet, naïve Emily.

The girl went to join her father, and Nathan strolled to

Maddy's side. Her husband looked extraordinarily attractive tonight in a form-fitting black coat and stark white cravat, his long dark hair tied neatly at his nape. The bruise on his cheek had faded. The past few weeks had been wonderful, for in the aftermath of their quarrel, he and Maddy had grown closer. Though he'd never voiced words of love, Nathan had escorted her to shops and parties and the park, seldom straying from her side. Lately, she'd even allowed herself to entertain the hope that he might change his mind about leaving England.

Bending close, he murmured, "You look dazzling, darling. You'll outshine every woman here."

She had dressed with great care tonight, donning her finest ball gown, a rich cobalt-blue silk that enhanced the color of her eyes. Shunning the elaborate curls of the other ladies, she had arranged her blond hair in a simple twist with a few wisps framing her face. A sapphire necklace from the family jewels gleamed above her breasts.

Before she could do more than smile at the compliment, he lifted her gloved hand to his lips and kissed the back. "You've been very quiet tonight," he said, studying her quizzically. "Don't worry, Dunham won't come near you. I'll make certain of that."

"And you're to be civil," she reminded him. "Promise me there will be no fisticuffs in the midst of the ball."

He grinned. "As you wish."

A quiver ran through her as he tucked her gloved hand in the crook of his arm. Little did he know, she feared Dunham's venomous reaction when he learned of their blood relationship. Even though she'd decided to confront Houghton in private, the truth would still find its way to her two cousins. Once Dunham and Lord Theo knew, the news would not remain hidden for long from society, as well.

And what would her husband say when *he* found out?

Nathan would be very displeased that she'd kept such a vital secret from him.

But that could not be helped now. Had she told him, he might have tried to interfere in some way, and this was something she had to do for herself.

They proceeded up the steps, following the earl and his mother, with Emily and Lady Sophia close behind them. Maddy's knees felt ready to buckle. She had never been more grateful for Nathan's support as they passed through the open doorway and into a magnificent entrance hall lit by blazing candles in a crystal chandelier.

An array of guests mingled in the large space, the hum of voices echoing in the vast room. Gentlemen in formal black coats escorted ladies adorned in dazzling jewels and exquisite gowns. Her gaze followed a broad staircase that led upward to the reception rooms. The wrought-iron balustrade was festooned with swags of gold ribbon. How many times had her mother walked down that staircase? Had Mama regretted leaving this splendid mansion for life with a traveling band of players? She had once called this house a gilded cage.

To be standing here now seemed unreal to Maddy. She had dreamed of this moment for so many years. It was upon her now, and she could scarcely contain her nervous anticipation.

She clung to Nathan's arm as they joined the slow-moving receiving line. She tried to peer ahead, but there were too many people blocking her view. In front of her, the Earl of Gilmore stood in line with the dowager, who was clad in green satin and leaning on her cane. Nathan turned to chat with Emily and Lady Sophia, laughing at something they said, though Maddy could make no sense of the conversations swirling around her. She felt caught in a bubble, her hands damp inside her kidskin gloves.

At last they approached the front of the line. The Earl of Gilmore and the dowager greeted flaxen-haired Lord Dunham with his thin features and, beside him, Lord Theo, with neatly combed sandy hair, looking scholarly in his gold-rimmed spectacles.

At least Emily would be happy tonight.

Even as that thought flitted through Maddy's mind, it was her turn. Nathan uttered a cool greeting to the two men. She could see no lasting damage to Dunham from the fistfight with Nathan. As she briefly touched hands with her cousins, they spoke to her, but the meaning of their words failed to register in her mind. Her attention already had shifted to the old man beside them.

The Duke of Houghton.

With a jolt, she realized that her grandfather sat hunched in a wheeled invalid's chair. Stoop-shouldered, he had a tonsure of wispy gray hair that encircled his bald pate. His dark attire hung on his emaciated form, his chest sunken beneath a white waistcoat. Despite his scrawny appearance, however, he held his chin at a haughty tilt.

He gave a curt nod to Nathan.

Only by rote did she manage to dip a graceful curtsy. Her mouth felt dry, her heart pounding. "Good evening, Your Grace."

Rising slowly, she gazed straight at her grandfather's withered features. So this was the man who had shunned Mama. Over many years, hatred of him had formed a calcified knot inside Maddy. But she should not have dreaded this meeting. He was just an arrogant aristocrat at the end of his days.

He peered at her through rheumy blue eyes. She stared back, unable to tear her gaze from him. His face was so gaunt, his nose looked very prominent. She saw in him her mother's high cheekbones and a certain similarity in the oval shape of their faces.

The duke leaned forward suddenly. His crablike hand groped out, his skeletal fingers closing around hers.

"Sarah?" he croaked.

Her heart took a tumble. Dear God, he had mistaken her for her mother. Papa had always remarked on the resemblance between them. "No," Maddy whispered, then said, louder, "No, that isn't my name."

She tried to pull her hand free, but his gnarled fingers held on to her with surprising strength. "You're Sarah. Don't try to bamboozle me, girl. You always did try to do so."

Nathan intervened, saying gently, "Your Grace, I'm afraid you're mistaken. This is my wife, Lady Rowley."

She wanted to back away. They were drawing attention from the nearby guests as people turned and stared. She spied Lady Milford in the crowd, her lips pursed in concern. A short distance away, Lady Gilmore stood frowning, the quizzing glass held to one eye.

Maddy couldn't retreat. The duke clutched her hand in a death grip. She tugged again. But she was afraid to pull too hard lest his ancient bones snap.

His sunken blue eyes grew watery, his once haughty chin wobbling. "Of course you aren't Sarah," he said brokenly, as he released her hand. "You can't be. My daughter would be much older now. It's just . . . I was hoping to see her again . . ."

That display of anguish whipped up a frenzy of rage in Maddy. How dare the Duke of Houghton pretend sorrow when he himself had driven his daughter away? When he had cut Mama off from his family and told her she was dead to him?

Maddy didn't stop to think. The words poured out in a bitter rush. "Lady Sarah Langley is dead, Your Grace. She was my mother, and she died over ten years ago. I'm your granddaughter, Madelyn. The granddaughter you never knew existed—because you'd shunned us."

Gasps eddied from the bystanders. A buzz of whispers spread throughout the entrance hall. She sensed movement around her, though she kept her gaze on the duke's slack-jawed face. She wanted him to say something, to lash out at her in anger, to look down his long nose and rebuke her.

Nathan's hand tightened convulsively on her arm. She glanced up to see his stark, astonished features. The others were staring at her in disbelief, Lord Gilmore frowning beside his mother, Emily clinging to Lord Theo's arm, Lady Sophia with her mouth agape.

Maddy felt faint. What had she done? This was not what she'd intended. But it was too late to turn back now.

Lord Dunham sprang to the duke's side. His icy gaze bored into Maddy. "What the devil is this nonsense? How dare you make such an outrageous claim! You're nothing but an upstart actress. Leave this house at once."

Nathan uttered a growl low in his chest. Sensing him about to spring, Maddy dug her fingers into the hard muscles of his arm to stop him. "Every word of it is true. The Duke of Houghton is my grandfather. You are my cousin. So is Lord Theo."

"Impossible—" Dunham sputtered.

"His Grace tried to force Mama into a betrothal with a nobleman when she was eighteen. But she'd fallen in love with a traveling actor, Jeremy Swann. For the sin of running off to marry her true love, she was cast out of this family forever." Maddy gestured at the duke. "Ask my grandfather. He'll confirm it. I'm sure he remembers exactly what happened."

The Duke of Houghton said nothing at all. He sat staring up at her, his bony fingers gripping the arms of his invalid's chair. A single tear trickled on a slow path down his withered cheek. He looked old and broken, and Maddy knew it must be a shock to learn that his daughter was dead. Then she chided herself for feeling even a shred of sympathy for the man.

Nathan placed his firm hand at the small of her back. "Pray forgive this outburst, Your Grace. My wife and I will be leaving now."

His frigid tone chilled Maddy. All the fire seemed to have burned out of her. She didn't feel relieved or triumphant—just hollow and wretched.

Her legs moved woodenly as Nathan thrust her toward the door. The multitude of guests parted to give them wide berth. She felt their stares and heard their whispers as if in a dream. None of them mattered to her. Let them think what they willed. She wanted only to go home and bury herself beneath the covers of her bed. To hug her pillow and escape all the prying eyes.

They went outside into the cool night and down the porch steps. Nathan propelled her past a line of carriages. Coachmen gathered in small groups, conversing and trading jests. A burst of hearty laughter came from the carriages parked across the darkened square.

Nathan's footsteps were quick and sharp on the pavement, and she had to half run to keep up with him. As they hurried by Lord Gilmore's vehicle, the stout coachman doffed his hat in surprise. "Milord—"

Her husband didn't stop to answer. He ploughed ahead, his hand pressing at Maddy's back. As they passed beneath a street lamp, the glow of gaslight cast harsh shadows on his grim features. Never had she seen him look so coldly furious. Not even when confronting his father.

Stepping off the curbstone, she nearly twisted her ankle in her new dancing slippers. "Nathan, do slow down. Where are we going?"

He moderated his pace only slightly. "Gilmore House. It's eight blocks away."

"Oughtn't we take the coach?"

"No. My family will need it when Houghton ejects them."

A huge lump crowded her throat. She had ruined the ball for everyone, Emily in particular. How disappointed the girl would be to miss her only chance to flirt with Lord Theo.

Clearly, Nathan believed no one in his family would want to ride in the same coach as her. How they must all resent her. She had lied to them. She had hidden her past and tricked them into taking her to the Duke of Houghton's house.

They would all realize, too, that confronting the duke was the real reason she'd married Nathan.

Tears blurred her eyes, but Maddy blinked them back. She swallowed to ease the tightness in her throat as she strove to keep up with his long strides. "Nathan, I'm . . . I'm so very sorry. I should have asked to speak to the duke in private. That's what I had intended to do. I never meant to make such a confession in front of everyone. It just . . . spilled out."

"Spilled out," he mocked, urging her past a row of tall, darkened town houses. They had left the square and now proceeded down a side street, their footsteps echoing in the quiet night air. "All this time, you've kept your past a secret from me. You should have allowed your connection to Houghton to *spill out* when I asked you to marry me."

"I—I couldn't. You would have withdrawn your proposal."

He gave a harsh growl. "Precisely. You played me for a fool. You saw my offer as your big chance. You wanted to use me to enter society. All so that you could gain entry to Houghton's house."

Everything he said was true. But she was done apologizing. "You used me, too, Nathan."

"And I paid you well for the privilege! Dammit, I *knew* there was something odd about your interest in Dunham. I knew it and I let you hoodwink me." He ran his fingers through his hair, mussing the long black strands. In the gloom, his face looked taut with fury as he hauled her down the street. "Blast you, Madelyn. You lied to me. You led me to believe you were a commoner. But your blood is bluer than mine."

It seemed an odd thing for him to say. "What do you mean? My father was an actor."

"And mine was a damned footman."

Startled, she stopped in the halo of light from a street lamp and spun to face him. "No. The Earl of Gilmore is your father."

He glanced around as if to assure himself there was no one out on the street. "My mother had numerous affairs. She saw no need for fidelity in marriage. She was caught carrying on with a footman nine months before I was born."

Disbelieving, Maddy slowly shook her head. "That can't be true. Who told you that?"

"Gilmore himself," Nathan snarled in a harsh undertone. "It was his gift to me on my twenty-first birthday. He was angry about having to pay off my gaming debts, and he attributed my depravity to my bad blood. Needless to say, we had the row of the century. The very next day, I left England, intending never to return."

Shocked, Maddy leaned back against the hard post of the street lamp. It all made perfect, awful sense now. No wonder the earl had treated Nathan so coldly in his childhood. No wonder he had favored his elder son. No wonder

Nathan had gone abroad and returned ten years later with vengeance on his mind.

And no wonder he had offered marriage to a disreputable actress. It was the perfect way to punish Gilmore.

"Who else knows this?" she asked faintly.

"Only the dowager. But I'm sure there were rumors, given my mother's notoriety."

Maddy felt sick at the realization that she'd proved to Nathan that she, too, was an untrustworthy wife. She had tricked him, concealed the fact that she had blue blood. But didn't that make them equals?

"We're alike then, you and I," she asserted. "We're both half noble. And if the earl resents you, it stands to reason he will continue to resent me, as well. Perhaps even more so since I caused such a great scandal tonight."

"No. You're wrong." Nathan took hold of her arm again and pulled her along the foot pavement. He seemed too full of rage to stand still. "Consider it from his perspective. Gilmore was forced to accept the footman's son as his heir. And when the footman's son married a common actress, it was the worst possible circumstance, for it meant the Gilmore bloodline would be further diluted. But now, the actress reveals her connection to one of the most powerful peers in England. And that changes everything." In the shadows, Nathan clenched his jaw. "Trust me, once he overcomes his shock, Gilmore will be very, very pleased by this new development."

Maddy took a shaky breath. "But . . . the scandal . . ."

"Will die down eventually. In a matter of months, you'll be cozy with the ton, especially if Houghton decides to accept you as a family member. So in Gilmore's way of thinking, he's won. Because if you were to bear me a son, the boy needn't be hidden away. He would be eminently worthy of the title."

"Surely the earl can't be that petty."

"Yes, he can be. Pedigree means everything to him."

The deep bitterness in his tone distressed her. It reflected the estrangement he had suffered in his own family. The Earl of Gilmore had made Nathan believe he was unworthy and unloved.

They walked for a few minutes in silence, turning a corner and heading down another dark street. Her feet hurt from the new shoes, but the pain in her heart was far greater. Now she understood the full extent of Nathan's fury. She had completely overturned his plans. He had craved retribution for the Earl of Gilmore's cruel treatment of him. Nathan believed he'd finally achieved the perfect revenge in foisting a notorious bride on his family.

But she had ruined everything for him.

No longer could she blame Nathan for despising the earl. He had been justified in his resentment. The circumstances of his birth had not been his fault, yet he had suffered the consequences. In childhood, he had been denied the love of a father. All because of his mother's folly . . .

Abruptly, he demanded, "When did you last have your courses? It must be nearly a month already, isn't it?"

Startled, Maddy blushed, grateful for the cover of darkness. She turned her face downward, watching the kick of her slippers against the hem of her gown. "Um . . . yes, I believe so."

"Then you must tell me when they start. I've no wish to give Gilmore a grandson—not anymore. Then he truly *would* win."

His cold, cutting tone sliced into her. Any hope she'd had of reconciling their differences died with that harsh statement.

Because she had fudged the truth. It actually *had* been longer than that since last she'd bled. Her courses were a week late. And for the past few days, she'd been feeling weary and nauseous. With the confrontation with her grandfather looming, she hadn't allowed herself to consider the possibility of pregnancy.

But now Maddy feared it might be true. And she couldn't bring herself to tell Nathan, either. He would be all the more furious.

He didn't want their child.

Chapter 21

The brightness of daylight pulled Maddy out of a deep slumber. She struggled to lift her heavy eyelids. Through the screen of her lashes, she saw a dark-clad, stout woman moving briskly from window to window in the bedchamber. It was Gertie, drawing back the draperies to let in the morning sunshine.

"Lord Gilmore sends a message, milady. He requests yer company in the library at eleven. And 'tis half past nine already."

Maddy tried to focus her fuzzy thoughts. She had never before been invited into the earl's private sanctum. She'd always waited until he was gone to venture into the library to select a book. Why would he want to speak to her?

Then the events of the previous night returned in a sickening flood. The Duke of Houghton in a wheeled invalid's chair. A single tear sliding down his withered cheek. The angry words that had spewed out of her. Nathan hauling her out of the house in a fury and confessing that he'd been sired by a footman.

Of course Gilmore wanted an audience with her. He knew she'd concealed the truth about her background. She hadn't seen him after leaving the duke's house, for she'd gone straight to bed . . .

As Maddy lifted her head from the pillow, an overwhelming rush of nausea struck her. She scrambled out of bed and barely reached the chamber pot in time to retch.

Afterward, gasping and miserable, she pressed her forehead to the side of the bed. She felt Gertie's hand gently rubbing her back. "Poor dear. But 'tis happy news, I'll guess. Ye must be with child. Lady Gilmore will want t' send fer the doctor—"

"No!" Maddy took a linen towel from the maid, using it to blot the cold sweat on her face. "No, you mustn't bother anyone. Not just now."

" 'Tis no bother. And Lord Rowley's gone out. But he'll want t' know when he returns. Won't he be pleased!"

Nathan wouldn't be pleased. Not at all. He had made that perfectly clear the previous night. *I've no wish to give Gilmore a grandson—not anymore. Then he truly would win.*

The memory of his icy wrath weighted down her spirits. He had walked her back to Gilmore House and then had taken his leave, his manner cold and formal. A shudder ran through her. He didn't want a son. And he had not come to her bed last night.

Did it mean their marriage was over?

Maddy tamped down an incipient panic. Somehow, she had to get through the hours until she could speak to him again. Especially since Gertie knew nothing of their quarrel. The previous night, she had given the maid only an abbreviated version of the events at the duke's house. Just enough to allay her curiosity.

She caught hold of the woman's careworn hand. "You mustn't tell anyone, Gertie. Not even a whisper. Please. It's too soon and . . . I just want to wait for a little bit."

Clucking in sympathy, the maid helped Maddy to her

feet. "Mayhap 'tis wise since ye only just met the duke. 'Tis a lot fer ye t' swallow all at one time."

"Yes, that's right." Maddy seized on the convenient excuse. "I should like the uproar to settle down first. This house has had quite enough excitement for one week."

An hour and a half later, Maddy heard the musical dinging of a clock chiming the hour of eleven as she approached the library. She had girded herself for battle in a jade-green gown with her hair drawn up in a simple twist. The awful nausea had subsided. She felt much better now after a breakfast of dry toast and weak tea. Almost normal, in fact, except for the ache in her heart.

She still had not seen Nathan. He'd gone out early this morning without leaving word when he'd return. Somehow, she must find a way to make things right between them. She *would* find a way.

After this meeting with the earl.

The library was located on the ground floor overlooking the garden. As she stepped through the doorway, Maddy could see the green of the outdoors through one of the tall windows. The floor-to-ceiling shelves held a vast array of leather-bound books, so many she could be happy for years perusing them.

But that wasn't likely to occur. She didn't know if she would be allowed to stay at Gilmore House. Or even if she wanted to do so.

Her gaze went to the two people seated side by side in chairs by the unlit hearth. She faltered a step before continuing toward them. Of course, this summit also would include the dowager.

The Earl of Gilmore rose to his feet and watched her approach. His pitted features looked as harsh as ever, his graying auburn hair neatly combed, his dark garb impeccable. Only a certain keenness to his brown eyes gave any indication of a change in how he viewed her.

She performed the requisite curtsy. Then he waved her into a straight-backed chair that faced the two of them. "Good morning, Madelyn. Pray be seated."

Clad in dark gold, the dowager lifted the quizzing glass that was pinned to her bodice and peered closely at Maddy as she sat down. "Ah, you do indeed have the look of Houghton. I can see it now in your cheekbones and eyes. And in the fair hair, too."

Maddy folded her hands in her lap. She resented being examined like a butterfly pinned under glass. "People see what they wish to see."

"Indeed," the earl said. "And *you* wished for us to believe you were a baseborn actress. Why?"

"I never said I was baseborn," she corrected sharply. "My parents were lawfully married."

He gave a cool nod. "Of course. Forgive me. But you have not answered my question. You must have known that you would be far more acceptable to me as Nathan's wife had I been informed of your close connection to the Duke of Houghton."

Maddy pursed her lips. He was too astute not to have conjectured the answer. "My husband and I had made an agreement. I would play the vulgar strumpet, and in return, he would provide me entry to society. It was as simple as that."

"Aha!" the dowager said, thumping her cane on the carpet. "So you were playacting when you first came to this house. All that nonsense and babbling was designed to fool us. But you already knew proper behavior. You'd learned it from Lady Sarah Langley."

The earl held up his hand to silence his mother. He kept his gaze trained on Maddy. "Nathan didn't know about your connection to the duke. He appeared every bit as shocked as we were."

"I thought it best not to tell him. You see, both he and I have had our secrets."

Maddy coolly returned his stare. She wanted the earl to wonder if she knew that Nathan had been fathered by a footman. Despite the estrangement in her marriage, she couldn't bring herself to forgive this man for making Nathan's childhood a living hell.

To her amazement, Gilmore looked away first. He abruptly stood up and paced to the fireplace before turning to regard her. "You should know that I had a conference in private with His Grace last night after you'd left. He wanted to know your background, where you've been all these years. I'm afraid I couldn't enlighten him, at least not much."

She tensed. "He asked about me?"

"Of course. You're his granddaughter. He expressed a very strong desire to see you again."

Agitation gripping her limbs, Maddy surged to her feet. She had not thought beyond the confrontation, except to fantasize about the duke hanging his head in shame for all he'd done. "Why would I wish to see *him*? After the way he treated my mother?"

"Come now, Madelyn. You cannot fault him for showing an interest in his long-lost granddaughter. In fact, that is why I called you here. He asked me to convey an invitation to you to come for tea this afternoon."

Maddy followed a footman in white wig and crimson livery up the grand staircase at the Duke of Houghton's house. Their footsteps resounded loudly in the large entrance hall. In stark contrast to the throngs of guests the previous evening, the place was empty and echoing, the candles in the chandelier burned to nubs and the gold ribbons gone from the balustrade.

The Earl of Gilmore had wanted to accompany her to this meeting. He had been most insistent. But she had been just as adamant about coming alone. She would not defer to her father-in-law. Especially when he clearly favored her making amends with the duke.

She reached the top of the stairs. Her jade-green skirt rustled as she followed the servant down a long, ornate corridor. Was she doing the right thing in returning to this house?

Maddy stiffened her spine. It had been very tempting to reject the invitation. She owed no courtesy to the Duke of Houghton, not after the way he'd spurned her mother. Blood might make him her grandfather, but there was no other bond between them. Nor did she seek one.

Yet there had been things left unsaid last night in the heat of the moment. This would be her opportunity to make her position clear.

The footman stepped through a doorway and bowed. "Lady Rowley, Your Grace."

As the servant retreated, Maddy stepped into a spacious morning room decorated in autumn hues of gold and russet. Several tall windows let in the afternoon sunlight. Hunting scenes were displayed on the walls, with small porcelain dog figurines scattered here and there.

The Duke of Houghton did not occupy his wheeled invalid's chair today. He sat on a chaise beside the fireplace, where flames burned on the grate. Despite the warmth of the room, he had a rug draped over his knees. He leaned forward, his eyes squinting at her as if his vision were poor and he hungered for a look at her.

Then her gaze was caught by a portrait that hung above the marble mantel. Her steps came to an abrupt stop. The painting showed a young woman in an old-fashioned white gown with pale pink ribbons, a string of pearls at her throat, her blond hair drawn up in a mass of curls. She looked so hauntingly familiar that Maddy felt her heart catapult into her throat. Her lips formed the name without uttering a sound. *Mama.*

"Well, well, if it isn't our newfound cousin."

The aristocratic voice broke into her reverie. She realized to her surprise that two other gentlemen had arisen from their chairs. Lord Dunham and Lord Theo. Of course. How foolish of her not to have anticipated the presence of her cousins at this meeting. They would want to protect their grandfather—and they must be curious and resentful of an interloper into their exalted family.

It was Dunham who had spoken, and he strolled forward to greet her. "Do give me a kiss, dear cousin."

Maddy noted the angry resentment in his ice-blue eyes and in the curl of his upper lip. As he drew near, she sidestepped him. "There is no need for any pretense of affection, my lord."

"Alfred," he corrected. "Surely now we can be on more familiar terms . . . my dear Madelyn."

"You are presumptuous, *Alfred*. I'm afraid we scarcely know one another." She slipped past him and went to his brother, offering her hand. "Hello, Lord Theo. I'm truly sorry for disrupting the ball last night. I do hope you had a chance to speak to Lady Emily."

His dark blue eyes lit up behind his gold-rimmed spectacles. "Oh! Yes, I did for a few moments. Though she left early, dash it all."

Maddy's spirits lifted. Perhaps there *was* an advantage to her secret being exposed. Perhaps now she could arrange for more meetings between Theo and Emily. It was something to consider, anyway.

"Come here, girl," the duke rasped, beckoning with his

skeletal hand. "You're to sit right beside me." He patted the striped gold cushion of the chaise.

She hesitated. It was the only possible place for her to sit since her cousins already had laid claim to the pair of brown upholstered chairs opposite the duke. Everything in her resisted the notion of being within touching distance of the man who had shunned her mother. Yet if she refused to share the chaise with him, she would be forced to go across the room and drag over another chair.

That would only make her appear childish when she needed to be strong and fearless.

Maddy glided to the chaise and sat down, staying as close to her end as possible. Despite her best efforts, her skirt brushed against her grandfather's bony legs. Alfred and Theo resumed their seats as well.

She didn't want any of them to direct the conversation. So she said quickly, "I'm sure we can all agree there is no need for chitchat. I accepted this invitation only because I wanted to say—"

A movement at the door interrupted her as a footman entered, pushing an elaborate tea trolley. He wheeled it into the space between the chaise and the chairs, then bowed and departed.

"At least there's one advantage to having Madelyn as our new cousin," Alfred said. "We now have a *lady* in the family to serve our tea."

His emphasis on the word "lady" indicated that he hoped to trip her up, to prove that she lacked the proper refinement to perform the simple task. Of course, he didn't know about the endless hours she'd spent under Lady Gilmore's tutelage. Maddy arose gracefully and poured the steaming tea into the four cups, took orders for sugar and cream, then passed around a plate with slices of seed cake.

As she delivered a porcelain cup to the duke, he took it with shaky hands and balanced it in his lap. He looked down at it, then said, "Sarah always prepared my tea. She knew the precise shade of whiteness that I prefer. And it appears that you do, too, Madelyn."

Passing out the other cups, Maddy tensed, remembering how he had mistaken her for her mother the previous night. "I am not Lady Sarah, Your Grace. It was merely a lucky guess."

"Yet you look so much like her, it's uncanny. The portrait up there proves it."

Maddy's gaze was drawn again to the painting over the mantel. Papa had often remarked on the resemblance, and today she could see it, too. It brought a lump to her throat to behold her mother's gently smiling image captured as a debutante. The features that had grown fuzzy in her memory were now brought into clear focus.

"Grandfather had it brought down from the attic today and dusted off," Alfred said, watching Maddy over the rim of his cup. "Had I viewed it earlier, I'd have recognized you and guessed your game at once."

"Game?" she asked sharply, sitting down on the chaise with her own cup of tea. "This is no game. I came here today to clear the air. I grew up hearing stories about how Mama had been cut off from her family for the sin of having fallen in love with an actor."

She looked from her cousins to the duke. "I wanted all of you to know that my father was a fine man, moral and kindhearted, and he earned an honest living with his talents. He was nobler than many I've met in the aristocracy. And he adored my mother more than life itself." Maddy remembered him kneeling at Mama's gravesite, heartbroken at her loss. Tears welled in her eyes, but she blinked them away and focused on her grandfather, her fingers taut around the saucer in her lap. "You should never have passed judgment on Papa without even knowing him. It was wicked of you. Wicked and cruel!"

Alfred started to rise from his chair. "You would dare speak to His Grace in such an insolent manner—"

Houghton waved her cousin back into his seat beside Theo, who watched silently, his eyes wide behind the gold-rimmed spectacles.

"Madelyn is right," the duke said in a saddened tone. "I *was* cruel. And as punishment, I lost my only daughter. I never saw Sarah again." His chin wobbled as he returned his attention to Maddy. "How . . . how did she die?"

His remorse caught Maddy off balance. She had believed his sorrow of the previous night to be the result of shock, and that today he would be arrogant and disdainful. She had expected him to lift his haughty chin and stare down his hawklike nose at her. She had prepared a series of cutting remarks designed to bring him down a peg or two. But now it seemed churlish to be so harsh toward him.

"She suffered an accident when I was thirteen years old." Maddy described what had happened, that an axle had broken on their wagon and her mother had fallen beneath a wheel. She told them that her father had died of a lung ailment two years later, never having fully recovered his high spirits after her mother's untimely death, saying in conclusion, "That was when I left the traveling players and took a position with the Neptune Theater."

"I've seen several of your plays," Theo piped up. "You're smashing good."

Maddy smiled warmly at him. "So was my mother. She was a very gifted actress. She taught me everything I know." Her gaze went to her grandfather and she pursed her lips. "Did you even realize her talent? Did you ever try to find her?"

Houghton slowly shook his head, his shoulders slumped. "For many years, I wouldn't even let Sarah's name be uttered in my presence. I banished her portrait and pretended she'd never been born. But when a man grows old, he looks back on his life and sees all the mistakes he's made. I only hope you can forgive me."

"Stuff and nonsense," Alfred said crisply. "Aunt Sarah disobeyed your wishes. She chose her own fate. I don't see why we should even care what happened to her."

Maddy's spine went rigid. "If our grandfather wants to know about my mother, then I will tell him. It is no concern of yours."

The moment the words came out, Maddy was startled to realize she'd taken the duke's side. Was her heart softening toward him? What had he done to deserve it?

He had expressed regret, that was what. He'd blamed himself, not her mother. And he had placed Mama's portrait in a place of honor above the fireplace. Never in her wildest dreams had Maddy imagined she might actually *like* her grandfather.

But could she forgive him? It was far too soon to decide.

The duke took a sip of tea and the cup rattled slightly as he replaced in its saucer. His stern gaze was fixed on his elder grandson. "You would do well, Alfred, to accustom yourself to my granddaughter's presence in our lives. I have every intention of writing her into my will. Along with you and Theodore, Madelyn will inherit an equal portion of the wealth that is not entailed."

The announcement hung in the silent air. Maddy's shocked brain could not quite grasp the enormity of what he had said. Did he truly think she had come here for *money*?

Alfred shot to his feet. "Good God! You can't do that. She's a nobody."

"I can indeed," Houghton said, his chin lifted as he stared down his grandson. "And I shall. You have no say in the matter."

An ugly fury came over Alfred's narrow features. "I'll have you declared incompetent, then. You can't change your will on a whim for a blasted fortune hunter."

Maddy set down her teacup. "That isn't why I came here," she said sharply.

But no one was listening to her.

The duke reached over to a side table. He picked up a bell and rang it imperiously. The tinkling sounded incongruous in the thickness of tension.

A moment later, a portly man in a sober dark suit stepped into the morning room. It was as if he'd been waiting just outside for this very summons. "Yes, Your Grace?"

Glowering at his grandson, the duke said, "Alfred, I'm sure you remember Dickenson, my solicitor. Tell us, Dickenson, is there any chance the courts will declare me incompetent?"

"No, Your Grace. I am prepared to swear to the soundness of your mind before a tribunal of judges."

"Excellent. You may go."

Dickenson melted out the door as swiftly as he'd arrived.

Maddy was stunned by the change in her grandfather. Compared to the mournful old man who'd regretted losing his daughter, he was now every inch the autocratic duke. And she easily could see him as the strict authoritarian who had denounced her mother.

Nevertheless, he must not dictate to *her*.

Springing to her feet, she turned to face him. "Your Grace, there is no need for you to alter your will," she said firmly. "I will not accept a penny from you."

"Nonsense, no one would turn down such a generous offer. Nor shall you. You will have the inheritance. My mind is made up on the matter."

The steely expression on his wrinkled features told her that arguing would serve no purpose. Glancing at her cousins, she noted the poisonous resentment on Alfred's face. Even Theo looked mistrustful and didn't quite meet her eyes.

As if he, too, thought her a fortune hunter.

Chapter 22

Nate stepped into an unoccupied bedchamber at the end of the corridor. Protective cloth covered the bed and other pieces of furniture. The closed curtains blocked the late afternoon sunlight, though dust motes danced in a few rays that slipped through a crack in the draperies.

His gaze strayed to a chair by the fire. Memory transported him back to the day after his wedding when he had pulled Madelyn into his lap and made love to her right here. He could recall in excruciating detail every exciting sensation, the scent of her hair, the undulation of her hips, the erotic sound of her moans. With every ounce of his being, he craved to experience it all over again.

But torturing himself served no purpose. He must never again make love to his wife. To do so carried the risk of conceiving a son who would secure the line of succession and please Gilmore mightily.

The only way Nate could salvage his revenge was to stay far away from Madelyn. He was still furious at her for concealing her noble blood, and he'd resolved to depart England at once.

He shouldn't feel so torn apart by the decision. Leaving her should be no different than casting off a mistress who'd displeased him. Yet somehow, in the two months of their marriage, Madelyn had become central to his happiness. And all the while, she had been deceiving him. What a fool he had been!

Nate strode toward the far end of the room. This bedchamber had once been his, though he hadn't told that to Madelyn. The décor had been changed after he'd departed London a decade ago, and everything of his had been removed. The room no longer looked like a young man's quarters with paintings of horses on the walls, his coat thrown over a chair, his collection of maps strewn over the bed.

But the mahogany writing desk was still here. It stood against the wall in the corner, the lid closed to hide the niches where he'd once kept paper and pens. He had no interest in those things now. Rather, he was looking for something else he'd concealed many years ago.

He crouched down on his haunches in front of the desk. Reaching into the kneehole, he found the secret compartment that was hidden from sight. The latch popped open to the manipulation of his fingers. With a flare of success, he felt a familiar rectangular shape inside, the object of his quest.

He drew out a little wooden chest, undisturbed for over ten years. Rising to his feet, he strode to the window, blew off a coating of dust, and opened the box. Inside lay an assortment of treasures from his youth. A little book of aphorisms given to him by his godmother, Lady Milford. A rock with an imprinted fossil. A baby curl of Emily's russet-brown hair.

Nate picked up a folded square of fine linen embroidered with a border of flowers. The *C* in the corner stood for "Camellia." He brought the handkerchief to his nose and breathed deeply. Even after all these years, he could still detect the rose scent that his mother had always worn.

She'd given the handkerchief to him on her sickbed to clean his face, when he'd come to visit as a twelve-year-old with dirt smudges from a vigorous game of cricket. She had died several days later from complications related to Emily's birth.

A nostalgic ache tugged at him. With the passage of time, the memory of her face had grown indistinct. He had an impression of dark hair, dancing green eyes, and a brilliant smile. Most of all, he recalled her joy for life. Once, she'd awakened him and David at midnight to go out into the garden and play in the first snowfall—until Gilmore had come to angrily order them back inside.

Nate had seldom seen her, for she'd spent most of her time at society events or away on trips to the country homes of various friends. Yet he had adored her nonetheless. He could still feel his fury to hear Gilmore's disparagement of her. He hated that his memory of her had been sullied ten years ago by the earl's accusations about her infidelity.

Replacing the handkerchief in the box, Nate picked up an old note from his brother and unfolded it. "I am very sorry that Papa thrashed you. It was my fault for smuggling biscuits to you after tea. I promise to try to convince him to be more fair next time. David."

Nate ran his fingertip over the neat black script. He'd never felt that he measured up to his brother. David had always been honorable and well behaved, while Nate had been the troublemaker, being sent to bed without supper for one infraction or another. Whenever David had tried to help him, Nate had been the one blamed for leading him astray. Back then, Nate had been too defiant and resentful to thank his brother.

When he'd told that to Madelyn, she'd said, *You took David's thrashings for him. That's something.*

Perhaps she was right. Nevertheless, Nate wished he'd

had the chance to express his gratitude. In the decade of his absence, he'd never even written to David. He'd allowed his bitterness to carry on into adulthood. Then, because of Lady Milford's letter, he had returned to England believing his father had died and David was the new earl.

He'd hoped to see his brother again, to make amends. Instead, David was gone. Forever.

Nate rubbed his stinging eyes and told himself not to dwell on the past. He could not change the chain of events. He could only try to do what was right in the here and now.

He folded the note and put it back inside the small box, closing the lid. Gripping it in his hands, he headed out of the bedchamber. This time, he would take these few mementos with him because he wasn't planning to return. Perhaps he'd add something of Madelyn's . . .

No. It was best to forget his wife. Already, the prospect of parting from her twisted in his gut. He had to go before he succumbed again to her powerful allure. He had to recoup what he could of his revenge.

He'd be damned if he gave Gilmore a blue-blooded grandson.

Maddy hesitated by the connecting door in her bedchamber. She had returned from the duke's house a short while ago. The shocking interview with her grandfather still resonated in her mind. He intended for her to inherit an equal share of his wealth along with her two cousins. She had no inkling as to the exact amount, but judging by the magnificence of his house and the outraged reaction of her cousin Alfred, it must be a staggering sum, indeed.

She didn't want a farthing from the Duke of Houghton. It would feel like blood money, a bribe to compensate for the mistreatment of her mother. Not even a king's ransom could make up for the pain Mama had suffered in being cut off from her family.

To calm herself, Maddy took a deep breath. She must not allow herself to become overwrought. For the moment there was nothing to be done on the matter. But she could try to reconcile with Nathan. Gertie had said he was back home now from wherever he'd gone.

Maddy rapped on the white-painted panel. When there was no answer, she cautiously opened the connecting door. In all the weeks of their marriage, Nathan had always come to her bedchamber. How odd to think she had never even set foot in his.

Stepping inside, she found herself in a large dressing room with a number of masculine accoutrements on display. On top of the clothes press lay a stack of linen cravats, another of folded shirts, and yet another of trousers. Boots and shoes stood in a neat line against one wall. A mound of coats and waistcoats sat on a dressing table. Even the pitcher and basin on the washstand had been moved aside to allow space for a pile of stockings and undergarments.

Why was everything pulled out of the cabinets? Had there been an infestation of mice? Or was a spring cleaning under way?

Then she noticed an open trunk. It was an oversized traveling trunk made of leather with brass fittings.

Cold apprehension swept down her spine. Dear God. Nathan couldn't be preparing to depart already . . . could he? It was only mid-May and he'd promised to stay until the end of June.

She hurried through an open doorway and into his bedchamber. The spacious room was similar to her own in size, with a canopied bed bedecked in shades of blue and an assortment of mahogany furnishings. A clock on the mantel chimed the half hour. In the aftermath, the silence felt heavy, ominous.

Nathan wasn't here. Could he have left already, giving

instructions to his valet to pack the trunk and deliver it to the docks?

She trembled, her hand moving to cup her flat belly. He couldn't go just yet. It was too soon. He didn't even know about their baby.

But of course that news wouldn't keep him in London. He didn't want their child. The previous evening, he had made his opinion on the matter perfectly clear. *I've no wish to give Gilmore a grandson—not anymore. Then he truly would win.*

Maddy was trying to decide whether to wait here for Nathan or to go look for him when the door latch rattled and he strode into the bedchamber. He spied her standing near the dressing room and stopped dead in his tracks.

For a long moment, they stared at one another. Her heart leaped with untimely yearning. From their very first meeting, she had admired his broad shoulders in his tailored coat, the unfashionably long hair drawn back at his nape, the strength and confidence that he exuded. She'd loved his green eyes with the flecks of gold and the dimples in his cheeks when he smiled.

He wasn't smiling now.

He shut the door, then strode to the bedside table and set down a small, rectangular wooden box. The care with which he handled the box caught her attention. She'd hadn't even noticed him holding it.

"What is in that box?" she asked.

"A few odds and ends, things I intend to take with me." He turned to face her, his expression cool and remote. "I'm leaving, Madelyn. I'm going back to the Far East. I went to the docks today and made the arrangements. My ship sails at dawn."

His announcement stabbed into her heart. For a moment she couldn't breathe for the pain. Did he truly care so little about her that he could walk away from their marriage—just like that?

She folded her arms and sought refuge in sarcasm. "Yes, I noticed your trunk in the dressing room. Were you intending to tell me if I hadn't come in here? Or would you have just disappeared?"

"Of course I intended to tell you. You were gone this afternoon, visiting your grandfather." His face hardened. "Have you made up with Houghton, then? Has he accepted you into the family fold?"

"Never mind the duke." Her momentary show of pluck drained away and she mourned the lack of warmth in his expression. She knew the situation was her own fault, at least in part. "Oh, Nathan, I'm so very sorry for what happened last night. I truly regret deceiving you. Can't you at least stay until the end of the season as you promised?"

He prowled back and forth, his narrowed gaze on her. "May I remind you, Madelyn, *you* broke our agreement. You lied to me. You led me to believe that you were common. Had I known the truth, I wouldn't have married you."

His words hurt. But he had concealed his own explosive secret. He had not told her *why* it was so important that his wife be a scandalous actress, purchased at auction. So how could she have guessed that the earl had cruelly scorned Nathan all his life for being fathered by a footman?

Yet pointing that out now only seemed futile. He was too caught up in the poison of vengeance.

Nevertheless, Maddy couldn't just let him walk away. The prospect of never seeing him again was too dreadful to contemplate. She needed him in her life—and he needed her, too. They were two halves of a whole, though his hatred for the earl had blinded him to that fact.

She went to him, stopping in his path and forcing him

to cease pacing. "I understand why revenge has ruled your life for so long, Nathan. But it isn't good for you. I do think you ought to try to make peace with Gilmore instead of running away again."

"Don't be ridiculous!"

Determined, she reached up and cupped his jaw in her hands. "If you won't do that, then at least stay in England. We could move out of this house, you and I. We could make our own home somewhere else. You needn't ever see him again—and we could be together. I love you—enough for both of us."

Something flickered in his eyes as he stared down at her. Something hot and hungry. Then abruptly, he took hold of her arms and put her aside. "No. It's over, Madelyn. I'm sorry."

He stepped away to the window and gazed out, his broad back turned to her. His manner could not have been colder or more hostile.

Tears blurred her eyes. So much for opening her heart to him. Half of her wanted to sink into a weeping puddle at his feet. The other half wanted to rail at him, to pound her fists on his chest and demand that he see reason.

Turning, she walked out of his bedchamber. She couldn't forget that brief flash of need in his eyes. It gave her a tiny crumb of hope. And an idea for one last desperate campaign to change his mind.

A short while later, after Maddy had dried her tears, she went down to the library to seek out the Earl of Gilmore. She paused in the doorway and spied him at his desk by one of the windows.

He didn't notice her at first. He was concentrating on the notebook that lay open before him. He had a quill in his hand, and as she watched, he dipped the nib into a silver inkwell and made several notations on one of the pages.

She blinked in surprise. It had to be a miracle that she'd come in at this particular moment, for his actions jarred a memory in her mind of watching Nathan signing papers at his warehouse.

Was it possible—

She weaved a hasty path through the tapestry of tables and chairs. All the while, her mind turned the half-formed notion over and over. She had to find out the truth. And if she was wrong, then she'd do as she'd originally intended; she would somehow convince Gilmore to make the first move toward reconciliation.

He looked up at her approach. A slight smile easing his stern features, he waved at a chair with his quill. "Ah, Madelyn. Do sit down. You've returned from your tea with the duke. How did it go? Is His Grace still intent on welcoming you into his family?"

"Yes, Papa," Maddy said, seating herself. "But that isn't why I came here. I apologize for my abruptness, but I thought you should know. Nathan has decided to leave England tomorrow morning."

The earl's face paled. He threw down his quill without a care for placing it neatly in its holder. "What? That can't be. I passed him in the corridor early this morning, and he never spoke a word of it."

"Nevertheless, it's true. His trunk is being packed. He has arranged for passage at dawn." Her fingers clutched at the fabric of her skirt. "I realize this is my fault for lying to him about my background. But I need your help to stop him."

Gilmore pursed his lips. "I'm afraid it has been quite a long time since I was able to prevent Nathan from doing as he wished."

"Please, you have to try. He's your heir." She lowered her voice. "Even if he isn't of your blood."

His nostrils flared. She was afraid she'd overstepped her bounds. Especially when he scowled at her with flinty brown eyes. Under his breath, he bit out, "What exactly did he tell you?"

She kept her tone as hushed as his. "That on his twenty-first birthday, you were angry about having to pay off his gaming debts. That you attributed his depravity to his bad blood. And you revealed that . . . he'd been sired by a footman."

Closing his eyes, Gilmore pinched the bridge of his nose between thumb and forefinger. Half a minute ticked past. When he looked at her again, his expression was bleak. "Good God. I hope you haven't repeated that to anyone."

"No! Of course not. I would never tell a living soul."

He gave her a measuring look. "I suppose you *have* proven your ability to keep a secret. It would behoove you to continue to do so. If word were to slip out, it would harm this family—and Emily's chance of making a good marriage."

"Yes. I believe that's why Nathan has never told anyone, either. He does love his sister." She swallowed, then added, "My lord, forgive me for asking, but . . . is there any possibility that you might be wrong about Nathan's parentage? That you might indeed be his father?"

His expression turned thunderous. "That is most impertinent."

She would not let herself be intimidated. There was too much at stake. "I only ask because when I came in here just now, I noticed you were writing with your left hand. Nathan is left-handed, as well. Is that not an inherited trait? I believe it's rather rare, and to have two of you in one family . . . well, it does make me wonder."

He stared at her. Then he turned his gaze downward, picked up the quill, and stared at it as if lost in thought. Maddy tensely watched him, wondering what he was thinking, if he was at least considering the possibility. It would change everything. If she could soften his rigid convictions about Nathan, there might be a chance . . .

"He looks nothing like me," he growled as if to himself. Then he looked up at her. "It can't be true."

"Does he resemble his mother, then? Or . . . this footman?"

"From birth, Nathan was the image of Camellia, the black hair, the green eyes. Behaved like her, too, cheeky and insolent—" He broke off abruptly. "Why am I telling you this? You have no right to interfere."

"Yes I do. Nathan is my husband. I love him, and I don't want him to leave England. Surely you don't, either."

"As I've already said, I cannot stop him."

She leaned forward, her elbows on the hard surface of the desk. "Will you give up so easily, then? Nathan is still hurting from events that happened in the past. This estrangement between the two of you goes back to his childhood. From what little he's told me, you treated him with a coldness and cruelty that you never showed his elder brother."

Pausing, she braced herself for a rebuke. But when he merely stared at her, she went on, "Besides, even if Nathan is *not* your son by blood, the circumstances of his birth were never his fault. You should have been a loving father to him regardless. He was just a child. He did not deserve to feel the brunt of your hatred."

Maddy fell silent. She tried not to hope too much. The Earl of Gilmore was a proud man who did not suffer intrusions into his private life. He would not be amenable to heeding the frank opinions of an outspoken daughter-in-law. And he would be loath to admit his mistakes.

Yet, to her amazement, a sheen of tears glossed his eyes. He lowered his head into his hands and gave a sigh. He said heavily, "It is difficult for me to say this. But perhaps I *have* wronged him. And I *would* like to mend fences—if it isn't too late."

Relief bathed her heart. She could scarcely believe he'd yielded to her pleading. "It's never too late. If you could speak to him, extend a hand of reconciliation, then perhaps he might be persuaded to—"

"What is this?" Nathan's caustic voice interrupted her from the doorway. "A conspiracy?"

Startled, Maddy turned in her chair to face her husband. He strode purposefully into the library, coming to a stop a short distance from her, his suspicious gaze shifting from her to the earl.

He went on, "I came here looking for Gilmore and who do I find but you, Madelyn, no doubt tattling about my departure. How quickly you've shifted your allegiance, now that you're one of the nobility."

Frowning, the earl rose to his feet. "Don't speak to your wife with such disrespect."

"I learned it from you, *Father*. I grew up hearing your contempt whenever you addressed my mother."

Afraid the exchange would turn into a shouting match, Maddy jumped up from her chair. "Nathan, there's no need to quarrel. He's willing to make peace with you. If only you'll let him."

"Peace on his terms? Absolutely not."

"Please, if you'll just listen to him—"

"It would *please* me if this is the last time he and I ever come face-to-face." A muscle worked in Nathan's jaw. "In fact, I came back to England only because I thought he was dead."

The earl frowned. "Dead? What do you mean?"

"Lady Milford wrote to me that you lay on your deathbed from the smallpox. She sent a second letter a week later, but I never received it. So you see, I came back with the intent of visiting my brother and sister. Had I known you were still alive, I would never have returned."

His coldness made Maddy shiver. It had been many weeks since she'd seen him display such viciousness toward Gilmore. Nathan's revelation appalled her, and she could only imagine its effect on the earl.

Gilmore's face had turned ashen. His breathing harsh and shallow, he stared at Nathan. His lips parted as if he intended to say something.

He suddenly clutched at his chest. While Maddy watched in horror, he uttered a low moan and swayed on his feet. Nathan took a quick step toward him. Too late.

The earl lost his balance. He struck his head with a thud on the edge of the desk and landed in a heap on the floor.

Chapter 23

The following morning, Maddy stepped into the drawing room to receive a visitor. Lady Milford stood by one of the tall windows, gazing out upon the square through the rain-spattered glass. Elegant in a lilac gown and crimped bonnet with ostrich feathers, she turned toward Maddy with a somber expression.

"My dear, I do hope you don't mind the intrusion so early," she said, coming forward to greet Maddy. "I came as soon as I heard the news. How is Lord Gilmore?"

"He's still unresponsive, I'm afraid. He suffered an apoplexy and then hit his head as he fell. The doctor was with him all night. We won't know until the earl awakens if there is any permanent damage."

If indeed he *did* awaken.

Maddy shuddered. She relived the awful nightmare of seeing her father-in-law collapse. She'd hurried for help, then Nathan and a footman had carried the earl upstairs to his bedchamber. The household had come running. The dowager had needed smelling salts, Emily had cried brokenly, and Lady Sophia had given Maddy an accusatory look as if *she* had triggered the attack.

Maddy drew a breath that ended in a choked sob. Her

fingers dug into the blue velvet bag that she'd brought from her bedchamber. Perhaps she *was* guilty. Perhaps she shouldn't have troubled Lord Gilmore by stirring up the past. Perhaps if she'd never sought the earl's counsel, Nathan would never have said such cutting things to him . . .

A comforting arm settled around her back. Lady Milford led her to a chaise. "There, there, my dear. Shall I send for tea?"

Maddy sank down and wiped away a tear. "No, thank you, I'll be all right. It's just that . . . I'm afraid this whole mess may be *my* fault."

Lady Milford sat down beside her, taking hold of her hand and patting it. "Why, what do you mean?"

The story came pouring out. "It all started when Nathan learned that I'd lied to him about my past. He didn't know that I was related to the Duke of Houghton, and he was furious to find out the truth. He'd married me to anger his father, you see . . . Well, anyway, he made arrangements to leave England this morning—"

"Leave! Has he gone, then?"

Maddy shook her head. "He was forced to delay his departure due to the earl's illness. Though I don't know for how long."

When she had visited Gilmore's bedchamber earlier in the morning, Nathan had been there, looking grim-faced and weary. His manner had been remote, so unlike the warm, affectionate husband of the past weeks that she felt utterly dispirited.

"I shall have to have a word with him later," Lady Milford said firmly. "But I still don't see how any of this is *your* fault."

"I went to the earl yesterday and begged his help. I . . . spoke to him quite frankly about how unfairly he'd treated Nathan in the past. Unfortunately, Nathan came upon us, and he accused Gilmore and me of conspiring behind his back. Then he told Gilmore he'd never have returned to England had he known the earl was still alive."

Lady Milford pursed her lips. "Ah, yes, that letter. You cannot imagine how many times I've wished that I'd refrained from sending it. The news that his father lay on his deathbed was premature. Gilmore recovered, and the smallpox spread to Nathan's brother and sister. So I wrote a second letter, but apparently he never received it."

Maddy tried to look on the bright side. "Well, he ought to have come back to England anyway. And he should stay now, too. I've told him so, but he refuses to listen."

"Now, now, you mustn't fret, my dear. It truly isn't your fault. One could just as easily blame it on the letter that *I* sent. And Nathan should never have uttered such a dreadful remark to his father."

But the earl wasn't his father, or least they couldn't be certain. Maddy kept silent about that part. She felt honorbound by her vow to Gilmore to guard the secret of Nathan's parentage.

"I mustn't keep you," Lady Milford said, rising to her feet. "I shall return in a day or so. If Nathan attempts to leave London, pray tell him he is not to do so without speaking to me first."

"Of course, my lady."

As Maddy stood up, she remembered the blue velvet bag in her lap. It contained the garnet dancing slippers. She handed the bag to Lady Milford. "I nearly forgot. You lent these shoes to me when we first met. I thought it best I returned them."

A mysterious gleam entered Lady Milford's violet eyes. "I'm pleased you were able to make good use of them. And never fear, all will be well soon, you'll see."

Maddy smiled wanly, though she knew all would *not* be well. She had returned the shoes because she'd come to a decision. She would not be going to any more parties or balls. If the earl recovered, and if there was any hope of Nathan making amends with him, then she must not be a thorn in their sides.

It was time that *she* left Gilmore House—not Nathan.

The combination of an overcast day and the closed draperies rendered the sickroom dim and shadowed. On the bedside table, a single candle cast a meager light on the man lying beneath the bedcovers. His pitted features were pale, and if not for the slight rise and fall of his chest, Nate would have thought him dead.

Pacing the floor, he kept a watch on the earl. Gilmore lay unmoving, as he'd been all night and into the afternoon. It was unclear yet if he'd been rendered insensible by the attack of apoplexy, or if it was from the purplish knot on his forehead from his fall. The doctor had left to tend to other patients, with instructions to summon him if there was any change. Nate was here alone; he'd sent his grandmother and sister to rest since they'd all lost sleep the previous night.

Nate himself had dozed in the chair by the fire. He hadn't left this room except to change his rumpled clothing and to send a message to the docks. He'd felt strangely compelled to remain at his father's side.

His father.

His steps faltered. Strange, how he still caught himself thinking of Gilmore as his father, even though he'd sworn not to do so. Strange, too, that he could feel dread in his gut at the possibility of the man's demise. It wasn't just guilt over his own harsh words, either. Somehow, in the past few weeks, without knowing quite how it had happened, Nate had arrived at an uneasy truce with the earl.

Perhaps it had been Madelyn's influence, but as the season progressed, he and his father had behaved civilly toward one another. They had ceased shouting at each

other—at least until yesterday when Nate's angry tirade
had caused the earl's collapse.

According to the doctor, the bout with smallpox had
weakened Gilmore's heart. Nate had had no inkling his
father was anything but hale and fit. Or perhaps that wasn't
quite true. On the day he had returned here with Madelyn
as his bride, Grandmamma had alluded to the earl's ill
health. But at the time, Nate hadn't paid much heed. He'd
been too intent on his revenge.

He paced to the bedside table and flattened his hands
on the surface, squeezing his eyes shut. Yesterday, he had
gone to the library for the purpose of informing Gilmore
of his departure. Then he'd spied Madelyn talking earnestly with the earl.

Nate had come unhinged at the notion of the two of
them joining forces. Seeing them chatting like friends il-
lustrated everything that had gone wrong with his plan.
She was supposed to be his vehicle for vengeance, but
overnight she had become an acceptable confidante to his
father. And Nate had not been able to contain his fury . . .

*Had I known you were still alive, I would never have
returned.*

Those words had been corrosive, juvenile, and utterly
needless. There had been no real reason to tell Gilmore
about Lady Milford's letter. Nate already had decided to
deny the man a grandson. Yet that hadn't been enough to
satisfy his driving need to punish the man.

How had he become so bitter? So callous? He had never
felt more chained by the shackles of the past. On top of
that, he'd felt betrayed to think that Madelyn had shifted
her loyalty from him to his father.

I love you—enough for both of us.

His chest tightened at the memory of her speaking those
words, even though he didn't believe them. After her de-
ception about her noble background, he couldn't trust any-

thing she said. If she truly loved him, she wouldn't have lied . . .

A small rustling noise interrupted his morbid thoughts. Then a low moan came from the bed.

He whipped up his head. Jolted, he realized that Gilmore was awake, his eyes halfway open. His fingers grasped convulsively at the gold-embroidered coverlet.

Nate leaned over him, bracing his hands on the mattress. "Can you speak, Father? Do you know me?"

The earl frowned, his eyelids straining as if he were trying to focus. His lips parted. In a dry, guttural tone, he whispered, "Na . . . than."

He was thirsty. Of course he would be thirsty after being unconscious for nearly twenty-four hours. "Would you like a drink?"

Without waiting for an answer, Nate grabbed the pitcher on the bedside table and sloshed water into a glass. He wasn't usually so clumsy. How absurd that his hands should be trembling.

He slid his arm beneath his father's upper back and helped him sit up to take a few sips. Some of it dribbled down his chin. After a moment, Gilmore weakly waved away the glass.

Nate laid him back down on the pillows. "I'll notify the doctor that you've awakened. He'll want to know straightaway."

Gilmore grabbed hold of his hand. "Don't . . . go."

His father's grip was weak. Nate could have easily pulled away. But he didn't. He couldn't remember the last time the earl had held his hand. If ever. "I'll be right back. It will only take a moment."

"I meant . . . don't leave . . . England. We have to . . . talk. I'm sorry . . . I've been wrong . . ." Gilmore stopped, breathing heavily, as if the effort had exhausted him.

Nate stood transfixed. Gilmore had always ruled this

house with an iron fist. He'd never apologized for anything. And what did he mean by "wrong"?

Nate burned to know. At the same time, it could be dangerous to overtire the man. "Quiet now," he said. "We can talk tomorrow if you're feeling better."

Gilmore gave a slight nod, then closed his eyes again. His fingers relaxed and fell back onto the coverlet. Though his hand was now free, Nate remained standing at the bedside, gazing down at his father as Madelyn's words of the previous day sprang into his mind.

I understand why revenge has ruled your life for so long, Nathan. But it isn't good for you. I do think you ought to try to make peace with Gilmore instead of running away again.

Those words had infuriated him, and they still rankled now. She had labeled him a coward for wanting to live his life free of his father's poison. She didn't understand—she *couldn't* understand what it was like to grow up under this man's thumb. Leaving England to pursue his business interests didn't constitute *running away*.

Or did it?

Blast it, he didn't see how he could make peace with his father after all these years. Too much had happened. The past could not be changed. He had never known any affection from this man. Nor did he desire any.

To prove Madelyn wrong, however, he would give Gilmore a chance to speak his mind. Tomorrow. He could delay his departure for a few more days until he was certain of the earl's recovery.

But he had no intention of remaining in London any longer than necessary.

Chapter 24

The following afternoon, Nate was relieved to see that Gilmore felt able to sit up in bed. The dowager spooned broth into him, coaxing him to take more, and Nate found it somewhat amusing to see his grandmother scold her middle-aged son as if he were a wayward child. Then Gilmore sent his mother out of the room so that he and Nate could have a brief, though extremely startling, talk.

Afterward, Nate left the sickroom and walked aimlessly down the corridor. He needed time alone to think, to absorb the revelations he'd just heard. Gilmore had admitted he couldn't be absolutely certain that Nate was *not* his son, even though Nate's mother had been caught in bed with one of the footmen.

Nate felt stunned, his thoughts in a jumble. He had adored his free-spirited mother. But now, as a married man himself, he could see her through Gilmore's eyes, a wayward wife who'd flirted with so many men that her husband had had reason to doubt the paternity of her three children.

David and Emily had resembled the earl's side of the family. Only Nate had taken after his mother. Since he had been the child most like her, rebellious and wild, he had borne the brunt of the earl's wrath. For that, Gilmore had apologized. He'd expressed regret for having failed as a father. Judging by the tears in his eyes, his remorse had been sincere.

It was too much for Nate to take in all at once.

Nevertheless, he understood his father's anger now. He himself had experienced the choking tentacles of jealousy. The thought of Madelyn with another man made him livid. He could no longer fool himself, either, that it was due to the fact that he'd paid her to marry him. Rather, they had become close friends as well as lovers.

Was it any wonder that her lie still stung?

Trying to sort through the tangled state of his emotions, he found himself standing outside Madelyn's bedchamber. He could hear muffled voices inside. An instinctive impulse had brought him here. He felt the urge to tell her about the conversation, to ask her opinion on those earth-shaking disclosures.

But he was supposed to stay away from his wife. For all intents and purposes, their marriage was over. They would go their separate ways very soon. It was best to make a clean break and not put himself through the torture of seeing her again.

As he was turning away, however, the door opened. His sister walked partway out, then stopped. Clad in a leaf-green gown with a matching hat, she wore the jade dragon necklace he'd given to her.

Her face glowed with a smile. Her skin had been made up skillfully so that her pockmarks were barely visible. "Nathan! I'm so glad to see you. How is Papa?"

"Much better today." Nate looked beyond her and his heart lurched at the sight of Madelyn, her eyes very blue and solemn inside the frame of a straw bonnet. "Though I believe he intends to take a nap. Were you going out?"

"Lord Theo invited me on a walk around the square,

and Madelyn is coming along as chaperone." Emily paused, her face falling. "But perhaps you wish to speak to her?"

Nate hid his disappointment. "It's quite all right. It can wait until another time."

"Actually," Madelyn said, stepping forward, "I've a matter of some importance to discuss with you, Nathan. Emily, I'm sure it would be fine for you to go on your walk with Theo. Just stay in the square and don't go anywhere else. I'll join you shortly."

Emily beamed. "Thank you!"

As his sister scurried down the corridor, Nate turned his gaze to his wife. Her beauty erased all other thought from his mind. She looked delectable in a sky-blue gown with a form-fitting bodice that hugged her bosom and waist. He felt a powerful desire to wrap her in his arms and taste the sweetness of her lips. The painful craving clutched at his insides. But her air of cool reserve held him at bay.

She stepped back to allow him entry, untying the ribbons of her bonnet and placing the hat on a chair. He hungrily watched her graceful movements as she smoothed her hair and then turned to face him, her fingers clasped at her waist.

"Has the earl spoken to you yet?" she asked in a formal tone.

"Just now. That's why I came here." All of his muddled thoughts returned. "I don't know quite what to think about what he said to me. You see, he admitted that even though my mother had affairs, he has no absolute proof that he isn't my father. Do you realize what that means, Madelyn? I could actually *be* his son."

The revelation shook Nate. It still hadn't quite sunk in. He felt too numb to sort out if he should be elated or angry.

She smiled slightly. "I'm glad to hear it. I hope he apologized for treating you so coldly as a child."

"Yes, he did." Nate trudged back and forth, feeling not quite so burdened anymore by all those years of pain and unhappiness. "He said . . . I'd reminded him of my mother, and he didn't want me to turn out like her. He also confessed to taking out his anger at her on me. The trouble is, I don't see how I can forget the past with a snap of the fingers."

"You'll have to give it time. I imagine it will be hard for the earl, too. He has to live with the memory of what he did to you."

Nate wasn't ready yet to forgive Gilmore. How much time would it take? If he stayed in London for a while, could he resolve his differences with Madelyn, too? Perhaps right now . . .

"Forgive me for going on," he said. "You wished to speak to me?"

She glanced away, her secretive gaze going to the bed, as if she were remembering the many happy hours they'd spent there, wrapped in each other's arms. Heat tightened his groin. Did she mean to beseech him again to restore their marriage? To propose that they make love?

By God, he didn't think he could resist her this time. And why should he? After the talk with Gilmore today, the notion of denying him a grandson no longer seemed of such vital importance.

She returned her gaze to him. "Nathan, I've decided it's best that *I* leave Gilmore House, not you."

Her statement struck like a blow to his gut. It knocked the breath right out of him. He couldn't speak, he could only gawk at her in shock.

"That way," she continued, "you'll be able to remain here for a time and settle things with your father. You don't love me, and my presence would only serve as a reminder that you used me to take revenge on him."

You don't love me. Nate wanted to deny her statement, but the words stuck in his throat. He didn't believe in love. It was an invention of poets and playwrights to put a pretty gloss on raw sexual passion.

Nevertheless, he didn't want Madelyn to go. This house wouldn't be the same without her. He liked talking to her over the breakfast table, escorting her to parties, visiting her bedchamber at night. Yet they'd made a business arrangement. They'd agreed to part company once she'd fulfilled her purpose of being an embarrassment to his father.

"Where would you go?" he asked hoarsely. "To your grandfather?"

"No. Perhaps . . . back to the theater."

"The theater?" Disbelief pierced him, and he took an angry step toward her. "Absolutely not. My wife will not perform on a public stage. It's out of the question. I'll contact my banker in the morning. He'll arrange for you to collect your stipend."

"I won't accept it," she said quietly. "I don't want your money anymore, Nathan. I should never have entered into this devil's bargain in the first place." She tugged the diamond ring off her finger and held it out to him. "Here. You may have this back, too."

"What the devil—That ring was your wedding gift. It belongs to you!"

"I'm not taking it." Gliding to the bedside table, she placed it there, the square-cut gemstone glinting in the light from the window. "I won't take anything of value."

Staring at her, he rubbed the back of his neck. She'd gone stark, raving mad. He'd never seen her this way— except perhaps on the night they'd met when she'd been adamant about not considering his bid in the auction. "Madelyn, this is absurd. How will you live? What about your shop? You'll need the funds to open it."

"I'll work and save by myself." She made a harsh sound in her throat. "But I don't expect you to understand that. The duke, too, thinks my affections can be bought with the promise of an inheritance."

Nate frowned in surprise. "Houghton is adding you to his will?"

She nodded stiffly. "I'm to be given an amount equal to that of my cousins. I tried to refuse the duke, but he wouldn't listen. You nobles are all alike, using money to control people." With that, Madelyn turned away to stare out the window. "I think you had better go now."

Nate felt the powerful urge to take her by the arms and shake the sense back into her. No, he wanted to coax her into bed and persuade her out of this irrational scheme. He wanted to plant his child in her and bind her to him forever.

But he had sworn not to do that. He was supposed to be angry with her for lying to him about her noble blood. Dammit, he didn't know what he felt anymore. Except that he desperately wanted her to stay.

Caught up in painful turmoil, he stalked out of her bed-chamber. How bitterly ironic that the tables had been turned. She was doing to him what he'd intended to do to her—walk away from their marriage without a backward glance. And he didn't know how to stop her.

Maddy ordered a dinner tray in her bedchamber. With such pain in her heart, she preferred not to see anyone. Even Gertie had detected her gloomy mood and wisely left her alone to brood.

Sitting at a table by the window and gazing out at the

pink streaks of dusk in the evening sky, Maddy trailed the tines of her fork through the remains of her roast beef and potatoes. She told herself to be happy for Nathan. He and his father had taken the first important step toward making amends. It appeared as though their lifelong rift finally might have a chance to heal.

Unlike the rift between her and her husband.

Her hand slipped downward to cradle her womb. She would have to tell Nathan about the baby eventually. But not until after she'd moved away from here. He would only use their unborn child as leverage to force her to remain under his control until *he* decided to leave.

She could not bear to live at Gilmore House so long as he was here. Nathan didn't love her. To him, she was nothing more than a possession purchased at auction. That was why she'd refused his stipend.

In retrospect, though, Maddy knew she would have to accept a small sum of money, perhaps from her grandfather or from the earl. Nathan was right; it was impossible for her to return to the stage. That life was behind her. She couldn't bring shame down on his family when she'd come to love them. Nor would it be fair to raise her child in poverty. If it was a boy, he would be the Earl of Gilmore someday.

She forced herself to face reality. Yes, it would be selfish and prideful to deny her son or daughter the benefits of living at Gilmore House. But she still couldn't remain here at the moment. She would leave for now and then return only after her husband left England.

A knock sounded on the door. Her heart tripped over a beat. Could it be Nathan again?

Abandoning her half-eaten dinner, Maddy arose from the table. She smoothed back her hair and brushed a few crumbs from her skirt. Then she opened the door.

To her relief or disappointment—she couldn't decide which—a footman stood there holding a silver salver. On it lay a folded note. "For you, my lady."

Surprised, she picked it up. Only her first name was written on the outside—and it was misspelled. "Madeline."

She thanked the servant, then closed the door. Breaking the unmarked red seal, she unfolded the paper and read the message. "You must come outside to the square at once. I can't find my necklace. I must have lost it on my walk with Theo this afternoon. Pray don't tell anyone, for Nathan will be angry at my carelessness. Please hurry! Emily."

Maddy frowned. Why hadn't Emily come here herself on her way outside? Why take the time to pen a note? Unless she had written it downstairs in a hurry. Whatever the reason, the girl should not have ventured outside by herself when it was nearly nighttime. Even in Mayfair, footpads and other ruffians could be lurking in the shadows.

Maddy dropped the note on the bed. She threw a fringed paisley shawl over her shoulders and grabbed a small candle lamp, the flame flickering inside its glass chimney. Then she hastened out the door.

The house was silent as she went down the long corridor. The dowager and Lady Sophia, along with Nathan, were likely visiting Lord Gilmore in his chambers. A wretched despondency tugged at Maddy. How she longed to be in there with the family. She had grown especially fond of the earl, for beneath his gruff exterior, he had proven himself to be a good man who could admit when he was wrong.

Her footsteps echoed as she descended the grand staircase to the entrance hall. Because the hour was late and the family was at home, no footman stood on duty. She opened the door and slipped outside.

Maddy paused on the curbstone and scanned the large

square. At just past nine o'clock, the park was deserted. Although a few last feathers of pink brushed the horizon, dense shadows gathered beneath the plane trees. The deep gloom prevented her from spotting Emily.

Where was she?

Perhaps she'd gone to the far side of the square, where clumps of overgrown rhododendrons crouched like sentinels. She might be bending down, searching the ground for the necklace. But there was barely enough light left to see. Had the foolish girl not brought a candle?

A cold breeze snaked down her spine and Maddy shivered. The night air was chilly. She started across the street, vowing to give her sister-in-law a sound scolding for taking such a risk.

From out of nowhere, a black carriage rattled toward her, the clip-clopping of the horses loud on the cobblestones. She scurried quickly toward the square. Even as she reached the other side of the street, the vehicle veered straight at her.

Gripping the lamp, she backed up to the low iron railing that surrounded the little park. The closed carriage drew to a stop just ahead of her. A burly coachman clad in black sat hunched on the high seat. If it was a visitor for a neighbor, why hadn't he drawn up closer to the houses?

The carriage door opened. A man in a hooded cloak stepped out. She frowned at him, realizing in alarm that a demimask obscured his upper face.

He sprang straight at her.

Terror leaped inside her. Even as she parted her lips to scream, his hand clamped a cloth over her mouth. A sickeningly sweet smell filled her senses. In an instant, the world melted away into darkness.

Chapter 25

Nate had been reading to his father by the light from a branch of candles. He quietly put down the copy of Alexander Pope's translation of the *Odyssey*. The earl had fallen asleep, his chest rising and falling beneath the coverlet. Aside from the knot on his forehead, he looked much better tonight, with natural color in his face rather than that ghastly paleness.

Nearby, Emily sat on a hassock, absently fingering the jade dragon of her necklace as she watched their father. A warm softness squeezed Nathan's heart. He liked knowing that she might very well be his full-fledged sister. Maybe it shouldn't matter—yet it did.

Her lips parted in a yawn that she tried to stifle with her hand.

"You're tired," Nathan whispered. "It must be all that fresh air from your walk with Theo. Go to bed before you keel over."

Emily smiled, but before she could reply, a light rapping sounded in the room. He glanced up sharply to see the door opening. It was past ten by the mantel clock and the dowager had already retired for the night, as had Sophia.

Could it be Madelyn? He hoped so. He'd botched their earlier talk. He should have been more persuasive in convincing her to stay. He should have coaxed her . . .

But it was Madelyn's stout maidservant who stepped into the bedchamber. Gertie beckoned urgently to him. It was such an odd gesture for a servant that he knew at once something was amiss.

He followed her out into the corridor. "What is it?"

Her plain features were taut with worry. " 'Tis me mistress—oh, milord, I fear she's gone."

Shock jolted him. He hadn't expected Madelyn to depart so swiftly. "What do you mean, gone?"

"This was on her bed just now. Maybe I shouldn'ta read it, but 'tis glad I am that I did."

Gertie held out a paper, and Nate grabbed it. Scanning the brief message, he felt an icy chill seep into his bones. Emily couldn't have written this note. She'd kept vigil in the sickroom with him for the past several hours.

Still, he had to make certain.

He stepped back into the earl's bedchamber and motioned to his sister. She trudged out, her hazel eyes impish. "All right, all right. I'll go to bed. You needn't be so dictatorial—"

"Did you write this?" he demanded.

She read the note he thrust at her, and her smile vanished. "No! I never lost my necklace. I'm wearing it." Her hand went to the jade dragon at her throat. "And this isn't even my penmanship. What is the meaning of this?"

Nate didn't want her fretting. Nor did he wish to raise a hue and cry that could be damaging to Madelyn. "Never you mind. It's likely just a prank. You'll leave the matter to me."

With that, he went striding down the staircase, his quick steps sharp and echoing in the entrance hall. Horrible images of her possible fate tormented him. Had Madelyn been attacked out in the square? If she'd been struck over the head, she might be lying in the shadows somewhere, hidden from the view of any passersby.

He threw open the front door and plunged out into the night. The note had alluded to the time being nearly dark. Twilight had been an hour ago.

Driven by fear, he dashed across the street. All the while he scanned the darkened park for any sign of her. Despite the star-studded black sky, it was impossible to see much of anything in the murky gloom beneath the trees. He might have to organize a search party—

Then he saw it. The glitter of broken glass.

Dropping down on his haunches, he spied a lamp lying on the ground, the chimney shattered, the candle extinguished. He recognized it straightaway. That lamp usually sat on Madelyn's bedside table.

Dread knotted his insides. If she'd dropped the lamp, someone must have been lying in wait to grab her. Where was she? He couldn't see her anywhere in the darkness. Had she been abducted?

Taken somewhere to be misused—or even murdered?

A sudden certainty gripped him. He could think of no other logical explanation for someone to have concocted the elaborate scheme of a forged note in order to lure her out here.

But who? Why?

In a fit of anguished fury, Nate sprang to his feet. Only one name stood out in his mind. One man who surely resented her now that she'd been named heiress. Her cousin, Alfred, Lord Dunham.

Where the devil would he have taken her?

Where was she?

Her brain groggy, Maddy opened her eyes and blinked at

her dark surroundings. She was seated in a straight-backed chair, her hands tied behind her back. The faint light from an uncurtained window revealed a shadowy bedchamber. She could discern a four-poster bed along with a few other black lumps of furniture. The rug had been rolled up in a corner and a smell of mustiness pervaded the air as if the room had been closed up for a long time.

Memories flooded her mind. The carriage coming straight at her. The masked man jumping out and seizing her. He had pressed a smelly cloth to her face. Then everything had gone dark.

Now, a rhythmic rumbling noise in the distance caught her attention. She cocked her head in puzzlement. It sounded like waves crashing onto rocks. As a child, she had visited the seashore . . .

Horror seeped into her. Dear God, she was no longer in London. The coast lay many hours distant. Nathan would never find her here.

Her heartbeat raced and her body trembled. She jerked frantically at her bonds to no avail. If only this were a bad dream. If only she could close her eyes and wake up in her bed at Gilmore House . . .

Maddy took several deep breaths to calm herself. Succumbing to panic wouldn't help matters. She must keep her wits about her and formulate a plan for escape. Surely her captor would show himself soon.

Who was he? Who could have planned such an abduction?

A name pushed its way into her beleaguered mind. Loath to believe it, she considered the matter from all angles. Truly, there could be no other explanation . . .

Her senses sprang to the alert. Amid the muffled crashing of the waves, the tramp of footsteps approached from out in the corridor. Maddy braced herself, her gaze glued to the dark outline of the door. A strip of faint light appeared on the floor. Then the door swung open and two men stepped into the bedchamber.

The burly stranger in the rear held a lantern that illuminated his coarse, whiskered features and thick eyebrows. The glow also fell upon his leader's flaxen hair and narrow, aristocratic face.

Maddy's insides squeezed. Just as she'd suspected, the villain was her cousin Alfred. And he surely meant her grave harm.

He sauntered forward to stand in front of her. A sly smile of triumph tilted his lips. "My dearest Madelyn. It's good to see you're finally awake."

The urge to spit in his face boiled up inside her. But that would be foolish. He'd strike back, and with her hands bound, she'd be unable to defend herself. Or her baby. She would have a better chance of escape if she used her acting talent to play the meek, frightened female.

She looked up at him fearfully, her lower lip quivering. "Lord Dunham! I—I don't understand. Why am I tied to this chair? Was it *you* who brought me here?"

"Of course it was me, you fool. You didn't think I'd let you get away with stealing my inheritance, did you?" Reaching inside his coat, he drew out a small pistol and caressed the barrel.

Maddy gasped in true alarm. "Please don't shoot! As I told you before, I don't want the money. I mean that!"

"Stop your sniveling." Grinning at her distress, he lowered the pistol. "I want you to remember who's in charge here, for you'll live if you cooperate. The boat should arrive soon."

"Boat?"

"I'm sending you somewhere far away so that you can't ever claim your inheritance. Pidgeon will accompany you."

The brute with the lantern leered at her.

Alarm surged in Maddy again, though she struggled to keep her expression cowed. Alfred was lying to her. He would never allow her to survive. He'd never risk the chance of her returning. He'd probably instructed Pidgeon to sail far offshore and dump her into the cold black sea.

"Where—where are we?" she asked. "What time is it?"

"It's nearly dawn. We're at a small estate our grandfather owns on the Sussex coast." Alfred's face twisted in a sneer. "Too bad you'll never inherit it—or any of his many other holdings."

Maddy struggled to think. Her cousin was chillingly intent on his plot to get rid of her. She couldn't expect help from Nathan, either. Even if he realized she'd been abducted, he couldn't possibly know where to find her. She was utterly on her own.

Then the perfect solution struck her. It might also act as a deterrent to Alfred abusing her in any way. "You needn't threaten me," she said. "I'll gladly sign over my portion of the inheritance to you."

"What? Don't be absurd."

"I assure you, I'm quite sincere. Nathan has given me more than enough funds. Anyway, I don't want blood money from the duke after the terrible way he treated my mother."

"You can't mean that."

"I do, indeed. And I would be pleased to sign a legal paper to that effect." Striving for a look of sincerity, she leaned toward him. "You see, this would work out even better for you. As of now, the inheritance is split three ways. If I disappear, you and Theo will each have a half share again. But if I stay and sign over my portion to you, then you shall receive two-thirds."

One of Alfred's blond eyebrows arched. His pale blue eyes shifted away from her as if he were weighing all the ramifications. Greed showed plainly in his look of concentration. The inheritance must be a tremendous amount of money, indeed.

He swung his attention back to her. "I know your game. You're planning to tell Rowley that I abducted you. He'll come after me and have the agreement overturned."

"No! Nathan and I have quarreled. I told him I'm leaving Gilmore House. He probably doesn't even realize that I'm gone." This time, she didn't have to pretend anguish. Even if Gertie had informed him she was missing, he was likely to assume that Maddy had moved out early.

Alfred shoved the pistol back into his coat. He prowled back and forth, his hands on his hips. "I don't see how this could be legal."

"Why not?" she countered. "We must return to London posthaste. Surely we can be there by late morning. The moment your solicitor draws up the papers, I *will* sign them, I promise."

Her cousin stared intently at her another moment. She held his gaze, hoping and praying he would agree to her plan. "All right, then," he said. "But I'll fetch the papers and bring them here. Pidgeon can watch you during my absence."

Maddy drew in a searing breath. As she glanced at the guard with the lantern, he smirked at her, his curled-back lips revealing several blackened gaps in his teeth. Dear heavens, she couldn't remain here at the mercy of this cold-blooded brute.

But Alfred was already starting toward the door.

"Wait, please!" she begged. "If you insist upon leaving me here, then pray be so kind as to untie me. My arms are quite numb, and by the time you return, I won't be able to sign anything."

To her great relief, Alfred jerked his head at Pidgeon, who lumbered over to unbind her. As the ropes fell away, she rubbed her wrists as if they pained her. She slumped in the chair and bowed her head dejectedly, wanting both men to view her as weak and beaten.

The door closed. A key rattled in the lock. Two sets of male footsteps stomped away.

Maddy jumped up from the chair. She had to find a way out. She first tried the door in case the lock hadn't fully engaged. But the latch refused to budge. Whirling around, she darted to the window.

To her frustration, the casement was stuck. She jerked on it numerous times, hitting the latch with the heel of her hand, until finally the window opened to a loud creaking of hinges. She froze, glancing back at the shadowed door. Luckily, no footsteps came running.

Pushing the window all the way open, Maddy leaned out onto the stone ledge. The crashing of the waves sounded much louder now. A chilly wind blew at her face. The moon had risen to scatter a thousand diamonds over the vast blackness of the water.

Looking down, she blinked in dismay.

The house perched on the edge of a cliff. It was a long drop to the water's edge, where the surf collided with a great pile of rocks. The foamy waves hissed and growled like a beast waiting to swallow her.

She was trapped. Escape seemed impossible. Yet what other choice did she have? If she stayed in this bedchamber, Pidgeon might very well come back and force himself on her. She had no guarantee, either, that once she'd signed the agreement, Alfred would let her go.

Maddy forced herself to look down again at the steep slope. She realized her mistake in thinking the house was situated on the very edge. A narrow verge of grass lay two stories below. From it, a hardy tree had grown up to hug the stone wall, its roots sunk into the side of the cliff.

Leaning out, she could easily touch one of the stout branches. She had climbed plenty of trees as a child. She also had clambered like a monkey over stage sets. Surely this should be no different. At least not much.

Maddy quickly prepared herself. She reached beneath her gown to untie her petticoats, kicking them aside. Freed of that bulk, she placed a stool beneath the window and scrambled up onto the ledge.

Her courage nearly failed her as she glanced down at the long drop. Instead, she focused her steely gaze on the tree and stepped to the end of the ledge. Her palms felt damp. A cold breeze nipped at her skin and tugged at her hair, sending loose tendrils blowing around her face.

It was now or never.

Whispering a prayer, she stepped out onto the branch. It swayed beneath her weight and her fingers scrabbled at the bark of an upper branch. Bit by bit, she inched toward the trunk. Luckily, her shoes were soft-soled to prevent slippage. Several times, she had to stop to yank her skirt free from a twig or another protrusion. Finally arriving at the trunk, she felt her way down, branch by branch.

Despite her best efforts, however, she half slid down the last section, her arms hugging the tree. As her toes met the earth, a sense of triumph filled her and she eased her grip. She'd made it!

Abruptly, the sandy soil began to crumble beneath her feet and she grabbed at the trunk again. Her heart thumped wildly. Hearing the waves booming onto the rocks below, she feared to let go. But she couldn't cling forever. Taking a fortifying breath, she edged over to the stone wall and then crept toward the corner of the house.

At last she emerged onto a wider, grassy stretch. Maddy allowed herself a moment to recover. Her cheeks stung from several scrapes and her nerves felt battered. Setting her hand over her belly, she gave thanks to God Almighty that she and her baby had survived the first hurdle.

Now, she just had to find her way back to London.

She mustn't linger, either. The moment Pidgeon discovered her absence, he would mount a search. He looked a rather dull-witted sort, but it wouldn't take a genius to realize she'd escaped out the window.

After readjusting her gown, Maddy hastened along the side of the house. Scrubby bushes impeded her progress and the darkness made it difficult to keep from stumbling on stones or dips in the ground. There must be a lane ahead. She'd follow it to the main road. After that, she'd have to use her wits to convince someone to return her to the city.

Nearing the front of the house, however, she heard something over the roar of the waves. Voices.

She crept forward and peeked around the corner. Two shadowy figures loomed in the darkness a short distance away. Her eyes widened on Alfred's wiry form standing on the graveled drive. He appeared to be giving orders to Pidgeon, who held the team of two horses.

Maddy had imagined her cousin would already be on his way to London. It seemed a lifetime since he'd left the bedchamber. But perhaps no more than fifteen minutes had passed. Since the horses would have been stabled for the night, it must have taken Pidgeon that long to attach the harness and hitch the team.

His dark cloak flaring, Alfred bounded up onto the high seat of the carriage. He grabbed the reins and snapped them. The wheels rattled as the horses went trotting down the drive. Pidgeon clomped back up to the porch and vanished inside the house.

Knowing that the servant might go upstairs and discover her gone, Maddy lost no time in hurrying after Alfred. She kept parallel to the drive while staying out of sight beneath the cover of the trees. The thorny underbrush snagged her skirts. Scarcely able to see her way through the gloom, she stumbled more than once on some invisible obstacle.

The damp sea air made her shiver. Until this moment, fear and determination had kept her warm, but now that she'd made her escape and felt somewhat safe, the full effect of the night chill enveloped her. She crossed her arms, her teeth chattering. She'd cheerfully sign away her inheritance for a thick, warm cloak.

Instead, she would just have to walk briskly to keep herself warm.

Maddy had no sooner formed that thought than a sound came from somewhere ahead of her. A shout.

No, she had to be mistaken. It must have been the hoot of an owl or the distant howl of a dog. Then she heard it again. This time, it sounded distinctly human and definitely masculine.

Prudently keeping to the trees, she rounded a bend in the lane. The sight ahead made her stop dead in her tracks. Moonlight bathed Alfred's carriage with its team of horses at the side of the road. Another horse, riderless, cropped the grasses alongside a ditch.

In the middle of the lane, two men grappled with each other. Alfred's flaxen hair gleamed in the darkness. As he tried to scramble away, his assailant lunged at him, catching his legs and knocking him down. A glimmer of moonlight lit the newcomer's resolute face.

Maddy stared in wide-eyed, glorious astonishment. "Nathan!"

Chapter 26

Neither man heard her; they were too intent on their battle. She had to help Nathan. Seeing a stout branch lying on the ground, she snatched it up and hastened toward the combatants.

The smack of punches filled the air. Both men taunted each other in between gasps and strikes. They parried and struck.

Maddy brandished the stick like a sword. But she couldn't find an opening. They were too close together and she feared to hit her husband by mistake.

Then Alfred kicked him hard in the shins. As Nathan crouched in reflexive pain, her cousin stepped away and reached inside his cloak.

Terror galvanized her. "Nathan, watch out! He has a pistol!"

In the next instant, a shot rang out. Her husband stumbled backward and fell to the ground in a crumpled heap. Horrified, she started toward him.

But Alfred was getting away.

Her cousin lurched toward the carriage and pulled himself up onto the coachman's perch. A savage rage fueled Maddy. If he'd killed Nathan, by heavens, he would pay!

The branch upraised, she ran toward Alfred. He fumbled for the reins. As she swung out at him, the team abruptly danced toward her.

Instead of hitting Alfred's leg, as she'd intended, her makeshift weapon glanced off the hindquarters of the nearest horse. The animal squealed and then charged forward. The carriage traveled for only a few yards before it careened into a ditch and tilted to the side.

Alfred howled as he slid off the high seat and vanished from sight. She heard a thud as he struck the ground on the other side.

The carriage leaned at a crooked angle, one set of wheels in the ditch. No longer able to pull the disabled vehicle, the pair of horses stopped in place. They snorted in alarm, their front hooves pawing the ground, but appeared otherwise unharmed.

Dropping the stick, Maddy dashed around the carriage to see her cousin sprawled unmoving in the shadows a few feet away. That was close enough for her. She cared nothing for his fate.

Only Nathan's.

Running toward her husband, she saw to her great relief that he was pushing himself into an upright position in the road. She dropped to her knees beside him, reaching out to caress his whisker-roughened jaw.

"Nathan, darling! Are you all right? When you fell, I feared you were dead!"

In the pale moonlight, his face was twisted with pain. "Damn bullet ploughed a furrow in my arm. But I'll survive. And Dunham? I saw him take a tumble."

"He's lying over there," she said shakily. "I—I didn't look very closely at him."

"I'd better go see, then. Lest he come to his senses and draw another pistol."

She gently touched his upper arm and her fingertips came away sticky. With her hand on his shoulder, she stopped him from rising to his feet. "Don't move! You're bleeding."

"It's merely a scratch."

"Then at least let me bind it."

With trembling fingers, she untied his cravat to use as a bandage, the white folds barely visible in the shadows. He didn't protest. At least not until she began to wrap the strip of linen around the wound, right over his sleeve.

He sucked in a breath through his teeth. "Have a care!"

"It has to be tight or it won't stop the bleeding. And you're to see a doctor as soon as possible!"

Nathan gave a low chuckle. "Well, I'm glad you don't wish me dead, anyway, after the way we parted."

Her fingers froze on the binding. Maddy glanced at his moonlit features, realizing she'd forgotten all about their estrangement. It seemed a lifetime ago that she'd informed him of her plan to leave Gilmore House. A lifetime since she'd told him she loved him and he had not returned those tender words. Yet he had come after her, anyway. He'd cared enough to ride for hours through the night just to rescue her.

She didn't dare let herself hope he had changed.

Too shaken at the moment to contemplate their future, she tied off the bandage. "How in the world did you find me?"

"I'll tell you in a moment. First I'll see about Dunham."

Nathan sprang to his feet, wobbled a step or two, then caught his balance and paced across the road to the lop-sided carriage. As he vanished from sight, Maddy arose, too, following cautiously in his wake.

Her arms crossed to subdue her shivering, she watched as he knelt down and leaned over her cousin. A sick apprehension stirred inside her. There was something about Alfred's stillness that looked unnatural. She wanted to close her eyes and go to sleep and forget all about him.

After a few minutes, Nathan arose and trudged toward her. His face looked grim in the moonlight.

"Is he—" she whispered.

He tightened his lips. "He isn't breathing, I'm afraid. The fall must have broken his neck."

"Oh, *no* . . ."

Maddy felt herself sway; then Nathan's arms came around her, cradling her against him. All of a sudden, she found herself sobbing into his coat, her breath shuddering. It was out of character for her to fall apart. Especially since she hadn't even *liked* her cousin. Yet she felt miserable to know she'd been the cause of his death, however inadvertently.

Nathan pressed a folded handkerchief into her fingers and she dried her cheeks. "This all happened because Alfred wanted my inheritance," she said, sniffling. "He was intending to take me out on a boat and dump me overboard."

"Thank God he didn't succeed," Nathan said roughly. "But why was he leaving here, then?"

She swallowed, gaining control of her emotions again. "I convinced him that I would sign over my share of the inheritance to him. He was returning to London to have the papers drawn up by his solicitor."

Nathan frowned. "Without you?"

"He left me locked in an upstairs bedchamber. Pidgeon was supposed to be guarding me."

"Pidgeon?"

"He's a treacherous brute in Alfred's employ. I escaped out a window and climbed down a tree."

"Good God! *You* might have been the one with the broken neck—" Nathan's appalled voice broke off as he stared at a point beyond her. "Well, look at that. It would seem I am about to make the acquaintance of this brute."

Maddy turned to see the bulky man stomping toward them down the road. He'd either realized she was missing—or he'd heard the gunshot and had come to investigate.

All of a sudden Pidgeon stopped and peered at the scene ahead, the cockeyed carriage and the two of them standing beside it. Then he abruptly wheeled around and took off running back toward the house.

"Wait here," Nathan ordered.

He dashed after the man, though Pidgeon had a long head start. Maddy hastened after them. She didn't care what Nathan said. She had to stop him from engaging in another fight, especially when he was weakened by the bullet wound in his arm.

It was only a short distance to the house, and this time Maddy made better time by hurrying straight down the rutted lane rather than being forced to creep through the trees. Nevertheless, she found herself panting by the time she spied the outline of the roof with its many chimneys against the night sky. She ran across the scraggly front lawn to see her husband heading toward the edge of the cliff.

The terrifying vision of him tumbling down to the rocks seized her. "Nathan, stop!"

Amazingly, he turned and waited for her. She rushed to join him, and he pointed to a steep staircase cut into the cliff. Halfway down, a large figure was descending to the rocky beach. A fishing boat was moored out in the dark water.

"Don't you ever listen?" he asked tersely. "This time, you're not to follow me. It's far too dangerous."

Maddy held firmly to his good arm. "Let him go.

Pidgeon never actually harmed me, and it isn't worth the risk if he happens to have a pistol, too. I doubt he'll trouble us again."

Nathan scowled down at her. Resistance radiated from him, so she slid her arms around his lean waist and held tightly to prevent him from continuing the foolhardy chase. They watched together as the big man hopped into a small rowboat bobbing in a sandy cove. Then he paddled out toward the larger boat.

Maddy subdued a shudder. That must be the boat that Alfred had intended for her to board, to be sailed far out to sea and tossed into the deep waters. She tucked her face into the crook of Nathan's neck, breathing in his familiar, wonderful, masculine scent. How awful to imagine that she might never have felt his warm embrace ever again.

"So the Pidgeon has flown," he said, flexing one of his fists. "Are there any other brutes around for me to vanquish on your behalf?"

With a tremulous smile, Maddy looked up at him. "Just the two, no more. Oh, Nathan, I never thought you would find me in time. How *did* you?"

"Come along, and I'll tell you."

As they walked arm in arm back toward the carriage, he related how he'd read the forged note, then found her shattered lamp in the square. Having surmised at once that Alfred had abducted her, Nathan had saddled his mount and ridden to the Duke of Houghton's house, where he'd summoned Lord Theo and confirmed Alfred's absence.

As an alibi, Alfred had told his younger brother that he intended to spend the night with a whore. Once Nathan had convinced Theo of the gravity of the situation, however, Theo had confessed that he'd overheard a curious conversation the previous day between Alfred and a hulking fellow who'd come to the garden gate, something concerning a boat.

"Pidgeon!"

"Indeed," Nathan said, "and since the only coastal property owned by the duke is this one, we surmised that he'd brought you here. Theo drew me a map, but I can't tell you how many times on the long ride that I feared we might be mistaken."

"Thank God it was a clear night, or you'd never have found me."

"I did take a wrong turn once and had to backtrack. But all's well that ends well."

"Shakespeare would agree. And so do I."

He slipped his arm around her waist as they walked, and Maddy marveled at the joy of being close to him, feeling the heat and vitality of his muscled form. He had come for her, risked his own life to rescue her. Surely that meant he felt more for her than mere possessiveness.

But she couldn't bring herself to ask him if he loved her. She felt too weary and wrung out to chance a denial.

As they spied the carriage up ahead, she realized that the night didn't seem quite so dark anymore. A faint glow had appeared along the horizon. "The sky is lightening," she said. "It's nearly dawn."

Nathan drew out his pocket watch and flipped open the lid. "Indeed. And I should think the coach should be arriving soon."

"Coach?"

Even as he spoke, the drumbeat of hooves and the clatter of wheels could be heard over the hiss of the sea. A black coach drove into view, and as Nathan raised his uninjured arm and waved, the coachman drew the team to a halt. Nathan urged Maddy forward and they reached the boxy vehicle just as the door opened.

Much to her surprise, Theo stepped out. "Madelyn!" he

exclaimed. "You're all right! We've been terribly worried!" With that, he turned to lend a hand to a stout woman in the plain garb of a servant.

Maddy rushed forward. "Gertie!"

The maid caught Maddy in the pillowy comfort of her arms. "My precious dear! So ye're fine, then?"

"Yes, I am! But . . . I had no idea you were on your way here."

"Lord Theodore came fer me last evening. In case ye needed my help." She held Maddy by the shoulders to scrutinize her in the uncertain light. "A few scratches t' yer face, I see."

"There was no real harm done . . . at least not to me." With a jolt of distress, Maddy looked at Theo. He stood watching, his gold-rimmed spectacles glinting in the darkness. Her heart went out to her cousin, for he didn't yet know about his brother. It would be such a terrible shock.

Nathan placed his arm around the younger man's shoulders. As he led Theo to the other side of the tilted carriage, Maddy murmured the news to Gertie. "It was dreadful. I never meant for Alfred to fall." All of a sudden, weariness overwhelmed her and she swayed on her feet.

"O' course ye didn't." Gertie helped her into the coach. "Sit down, dear girl. Ye need a good long rest after such a night, and ye in such a delicate condition."

Maddy sank gratefully against the plush cushions. "Shh," she whispered. "Nathan doesn't know yet."

How would he react when she finally told him about the baby? *I've no wish to give Gilmore a grandson . . .* Did he still feel that way? Would he reject their child and sail off to China?

She didn't want to contemplate it anymore. She was just too exhausted. It would have to wait.

Gertie had brought blankets and pillows, and a short

while later Maddy was curled up half asleep when Nathan came to inform them that the coachman would drive them back to London. He and Theo would set the other carriage to rights. They would transport Alfred's body to Houghton House and relay to the duke the grim news of his heir's death.

Nathan's enigmatic gaze rested on Maddy for a moment. But he spoke nothing personal to her, saying only farewell before shutting the door of the coach. As the well-sprung vehicle started off, she had one last glimpse of him standing at the roadside, staring after them.

Chapter 27

The following morning, Maddy descended the stairs to the drawing room after a breakfast of tea and toast. She felt wide-eyed and clearheaded after sleeping most of the previous day and night. Lady Gilmore had sent a message requesting that Maddy come down to join the family whenever she felt ready.

Misgivings touched her. Would they rebuke her for causing the death of Houghton's heir? Had she brought shame down on them once again by stirring up another scandal in society?

Oh, she hoped not. Nathan's family had grown dear to her. Their opinion of her mattered now, and she would never deliberately hurt any of them. What a difference two months of living here had made.

Passing through the arched doorway, Maddy recalled the first day she'd entered this drawing room as Nathan's bride. Back then, she had naïvely assumed it would be easy to play the loudmouthed strumpet. Easy to regard his family as pompous aristocrats instead of real people with feelings and vulnerabilities. She had babbled nonsense to the Earl of Gilmore and called him Papa, and had relished the way the snooty dowager had cringed in disgust.

How long ago that all seemed now.

The long, stately chamber had the same rich tapestries on the walls, the same groupings of chairs and chaises, the same gold brocade draperies drawn back to let in the sunshine. And just as before, the family was gathered together by the hearth. The earl and his mother sat in thronelike chairs, with Lady Sophia and Emily on the chaise . . .

And there was Nathan.

Her husband stood by the fireplace, one elbow propped on the marble mantel, the other arm in a sling. Without expression, he watched her walk toward them. In his charcoal-gray coat and white cravat, his dimples hidden, he looked aloof and unapproachable.

Maddy's breast squeezed. She had not seen him since dawn the previous morning. She feared it meant the worst, that his heart remained hardened to her despite his gallant rescue.

He had taken back her diamond wedding ring, too. During their quarrel two days ago, she had placed it on her bedside table, and this morning when she'd looked, it had vanished. Nothing could be more symbolic of the end to their marriage. Or more distressing.

Upon reaching the family, she resolutely turned her gaze to his father. He appeared robust, and the discolored lump on his forehead had shrunk in size. "Lord Gilmore, should you be out of bed already?"

"I could not tolerate that sickroom one moment longer," he said, a slight smile softening his taciturn features. "And I should think it more appropriate that you call me 'Papa.'"

Touched, she leaned down and kissed his pitted cheek. "Of course, Papa. I'm so very glad you're feeling better."

Emily jumped to her feet and gave Maddy an exuberant hug. "We're so very glad you're back home again, Madelyn! I was ever so afraid for you. Why, I scarcely slept a wink that night you were gone!"

"None of us did," the dowager said, one withered hand wrapped around the gold knob of her cane, the other holding up her quizzing glass to peer at Maddy. "You gave us quite a fright, girl. We are pleased that the doctor gave you a clean bill of health."

At Lady Gilmore's insistence, the earl's physician had examined Maddy upon her return yesterday. In private, he also had confirmed her pregnancy at Maddy's request. She had sworn him to secrecy, and it seemed the man had kept his promise, for no one here showed any sign of knowing about the baby.

Her gaze strayed to Nathan. What would he say when he found out? Would he be as thrilled as she was? Or would he be irked that she might bear an heir with ducal blood, a boy who would make Lord Gilmore proud?

Maddy wanted to know—and yet she dreaded the worst, too.

Lady Sophia gazed anxiously at Maddy. "You and I have had our differences in the past. I hope that will change. And do allow me to say that I'm appalled Lord Dunham thought he could get away with murdering you—his own cousin!"

"Greed can twist a man," Nathan said. "The duke is an immensely wealthy man. Madelyn's share of the inheritance will someday make her one of the richest women in England."

Maddy emphatically shook her head. "I don't want the money—I never did. I would have cheerfully given every farthing to Alfred and his brother."

"Poor Theo." Emily sighed, resuming her seat on the chaise. "He always looked up to his brother. I should like to comfort him, but he's gone to Hampshire."

"Hampshire?" Maddy asked.

"Dunham is to be laid to rest at the chapel on the family

estate," the dowager said heavily. "At a private service two days hence."

Dispirited, Maddy sank down onto a chair. Her fingers twisted the deep rose silk of her skirt. "I shudder to imagine what the duke and Theo must think of me now. They surely resent me for coming into their lives at all."

Nathan strolled to her side. "Actually, they don't. I made certain of that. Come with me and I'll tell you what happened while you were playing Sleeping Beauty."

He held out his hand.

Maddy's heart fluttered. She gazed down at his broad palm, the strong fingers that could caress her with such gentleness—if not for that quarrel. Slowly she raised her eyes to his face. He was smiling slightly, his dimples barely visible, flecks of gold gleaming in his green eyes.

Her heart fluttered again. She placed her hand in his and he helped her to her feet. He turned to his family. "I would like to take my wife for a short drive. Will you excuse us, ladies? Father?"

How amazing to hear Nathan address the earl as his father. The thought passed fleetingly through her mind; then she realized they were walking out of the drawing room, their fingers entwined.

"A drive?" she asked. "Is that wise? Don't people know that I was abducted? That I'm responsible for my cousin's death?"

"Certainly not. Go fetch your bonnet and I'll fill you in on the rest."

Intensely curious, Maddy dashed upstairs to don her favorite straw bonnet, kid gloves, and a white silk shawl. When she came back down, her husband stood at the base of the stairs. Arm in arm, they went outside to find an open phaeton waiting for them, the black horse held by a groom.

Nathan had planned this excursion in advance, she realized in surprise. What was the purpose of it?

He helped her up into the high seat and then joined her, taking the reins. The horse set off at a brisk trot over the cobblestones. She tilted her head back, enjoying the cool breeze and the warm sunshine. The world seemed so much brighter with Nathan at her side. She felt as if she could face anything—if only he loved her.

Her heart aching, Maddy glanced over at him. As always, he looked like a rakish brigand in the tailored garb of a gentleman, his black hair drawn back in a neat queue, his arm in a sling. She marveled that he could drive one-handed. "How is your wound today?"

"A nuisance, nothing more. I don't really even need this." He slipped off the sling and tossed it away, so that it went tumbling along the cobbled street. "I only wore it to please Grandmamma."

"Nathan!" Maddy didn't know whether to laugh or to scold, but perhaps neither reaction was her right anymore. She still wasn't certain of his feelings for her, or if he intended to board his ship and sail out of her life forever. Unwilling to think about that, she said, "Perhaps it's time you told me what happened after we parted yesterday."

He cast a solemn glance at her. "Theo and I came back to London to break the bad news to your grandfather. Needless to say, the duke was exceedingly distraught. Any man would be in such a circumstance. But I can assure you, he knows nothing of your part in the incident."

"You *lied* to him?"

"Absolutely. You see, on the drive back, Theo and I agreed it would be best for everyone involved. A scandal would only sully your reputation and Dunham's memory, as well as bring more pain to the duke. Consequently, we told Houghton that Dunham suffered a terrible accident while on his way to an assignation with a woman."

"How did you explain your knowing about this accident?"

"Theo told his grandfather that he'd intercepted a messenger bringing news of the mishap. And that he hadn't wanted to worry the duke until confirming it to be true. He asked me to accompany him so he wouldn't have to go alone."

Maddy sighed. She'd had quite enough of deceit for one lifetime. Yet she could understand the necessity of it in this case. To learn of the treachery of his heir would only heap more anguish on the duke when he was already grieving.

Theo was the heir now, she realized suddenly. That was one thing for which to be grateful. Now he would be free to court Emily if he chose. Maddy hoped with all her heart that he would do so . . .

"I should like to attend the funeral," she said. "Alfred was my cousin, after all. Perhaps Emily might care to go, too."

Nathan nodded. "I'm sure Theo would appreciate the gesture. He was quite broken up over his brother's death. We should have ample time to drive to Hampshire tomorrow for the service the following day."

He was offering to accompany her, as if it were the most natural thing in the world that they'd go together. Was it just chivalry again? Or did he intend to commit himself to their marriage?

Afraid to hope, Maddy realized that the carriage was turning onto Bond Street. Numerous elegant vehicles thronged the wide avenue. On this fine sunny day, ladies and gentlemen strolled along the foot pavement, going into shops or stopping to peer at the window displays.

"Where are you taking me?" she asked.

Nathan deftly guided the briskly trotting horse past a lumbering black coach. "There's something I want you to see."

"What is it?"

His dimples flashed in a grin. "If I told you, it wouldn't be a surprise, now would it?"

Just then, he steered the carriage close to the curbstone and drew on the reins. He dismounted, secured the horse to a post, then reached up to circle her waist with his hands. As he lifted her down, their bodies brushed, and she trembled with longing at the pressure of his hard chest against her bosom. His enticing nearness made it difficult for her to thread two thoughts together.

"Are we shopping?" she asked in confusion, glancing at a tobacconist's on one side of an empty shop and a men's haberdashery on the other.

"Not quite."

Reaching inside his coat, Nathan withdrew a key. He led her to the large, vacant shop straight ahead, the bow window sadly devoid of any goods. He turned the key in the lock and opened the door, ushering her into the dim interior.

Why did he have the key?

The question faded as she found herself distracted by the sight of an enormous, bare room with a few glass display cases empty of merchandise. Her footsteps echoed on the wood floor. Venturing deeper into the shop, Maddy experienced a burst of enthusiastic vision.

"Imagine all that could be done with such an immense area," she mused aloud. "There should be gowns along that wall and hats on display by the window and perfumes near the front so the scents will entice customers as they walk inside—" A startling comprehension made her spin around to face Nathan. "Is this . . . for *me*?"

Smiling, he strolled to her side. "The shop can be yours if you like. I haven't signed a lease, but the landlord is holding it for me. *If* you approve, that is. The decision is yours, Madelyn."

Maddy's heart overflowed. He must have put a good deal of time and effort into finding this place for her. Why? Because he cared for her? Or because he thought it would soften the blow of him leaving England?

"It's perfect," she said, her gaze searching his. "But what will your father say? And your grandmother?"

"Leave them to me. They've had to adjust to my being in trade, so we shall both be rebels."

Yet if he intended to sail away to China, then she didn't want his stipend. It would feel too much like being bribed in order to blunt the pain of abandonment. "This is a prime location. What will it cost?"

"Consider it my gift to you on this very special occasion."

"Occasion?"

To her astonishment, Nathan dropped on one knee in front of her. "Although I'll always cherish the memory of that auction, I never did propose properly to you." Reaching inside his coat, he withdrew the diamond ring he'd given her many weeks ago, the one that had vanished from her bedside table. "Will you, Madelyn, wear this ring and be my wedded wife for always?"

A lump formed in her throat as she gazed down at his solemn, handsome features. She hardly dared to believe him. "How can I be? Aren't you departing England soon?"

"No. I've decided to stay right here, if you'll have me. I'll hire an agent to handle my foreign trade interests." Nathan gazed up at her earnestly. "You see, I'd like to change that cold-blooded bargain we made. Instead, I'll devote my life to you, darling. I do love you madly— with all my heart."

Joy shimmered inside her, spreading into every part of herself, body and soul. "Oh, Nathan, yes! I love you, too. So very much."

Smiling, he sprang to his feet and she removed her glove

so that he could slip the ring back onto her finger where it belonged. She admired the diamond sparkling on her hand, but only for a moment. Then she lifted her arms around his neck and brought her lips to his. Nathan kissed her so deeply and tenderly that she no longer had the slightest doubt that he loved her. His hands glided up and down her back, holding her close as if he couldn't bear to let her go.

He broke the kiss, his lips nuzzling her face. "I believe it's high time we returned home and locked ourselves in the bedchamber."

Home. She liked the sound of that. Not to mention the prospect of lying naked with him again. Yet one aspect still troubled her.

She cradled his jaw in her palms. "Nathan, I have to know. Do you still not want a son?"

A rueful look came over his face. "I should never have said such a terrible thing. I was furious at my father, but I've put all that behind me now. Can you ever forgive me? I do very much want for us to have children."

Taking his hand, she placed it over her abdomen. "Then this baby shall be my gift to you."

His green eyes widened. "What? Are you truly—"

"Indeed so," Maddy said, laughing at his stunned expression. "We're to have a child just after the new year. The physician confirmed it yesterday."

"My God! Did you suspect it when I made that awful statement to you, then?"

"Yes, you jackanapes, and you may spend the rest of your life making it up to me."

He fervently kissed her brow. "With great pleasure."

As they strolled arm in arm to the door, Maddy stopped to glance around the empty shop, envisioning it as it would be someday. She leaned against her husband. "I was an upstart actress who sold herself to you at auction. Now I'm going into trade. I'm afraid I won't ever be a proper society wife."

Nathan's mouth curved in a wicked smile that put his gorgeous dimples on display. "Then we shall be improper together. Today and every day for the rest of our lives."